Fierce Stranger

a novel by
Louis Anthes

Long Beach, California

Fierce Stranger

Copyright © 2019 by Louis Anthes
All rights reserved.

This is a work of fiction. All of the characters, names, incidents, organizations, and dialogue in this novel are either products of the author's imagination or are used fictitiously.

First published, except for all of Act II,
from July 2012 through July 2013.

This version has been edited for this 2019 edition.

ISBN 978-0-578-49472-2

louis.anthes@gmail.com

For Carrie Hall, who asked, "Who is Anthony Camarrata?"...

Aren't you dead yet already?

I am.

"And this is that if you look at any walls spotted with various stains or with a mixture of different kinds of stones, if you are about to invent some scene you will be able to see in it a resemblance to various different landscapes adorned with mountains, rivers, rocks, trees, plains, wide valleys, and various groups of hills. You will also be able to see divers combats and figures in quick movement, and strange expressions of faces, and outlandish costumes, and an infinite number of things which you can then reduce into separate and well conceived forms."

– Leonardo Da Vinci, Notebooks, Book III, "Art: The Precepts of the Painter" (early 16th century)

"Should some cool-minded Martian come to earth and check on the state of our music, he might play through 10,000 jazz records before he found one that wasn't in common 4/4 time."

– Steve Race, *Liner notes for Dave Brubeck Quartet's album, "Time Out"* (1959)

"It fitted in both categories at once, giving rise to infinitesimal surveillances, permanent controls, extremely meticulous orderings of space, indeterminate medical or psychological examination, to an entire micro-power concerned with the body."

– Michel Foucault, *History of Sexuality, Vol. I* (1984)

"Sometimes love gives us too many options."

– LCD Soundsystem, *"Drunk Girls"* (2010)

Table of Contents

ACT I: DEATH OF ANTHONY CAMARRATA
Bitter
Purpose
Mushrooms
Words
Violence to Violets to Violence
Blindfold
Villa Riviera al ¡Petróleo!
Digs
Blackmail
María de Tijuana
Friends of Friends
Abalone Cove
First and Subsequent Shocks

ACT II: SIXTH DIMENSION

ACT III: LAST INCARNATION
Martial Law
Bath House Plunge
Guilt
Contrivance of Vengeance
Strike!
Baja
1939
Return of the Octopus
Anxieties of Influences
Tango Showboat Texas Rex
Beer Barrel Polka
One for Her, One for Me
Dec. 8, 1941 A.D.: Rev. 13:1

Addendum: Acknowledgements

ACT I:
Death of Anthony Camarrata

Chapter One

"Bitter"

"Do I fear dying?" asked my reflection.
Upon which words must I first meditate before giving my reply?

* * *

In pneumonia there is revelation: bacterium amok serpentine bronchials engorged expectorating lymphatically distressed dehydrated delerium tremens fluids asphyxiating pulmonary cardiac arrest brain dead.

Aroused by the trivia of a trade magazine's pictures of a new Henry Ford assembly plant in Long Beach, California, my fevers conjured images of a manufactured land of derricks and irrigation, fantastic cars and stucco homes, but also seaside real estate surfing a tide of asphalt expanding like Tarzan's chest, chiseled from obsidian striations lacing the smooth, pale desert ivory hills dotted with sage. Did I ever imagine living life somewhere beyond America? As a child, Tokyo, 1905 – the Japanese Navy defeated Europeans. Did I deliberate upon the geological consequences of earthquakes? Alaska, 1929 – I was captivated by serial newspaper reports of an earthquake with waves recorded in Hawaii. Do we, Americans, speculate on real estate colonies, like the Philippines, their lies and partial truths, comfortably, almost naturally? My sickly thoughts trickled like water down an imaginary Colorado aqueduct flirting with Mexico, while those I left behind in New York, I dreamed, eventually drifted to that city five hundred miles northward on the peninsula, a good walking city draped in fog free of ice, while to their south, peering from the shore to the sea, I returned my eyes upon the land and saw running water that never freezes, oil percolating underneath desert sun.

Mulling over such fanciful thoughts on a splendid light-green velveteen divan in a rather pale room, for twelve days in the spring of 1931, I lay healing, not wishing pneumonia upon even Caligula. Looking back now, I gather Manhattan pushed my spirits lower than they had ever been in Brooklyn. Tree blossoms near the open bedroom window in the Village basement apartment let tiny, green-orange pollen dunes gather on either corner of the window sill. The never-ending pollen also stirred in me frequent reactions I had not experienced since childhood. Then, following a rare weekend of dance and drink, I succumbed to an unshakeable cold. Quickly exhausted, vulnerable to vivid, if infrequent, hallucinations, and falling into fits in step with urgent changes in my body, I felt doomed and boxed in. Like spoiling fruit I reeked – standing up, sitting down or sleeping. A doctor diagnosed walking pneumonia and prescribed rest, water, broth, and aspirin when tolerated, along with hot baths, steam remedies, a variety of coughing exercises, and moderate amounts of whiskey for insomnia. He speculated my condition might be related to sweeping economic depression. The odor and taste of dying. In it, I understood how long fortune had insulated me. Childhood memories of the pox or a few street trolley near-misses or my closest introduction, in fact, at the hands of the Rumrunners, or for that matter the record of my own idle threats towards others, still my illness led directly to death's insecurity, private and public (for the first time since the Great War, I visited a hospital – at the onset of the worst of my condition to receive diagnosis and treatments). The whole episode instilled in me an indelible and practical memory regarding the wealth required to regulate death and dying from a comfortable distance (as one would for an elder aging gravely in a room, maintained on her behalf after she is no longer able to do it by herself, and shortly, it becomes an impractical burden to be balanced by other considerations arising from an actuarial disposition accommodating an imperfect world, while letting her know, gently of course, little of only a very few of the so many necessary inconveniences – would anyone not?).

To me, before this episode, death seemed so much less a law, than the end of law. I knew life's end often initiated lawsuits, but the materiality of spirit seemed miniscule in a deferential view of the Cosmos, taken in grandly. My parents had common funerals, and I, their only child, expected nothing different for myself. Vincente, my father, passed in the influenza epidemic after the war. Everything he owned, or could have owned after quitting the numbers racket, was invested in my education because he abandoned his debts in Calabresia by emigrating alone to Brooklyn where his wife birthed me to create a record of grammar school truancy requiring paid priestly tutelage. At his memorial, I said few words. The affair was orchestrated with

"Mirror"

the assistance of his brother janitors working in the courts, as well as one patronizing lawyer who couriered to me a hand-written copy of a single, brief poem by Dante Gabriel Rossetti, "Look in my face; my name is Might-have-been/I am also call'd No-more, Too-late, Farewell…". And as for my mother, Verona, whose family had relocated to New Orleans following her marriage, she required my support after he died, but as she desired, her priest cared most for her, certainly after the catastrophe on the exchanges brought a speedy and concrete end to the assistance she received from me. A few months later, she passed in her sleep, having bequeathed what little she owned to charity, following a modest Roman Catholic service. My version of anarchism tolerates exceptional memorials on those occasions where the deceased deserve worldly celebrity or where some survivor reasonably asserts an interest in the legal consequences of another's passing. It is, however, only in these very specific, and uncommon, situations can anyone pretend to preach, while not be taken for a jester, that law is stronger than death

And in my case where one lacked any estate at all, fighting pneumonia, when does Manhattan turn a might-have-been, a no-more, a too-late or a farewell? Following our Niagara honeymoon, of sorts, Abraham and I tried to establish a domestic routine upon our romance, but it is akin to universal law that each person becomes another's most definite yes-no, true-false question. Even each of our loves is a decision to embrace them, continuously made, and remade, until the temptation to yield to an alternate choice develops into a feeling harder to resist, especially if nobody pushes you back towards equilibrium. In due course, at some moment, you commit your love, in one act, for commitment's sake, like Abraham commanded by his god to bring down a lethal weapon swiftly upon the submissive body of his son, Isaac; or, the projected future course of your love begins to change, as you sense the new coming into view long before you execute a deliberate plan that generously accounts for the contingencies unforeseeable by even fortune-tellers. I settled, however, into the bitter notion that, after more than two years of partnership, Abraham had slowly abandoned me. At first, it was trips to Brooklyn, where Abraham visited his wife, Ruth, and his two children, at their insistence, he confided to me. Then, the law firm he started in Manhattan with my regular help – it was hired immediately by Ford Motor Company to implement and administer legal innovations for Ford automobile dealers in New Jersey, New York and Connecticut accepting used cars, of all makes and models, as part of a buyer's offer in purchasing a new Ford car – consumed more, then more, of his time, although it was clear such investments failed to reap anticipated treasure after the country's economy abruptly collapsed less than two years later. He continued his oft-repeated claim he never wanted to see me change, but thereafter he accused me of changing. I pleaded with him that I had grown more deliberate and serious in the short time since leaving Brooklyn, and that I was now ready to live life, outside our domestic arrangement. Without regular employment available to me (at least Abraham's mere license kept happy a couple of paying clients), I fell victim to his accusations that my heart was dissembling and that, in fact, I had been plotting all along to become his dependent, in abdication of responsibility towards myself. I was at fault for my own hopelessness, he complained. When I pushed him to recommend a course of action to pursue in lieu of my old liquor trade or simply begging in the streets, especially at times of such austerity and unrest, he mounted the high ground, claiming our relationship had descended into an intolerable state of despair. I responded to his concerns by calling upon some last, few favors and arranging amusing trips to supper clubs and to speakeasies, remnants of the previous decade, which was to end, as we all knew, sooner or later. So, in the months preceding my illness, we felt isolated and, as money seemed to vanish slowly from our lives, he retreated to attending to my immediate needs, almost professionally, paying for our rent, food, and similar necessities, even keeping me laughing at times, but definitely unable (or unwilling) to deepen our intimacy. Only during my recuperation did I receive Abraham's affection previously felt so strongly, first upon our reintroduction and later upon the novelty of living together, outwardly as business partners. Pneumonia rendered my dependency temporarily justifiable, in his mind, so his caresses returned, releasing me. I observed my moods grow peculiar. Whereas before, I had felt consistently confident, masculine in my affections, especially in Abraham's active and assertive embraces, fever brought forth new inner feelings I considered, for want of better terms, passive and soft, and I entertained fantasies that these felt desirable. His simple broths, hot baths and mama's garlic steam remedy, plus potions of absinthe, lemon and aspirin, he administered to me with the silent devotion and tender caresses of a gentleman.

    At rest for days, I shut my lids, and beneath, my eyes darted. I looked up, blindly, and sensed climbing inside me a haughty sigh, as though directed at someone in dull conversation. Still unopened, I rolled them around, mockingly, which is a more expressive form of contempt, I suppose. Then, they flipped to the left, in my own private shadow. I felt the pleasing anticipation of flirtatious desire, as if somebody was there to look at, but I knew Abraham was at his work desk some streets away. I opened my lids. As there was nothing to see, I stared straight ahead. Had my domestic life unsettled into psychic nervous bouts, unfamiliar to Abraham's Talmudic demeanor, and did he perceive it yet withhold its mention? In all humility, I accept Abraham's belief in his faith, and not his faith itself, as having helped my healing. So many feelings to catalog and interpret, and in the course of my recovery, I made experimental movements, revealing my adult body was imprinted with an adventurer's disposition, to a point where I felt now merely afloat, unattached, anxious – in the home my lover and I could not quite complete. If the Rumrunners' guns had not shocked me into changing years before, I supposed I might have remained in that lost state, or worse, altogether disappeared from Earth. I believed Abraham provided me the only escape from this prison, as his eyes were steadfastly anchored in his books. And to the very end, I desired a return to the normalcy we invented together, but perhaps I am too young or ill to say such a thing, but disregarding miracles I've never witnessed outside the context of a successful murder with malice aforethought, each of us, in the end, saves his own life, if it is to be saved.

Lying on the divan, I dreamed Darwin would have wagered against the infertile offspring of charming people, speaking more than one language, smiling infectiously, mastering social and romantic arts, and heeding the Great Chain of Personal Needs before enticing others. Surely, predatory people own advantages as single-minded, hasty animals, but the charming, though seductively efficient, fail in the end. This private conceit fed my final pneumonic hallucinations upon far future visions of an emerging simian class, in the mode of H.G. Wells: in the early twenty-first century, charming people have become extinct, and so prowling brutes muddle about with apparent freedom yet pursue unalterably submissive lives, lacking the potential to enjoy the pleasures of a technical, complicated Fritz-Lang-like Metropolis, guarded from them, jealously, by citizens who employ old European codpieces and Japanese wax to humiliate and domesticate their subcivilized property into sharing, trading, and ingesting measured regiments of spirits and narcotics, since the body of each fit but drugged degenerate serves as a dynamo electrifying pagan debaucheries inside the rhythms of clandestine, subterranean music, disciplined beyond religion, industrial and agricultural work, nonetheless sheltered inside common wood and brick dwellings, decrepit and soon doomed, too.

At length, my lifelong sense of strength, inspired by conquest, of the flesh, the heart, mind, was vanquishing a biotic betrayal. The phlegm left more easily my body. Perspiration returned to a normal rhythm, syncopated with my surrounding environment. Feelings of hunger returned. My ability to remain awake and alert grew stronger. I no longer felt ashamed of my odor. And in this improving state, a day came when Abraham approached my side while I was resting on the divan in our apartment parlor. His voice spoke, "Anthony?" I lifted my head. Abraham was standing next to me. At his right was Dr. Isaac Parks, from Columbia University, I guessed, although I had never met him previously. His name appeared on three envelopes, all of which arrived during my illness, and now rested on Abraham's desk. It seemed foreseeable that Abraham should appear, one day, with this new doctor. "Anthony?" Abraham reiterated in an insistent tone.

"You don't have to ask a third time. Yes, what is it?" I answered groggily. There was a long pause. Dr. Parks moved a step behind Abraham, who approached me, and bent over, as if to examine my condition. "I'm feeling much better, if that concerns you," I joked.

Abraham retreated to his upright position, and looked at Dr. Parks, who returned the look, with one eyebrow arched. "It does concern me. It always has." His silence momentarily lingered. "I have made a decision."

"That doesn't surprise me... mea culpa for my ill-temper. About?"

"Our lease is terminated, as of the end of this month. I made the arrangements this afternoon. Dr. Parks..." Abraham continued, as though the legal matter between us had been adequately addressed and disposed of, first and foremost.

"Is this a matter of your concern, doctor?"

Dr. Parks looked, again, at Abraham, and both men nodded and stood silently, like a brick wall. Dr. Parks spoke, "Your pneumonia seems to be abating, yes?"

"Well, not being a medical doctor..." I coughed.

"Anthony Camarrata. My credentials are not the subject of this conversation."

I lied, "I was speaking about myself, not being a medical doctor."

"Yes. Of course, if you need my credentials confirmed, you may call upon the Dean of the Teacher's College at Columbia..."

I summoned my strength and sat up instantly, but remaining at least seated, until the passing of a brief dizzy spell, for which I hid outward signs. I refused to succumb to my obvious weakness. "Doctor, why are you even here?"

Abraham interrupted, "He's here at my invitation."

"Well, this is still our home, Abraham. Or, until the end of the month."

Abraham looked down at the ground and sighed. He said to Dr. Parks, "I can't," and he turned and began to pace back and forth in a corner of the room.

Dr. Parks began, "The matter of the lease is not..."

I protested, "...who are you, a shyster, too?"

The doctor spoke gruffly. "Listen, Mister Camarrata." I felt a chill upon hearing the word "mister." He resumed, "I have heard you are quite capable of vulgar and insulting discourse, which I had hoped to avoid in your present state, and yes, as you might guess, I thought about what I had to say, before agreeing to Abraham's request to come here today, which was planned some weeks ago, to be honest, before you fell ill."

"I see." My face felt flush in embarrassment.

Abraham briefly stopped pacing, and in a brief loss of composure, he barked at me, "You see nothing."

Without hesitation, I replied, "I see that you don't mind fucking me when I'm healthy and when I'm not." It was a pointless, but satisfying accusation.

"I've kept care of you, Camarrata. I even took care of you when you were shitting in bed."

Dr. Parks spoke deeply and seriously, "Enough, gentlemen."

Dropping my head down to the divan, I closed my eyes. "Fine," I stated. "Give it to me, Doctor Parks. Give me the truth."

Parks wiped his lips with his hand before speaking. "The truth is, Anthony, you need to cease cohabitating with Abraham, whom I have been consulting, along with his wife, yes, who has agreed to resume their previous consortium for their mutual benefit and for the benefit of their children."

"Fool!" I jerked up and screamed at Abraham.

"No surprises, Tony," Abraham replied.

"Forget you, Abe."

"Well, the same at you, Antonino."

Dr. Parks waited nearly a minute for the effects of that exchange to clear, before he cleared his throat and tried again. "Anthony, I have tried to approach this matter civilly, and without creating some sort of insulting ruse to gain your unwitting cooperation, which admittedly would have been too challenging, given your natural intelligence. I trust my being honest is sufficiently assuring that you won't betray my trust in turn." As he flattered me, Dr. Parks, seemed particularly black, blacker than he had ever seemed. His blackness screamed at me, as though emerging from the darkest Africa. Under any other circumstances, I would have asserted myself, but I still felt weak, and both he and Abraham knew that. "Do I have your trust?" Dr. Parks asked pointedly. I wondered if Abraham recognized how black Dr. Parks was.

"I don't have much of a choice," I pleaded.

"Surely, you do," Abraham and Dr. Parks both sang. Abraham sat down on the edge of the divan next to my feet, kept warm in navy blue socks.

Dr. Parks resumed his professional demeanor, "Anthony, to help you make this transition, I previously have made arrangements with someone, it is my understanding, whom you knew before, and who now is willing to assist you to move out and hopefully, after some time, move up. Glamour Jackson?" What does one say about someone who had once seemed all important to me, more than anybody else, but now had become a visceral but imperfect memory? I tried my best to forget her. I gave myself that much credit. But, here was the good doctor trying to force me to accept my forgotten past.

"What about her?" I pretended ignorance, suppressing memories of her kisses.

"She is expecting to meet you, at the old Automat."

"In Brooklyn?" I cried, sitting up so quickly, that this time I actually saw stars flying through the air.

"Yes," Dr. Parks confirmed. Abraham was still seated on the edge of the divan, and he looked at me, trying, I could tell, to disguise his true emotions, likely a cocktail of smiles and tears. "Near the…"

"…Childs restaurant," I butted in. "Yes, of course. She still works there?"

"No, no. Those days are over. She's chosen another path for herself, and is actually enjoying some success."

"Psychiatry"

"Those days?"

Abraham, growing anxious, interjected, "Hard times haven't hit everyone as hard."

"Just me."

"Well?"

"So, it's me, Dr. Parks, is that what you're saying?"

Dr. Parks clapped his hands once, and loudly. "Anthony, the time is now, for you to leave here, this. She is expecting to meet you at the Automat in Brooklyn, in about an hour, tonight."

"But..." I tried to argue, which was little more than desultory.

Abraham chimed, "There is no debate, Anthony. It has been arranged."

Dr. Parks prudently added, "And to be sure, Mr. Camarrata, your past associates, who have kept a distance before today, may surface in your life again. So, discretion is advised at all times."

Abraham placed one hand on my leg, "It is for the best, Tony. Go to her. She will help you. I can no longer help you."

I looked up at the ceiling. My clothing was kept in one large closet, separate from Abraham's belongings. We agreed to the arrangement very early. Perhaps a separation would not be so dramatic as I feared. But, Glamour?

Abraham stood and gave me his hand, which I declined, electing to stand by myself. "Abraham, if I were to put a fucking curse on you, I would bring down your whole..."

"...Bitter..."

I stopped. Ruth had taken years to seduce her husband into performing this scene, I speculated. First, there must have been some foundational conversation about the needs of children, their father. Abraham might have tried to buy time. Eventually, he agreed to secret visits, at his work, I told myself. Then, there were late nights we spent apart, when I thought he was working. He knew I was taking myself to dancing balls, one of Manhattan's outwardly eligible bachelors, about which Ruth probably made a great fuss, after Abraham confessed. As time passed and money became scarce between us, he talked openly to me about his children, perhaps trying to determine whether I had any paternal instincts. I never met Ruth, but I sympathized, and I felt hatred towards her, and she most likely felt hatred, too. My only hope was that Abraham spared me from such hatred and resolved to accept his infidelity towards Ruth, as I was now obviously to be cast as an excuse for his straying from their marital path.

"One hour," Dr. Parks emphasized. "Once you're resettled, Abraham will make adequate arrangements to return your personal property to your possession."

"The beach," I stated simply.

Abraham puzzled, "Sorry, what's that?"

"Nothing," I lied.

Abraham and Dr. Parks eventually made their way towards the apartment door, apologizing for the unavoidable urgency of the situation, but emphasizing that I had survived pneumonia and seemed sufficiently mentally strong to accept the mistake I had made by believing Abraham and I could live together as lovers and partners. In their absence, I removed my undergarments and stood in a full-length mirror that we positioned near the large bed we shared for years. It seemed I had lost weight during my illness and recovery. In a passing thought, standing there at the mirror, I pictured the Automat as replenishing, while Abraham merely seemed silly, having staged a dramatic encounter for my benefit with the aid of his wife's therapist (I recalled the daft article Abraham shared with me, in which Dr. Parks interviewed his wife for Ladies' Home Monthly Magazine, years ago). Perhaps it would be a matter of one year before Abraham returned to his senses and realized the folly of perpetuating the sham of his marriage to Ruth. I stared at the flaccid flesh hanging between my naked thighs, longing for the warmth of sun.

* * *

"Do I fear dying?" asked my reflection.

Upon which words must I first meditate before giving my reply?

"No."

Chapter Two

"Purpose"

I mind your mind.
Solstice Meridian winked at me, somewhere in New Jersey.

* * *

First cleansed by a warm shower and then dried, dressed in a collared shirt, pressed suit and polished shoes, I pushed my fingers through my wet black hair. I shaved my face two days ago, and now it showed.

I felt anxious, uncertain, sick. I recalled Dr. Parks' words about Abraham dispatching my belongings – nothing much, really, except cologne and some vases, a fan, radio, rug, and art nouveau lamp, besides a modest wardrobe – to a future address, but presently, upon finding inside an apartment closet an empty canvas bag with a shoulder strap, I neatly packed some undergarments, stockings, one tweed jacket and matching shirt, a pair of wool trousers, and toiletries. I spied a money clip with five twenty-dollar bills on Abraham's desk, and tempted to keep four of the bills, leaving one behind with a note, "For Ruth," I pocketed the cash and clip, itself soldered to a gold eagle coin, thinking to myself that Ruth and her children deserved only my genuine well-wishes, and nothing more. The bag resting on the floor, I briskly turned in the direction of the bedroom, before stopping at the water closet in the hallway. Above the sink, in the cabinet, my medicinal flask, still half-full of whisky, soon found a place alongside my packed clothes. Removing from my possession the key to Abraham's front door, which used a spring mechanism automatically locking the door upon being closed, I left the key in the same location where the money had been on the desk. My exit was stoic and efficient, and I estimated about forty-five minutes remained before I was to meet Glamour, a simple matter of leaving Prince Street and arriving at Boro Hall and, of course, strolling handsomely into the Automat out of the dusk.

If had the time, I would have walked to Brooklyn, requiring a healthy adult no more than two, perhaps three, hours, depending on the peregrination. To get across the Brooklyn Bridge, I would have had to pass through Chinatown and Little Italy, through city ghettos that were never mine, but beckoned nonetheless, and for that reason, I summoned my strength, slid my bag under the turnstile at Prince Street station and jumped it, rather than purchase a token by tendering one of my bills at the window, so as to bid farewell in my own fashion. As luck would have it, at the moment, the train was arriving, so my behavior failed to earn much public scrutiny amidst the rush of passengers boarding and alighting the BMT, but upon completing my jump, one of my feet slipped, perhaps because I overestimated my health, and I fell face-forward onto the platform. When I stood up, I wiped the bridge of my nose and forehead on the sleeve of the suit jacket I was wearing, and I noticed swaths of blood over its grey-blue hues. I quickly grabbed my bag and slipped successfully between two closing train car doors. In a few seconds, the train left the station, and notwithstanding my now disheveled appearance, and despite how any fellow passenger might have tried to interpret what just happened to me, I succeeded in finding a place to sit on a crowded Brooklyn-bound train. I used my fingers to touch my nose, then my forehead, and as it seemed hardly any blood flowed, I could only diagnose a mild abrasion, lacking a clean, unobstructed reflective surface inside the train car to return the appearance of my gaze. At least my teeth were unbroken.

The journey on the train was unmemorable, except for two Navy sailors, in white uniforms, laughing and leaning on each other, perhaps drunk, but certainly looking for good times and obviously expecting to find them, I figured while the train passed through a tunnel underneath the East River. I stared. The taller one was slouching so comfortably his legs split apart, showing precisely how tightly the uniform fabric was stretching across the snake nesting inside his lap. The shorter one watched me staring, and then pointed at me and showed the nerve to ask me, while seated some feet away, "Hey, mistah. Coney Island, they got lots 'em sailors like us?"

"Sure," I replied, coolly before I stopped staring, as now at least half a car of strangers noticed me with blood on my face and clothes, their faces showing variously concern, fear or contempt.

Finally, at Boro Hall station with my bag in tow, I briskly pushed through the train doors, moved properly through the turnstile and ascended the stairs to the sidewalk above, as I heard the train speed away. In such a state, it was hard reconciling the image of Abraham as belonging now decidedly in my past. It didn't feel right. If there only had been some way to convince him, is what I insisted to myself to be the necessary solution to our problem, in other words, some way to convince him it was a matter of time before I returned to my sturdy self. Sturdy doing what, I wondered, not knowing exactly what it was that I was supposed to achieve under the circumstances of our partnership. My life seemed to lack measurement. Perhaps, Abraham had been right. My despair had become overwhelming, and regardless of its cause, he did still have the responsibility of tending to two growing children, his wife fairly reminded him. As Abraham insisted, no divorce from Ruth had never been the subject of a formal ceremony, legal or otherwise, and therefore, their marriage remained an awkward fact in our lives, while I protected his feelings as a father and encouraged him to remain loyal to Boris and Mila, whom I never met, although I did ask once if I could. Without a divorce from Ruth, I could only accept Abraham's promises and assurances and brave admissions of emotions in the privacy of our Village home, while at an imposed distance observing Abraham living another life.

The time for dwelling on such matters passed as I walked the empty nighttime streets of downtown Brooklyn, until I faced the urgency of my present solitary situation, standing at the doors of the Automat and peering in with purpose yet failing to glimpse her presence. My face close to the glass, air left my body conjuring clouds of condensation and hindering my view of the interior. There were about four or five empty tables, as the restaurant appeared to be busy.

Two uniformed attendants poured coffee and cleared tables as they made rounds. At the back, a customer's brown leg impolitely showing itself beneath the edge of her modest dress caught my eye, but I figured the distance was too great to confirm whether I found her, or whether I was investing too much attention on an irrelevant detail, and at that moment, of a sudden, I felt the gentle tug on the waist of my coat demanding that my attention look to the street behind me. I turned.

"I'm Solstice Meridian."

If the aim of her clumsy introduction was to catch me off guard, it worked. It was not immediately obvious what I should make of a young white girl, smoking an exotic cigarette, and wearing ill-matched and ill-tailored clothes, greeting me in the manner she did, in public. I pulled my head out of her aura and looked both ways down the street. It was nearly dark now. Street lights cast long shadows on cars and trucks. More than a few brownstone windows were alive with light cast by cozy domesticities. When I moved my eyes to meet her browns, it seemed as if she had never left, or as if she had never been there. Her smile looked stupid, literally ignorantly happy. I found it impossible to read what she even might have wanted, introducing herself in the way she did. "What's up, kid?"

"You can call me 'Solstice'. I know I talk very fast. My friend says it's on count of eating too much sugar. But anyways, I talk really fast. Sorry for saying 'hi' like this. Are you looking for somebody, by any chance, cause so am I."

"Is that so?" I asked, my curiosity aroused by her speech which seemed mature in voice, but stunted in eloquence, and yet clearly she was a girl, not nearly a woman, and that was clear even under the light of one lamp illuminating the exterior Automat sign. "I might be, maybe," I finally said. "A woman, a black lady." I turned to look inside the Automat one more time, then returned my attention. "I thought it might have been her, but."

"Does she sing? Is the woman you're looking for, is she a singer?"

I smiled. "She sings."

"I think we're looking for the other, you and me."

"Pardon?"

Dropping her cigarette and crushing it under the heel of her boot, she extended her pale hand and pulled her index finger repeatedly towards her, like she was beckoning me to follow like her pet. Not taking kindly to such gestures, I hesitated a moment before I relented and joined her in the Automat, where we sat down at the back and ordered two cups of coffee. With some pocket coins Solstice tossed on the table top, I bought her a piece of pie, which she didn't eat right away, because, she insisted, she was eating too much sugar. I desired meatloaf, but waited some time without moving.

"Like I said before, you can call me 'Solstice'. I know it's a crazy name, that doesn't make no sense."

I tried to flatter her, to calm her down. "No, it's quite pretty, actually."

"My parents are gone and all I know is the name they gave me that they kept at the orphanage. But my name, as pretty as it is, is not why we're talking right now, is it?"

I laughed, "No, I guess you're right on that point."

"Thank you. I like your gentlemanly kindness. So, if I may, Mistah Comarati?" The sounds of my misspelled name earned my silent nod. I wanted to correct her, demanding a proper pronunciation, but I let it go. I assumed she didn't mean anything by it, as they say. "You're in a heap of trouble," and she started to speak in a whisper. "She sent me here to get you, told me what you look like, when you'd show up. You were the second guy I asked out front there, to be honest. But now we have to leave here and you have to trust me. Can ya do that?"

And it occurred to me there, in a flash of insight: should I have trusted Abraham? He could easily have turned me over to the Bureau or have made a backroom deal with Caligula. I feared I had lost my instincts and that even my very grammar and vocabulary created obstacles to clear-headed thinking, which at this point might be the only cause of my survival. I remembered I was still sick.

"I'm healing from a bad cold," I coughed. "So, what sort of trouble are you talking about, cause I'm not sure you can handle it, to be honest, young lady, pardon me for saying so."

"Mistah Comarati, look. I don't drive a car yet, but I know how to drive a car, cause I have, do you understand what I'm saying?" And at that second, a young man sporting a long black scarf slapped his shoes on the exterior sidewalk, racing into the distant dark beyond the Automat, and in chase, a police officer appeared out front, stopped, held his revolver at eye level, and pointing straight-ahead fired one shot into the night. Without any prior hint, he hastily shifted his eyes to his right, in our direction, and simultaneously, Solstice disappeared behind the table, next to my bag, and tugged at my jacket to join her, which I did instantly. From below, she watched the copper's face abandon the Automat window and resume his chase. We stretched upwards and returned to our seats, when Solstice said, "When I was a kid, I used to think about kid things, but you know. I'm on my own now mostly. By the way, how did you get that scratch on your face?"

Ignoring her question, I resigned, chuckled, "Just, show me the way then, sister. You're driving."

"We're just walking for now," she accidentally spit into her now half-empty pie plate for which she left a small tip on the table, before handing me my bag, leading me through the front door and into the night, then finally looking at me and tilting her head up on the sidewalk, "Thanks, pops."

Solstice talked about The Arms, Glamour's apartment residence, to keep me focused on and confident in her lead. She said it was a three-story, brick building that housed a few dozen people, more or less, though who was a legitimate tenant there or was a squatter, she could never say, she said. She claimed she was making conversation to put me at ease. She pulled out another rolled cigarette and lit it with a match, while we were walking and talking. The cigarette made her look childish to me, as she displayed dramatic affectations, such as the slight laugh accompanying every emission of billowing smoke. And then, I noticed her clothes—pants, boots, and underneath an oversized hand-knit sweater, an old top the color of milk, coming unstitched in a couple places, showing a few stains. As we moved through city blocks, Solstice pulled herself in closer to me.

She took my free hand, "Hey, hope you don't mind getting this close. It makes more sense this way, like you're my pop." I declined to argue, instead I kept my mind free of distractions. "Your hand feels guilty," she stated, as though it was obvious to her, and should have been to me, what she meant.

"Guilty?" I asked her, bringing my feet to a stop, which had the effect of yanking her hand, and then whole body, back in my direction. She sighed. I pulled my hand away from her and also used it to hold the bag strap clenched in my other hand.

"Yeah, your grip is cold. Like you're old. I mean, I can't say if your hand's more cold today, more than any other day." She laughed, as she exhaled smoke. And then, she pushed herself against my body, and took my cold hand in both her hands, her cigarette in her mouth, and she began to warm them up, rubbing briskly, like a Boy Scout trying to start a fire. She mumbled with the cigarette lightly clenched between her cracked lips, "take my warmf."

"I'm wondering why you used the word 'guilty'," I stated, and she pulled back, having accomplished her goal of making me feel better.

She took the cigarette out, "Well, am I wrong?" She laughed, then said, "Let's keep walking."

I didn't respond immediately, and resumed the pace she set for us previously. "I have an illness, and it is a cold night, so maybe that's why it feels that way, " I finally said, as I spied the faint words "The Arms" in relief on white limestone set above the front stairs and door on a brick building about a block away.

"Your hand is cold today more than any other day, I have decided. I mean, it takes me time to make decisions sometimes, slower than I can talk. You're guilty, that's my hunch. But don't worry, I believe... in you."

One last time, I stopped her, because it seemed important to me that, even if I was ignoring buried guilt, although about what it was I couldn't say, then at the least, I shouldn't enter Glamour's apartment with paranoia as well. The impulse to monitor my feelings turned into a nervous urge, and I started to shake, slightly. "Solstice?"

"Yes?"

"Hey, listen, kid. I came here expecting to meet Glamour, right?"

"Yes." She threw her cigarette down, and like the last, crushed it beneath her boot, but this time, she gathered the crushed butt, and put it into a pocket.

"How are you helping?"

"I take people places. Along the way, I kinda talk, I know. But I usually get people to where they want to be, or where they need to be, and who

"Solstice"

wouldn't? You would, wouldn't you? Anyways, it's a thing that… I mean, I know that… I might talk too much, but what I'm trying to say is, I'm still helping you on purpose." Finally, I took the lead, though I didn't know what to do upon reaching the front door of the apartment building. Solstice removed a key from her pocket, opened the front door, and directed me to the stairs down the interior hall. "She lives on the top, apartment 304." We took silently to the stairs. A couple of black women passed us. At length, we reached the correct apartment door, which was slightly ajar, and Solstice pushed passed me as she entered the light inside the apartment, nonchalantly, inviting me to follow and directing me to leave my bag in the kitchen at the left.

I entered, per Solstice's instructions, and took inventory of the messy kitchen, with dishes unwashed, collecting in the sink. There were several open paper bags on the little porcelain counter. A rug, sullied, covered half the kitchen floor. Unpleasant greasy odors filled my nostrils. I moved into the parlor, noticing movie magazine photographs pasted to the wall, randomly. A radio softly played piano music in a corner. A couple of large, leafy, green tropical plants extended up from their brown pots and over either side of a small sofa, the only furniture, resting on the parlor's hardwood floors. A paper bag with stains, rolled closed, was seated on the sofa next to a calm, gaunt black woman who appeared older, conservative, as though she was dressed to attend church, when it fact it was a common Tuesday night. Upon closer view, I later saw holes and stitches in her clothes. The toes of both her worn-out shoes were neatly wrapped in copper wire, several times. Both hands rested on a silver-handled cane standing between her legs. Draped behind the sofa hung a large red curtain, sheer enough to reveal, beneath, a window looking out to an alley light, attached to an opposing brick wall and shining downward. Meanwhile, Solstice disappeared into colorful, densely-strung glass beads suspended from the threshold arch separating the parlor from what I surmised was a bedroom.

I waited silently for some time and then spoke. "Evening ma'am," I politely said for the benefit of the older woman.

"Have you seen my celery?" her voice squeaked, as she removed her hands from the handle, causing her cane to fall to the ground. She grabbed the bag next to her, and clutched it in her bosom. And then with a slight plaint in her voice, she whispered to me, loudly, "I need my celery. There's some in the kitchen." I understood her to ask for my help, so I silently turned one finger in the direction of the kitchen. She nodded, "Yes, yes." Still waiting for Solstice, and I presumed Glamour, too, I turned to walk into the direction of the kitchen. Rather than rummage around the icebox, I looked first through the paper bags, full of fruit and yellow, red and brown vegetables, except for one, which had a stalk of fresh celery, and a tightly-folded newspaper sheet that appeared to have some mystery bulging inside. There was also a clean spoon. I folded the bag, and entered the parlor, to rest on the sofa next to the woman, whose sleeves were now pulled back, revealing bruises and sores on the skin under her exposed arms. She otherwise appeared free of blemish.

I was about to retrieve her cane, when Glamour's face, and not quite her whole head nor her body, could be glimpsed behind the beads hanging in the threshold. Her voice sang deeply, "It ain't time, sister. Ain't time. Anthony, do you have some drink on you, cause you might offer Bernadette a drink, instead of that bag of celery, which should stay back in the kitchen, if you don't mind." After Glamour's face vanished, I heard her voice speak fading words, "Not now, Solstice. No, no..."

I spoke loudly, for Glamour's benefit, "Yeah, I brought my whisky flask." Without receiving any rejoinder from beyond the beads, I softly addressed Bernadette, "Um, do you mind if I trade you the celery for some whisky?" Fortunately for the sake of peace, she quietly nodded and surrendered the paper bag with celery in it. I returned to the kitchen, dropped the paper bag somewhere below a cupboard, and took the flask from my bag. Before handing it to Bernadette, I enjoyed a quick, generous swig. Once she took it from me, she finished its contents with a few gulps and a large smile. She thanked me, as she lifted her cane and waved it in my direction. "Thanks" was all I could reply, as I took possession of the empty flask, and slipped it inside my pants pocket.

At that moment, Solstice raced through the wall of beads and, appearing in a fit of anger, approached me to say, "You want her time, but she only has to give tomorrow, Anthony."

"Solstice, bear with me, you mean, Glamour?"

Solstice backed away from me, and made a contemptuous, "hrumph," followed by some odd grinding noise coming from her throat.

From behind the beads, "And you ain't gonna ever if you don't get Bernadette to her room downstairs. And don't give her any your reefer, Solstice. Now git, girl, please."

Solstice turned to Bernadette and extended her arm, which Bernadette took, kindly, as they made their way out the apartment, slowly and quietly, whereupon their absence, Glamour Jackson burst into her parlor, quickly and loudly. Then, Glamour stood motionless, in front of her jangling beads. The effect was probably intentional, because it provided me a few seconds to appreciate the details of her ensemble, as well as its overall glow. She sported a short bob wig, black, straightened, combed just down to the lobes of her ears, the left of which supported a smallish white chrysanthemum. Her penciled brows tapered at the edges to meet the tip of the smokey eye-liner, framing long lashes. She chose bright red lipstick, and light powder foundation. No jewelry, except for jade bracelets on each arm. Her blouse, made of yellow-white silk, reached to her neck and featured five small, gold-embroidered flames, bordered in black lace, but the centerpiece of attention was a large gold and black embroidered dragon across the front of her chest. I hardly noticed the flowing red silk pants she wore above her golden evening shoes.

"Glamour Jackson calling Condé Nast," she boasted, before blowing me a kiss.

"You've been waiting to show me that all night," I smiled, as I inched my way towards her.

She came forward, too. "Anthony, I've been waiting to show this since 1926."

"It had to be me," and my self-confidence brought my Calabresian nose to her chrysanthemum. I whispered to the flower, "It had to be me."

She pulled back, looked into my eyes, and sighed, "It had to be you, Anthony." Her hands came up to my shoulders, where she rested her forearms, as she moved her waist between my thighs. "How did you get that on your nose?"

"The cut? Jumping a turnstile." A long pause. "Glamour, I should have defended, protected you," I confessed, as though contrite, but in fact, I knew this is what she wanted to hear, all these years. The words were not so much offered as an admission of some sin against her, but were rather intended as my overdue acknowledgement of her more perfect self. "Can you forgive me?"

Moving her head naturally, she pushed her lips against mine, which softened, into hers. Owing to my illness, my mouth closed, before my tongue pushed through to hers, until our hands clasped in the space between our bodies and slid apart, as we fell into each others' embrace. The time that passed felt immeasurable. We pulled back at precisely the same second, saving each other from the embarrassment of having to feel the other pull away first.

"Can I forgive you?" she laughed. "Anthony, it's over, you've known that. Forgiveness seems, so, oh, I don't know, church or something. Are you bringing church, Anthony?"

"You, Glamour, are funny."

"I invited you here for a reason, Anthony. A purpose."

"Solstice..."

"...Solstice!" she exclaimed impatiently. "You are going to have your hands full with that one."

"I don't understand. Does this have to do with Solstice?"

"Yes, and no. Which do you wanna hear first?"

"I should sit down on the sofa?"

Glamour moved with grace and poise towards the sofa and reclined into a seated position. She crossed her legs, pushed some creases out from her clothes, and patted her hand next to her knee, inviting me to relax alongside. I obliged, and let some moments pass before speaking. Comfortable with the pace of our conversation, Glamour began talking at length.

"Anthony Comarati, the 'no' of it is this: you are a marked man."

I felt shock, but spoke stoically. "Caligula?"

In Glamour's most honest voice, she asked, "Well, of course, isn't that why you turned to Abraham in the first place?"

"I feel accused," I admitted.

"It is, Anthony, a genuine question," Glamour said, pulling her arms back against her dragon, and folding them with an air of polite impatience.

How should I engage? I was aware of no conscious purpose in pursuing Abraham other than romance and genuine affection, except as I thought about her question, it did occur to me the timing of my reintroduction to Abraham, coming some months after the failure with Glamour, and then my indirect involvement in the murder of the orphan Joe, at the hands of Caligula and the Rumrunners. Indirect? Had I let myself off easy for dropping my gun, instead of murdering Joe? What I had believed was my good character now became cowardly personality. "Glamour, I..."

"...shhh," she interrupted, placing a long, black finger near my lips. "Caligula would have taken your life, if Abraham hadn't ran away to Manhattan with you, protecting you. Now...you wanna know why I know all this?"

"Tell me."

"Because, Caligula wanted you pushed out, one way or another, so he could get to me."

"You?"

"Yes, me, Anthony. And if I hadn't had the strength of mind, and the good fortune of meeting Solstice, just after you packed for Manhattan, I might have met my fate too soon."

Glamour and I discussed at length Caligula's history of threats towards Glamour, following her one, short trip to Paris in early 1927. Some time later, around the period as the nationwide crisis deepened, Caligula foresaw rumrunning offering little future, and he pursued Glamour for his own

"Glamour Jackson"

purposes, specifically, expanding into assassination, linking the two goals in an elaborate scheme. As she explained it to me, Caligula offered, for a price, the opportunity to decide the calendar date of passing for any relative whose existence was, for any family member willing to pay, "inconvenient," for lack of a better word. If two brothers stood to inherit a business or an estate, one of the brothers would be bitten by a snake, or suffer an automobile accident, or drink bad whisky. Glamour was to slip in and out of being variously a man or woman to deliver the fatal blow. It was Glamour's clever alliance with Father Profito of Our Lady of Sorrows Church that spared her from Caligula's scheme. At first, she moved into the rectory offices, where she received protection for one year, as Milton. She finished her story, "and that's how I started this boarding house under Father Profito, allowing me to live freely as a woman. It's a fair deal, and ain't nobody coming up those stairs, unless mama's saying so. And I would be mama." Not sure what to say, I asked Glamour about her future intentions, but she directed me to Solstice, again. "Don't you want to know, Anthony, about the 'yes' of your question?"

"The 'yes' of my question?"

She replied, sharply, "Does this have to do with Solstice?"

"That question, " I realized aloud.

"Solstice is a very, very special young lady, Anthony. She senses danger, through interpreting her own dreams. You may confirm that with Dr. Parks."

"I see. Is she a medium or something?"

"I'm not a scientist, but two-out-of-three times, roughly, Solstice is spot on. Wanna hear her most recent dream, from about a week ago?" I nodded, while she continued, "She dreamed you and her living in the desert, looking out on the ocean."

"Me?"

"You."

"California?"

"Anthony, California."

I murmured, puzzling Glamour, when instantly, screams of "Fire!" filled the hallway, outside Glamour's apartment door, startling Glamour, and sending me to the door, which I opened, to see Solstice standing in front of me and smoke rising up the stairs behind her.

"Fire! In the basement, all the phones are out. No time to call the fire department. We have to leave now!" Before the chaos coinciding with the late arrival of firetrucks, Glamour explosively leaped to gather a few items seeming desperately important to her—clothing, jewelry, a small, portable vanity—and handed me my canvas bag. Fleeing, we knocked on each of the tenant doors on all three floors, directing people to avoid danger and take to the safety of the fire escape. Every person was spared, but in the course of sharing arsonist rumors during the evening, the name "Caligula" surfaced more than once, who few knew, as I, to be the currently independent operator Claudio "Caligula" Adami, also former associate of international shipping mogul Carlo Garcia Villa. While the interior of the building endured an hour before it collapsed under the weight of fire department water and structural debris and settled into smoldering ash, Glamour directed all the tenants to Our Lady of Sorrows. Then, she led Solstice and I to a black 1924 Ford truck she said she rarely made use of, on loan from Father Profito, parked about a block from The Arms. Showing us a map of New York and New Jersey kept between the driver and passenger seats, she begged both of us to make for the Holland Tunnel, without delay, and offered vague promises to meet us in California, one day.

* * *

Taking the wheel, I drove next to the sleeping girl. In an instant, somewhere in New Jersey, in the middle of the night, a voiceless thought entered my head, persistent and clear, but it was a short, lonely fragment of a thought, too.

I mind your mind.

Solstice Meridian winked at me, somewhere in New Jersey.

Chapter Three

"Mushrooms"

"Upon receiving your letter, I read these first words, of course, 'It was good receiving word from you.'"

* * *

Smallish chocolate pyramids psilocybe infused. I am speechless as I am jobless. Jobless, jobless. What is my intention? What is my intention, speechless as I am jobless. Like a fourth-dimensional Cheshire cat clawing inside my guts underneath my dress shirt, my stomach aches, occasionally sending sharp pains to my brain. I imagine the center of a spiral, focused on a small seashell in the dead middle between where the ocean waves recede and return, in waves, in waves a space no more than ten feet. In waves, the spiral spirals tightly ever-outward. A sharp pain in waves.

'Olevaivai'olefe'e says to me, "Ah… yeah, you're opening up like a window!"

"I'm hungry, I think."

She says, "You're not. You growing a moustache?"

A moustache? I haven't shaved in two days, and she asks me if I'm growing a moustache. And I contemplate each hair above my lip, tickled suddenly at one corner, and I pull my upper lip inward, using my incisor to scratch the itch. My breath comes over me, a strong odor, like rancid acid. In waves. I reply, "no, or maybe."

"No, wait!" she screams. "You have a beard. Is that a beard?"

I laugh, and keep laughing, "just a moustache?"

"Like a window," she says and falls down, rolling several times, making angelic impressions on the beach, repeating frozen sand waves.

* * *

"E pei 'o se fa'amalama," she says and falls down, rolling several times, making angelic impressions on the beach, repeating frozen sand waves.

I am drawn to a small scallop seashell. I lay down on my empty belly, slipping one shoe off at a time, using the toes of the opposite foot. I hold the shell in my dirty hand and bring it close to my ear, listening to the sound of wind passing through it and creating illusions of ocean noises, more amplified than the ones filling the humid, salty air.

'Olevaivai'olefe'e crawls a few feet towards me and, giggling, pushes her nose against the shell in my hand. "Sole, fa'alogo mai!" I don't know whether she's talking to me or the shell or the sand. She turns her large brown eyes, long lashes towards me. "Manamea, fa'amatala mai se tala mālie, 'iā te a'u." I have no idea what she is saying, but I let her talk. "Se tala mālie!" she repeats two or three times, then finally she cries, "A story!"

I ignore her.

"Fa'alogo mai. E tatau ona 'e māfaufau mai 'iā te a'u. E lē 'o a'u se tagata 'ese. 'O a'u 'o lou au, 'o lou... fa'afāfine."

I kiss her soft, purple lips, quickly.

She pulls back, wipes sand from her mouth and scours, " 'Auē! "

* * *

In sand, with driftwood:

> *It was good receiving word from you.*
> *It was good receiving head from you.*
> *It was good receiving love from you.*
> *It was good receiving life from you.*
> *It was good.*
> *Good.*

In waves. Abraham.

* * *

Indecisive thoughts. I want to think in whole paragraphs, to speak in whole paragraphs, as if a whole paragraph is a whole idea. A thought is like the whole ocean, and I speak to 'Olevaivai'olefe'e in waves. If only we could.

Our sights are set on Pleasure Pier at the Pike, at low tide.

She.

I ask her why the pier is named as such, and she tells me to use my nose.

Him.

    The air smells like salt. And burning oil. "Oil creates pleasure," she tells me, and points away from the water and towards the north, towards Signal Hill, also called Pincushion Hill, because the oil derricks line up along the ridge. She adores Charles Lindbergh, an occasional Long Beach goer himself, she says, and one day plans to fly planes herself.

    The beach opens up, unpopulated for the most part.

Ours.

    A few people walk by, paying us no attention.

Them.

    Knowing that I am hungry, she takes me to buy ice cream. I buy chocolate, and she takes the same, smiling. Stepping back onto the sand, we approach the pier, designed to resemble the shape of a giant horizontal arc, a rainbow. Truly.

" 'Olevaivai'olefe'e"

Her.

In the late afternoon, I see the daytime moon, faintly caught in some middle phase, above the shore, and I want to remove my clothes, all of them. Along the horizon, out towards Catalina Island, anchored boats rest some miles away, while smaller skiffs ferry back and forth to the mainland shore. I walk into the sand and study the pier's construction, its shadows, near where ocean waves lap the beach, somewhere beyond the shore, where the breakwater meets the Pacific. I kick off my shoes and 'Olevaivai'olefe'e dutifully follows me to retrieve them. I lose my collared shirt, which she also takes, and roll up my pants above my knees. The late sun warms my skin, too pale for too long. She laughs, "Palagi…," then gestures in the direction of some dozens of yards beyond. I jog, sort of, and quickly grow tired from exerting myself in the dry sand softly absorbing my gently pounding feet.

Her laughter fades as I approach Pleasure Pier.

* * *

It may be hard being a man, but they say, God forgives you for anything you do, I whisper, to Abraham? I can't stand it anymore: God.

I follow the glow of tobacco moving up and down in the hands of a silhouette, one leg bent, foot propped up against a rock some distance away from the sand. I turn back, for a second, and see her hands covering her brow, shielding her eyes from the setting sun poking through clouds. At this moment, the pier is empty of people.

Shrouded, sweaty, filthy, I navigate the rocky boulders, pulling in closer as sparks fly towards me. The smoke disappears. He drops the butt. I give my lips. His tongue pushes inside, forcefully, as his hand reaches down and tugs my turgid cock. I love the word "turgid." I could repeat the word "turgid" for at least an hour, in waves, in my mind. My mind, inattentive, is overcome by his embraces. He is smaller in height, but thicker in frame, and to my surprise, assumes command over my body, falling passively to the waves of his strange noises. He bites my neck, I whimper, to my surprise, and he hisses, "ssssssiiii…" Both of his hands reach up to fall on my shoulders then press down while he sits. The pressure builds until I succumb, but even so my mind races, the word "turgid" in repeating mindwaves. And in a second I fall to my knees, nearly naturally. Why hadn't I done this sooner?

Without hesitation, he drops his trousers while the heavy atmosphere of seawater, urine and tobacco yield to the intoxicating aromas of his mushroom-headed… Bam! He throws the hefty weight of it against my face. Smack! Twice. My eye is closed but strands of fluid stick to my lids. I open my mouth and open it further still. He enjoys the stubble on my chin tickling his cannonballs, pulling into his body, until their skin turns tough as leather. Instantly, he forces his way in, holding my hair in his left hand, and gently rubbing his own nipples with the right. I can't breathe so hold my breath. There's no room inside my head for him to move in and out so he makes his own, pinching my cheeks until I open as far as I can. The friction against the roof of my mouth sends waves of electricity to my knees. My tongue turns dry. I take air for every five or six of his grunts. His enormous head, attached to a skinny pole. I turn my mouth to stop my teeth from interrupting our joy. In waves, I gag. The ice cream made my throat secrete viscous mucus, exciting him. He lets go my hair and drives his hips through my tonsils. Quickly thrusting in waves, until withdrawing, he finally grabs himself and moans loudly one long time as milky gallons crash like waves upon my cheeks, inside my nostrils, over my tongue, down my neck, and just as he seems about to end, my lips reach up and swallow his mushroom one last time, for the final blow. I swallow. In waves.

Her peering towards my direction, from the beach some yards away, I barely hear 'Olevaivai'olefe'e say, "'Oka, 'oka, 'oka."

* * *

Coming back down feels smooth and soft. I feel slightly hungry, tired, walking eastward, away from Pleasure Pier, and 'Olevaivai'olefe'e removes some reefer rolled tightly and snuggled in her hair, behind her right ear. She offers to share, I accept, and the orange glow of the early evening sky warms me, as we share.

"I feel..." I start to say, before taking inventory of what is happening to my body. "I feel so... lazy," I confess, although there is no guilt behind my words, just a sort of relief.

She says, "Fēfē. You're not lazy, valea. You're just low energy, as they say, and who cares? If you were lazy, you wouldn't have walked into the waves after your... love encounter... to wash your face." She hands me my shirt, which I don, and grabbing my shoes from her, I wince slightly cranky, perhaps, because in fact I am tired, having experienced nearly a month of insomnia, off and on, about every other night or so. She giggles, "Lazy? Lei! Look at me, they say I'm lazy, too. Lazy, because I smoke reefer, and lazy because I don't work at some cannery down the shore or cook for smelly sailors on some boat. Lazy for just being from Pago Pago. Lazy, because I only work two part-time jobs, one for a salon, they say is lazy, and another job for a florist, they say is lazy also." At this point, her fingers pop out a little cherry ember at the tip of the reefer, and she hides the rest behind her right ear. "But I know I'm not lazy. I do flowers and I do hair, and sometimes even, I do flowers for hair. That's three jobs!"

She has a flower in her hair above her left ear, a lovely white gardenia whose stamen have started to wilt, it seems, while the petals have kept their turgid shape. Suddenly, dwelling on the word "turgid" seems less urgent to me. Clearly, I'm coming back down. "No, you're right. The word 'lazy' just seems so moralizing."

" 'Ioe, yes. Don't judge yourself."

I smile, staring into her brown eyes, "then... 'not productive'?"

"Yes, pa'u. But even so, you're such a hard-working fa'ase'e..."

Finally, at long last, the urge to express my lack of toleration for her foreign tongue overwhelms me, and I ask, "What are you talking about?"

"Auē, valea, I'm saying..." she begins, before her eyes bulge and her voice turns rather unlike a lady's voice, "you are... supereasy," to which she gives emphasis by performing silly pornographic gestures, as she jogs some yards ahead, her gleeful cackles merging into the noises of wind and waves.

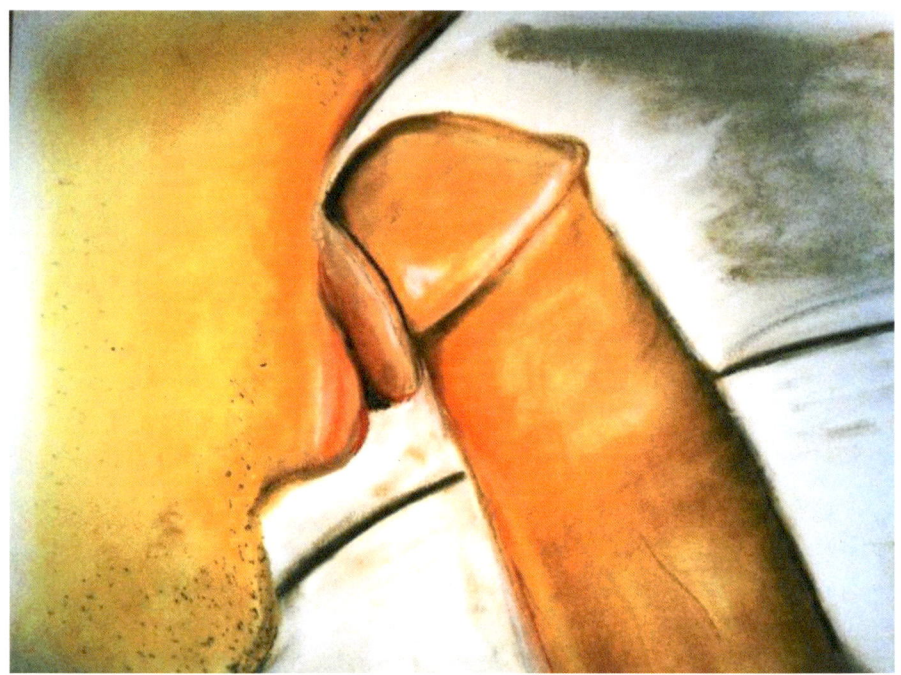

"Love Encounter"

***

Within minutes, 'Olevaivai'olefe'e appears lost to me.

I turn and my feet retrace the footsteps I took vainly following her into the dusk. When I reach Pine Avenue, I ascend the stairs and pass the State Theatre as I stand on the corner of Ocean and Pine. The streetlights' glow turns the sky yellowish-white. The Schuyler Hotel is in front of me, a few rooms lit. Lord & Taylor is closed for business, and city park is mostly empty now. The autumn air is cold and damp. Waves of patchy fog visibly pour onto the street. I head for the Pekin Cafe, right next door to Vogue Beauty Shop, some blocks down Ocean, at the intersection of Cedar Avenue. As I walk alongside parked cars on Ocean, the Long Beach Bath House, stately and majestic, almost gothic under the fog, dominates the horizon, and in the other direction, towards Signal Hill, distant fires from derricks glow upwards.

I recognize that some sort of geography has begun to take shape in my mind. But before long, everything resumes its unrecognized appearance, jumbled waves of different seaside cafes, hotels, barbers and the like, some of which have locked the doors for good, it seems. My legs feel heavy and my arms ache. An overwhelming need for water, and for sleep, takes me. I imagine waves of cars traveled up and down the boulevard just a few years ago, blocking intersections, filling the air with yelling and laughter, motor noises and smoke. But this night, everything seems tired, spent as though the happiness of the past had been an endless party exhausting itself, like I feel now. I reach into my pocket and touch a few coins, probably less than a dollar, maybe I guess, by feeling the size of the metal pieces, without retrieving them. I muffle the high-pitched noise of metal clinking against itself by making a fist inside my trousers, hoping to attract little or no attention. I cough.

I enter Pekin Cafe, a mishmash of Chinese cuisine and common fare. There are only a few tables and a counter. Maria comes up to greet me, "Hey, Tony." Maria is dressed as a waitress, keeping her hair underneath a net, appearing clean and kempt, except for her fingernails on her left hand. Two of her smallest fingers show thick nails with white and brown spots, and they curl towards edges that appear to be almost crumbling. Usually, she does her best to keep her left hand from touching anything except money, unless she has more than one plate to serve.

"Hello, let's see… what's the blue plate today?"

She smiles, "Same old, same old… the best chops, potatoes and gravy you'll find in Long Beach."

"Great, with extra fixins," I nod. "And a cup of coffee, black."

"Be right up. By the way, you saw Fe'e?"

My face appears puzzled, confused, until I realize she might be talking about 'Olevaivai'olefe'e. I ask her, "The Samoan?"

Maria scowls a little bit. "Now, now. She's more than that, Tony."

Curious, I ask, "Yeah? How'dya know?"

Maria giggles, "She's next door, at Vogue, and in here all the time. Sweet Christian girl. She mentioned during breakfast, some tall, handsome fella from the East Coast. I first thought of you."

"I see."

Maria shakes her head, "I'll be right back with your plate. Perk up!"

As she leaves, my hand takes out the change from my pocket. Two quarters and two dimes fall and shine on the tabletop. Over the soft chatter of a couple eating at a nearby table, I think about where I'm staying tonight, a small boarding house a few blocks up Broadway. I've slept there since Solstice and I arrived in Long Beach, more than two months ago. Although Solstice has found her own place to stay through St. Anthony's parish, we see each other, and in fact, she introduced me to 'Olevaivai'olefe'e. I quickly add up some figures: There's the advance on my room, already used up, taken from the last money Solstice and I made on the trip to California, but yesterday was the final day of an extension the management gave me, and they are expecting at least one night's rent tonight, exactly fifty cents.

Interrupting my thoughts, an older man and woman enter the Pekin, arguing about reports that Democrats might nominate New York Governor Franklin Roosevelt, in '32. "That goddamn cripple ain't gonna get elected, by God. Enough of these socialists running this country into the ground." He shouts towards Maria, "Hey! The usual, honey." As Maria peeks from the kitchen she waves her hand in their direction, then disappears. The older woman quietly seats herself, but her company is already seated, still talking. "I mean, a cripple? No one wants to talk about it. See, you... I curl your hair, take you shopping, cook and clean. How's a cripple president gonna work out? Might as well put a pansy in office, some weak sissy, like the ones hanging out at the beach all the time." He turns to me to ask, "Hey, mister. You got a light?"

I merely shake my head, because I do not have matches, and also because his words seem to lack sense or logic.

Finally, the woman speaks, "Dear, it's okay. I have matches in my handbag." Very slowly, her pale, frail hands shaking, she opens her purse and retrieves a small matchbox and hands it to the man.

"See, that's what I'm talking about," he continues. "These goddamn socialists are going to run this country into hell. People ain't all the same. God made some of us to serve the rest of us." He lights a cigarette and returns the matchbox to the lady. "Can you imagine? Two dames taking care of each other like I do for you? Or, some sick, fucking fairies taking care of each other? Ain't gonna happen, not in a million years. And, ain't no weak cripple gonna run this great country. I'm a Hoover man, all the way, and I don't care who those Reds put up."

Meekly, his companion says, "Yes, Hoover."

"Just give me the good book, is all I need."

Maria, returns from the kitchen, holding my blue plate order in her right hand, and a full coffee cup in her left. Carefully, she puts these on my table in front of me. I stare at the fungus destroying her fingernails. She says, "There you go, Tony. One blue plate and a cup of joe."

I notice that, in addition to pork chops and potatoes, there is also applesauce, and sauteed onions and mushrooms, on the same plate. I ask her, "Is this the special?"

"Yep," Maria replies, pulling her head back in surprise, and drawing the attention of the loud man seated near me. "With extra fixins, like you asked."

I realize that the money I have may not be enough for both the meal and for the boarding house. So, I try to see if she will help me, "Maria, thanks much. But, can I say that I thought the special also came with fixins?"

She crosses her arms, her pad of paper for taking orders in the same hand infected with nail fungus. "You asked for extra fixins," she says, emphasizing the word "extra."

"I see."

"Yeah," she clears her throat. "So, that's two bits for the chops and spuds, and an extra dime for the coffee and extras... the applesauce, the onions and mushrooms..."

Perhaps it is because I feel run down, exhausted. Perhaps it is because the older man seated next to me made me upset. Perhaps it is because I enjoyed a day on the beach, free of the concerns of life's necessities, and indulging instead life's pleasures. I become short with her, "I never asked for the mushrooms. Or for the sauce or onions for that matter."

"Listen, young man. I like you. But, you gotta pay for what you ordered."

Just then the older man adds his voice to the conversation, "What do you think this is, boy? Russia? What are you, a Red? The lady said you ordered extra, you pay extra."

I tender a quarter and two dimes to Maria, who silently nods, appreciating the tip. Within five minutes, I have finished my meal, and without saying another word to anyone, I leave, uncertain where I am sleeping tonight.

* * *

The day before eating mushrooms and walking along the beach, Solstice Meridian met me at the entrance of the Pekin Cafe, where she told me, "All set, Tony. 'Olevaivai'olefe'e will meet you tomorrow, by the outside front doors of the bath house, at about four o'clock. She'll bring little chocolate treats, so you can get your mind off everything, take a walk along the beach." Solstice also took out a letter from her pocket. "Tony, this came for you today, at the boarding house. I asked if there was any mail for me, or my uncle," she winks, "and they just gave me this."

It was a letter from Abraham. After opening the envelope and reading the letter's first sentence, I immediately conjured my first sentence in reply: "Upon receiving your letter, I read these first words, of course, 'It was good receiving word from you.' " Then, I felt the immediate need to find some paper to write on, before spending a day walking around Long Beach with 'Olevaivai'olefe'e, both of us forgetting the world and enjoying the benefits of what Solstice promised to be infamous chocolate candy. That was my intention. Instead, I finished writing my letter to Abraham about a week-and-a-half later.

Chapter Four

"Words"

November 16, 1931

Abraham,

Upon receiving your letter, I read these first words, of course, "It was good receiving word from you."

I can hardly remember now what words I shared in the letter I sent you, but I sincerely beg your strong yet tender heart to reveal its generosity and forgiveness, so you may read this second letter, at least once, pretending rivers and mountains separating us are vanished, and two separate seas we call home are one.

Before I write words about your wife, Ruth, and children, Boris and Mila, I must call attention to the cold tone in your missive, which leads me to wonder whether my words exerted here represent no more than wishful thinking on my part, and therefore, merely prop up vague but lingering feelings for you, as if written words create something more than the reality from which they are reduced.

So, instead of beginning deceptively, with grand, heartfelt declarations, I divulge my tormenting ruminations. By what right do I dare speak of love in a manner beyond childish cant? Need God ordain my right to do so? Is it only possible that an obscure divinity be the fountain of all imperfect sentiments, however they rise to the surface? Surely you recognize the self-love in my actions when I exited your life in Manhattan and pursued my own elsewhere, and if so, I hope you also recognize that I do not regard any kind of love, either for oneself or for others, as originating from devotion to the eternal, which has no truth for me. Without your recognition of me as I am truly, I fear the current state between us actually may perpetuate ancient intolerances. Given what we are witnessing in times like these, in Italy, Germany and always America, my fears of the consequences stemming from our difference are not unfounded, though at least I know I am brave enough to mention them. Is my ceaseless courage, in itself, not worth anything to you? After all, with respect to the distance separating us, it is only by writing to you that I may feel not merely friendship but a love that holds something over me and fills and surrounds me, almost.

"Almost," because my qualification is an emphatic restatement of what I believe is our imperfect human condition and all its temporary beauty and worldly possibility. And thus, I state objectively that I accept you are a father of two wonderful children, who are fortunate to have Ruth as their devoted mother. I accept you must love the person who delivered two children calling you father. My acceptance of, and not devotion to, your familial ties, perhaps, points towards the "almost" of my love for you, by which I mean, I can do no more than wish I held passionate feelings towards Ruth and your children, for the sake of your own happiness, yet this is impossible. I cringe at the thought of the pain I will cause you, if you dare open this letter and read the preceding sentence. But, causing you pain is not my intention, as I lack desire either to debate or to persuade. Motivated to share my emotions, I admit my immature and self-destructive jealousy towards Ruth, who has caused me neither insult nor harm in any way. And meekly, I confess it remains only a possibility that such jealousy could be remedied in time with effort, but regardless, it first must be acknowledged.

"Abraham"

I ask, in earnest, could it be any other way? Could I ever, truly appreciate Ruth with the same depth and commitment as you claim? Perhaps I could, in time, learn to love your children, if I felt some recognition as their father, yet such ridiculous thoughts only make me laugh aloud. It would take the imagination of H.G. Wells to conjure a fantastic future where I alone could marry you and raise two children, without the disapprobation of society and relations. And even in such a world, what place would Ruth occupy? I can hardly imagine a time when two men could be called fathers of the same children, and then to blend into the arrangement a woman? Would Ruth not laugh, too, if she were asked these same questions? For the sake of humor, I put the matter this way: appreciating what you and I have shared in the past, and also appreciating you need your family presently, it all makes me feel as though I dwell in Utah. I expect that last comment deserves your healthy laughter, which I believe permits me to grieve what seems to be the death of that which formerly existed, in fact, between you and me. Please take no offense. I write selfishly to lessen the weight of my perpetual anxieties. I have no one else to which to turn. Do you, besides Doctor Parks? I apologize if I sound presumptuous, but I would hardly believe you, if you were to tell me that you talk to Ruth about these matters, for it must be an enormous burden for her to carry even in silence, and you two simply care too much for each other to not exercise discretion, especially in your most private moments. And at that instant of supreme intimacy, you must feel challenged, I suspect, to choose to name it as honesty, pride, or authentic faith, and even more challenged to call it lust.

About such matters concerning that which is true and that which is convenient, I often find myself distracted, and I entertain my mind with philosophical questions about whether it is useful to talk about ourselves as beings that really make choices. Lately, I am vexed by scenes of sailboats on the Pacific Ocean, moving with the ways of the wind, eternally gliding until finally settled in some safe harbor. Is Doctor Parks your anchor? I can't imagine that he alone stopped your drifting about, but I can envision you giving up in his office around the time of the disaster on Wall Street, talking anxiously about your longing for the stability of home and routine, of the illusions Ruth kindly offers, divulging you eagerly want to return to a successful life, of relative wealth and normalcy—none of which would include me. I wonder if he surprised you, if he asked about homosexuals and watched your eyes dart back and forth, unwilling to stare at him directly and simply say, "yes." Surely I am a hypocrite for writing such words, after all I feel somewhat uneasy about taking on professional labels, or even the more vernacular ones often uttered with hate. But, alas, I have never visited the good doctor, nor any alienist for that matter, and therefore, I can truly say that at the end of the day I sleep, when I can sleep, knowing I am my own anchor, which offers me no particular pride, just a certain perspective, which I wonder if you ever miss.

Dare I tell you of my adventurous choices thus far? As you pointed out in your letter, my journey from New York to California mirrors the decisions of throngs of poor people, but I am certain that it is quite dissimilar in several aspects. First and foremost, I feel fortunate to have as a companion an orphan girl, who prefers to use the name Solstice Meridian, lacking true knowledge of her birth name, if she even was ever given one. Perhaps you have heard from Doctor Parks some rumors. In any case, our trip started at Glamour Jackson's Brooklyn home, where we narrowly escaped a fire, the cause of which was unknown, although Solstice suspects Caligula's gang was behind the incident. Fleeing in a 1924 black Ford truck carrying a variety of Catholic paraphernalia in the back, we transacted in Baltimore two dozen minor and major Saints painted on plaster figurines hollowed out to transport—how shall I put it—whatever one might be able to carry inside. The sale of these statuettes from the back of the truck, in addition to the money you kindly left me, purchased gasoline and food as far as Texas. There was a staged incident with the El Paso police involving a private financial settlement of an unpleasant matter in our favor followed by a hasty departure. Finally, by the time we arrived in Tucson, we had to sell the truck but earned a profit allowing us to purchase two rail tickets to Los Angeles. Thankfully owing to Solstice's wits wagering our last dollars on the train, we arrived in Long Beach with enough currency to keep us meagerly housed and fed through the end of October, about the time when your letter finally arrived.

In the last week or so since receiving your letter, I have been sleeping in a bed owned by a boarding house manager, from whom I have also rented a shared room, and to whom I offer my labor voluntarily. Such labor has included modest housekeeping but also personal favors, which I would rather not describe further, if only because I don't want to confuse you. Honestly, each and every day has been a struggle, yet I have no regrets taking whatever measures seem necessary to care for myself—perhaps in this regard you recognize something about your domestic situation in mine. As for Solstice, still a girl in appearance though more a woman in intellect, she encountered little difficulty persuading religious charities to provide her shelter and meals, and she volunteers in exchange for their assistance, while at the same time, we have developed a fruitful rapport between the generations, about which I cannot detail, except to say that, even after a decade, Prohibition continues to favor unlikely alliances. I feel certain that by the time she reaches the age of majority, she will know more about the ways of the world than any Princeton lad.

At times, I find myself reflecting on my parental instincts, which to be honest, do not appear so obvious to me. Solstice, perhaps eleven or twelve years old, could be my daughter, it is true. And while we do at times play the roles of uncle and niece, when it suits our mutual advantage, such ruses serve no other purposes than the temporary ones we devise for any given situation. There is nothing avuncular in my disposition towards her otherwise. And she seems to appreciate her independence, for indeed, it is all she has known. And so, even if I were to drop my guard, and to reflect on the meaning of your children to me, as though I could empathize with you, I still would arrive at a sense of my own limitations in such matters. Boris, who from your stories I recall, seems a wonderful and curious boy, filled with such light and joy that only his older sister Mila stands taller in my eyes, in terms of meeting the expectations these days placed on children living in homes with the loving and constant support of stable parents. Nonetheless, I would feel lost if I were to assume the responsibilities of being their father. It is to your credit that you succeeded in raising them. Whether your past separation from Ruth will have any adverse effect on their development remains to be seen, but I can say that children are resilient, and for every child there is a unique story. My instincts, however, concern you. Are you happy devoting all your energy to their upbringing, and is it possible they notice that your heart is troubled by matters they cannot comprehend? You will always be their father, there is no doubt. Yet, your devotion to Ruth must seem somewhat artificial to them. Children are wiser than they often appear. You carry on your shoulders the weight of professional and familial duties, but the joy that would come to you if you could live life truly as your desire, free from convention—that joy would radiate and fill Boris and Mila with a special understanding of the human heart. Of that, I am certain.

In matters of children there is yet one more matter that I feel compelled to mention. One of Solstice's gifts seems to be her ability to sense things as they are, and not merely appear to be. I might use the word "clairvoyant" to describe her, and I am sure she would giggle if she heard me use that word about her, but she consistently senses certain hidden feelings within me, in addition to the approach of certain events and coincidences. To be sure, I might be exaggerating. But immediately upon meeting me, in Brooklyn, she sensed feelings of guilt surrounding me, lurking like a stalking shadow. Meditation has brought to the surface a likely possibility of the source of such feelings, and it now seems that my story of who I thought I am, as a person, might need alteration, for as it turns out, there are causes of my guilt.

Specifically, it seems an incident in Brooklyn was the precipitating cause of my seeking you out shortly before we re-ignited the flames of passion between us and formed a domestic bond that forced your temporary separation from Ruth. The incident to which I refer concerns yet another orphan, as if some cryptic message is being sent through children regarding my fate.

Only days before I attempted to arrange a meeting with you, first through lawyer Rothman, and then surprising you with a visit at the courts, I was standing on the edge of the Brooklyn side of the East River, at the shipyards, with a shotgun in my hand at one side and an orphan, named Joe, standing at my other. Facing Joe and me, Caligula stood in person, surrounded by a cadre of his loyal and armed brood of young orphaned queers. He gave me a choice: to either join his gang by killing Joe then and there, or to be killed by Joe, an ambitious but desperate young man also wielding a pistol. I hesitated, which should have instantly led to my death, as Joe in fact raised his pistol towards me. Caligula, having secret goals, interrupted Joe by shooting him fatally in the face. I instantly escaped and spent days before resolving I had to turn to you for help.

It is shameful that I hid this tale from you. That it in fact happened I can substantiate by suggesting to you that Doctor Parks, and Glamour Jackson, may confirm certain details. Still, I feel a buried but heavy guilt for having been involved in the murder of a child at all. If there is any insight to be taken from this grim story it is that I failed as a so-called gangster. And in my failure, I recognized the need to seek cover in your strength and stability, with the hope that something enduring and exclusive could be built from our arrangement. Certainly, there are many who would cast me as unfit to rear any child, and I do harbor persistent doubts about myself. Of course, that I could be arrested as an accomplice to this crime also haunts me, and I beg you, as an attorney, not to betray my confidence that you will protect this letter and its contents. But also as important to me, personally, I suffer from a nagging worry that I am incapable of performing as a man who can execute decisions either in his own self-interest or in the interest of others. I do feel time has healed some of the scars I suffered in Brooklyn, and I intend to avoid similar entanglements in the future. But it would be dishonest for me to say I have not changed. And it seems obvious to Solstice that something hangs over me, as though I were a man constantly obscured by a foggy overcast.

It should not have to be said, but I will say it anyway. Among my anxieties resulting from having retreated to your protections following the murder of orphan Joe is an acute awareness of my financial indebtedness towards you. When I go through the trouble of making estimates regarding certain expenses incurred since we started living together at the end of 1927 through my departure to California last spring, based on the costs associated with most domestic arrangements where one spouse supports another, we might arrive at a figure totalling an amount of dollars approximating a number in the low thousands. And while I insist that there were times where I did make modest contributions, it would be dishonest of me to claim that mine would offset yours in any real significant way: I would estimate my contributions as ten percent of my total debt to you. Such cold statistics, of course, do not take into account the intangible benefits we exchanged from our mutual consortium and intimacy. How strange I should even write of these things to you, when in fact, our romantic arrangement was never simply matter of contract, as if it could have been, but was always an affair of the heart. Still, I must make these matters clear, if I am ever to feel like you may trust me again, and not merely dismiss me as a sly ruffian or, worse, a gutter prostitute. Put most simply, I owe you, so please accept my debt to you as a debt.

For that reason, and for the many reasons previously shared, I beg for your mercy, which is perhaps the ultimate strategy of a scoundrel. That I should even ask for your mercy is obviously desperate. That I know you are capable of such may even be presumptuous. After all, what romance was ever born of mercy? But mercy is the temper of all justice, and in an affair as complicated and ill-fortuned as ours, where justice dictates that you must have your life and I must have mine, mercy may be the only path through which we might imagine any sort of future which includes both of us living long, happy, rewarding lives. We have suffered enough cruelty and disrespect in this world that we deserve mercy from the other, and by mercy I mean to say that we must acknowledge the power in our feelings. If it is necessary to live our lives apart, even for the rest of our days, then it is necessary, and no amount of pleading will alter this necessity, and therefore, even contrived silence may be, finally, the only mercy we can offer one another.

But if in that silence, you care to remember that there was a day when you opened this letter for the first time—maybe when you first took it from the mail, or maybe the following day or year—then I want that memory to stay with you, as long as possible, especially after you read these last paragraphs, calling for you, begging for your return.

If you ever change your mind in favor of a blissful cure, do not read but taste these words: fellatio on a rollercoaster, sodomy on an airplane, our fingers in three holes at once, tongue tied, salivating anus, uninserted erectile ejaculation, hyperextended scrotum synchronization, the private massage parlor of our own devices, not twenty yards from the sea. Pouncing on each ounce punched out from each pouch. Beachside service, a room filled with coitus interruptus, in flagrante delicto, voyeuristic misdemeanor, masturbatory crescendo. Your thigh skin, taut in my fist, my unusual uncircumsized trunk shrunk, hung, swung out and in like a pendulum, in tempo with your pole teasing my fisted hole. Stoned, drunk. Blood gorged and gorgeous, enormous, inside us, scissor-like and spread-eagle, lifted over and up, illegal, bowed down before your regal eminence, urinating prostrated, stimulating prostates, protesting pains ignored. Hog-tied, belly-down, jelly-stuffed and unjammed-up, semen-soaked, choked, cloaked in smoke, hot wax playing with flames burning in oil, in a vessel teetering above your urethra, your polished knob, teardrop emissions. Limbs extended like lambs over a spit, muscles exhausted, screaming beings, surrender and submission, completion in somnambulence, an out of body existence. The vocabulary of experience.

We may yet uncover the true kindness meant for the other hidden inside our skins.

And maybe you squander the moment by telling me to lie down, lie down for a moment longer than the moment passes, until we only dream: soft hairs on your arms emit notes, humming phrases, orchestrating movements, singing songs leaving earth, taking atmosphere and filling the city with unrecognized joys competing for oxygen, an all-consuming masculine energy powered by executive decisions made in our private committee, a two-man boardroom fashioned from our bedroom, a window to gaze upon a realm of colored, oceanic transitions like moon phases passing between bluish days and starry nights, indistinguishable from one another, unless we choose to name them so.

From sleep, we wake to the laws of private property twisted for our comforts, conveniently recorded in the judicial excrement that deploys categorical fictions, yet mere impermanent obstacles to our liberation. Testicular consequences are not merely human offspring in our world, as we become dirty old men, in our forties, fifties, sixties, seventies and perhaps eighties, who appreciate a respectful, asexual distance from the younger generation, who in turn honor and obey us, queer creatures that choose to keep an eye on the sea, the only true unitary reality surrounding all territory.

We have become our island for two.

Two, the only two. And yes there is Ruth and Boris and Mila, but there is also Solstice and maybe others, too. Our island is but part of an archipelago, encompassing more than fantastic domesticities, more than subterranean confidentialities, more than homosexual proclivities. In this fantasy, we have earned a certain reciprocity, according to which we are able to give those we love, and need, a lifelong stability. Error and confusion are banished, and the world becomes a practical problem, more prosaic, ending the linguistic taunts of pornography in favor of the delicate arrangements necessary for spending the rest of our lives together.

So, in concluding this letter, I retreat to a common discourse to beg for your return. I hope we can solve the puzzle of our mutual happiness. I am presently set on southern California as my home, although it is certainly the biggest con, the largest tourist trap in the world, as though one could live here for decades and never be allowed to claim a parcel of it as owned. So, yes, as you say, I will start over and live my life here. I have already started. But, I'm sorry, my beloved, it is impossible for me forget about you, no matter how much time and distance divides us. How could I? And unless I am truly lying to myself, I proudly declare I foolishly believe it is also impossible for you to forget about me, too.

Until you return to me,

Anthony

"Fantasy"

Chapter Five

"Violence to Violets to Violence"

There is nothing natural about protecting oneself. All homicides, even later construed as not immoral, necessitate a living soul either to execute or to allow to be executed in one decisive moment some obviously concrete criminal action, which reveals the lexicon of self-defense, coercion and even incapacity serves no other purpose than judicial artifice.

* * *

Each new year promises hope, but winter also comes mildly to Long Beach, so that the relief of warmer, sunny days appears muted in December, and especially so amidst signs and rumors of sweeping global depression.

In the confines of the boarding house at which I managed to find shelter, the world seems to grow ever more tired and slow, winter appears suitable, and my otherwise cheerful disposition takes on an appropriate mild-mannered, everyday grey. When we do see each other, about two times a week, Solstice jokes and calls me "Clingy," and I can't imagine what she might mean, as she also is held fast to life by the routine of her chores at St. Anthony's parish, which provides her room and board, similar to my own domestic arrangement, except hers is given to her freely, while my labors earn me five dollars weekly, before deducting seven-days room and board of three dollars. Outside, along Boardwalk Boulevard, some blocks down, small single-floor houses line up, row to row, sheltering families trying to make do with what seems available. Surely, the tourist hustle, once it returns in vigor in early summer, will bring some relief to Long Beach, they hope. But otherwise, it is the oil derricks on Signal Hill and Wilmington, and the traffic inside the ports of Los Angeles and Long Beach, that circulates most local currency to make survival more possible and less odious than it would be otherwise.

The boarding house itself is a two-story construction, containing four separate apartment units on the top floor, each one housing about three girls and women, and on the bottom floor, there is a single apartment divided into three rooms, each of which has about four men. There is also an empty garage with a couple pieces of gym equipment and a kitchen on the bottom floor, and a bathroom and living room with a new radio. It has become my responsibility to participate in daily activities which include some simple cooking and cleaning, but also giving attention to the manager of the facility, Daryl Williams, who not only sleeps in one room with three other boarders on the bottom floor, but spends his days issuing orders to everyone, as if the communal living arrangement is his own private experiment to determine who shall live under his supervision, until he expresses his dissatisfaction with any particular individual for whatever private reason.

When I first came to the premises, I had enough savings to survive a couple of months without laboring under the manager's direction, but nonetheless, I recognized the perilousness of my situation. After my savings ran out, I knew I had nowhere else to turn, as St. Anthony's parish was more inclined to assist orphans like Solstice than to assist able-bodied men like myself. Sleeping on the street or in parks has always been out of the question, if for no other reason than spending a night in jail—the inevitable result of sleeping outdoors overnight—seems not only unnecessarily damaging of any hopes to improve my situation but also dangerous in and of itself, as I have never heard of the police—who were rumored to be the same thing as the local Ku Klux Klan in Long Beach—dealing with unmarried, childless hobos except impatiently and, more often, brutally.

Resigned to accepting whatever it was my fate had in store at the boarding house, one night I returned from Pekin Cafe, with only two bits in my pocket, my toleration was tested when a wrestling fight broke out between the manager and a resident, Dennis Carpenter. It happened, without my exaggerating to any degree, as soon as I opened the house door. Pale, usually unshaven and a generation older than Carpenter, Williams stood tall in baggy, dingy clothes, screaming about rules for use of the communal radio. Carpenter, who had just finished cleaning himself in the bathroom, and who likely hoped to repeat a routine evening working as a dishwasher in a diner, stood completely naked in his dark brown, tattooed skin, except for a thin green towel wrapped around his waist. He protested Williams' accusations. As if I didn't exist, I entered the living room and tried to make my way peacefully through, but the two men ceased yelling only to take to wrestling each other, which caused me to retreat. Carpenter, being far more muscular, determined and younger than the manager, used both of his hands to push Williams backwards onto a small glass table in front of an old, broken sofa. The glass shattered as Carpenter's clean body fell down on top of Williams, forcing two other residents to jump in and separate the men. Williams received a severe cut to his shoulder, splattering the ceramic floor tiles with continuously oozing blood. Carpenter stood up unscathed, and even his towel kept snug against his waist, revealing nothing, as he returned to his room to dress for work. The two men did not look at or say anything to each other for a week thereafter.

Since agreeing to work under the manager's direction, I have avoided talking to Carpenter and the other house guests, by continuously making excuses of looking for work I know is not easy to come by and spending my days out and about, away from the illusory security of my shared bedroom. At night, I sleep in a room shared with three other men, all in wooden bunk beds. My roommate, Carl, sleeps in the same bunk as mine, below me. A heavy-set fellow, whose family is originally from Puerto Rico, he lives here because his wife kicked him out of the house after he threatened her with violence, which he swears never happened in fact. Often jolly, but occasionally edgy, Carl keeps to himself and returns every night with soup kitchen tales. Rarely, I invite Carl to a diner for breakfast, to keep him happy with me, and in fact he has been my only ally. His flaw is that he snores so loudly that I am forced to stuff cotton balls into my ears as far as possible, each night. Between Carl's snoring and the bed I sleep on, I frequently wake at night, insomniac, but never leave the house, as the manager locks the doors with a bar, from the inside, to keep us from exiting and entering after ten o'clock at night and before five o'clock in the morning, and this despite the obvious fire hazard his infantilizing security arrangement creates. As for my other two roommates, a black kid named Harold and an old pasty-white military veteran, Charlie, who served in the war in the Philippines, I pay them little attention. Harold hardly washes himself and is always coming into the house looking like he has no regard for the opinions or concerns of anyone. He never causes any problems as far as I know, but he usually keeps to himself, denying himself education and ignoring the manners and hygiene that most working people take for granted. Charlie is simply impossible. He always has something to say about the respect he was due as a veteran but spends most of his days reading novels, at times aloud, particularly late at night, about battle-weary soldiers then addresses everyone like he is still a training sergeant.

From the other rooms' inhabitants, I have made few allies or acquaintances. In the room across the hall sleeps James Carver, a sly, skinny father, who passes as white. I only learned he was black, because Harold once said something to Charlie I overheard one night. The next day, I confirmed it myself by asking Carver where he went to church, and he mentioned Christ

"Dennis Carpenter"

Second Baptist Church, which upon my investigation appeared to be a community of black believers. Carver insists everyone address him properly and formally, and only Dennis Carpenter has permission to speak with him on a first-name basis. Carver and Carpenter share their room with two other men, whose names I never have learned. One appears to be slowly dying, possibly from cancer, or something similar that produces foul odors and unsightly skin lesions. Another fellow is drying out from opium addiction, I hear, and he keeps busy during the day rereading the same book by Ernest Hemingway. In Williams' room, there are three more men, all of whom are either former convicts or extremely ill, or some combination of the two. Except for Carl, I trust nobody.

Daryl Williams, the manager, is an entirely different matter, for I have learned to trust him in a certain kind of way. He knows he can summon the police at any time and order the eviction of anybody for any reason he gives, tempered only by considerations of subsequent vengeful retaliations. Since Williams lost his fight to Carpenter, I have made it a point of displaying my healthy body by taking the liberty of walking around our dwelling in a towel, otherwise naked, each morning, copying Carpenter's swagger. I calculate he might see my healthy body as a counterpoint to the power of Carpenter, from whom I seek no trouble, so I make sure, walking in my towel, to greet Williams, who by the way neither talks about having a love in his life nor receives any visits from the opposite gender. To confuse my housemates, I once spent a series of mornings walking outside covered only in my towel, to arouse the curiosity of the women upstairs, calling for me, begging me for marriage, asking for assistance with the plumbing, claiming to need my help shopping. I almost always, politely, declined. Each time, Williams demanded that I return indoors in the name of decency, and I submitted, making him feel empowered. I even grew aroused rubbing against the towel I was sporting. As though unwittingly cast in a vaudeville routine, Williams scanned then chastised me, ordering me to get dressed then making me prove to his satisfaction I was decent enough to leave the house.

Of the many benefits I earn from Williams' favor, including the meager compensation for my domestic services, is riding in the car he uses. There have been occasions when Williams inquires about my agenda for the day, and I pretend as though I were busy, until he insists he needs help moving out items from grocery stores into his vehicle, a 1930 Ford Model A automobile that, at first, he claimed to own. In fact, his car requires making installment payments to Farmers and Merchants Bank, which also owns the deed to his boarding house. Payments for both the home mortgage and the Ford are made by Long Beach pastor, Dr. George Taubman, and offered free of charge to Williams. Dr. Taubman is reputed to have the largest Bible class in the nation, and anyone as white and self-important as Daryl Williams, who wants to get ahead in Long Beach society, has to belong. In exchange for his attendance and moral support, Williams enjoys a free bed at the boarding house, a line of credit at a couple of grocery stores and the use of the Ford, all courtesy of Dr. Taubman. The manager also collects as his personal income the rent he receives from women and men at the boarding house. He volunteered this information to me, likely as an effort to gain my confidence, and perhaps, to join my soul with Dr. Taubman's flock. But every time he reveals to me another detail about his personal life, while we take our weekly trips to and from the grocery store, he also uses the opportunity to place his hand on my knee, which he tries to massage, casually, before he quickly moves up towards my thigh then pulls away.

On those occasions, we usually have a conversation that begins with me stating, "You're touching my knee."

Williams pretends innocence.

"Go on," I say gruffly, then add, "but don't get queer on me." My aggressive tone usually causes him to become passive, and he apologizes by calling me "dear boy," pleading he is misunderstood.

But then, one day shortly before Christmas, silently riding in his car, he wipes his brow and asks me to bring him flowers. I ask him what kind of flowers, and he tells me to surprise him.

The next afternoon, at a little shop called Petal's near the corner of Pine Avenue and First Street, 'Olevaivai'olefe'e shouts to me from across a counter, "Anthony! I haven't seen you in forever. Where you been?"

Before answering her question, I tease her, "'Olevaivai'olefe'e! You're not at the salon?"

"You call me Fe'e, okay? It's my day off. I do flowers today," she responds.

And keeping the rhythm of our banter, I ask, "And flowers for hair?"

She laughs, "Very good, palagi. You remember me. Why, do you need some flowers for someone special's hair?" She watches me studying her dress, designed with repeating rectangular geometries in hues of black and brown over a background of yellow. "You like my puletasi? It's pretty, yes?" She moves her hands from her shoulders to her waist, turning her hips and head to one side.

"Yes, Fe'e. And yes, I need flowers for someone special's hair." As I approach the counter, I bring my hands close to my mouth, as if to invite 'Olevaivai'olefe'e to hear a secret. Before talking, I look around the store dramatically, and she follows my eyes, as if she, too, is concerned for keeping our privacy. Then, satisfied we are alone, I speak softly, "Ugly flowers... for the hair."

She pulls back, " 'Auleaga...?" She mulls my request. "I think the most ugly hair flowers are violets. They're so small and purple, and purple is so sad, don't you think?"

I turn my head in confusion. "Violets are sad? Huh."

"Yes, so let me get them." She scurries to the back of the store and speaking loudly asks if I want to walk with her on the beach again, but without her chocolate candies next time.

When she returns with the flowers, I tell her I accept her invitation, and then I suggest a topic of conversation. "Yes, the beach, but I want to hear about you and Pago Pago, about how you came to California."

"Only if you tell me about New York City."

I smile, "Maria was the one who told you then."

"Yes, she did. I love her."

I tender a dime for the violets, promising to visit 'Olevaivai'olefe'e again, soon, to make a date for a sunset stroll over Rainbow Pier.

Before I turn to the direction of the boarding house, I visit a newspaper stand on Ocean Boulevard. I ask the paperman if he has any copies of yesterday's news, and he hands me today's morning edition of the Press-Telegram. I offer to pay him a nickel, and seeing the violets in my hand, he waves me off and I thank him. I am about to take the first sheet of the paper to wrap the flowers and discard the other paper, when I realize I have a good deal of time, even though the news kiosk is already starting to close for the day. I walk to buy an apple from a street vendor and then make my way to a small grocery store to purchase some bread and milk. I head down to the sand and water, where I seat myself and read the paper: police reports of crimes and accidents, a couple of stories about Europe, socialites and book readings, tales about the Japanese empire, reports about the United States Navy, advertisements, market statistics, obituaries. I finish eating, and soon I fall asleep.

When I wake, the sky appears dark, and few people seem to be enjoying the damp evening atmosphere. I wrap the violets in one sheet of newspaper, walk up to Ocean Boulevard and spy a clock face on a bank building. It reads a few minutes past nine o'clock, and I feel somewhat shocked I had been napping on the beach for so long. I take an inventory of my body, stretch my aching back, pinch a bit of loose skin on my belly. Without much to keep me busy, I have lost tone and muscle mass to my physique. Even walking seems somewhat of an effort. If I walk my legs too quickly, my calves grow weak and sore after only a block or two. I adjust my gait to a slower pace, which feels more comfortable, but also makes me appreciate the relationship between routine inactivity and poor fitness. As I causally head for Broadway, I resolve to spend more energy devoted to exercise and concoct a personal training regimen using the few pieces of gym equipment in the garage at the boarding house. Aside from mismatched dumbbells and barbells, the garage has a rowing machine, well-maintained with a wood base, an aluminum seat with a cutout deco design, wooden pulleys and frame, and a fastened cloth belting.

Finally, when I arrive at the boarding house, about thirty minutes before the door is locked, I find the radio silent, and most everyone has turned early to bed. It is nearly impossible to see my way through the living room, except that a small sliver of yellow light seeps through the bottom of the garage door at the back of the kitchen area. I hear the soft noises of repeated squeaking and the gentle grunts of a man breathing. Curious, I open the door to find Williams using the rowing machine. I guess he parked the car on the street this evening. He pauses for only a moment to waive me inside, and as I comply, I close the door behind me. Without talking, he directs me to put the violets on a small, simple wall shelf, and then he resumes rowing.

He whispers loudly, "Anthony, come here."

I approach him and he asks me to come closer, and then closer still. I approach him, straddling my legs across either side of the machine, and position myself in such a manner that, as he rows pulling his arms back and his torso forward, his head comes within inches of my waist.

"Closer," he begs, keeping his head down, but his eyes look up at me.

I carefully inch forward, and as soon as he feels comfortable, still rowing, he begins to kiss the fabric of my trousers, which excites me, and the more it excites me, the more he pushes against my clothes. My hands reach down and open up the buttons on the fly-front, and as I had stopped wearing my old, worn-out undergarments for some time, his lips touch my skin each cycle of his rowing strokes. Studiously, he uses his exercise technique, as though to tease himself, trying carefully, without allowing his teeth to make any contact with my skin, to coax his mouth around my flesh, which he takes into his slippery throat, deeper with each rowing stroke. I merely stand above him, until reaching the point of climax, I pull back more than several inches, to his disappointment, and give orders. "Get up, so I can poke you out back," I command, pointing at him, first, and then the wall, second. He unbuckles the cloth belt attached to the machine, and he stands, drops his trousers, and places both hands against the garage wall and straddles the rowing machine, jiggling his pimpled, curvy bottom in front of me. Taking spit from my mouth, my fingers gently massage his rear, pushing patiently inside, using more dribble falling from my tongue. Finally satisfied with my efforts, I stand behind him, and with the same patience as before, I enter, and my hands take control of his hips, which I hold still, at first, but then let go so he may continue his exercises.

In a couple of minutes, he grows so excited that we both grunt, quietly, in unison, and without touching himself, he spills his seed on the rowing machine. After we dress ourselves, I walk to the table where the flowers are, and pick them up only to remove the newspaper covering which I hand over to Williams, who instantly takes it to clean the mess, as best he can. I then hand him the violets, we both smile, and without kissing or embracing, we leave the garage, turn off the electrical switch to the light, and make our way through the dark for our separate beds.

"Violets"

The next morning, I begin my day making eggs, toast and coffee for my housemates, after using the bathroom, and in the middle of my routine, Williams enters the kitchen and asks me about helping him with grocery shopping, which I decline, if merely to demonstrate my independence. The manager starts talking louder, whining about responsibility and demanding that I give him my attention. I ignore him, but he doesn't stop, and at this point, Carver and Carpenter who are also starting their day, notice things seem tense in the kitchen, and they hover interested in seeing where things will go. Rather than placate him, I decide to intimidate Williams by admonishing him, rudely, "Ya know what, Williams? You sound like a goddamn bitch," which has the effect of shutting him up. I wait for his reply, and he looks at Carver and Carpenter who leave us alone in the kitchen. Williams recognizes he has no allies in his own house, and although he probably thought about evicting me, he retreats and asks me if he can talk to me in the garage.

We leave the kitchen, close the door behind us, and he opens the garage door to let morning light enter. Then, he turns to me and says, "I don't appreciate how you talked to me in there, Camarrata."

"Well, what the hell is with all the nagging? I thought you were different, Williams—that you could handle our arrangement. But you can't, can you."

He then crosses his arms and says, "I feel threatened."

Impatient, I slap him across his face. "You know what, you little tyrant? You are the shittiest manager I've ever known, and if you want to keep things peaceful, you need to stop talking the way you talk to me and everyone else around here. It's too much."

Recovering from his embarrassment, Williams replies, "Yeah, well, Merry Christmas to you, too," and he storms back into the house, leaving me alone in the garage, where I stand for about two minutes in silence.

Right around New Year's Eve, after Williams and I ignored each other completely for about a week, without any holiday celebration or meals for the boarding house tenants, he invites me for another ride in his car trip to the grocery store, I accept his invitation, and he continues to put his hand on my knee, as I grow more determined to spend 1932 looking for better employment and shelter.

* * *

December 25, 1931

Anthony,

You have the confidential ear of this lawyer.

There is nothing natural about protecting oneself. All homicides, even later construed as not immoral, necessitate a living soul either to execute or to allow to be executed in one decisive moment some obviously concrete criminal action, which reveals the lexicon of self-defense, coercion and even incapacity serves no other purpose than judicial artifice.

As for the other matters you share in your letter, truthfully I am at a loss for words.

Warmest regards,

Abraham

Chapter Six

"Blindfold"

If it is a choice between my own suicide and promiscuity, then it seems rather obvious to prefer the latter. Daryl Williams, fortunately, ceased requesting flowers after our one and only encounter, and I happily obliged his further disinterest in me by requesting his assistance in helping me secure a California driving license in exchange for adding grocery shopping to my list of his assigned house chores, without expectation of further compensation. After mulling for a couple of days, the boarding house manager signaled his acceptance of my offer by leaving on my pillow a copy of the California Driver's Manual, needed for self-preparation before taking the written portion of the licensing examination. As my New Year's resolution, I saved my extra dollars, and by the dull and dreary end of the new year's first month, I managed to have stashed a small amount in a secret location, with the kind help of my trusty bunkmate Carl. The written test and driving exam date came, which I passed using Williams' offer of his Ford, and soon I owned a license and was granted the privilege of driving upon prior request for approved purposes, if I purchased my own fuel to be deducted from my weekly earnings.

Meanwhile, shortly before passing the test, I met up one day with Solstice, who knew I was aiming for a driving license. She mentioned that, in Vogue, she had seen 'Olevaivai'olefe'e, who in turn asked her to invite me for a St. Valentine's Day affair, and while both ladies felt the holiday likely meant little to me, Solstice mentioned it would be feted among a certain circle of 'Olevaivai'olefe'e's friends and acquaintances. They just started meeting at a secret location only recently agreed upon in nearby Wilmington, on the other side of the Los Angeles River from Long Beach, to spend the evening with decent Prohibition beverages and a bit of mirthful chaos—all taking place in an unnamed, unpublished location so as to stymie rumors that invariably circle back to the police, Solstice explained. The police just recently raided, simultaneously, two illegal hot spots in Long Beach called the 606 Club and the 96 Bar favored by 'Olevaivai'olefe'e's social set. Solstice said I was requested to borrow the Ford from the night of February Fourteenth through the following morning. I promised nothing about inviting Solstice, but told her to let 'Olevaivai'olefe'e know that if I passed the licensing test, I would take the two of us out for fun. Besides, I figured that after a month of near solitary confinement in the boarding house, for the purpose of saving a few dollars, I not only owed myself release, but also I needed an opportunity to meet people, to see if there was some social path out of my hopeless and unstable living situation.

"Daryl," I start to say, some days into February, "I want to talk to you."

"Shoot," he says. "Give it your best shot."

I stop washing the breakfast dishes and turn the water off. Rinsing both my hands on the towel, I then point double-barrel at him, "Right, so, I'm trying to meet people, you know…"

"Moving up and out, huh?"

I nod, "That's the idea, yeah. But I got to meet them first. So I've been invited to a little get together at a friend's house in a week or so, and I wanted to use the car."

Williams, still finishing his coffee, takes a sip to think about my request. "How late, would you say, young man?"

I speak honestly, "Can't say."

He quickly asks, "'Can't' cause you won't, or 'can't' cause you can't?"

"It ain't like you think. I just don't know how long it all will go. Tell you what, I'll park the car outside…"

He interrupts, "…and you'll sleep in it, cause I'm not opening the house late, and I'm not leaving it open for anyone." He appears to be in a good mood, because at least he acts cooperative.

"That's just about what I was gonna say. I'll sleep in it and get in at five."

Finishing his coffee in one gulp, he hands me the cup to wash, "Remind me the day before."

I smile, "You got it," and finish washing the dishes in the sink.

"Yep," he calls back and walks away, yelling from inside his bedroom, "And that's a week's notice if you end up moving out and up, please, otherwise I'll hold your pay."

As the days pass without event, and winter holds to its pattern of morning clouds and afternoon sunshine, I reflect on the matter of a club serving alcohol in this year of 1932. I think about whether it's cut, even though Solstice said 'Olevaivai'olefe'e described it as "decent." I think about, if it is in fact decent, imported from Canada or Mexico, how it might be transported from its source for distribution. And I think about what sort of people might provide decent liquor to the kind of people otherwise hated by most of society, nearly universally, as the police raid every new hot spot, put the names and home addresses of at least a couple dozen people in the papers, charge them with crimes involving moral turpitude—a series of events which usually lead to somebody's suicide, also usually reported in the papers, including that suicidal somebody's name and home address. And I imagine that among these kind of people there is always some inner circle whose anonymous members survive police arrests and newspaper reports and who ensure life goes on even after each raid.

With some cash saved from January and early February, I visit a small clothing shop on Ocean Boulevard and purchase a crisp, striped dress shirt, before I take my worn-down suit for cleaning and stitching. I polish my shoes and darn my socks. I sleep early the night before, and shave my face clean the next morning. After finishing my chores for the day, I visit 'Olevaivai'olefe'e at Vogue Salon, which is just as busy as Petal's, she tells me. She hardly has time to chat with me, but we meet in the back of the salon, and she tells me to drive the Ford onto Rainbow Pier, where she'll meet me at about ten o'clock tonight—a perfect time for me, as the boarding house doors will be locked, and no one will notice my departure, except perhaps Carl. She adds that Solstice is permitted to come, and that it was petty of me not to invite her, too, and she teases me for my ungentlemanly pettiness by calling me "Clingy" as we say goodbye to one another.

"Vogue"

When I return home, still dressed in the only pair of casual clothes I own, I make dinner for my housemates by roasting a whole chicken, already marinated the night before with garlic and butter. I toast some stale bread and cook it in a pan with half a can of vegetable soup for a few minutes. Once it's cooled, I stuff the bird, about seven pounds, and put extra stuffing in some foil, before I bake it all at a low heat for a couple of hours, telling everybody dinner will be a little later tonight, but worth it. The radio plays Al Jolson and popular music while they wait. The manager and all my roommates are waiting for dinner, and James Carver, too, while, Dennis Carpenter is already out, and most of the men sleeping in Williams' room keep to themselves tonight. After finished basting and thoroughly cooking, I take the bird out of the oven, filling the house with pleasant aromas, and prepare the kitchen table with plates, forks, knives, cups and clean cloth napkins.

As I invite them to the table, Carl starts, "What is this, Thanksgiving?"

"Nah," I smile. "Why not?"

Williams elbows Carl, "It's Valentine's Day, stupid."

Harold breaks his usual silence and jokes, "Anthony's in love..."

Carl cuts him off, "In love? With whom... one of them girls up the stairs?"

I finally end the conversation by saying, "Gentlemen, and you are all gentlemen, please be seated, and enjoy this meal, which I figure if it brings you happiness, may it come back to me many, many times."

Williams takes the first seat, "All right, boys. Let's eat."

The dinner conversation is actually pleasant and polite, which is a break for the house, as the members of our community usually fend for themselves, coming in and out of meals without rhyme or reason, except for Williams, who always joins me. Afterwards, they return to the radio or prepare for bed, and I clean the table and wash the dishes. Finally, shortly before ten o'clock, after the radio has been silenced, and after nearly everyone is either in bed or asleep, except for Williams who is rowing in the garage, I lock the bar to the front door and enter the garage, dressed properly for the evening.

Williams stops rowing, "Take care, kid. And thanks for dinner. Good job."

As I seat myself behind the wheel, I leave the garage and Williams closes the garage door and locks it for the evening.

I drive down Broadway Avenue, turning on Pine and follow the signs directing me to Rainbow Pier, which seems closed for the evening. 'Olevaivai'olefe'e is standing there, along with Solstice, who is jumping up and down, excited to see me behind the wheel of the sleek black Ford. I park the car and open the side and back doors for the ladies.

"Anthony!" 'Olevaivai'olefe'e cries, happy to see me. "You look so good."

I reply, "Good evening, Ladies." Solstice approaches me with a long white towel, clean, wrapped around her hand. "Solstice Meridian, are you okay?"

She laughs, "What? The towel? I'm fine." She keeps laughing.

'Olevaivai'olefe'e adds, "Anthony, Clingy, darling, the towel isn't for her hand, valea, because it's for you. Your eyes."

"Fe'e? What?"

Solstice starts jumping up and down again, laughing more, "I'm driving! I'm driving!"

Confused I step back, "Fe'e, what's the meaning of this? She can't drive. She's ten or something."

Solstice stamps her foot down, petulantly, "You know I can drive, Anthony. Besides, I'm thirteen, and the driving age in California is fourteen."

'Olevaivai'olefe'e adds, "She'll be fine. It's only Wilmington, and not across the country. And besides we need to cover your eyes. Club rules."

"Rules?" I ask. "But what about..."

"...Us?" 'Olevaivai'olefe'e interrupts. "Manamea, I am treasurer of the club."

"And Solstice?"

'Olevaivai'olefe'e giggles, "Le teine? She's just a girl. Nobody cares about her." Solstice sticks her tongue out, and I stick my tongue out back at her. I show my consent to have the blindfold put over my head by turning my back to 'Olevaivai'olefe'e. She takes the towel from Solstice, who immediately jumps in the driver seat, using all of her strength to turn back and forth the large steering wheel of the parked Ford. I ask 'Olevaivai'olefe'e, "Are you sure about this, Fe'e?" And she snugly ties the towel around my head, guides me towards the back seat, closes the door, and assumes the front passenger seat herself.

Solstice, still laughing, cries, "Hold on, Clingy!"

As we turn away from Rainbow Pier, Solstice focuses all her attention on operating the vehicle. I cannot see anything. I try to sit back and relax, but if necessary, I ready myself to insist that Solstice stop the car and let me drive.

After some time, 'Olevaivai'olefe'e directs her words at me, "When was the last time you were intimate with someone, Anthony?"

Surprised, I raised my hands in the air and drop them down on my lap. "Sex?"

"Yes," 'Olevaivai'olefe'e replies.

"Why are you asking about that in front of Solstice, Fe'e?"

"Fēfē, Anthony. She's driving the car. She can handle it, so what's your answer?"

"Um, ah..." I stutter wiping my mouth with a free hand. "I guess that would have to be last month. With..."

Solstice interrupts, "...with someone in your house."

"Yes," I admit. "Keep your eyes on the road, my little psychic. Are we there yet?"

'Olevaivai'olefe'e answers, "Gross." She pauses. "We're turning on Anaheim, west. Stop asking questions, Clingy."

"You're so easy," Solstice giggles.

"We call him a 'pa'u', Solstice," 'Olevaivai'olefe'e reveals. And just as I am about to use my fingers to peek from underneath the blindfold, she chastises me for even trying. "Sole! Valea! Stop that. Don't touch it. For the rest of the night."

Giving up, I sit back, frustrated, "The whole night?"

Solstice says sternly, "All of it, pa'u."

"Did you bring a flask, Anthony?" 'Olevaivai'olefe'e asks.

Surprised she asked, I reach into my inside coat pocket, remove it, then hand it to her, explaining as she twists open the squeaky cap, "It's empty, Fe'e."

Solstice chimes in, "I knew you'd bring it."

"Right," I say.

"Don't worry, manamea. I'll fill it up. Have you ever had tequila, palagi?"

"Me? No, I don't think so, Fe'e." I ask.

"From Mexico. Mmm. You'll like the tequila." And I hear her close the flask cap. After some time passes in silence, we approach a potholed road that winds some distance over gravel. Eventually, Solstice brings the Ford to a complete stop, parks it, cuts the engine, and removes the keys, which she hands to 'Olevaivai'olefe'e upon her request. The front doors open and both ladies step outside and close the doors behind them, while I wait. A minute passes, and I'm tempted to peek outside, but honoring the request of me, I continue to wait. Finally, after a couple of more minutes, Solstice opens the door closest to where I am sitting, slightly behind the front passenger seat, and she gives me one-word commands to come out, follow her lead, as we walk on gravel some feet forward.

'Olevaivai'olefe'e shouts from some short distance ahead, "Solstice, girl, kill the lights on the car!" Solstice lets go of my arm, and I stand still, while she returns to the car to turn off the lights, and hopefully, lock all the doors. When she returns, she grumbles and takes my arm, hurrying me forward. As we approach, we hear the muffled sounds of a loud radio playing unfamiliar festive music, mixed with cackles and infrequent shouts. The air smells like tobacco and reefer. My clean shoes occasionally stumble on small rocks.

We move through a door, hearing a familiar-sounding, low masculine voice, which politely says, "Evening." And suddenly, the air feels smoky, heavy with laughing chatter of what sounds like dozens of people enjoying themselves. Solstice takes me to a chair at a table, assists me as I sit, and places my hands upon the table, then abandons me.

"Well, hello, dearie. What's your name?"

I move my head in the direction of the question. "Do you mean me?" Then, I hear laughter from three or four people.

"Why, of course, you, silly. Whadya think? I know everybody else here. My name is Douglas Fairbanks."

From behind, I hear, "and I'm Catherine of Aragon." Then, "I'm Alfalfa." Then, "Baby Ruthie, over here."

'Olevaivai'olefe'e leans her lips close to my right ear to say, "It's like a masquerade, so make up a name. Mine is Lady Octopus."

I shout, "Uh, I'm... I'm Clingy!"

Everywhere around me I hear laughter, including 'Olevaivai'olefe'e, who leans back in to say, "Remember only you are blindfolded. Everyone else can see you."

Somebody shouts out, "Clingy what?"

I'm unable to answer right away.

"Clingy the Stutterer?"

And instantly, I shout back, "Clingy Calabresia!" The room purrs with, "ooo..."

From the sound of his nearby voice, I sense an older man has taken a chair to my left, and he speaks closely in my ear. "We are very, very happy you could join us. We hope you are happy, too. Sorry for the little game of the blindfold, but we want to see what you're made of. I brought some jewelry for you to wear, so would mind putting your hands under the table, on either side of the table leg, so I can put it on you?"

I comply with the request, and before anything else happens, I hear what sounds like three small glasses in front of me slammed on the table, before some liquid gurgles and some droplets hit my face. At that moment, I feel linkless handcuffs quickly folded over my wrists, while the entire room of people erupts in laughter.

"Hold your head back, Clingy, and open up your throat," the old man says. For at that moment, what smells like cigar smoke blows across my face.

Someone behind me adds, "Surely, he's heard that before..." More laughter.

The old man's fingers pry my mouth open, and I tilt my head back, open my throat, as three small glasses of a liquor I've never tasted before pour back. At least I don't cough. When finished, I hold my head still, and the old man place a piece of lime against my teeth and tells me, "Suck it, boy!" More laughter.

"I wish I could see what I'm sucking!" I joke, which earns a chuckle or two.

"What, you afraid it's a gun or something, and you might like it?" someone teases.

Then another voice, "What would it take... to just give up like that?" A couple people sigh at the stupidity of the last comment.

In the time that passes, I lose my sense of minutes, being held like a zoo animal for the indefinite enjoyment of an audience. I'm given no opportunity to make conversation. I never hear Solstice's voice, and 'Olevaivai'olefe'e speaks briefly to me, only once. Towards the end of my ordeal, I hear frivolous banter and drunken arguments over nothing, and I count the glasses of liquor I drink, until I stop at the number eight or nine. Someone near me gags at some point and races out, causing a stir, to vomit, I presume. But, by the end of what I estimate has been at least an hour, tired of my incapacitation, I ask if someone will unbind my hands and remove the blindfold, which earns disappointed sighs and complaints, as if I'm the bad sport for not playing this game longer.

Finally, the old man returns to the seat next to me, and says in a drunken slur, "No harm, my boy. We don't... mean no harm. There's a couple of fellas I want... you to meet. The first guy is... over there, on your... right."

Trying to keep focus, I turn my head and say, "Hello?"

The voice is mature but strong, unclouded by drinking. "Yes, my good man. I hear you need some work? Is that true?"

"Yes," I declare, as if finally able to reach out into the world.

"You like the tequila?" he asks.

"Yes." Then I add, "Would like it more, if I could move about freely."

"Very good. Well, seeing that you have a driving license, what do you say about some driving work. Does that sound good to you?"

Pulling back, I reply, "I have no car."

"Of course," he chuckles. "We'll take care of that. In the meantime, be down near Farmers and Merchants around six tomorrow morning. We'll pick you up and get you working on the derricks on Signal Hill. You know what those are?"

"Yes."

"Very good. Hopefully, you'll take orders and cause no trouble. The pay's good. And we'll work on the driving part pretty soon."

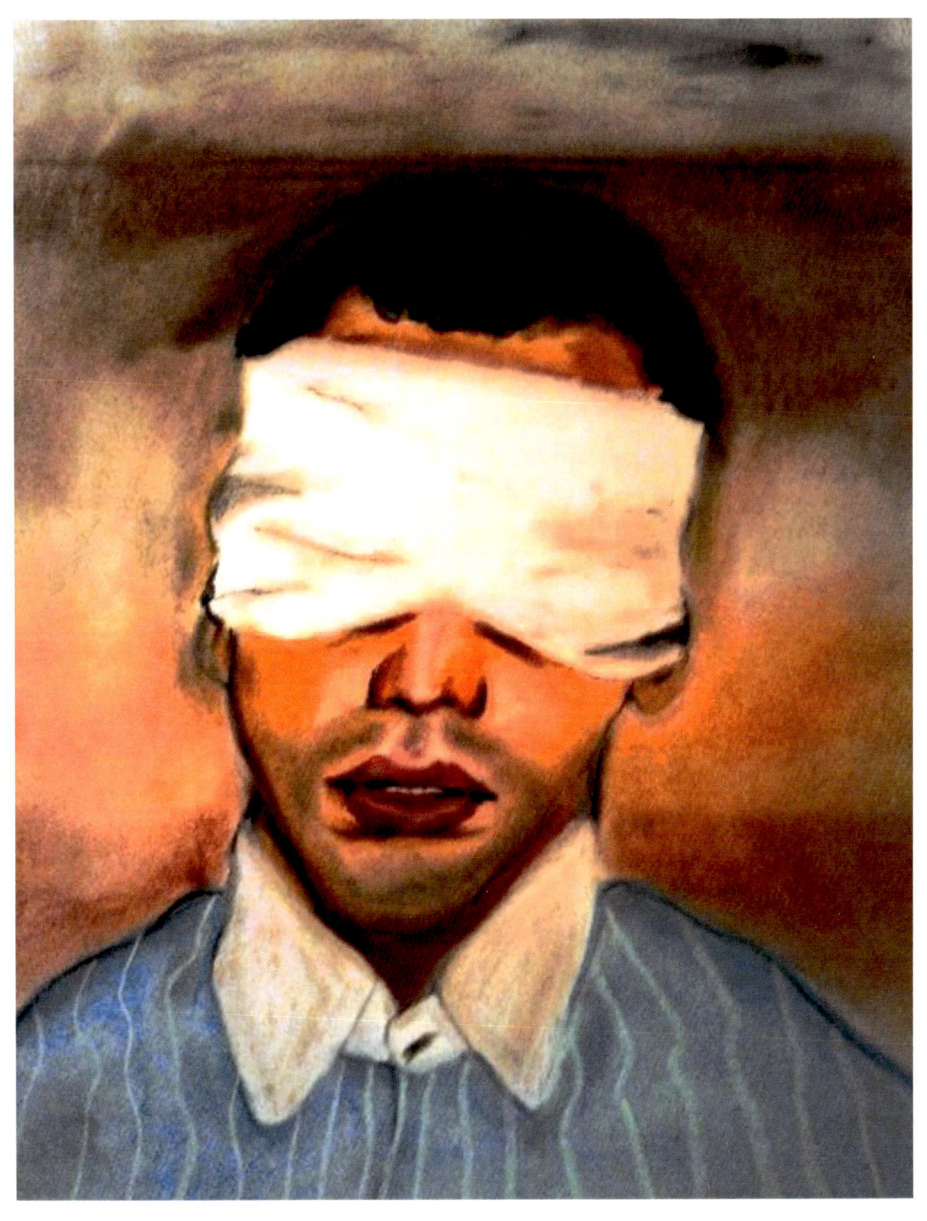

"Clingy"

At that moment, which must have been around midnight, I hear the bar go completely silent. Someone storms into the club, breathing heavily, claiming that the bouncer is dead outside. And yelling, "Suicide!" over and over. I get off my chair and bring my hands down the leg of the table, which I lift with my head to slip the cuffs underneath, freeing my body from the table. I lift my fingers to my head and remove the blindfold, to see a mass of people running everywhere. The old man suddenly appears. He's about eighty, short, wrinkled white. Without speaking to me, he takes a small key, and nervously drunk, he unlocks the cuffs on my wrists. By the time he has finished, 'Olevaivai'olefe'e and Solstice appear before me, and we join a few people, including the old man, trying to exit the front door to investigate. The rest of the crowd makes their way towards the back of the bar, likely anticipating police sirens, hoping they arrive later rather than sooner.

Outside the door of the club, staring at the dead body some twenty feet away from the door, in the dark, I ask 'Olevaivai'olefe'e, "What would it take... to just give up like that?"

Two club-goers approach the body and each light a match.

'Olevaivai'olefe'e hands me my flask, slightly heavier than when I handed it to her earlier, then points her finger outward, "He didn't give up. Two men did it, there in the neck..."

A pool of blood appears underneath a clear line carved in the body's neck. I mumble "...Garroted?" At that moment, someone turns the body over, and I walk a few feet closer, yet keep my distance to scan the face.

"But... there in the chest, a deep cut," she scowls, pointing to a blood-dripping tear in the man's shirt, about one foot long.

Stunned, I keep mumbling, "...but... Wait!" I shout, then speak more softly, "I know him... from the boarding house."

"'Oi, tālofa e! Le Ali'i e, alofa mai... tama uli, 'ua oti..."

I turn back to 'Olevaivai'olefe'e to say, "That's Dennis Carpenter." I sigh.

Seeing that I am both fascinated and upset, she takes charge, waving the car keys towards the Ford, "I don't know how to drive... at all, Clingy. I know you had a lot to drink, but you drive and spend the night with me." Before Solstice says a word, she adds, "Solstice, get in the back—make up your excuses before we drop you off."

Chapter Seven

"Villa Riviera al ¡Petróleo!"

I long for Abraham, hating his cowardice. Time?

* * *

  One's internal arrangement of melancholia and joy, including indifference, too, can be orchestrated with some intelligence, and there are certainly those among us who are either imbicilic or genius, or more likely still, some average in between, but even so, whatever equilibrium towards which any person tends psychologically will be thrown into imbalance after imbibing copious amounts of alcohol, especially the consequences observable the following morning—consequences which always make clever discourse, uninterrupted by vomit cascading near one paranoid detective seated and two stentorian patrolmen hovering, difficult. To my credit, whatever hang-over I am feeling, I remain remarkably confident in my ability to behave myself, most usually.

  However, forgive me.

  An unprecedented (for me), foot-long projectile of pink ooze and chicken bits publicly exits my wide-open lips, unpleasantly landing on the dirty tile floor in the area between my feet, my house manager's feet, the detective's feet, and the feet of two attentive patrolmen standing some feet away. After coughing twice, and dribbling out some last offending content, I gag dryly one last time. In silence. Williams, whose mouth is open, stares at me incredulously, but the room keeps quiet. Finally, I ask for some water.

  "Fuck you. Get your own fucking water, you sick fuck. And while you're fucking at it, get the fucking pail and fucking mop, and fucking clean up your own fucking shit. And hurry the fuck up about it, you dumb fuck," Williams says, then mumbles, "fucking water." He turns, and after one deep breath, speaks politely to the police, "Gentlemen, should we pick up our conversation another day, then? Apologies for the mess."

Detective Berger speaks beneath a frosty, white moustache while I gather the required supplies, fill the bucket with some water and grab some rags and bar soap from under the kitchen sink. He speaks, clearing his throat first, "Nah. It's alright, Daryl. But I'd rather not have to smell all that, would you boys?" He laughs.

As if carved from the same pale marble, magically animated, the two patrolmen, otherwise silent during the conversation, at the same time chime in, "Uh huh." They laugh, too.

Berger, again clearing his throat, "Right. So, if it's all the same to you, Daryl, we'd like to get on with this, while Camaratta's cleaning up."

Finished drinking a handful of water, I stoop down underneath the sink for the bucket and bar soap. Williams shouts extremely loudly at me, probably waking the whole house, "Will you hurry the fuck up? What's your fucking problem?"

Berger stands, putting his hand out towards the manager, "He's drunk, or he was drunk, Daryl."

By this time, I am kneeled down, cleaning up the mess with a rag, while the manager and the detective talk over me, like I wasn't even there.

Raising his bushy eyebrows, Williams says to the detective, "How can you tell?"

"His emesis has the faint odor of illegal liquor," Berger replies, using the word "emesis", the meaning of which I could only infer from the context was "vomit." I suppose such linguistic formality also has the effect of putting Williams on notice regarding his profanity, which he stops using after that point in the conversation.

The detective returns to his seat, and begins interrogating me as I clean and mop. "So, you were drinking, yes?"

"Yes."

"Where was that?"

"On the beach last night, late."

"About what time?"

"Oh, I don't know. Midnight, maybe."

"How much?"

"About a bottle."

"Of what?"

"I don't know. Maybe whisky."

"And where did you get it?"

"I'd rather not say."

"I asked you a question, boy."

"I'd rather not say."

I finish cleaning up the mess, using the mop to remove any offending emesis from the floor, and I dump the bucket's contents in the bathroom toilet, use the shower to wash the mop, rinse it and the bucket, wash my face and hands and return the cleaning items to their proper place. When I resume the conversation, I take my seat next to the detective. "Apologies, gentlemen," is all I say.

"Mr. Williams, here, wants to know where his car is," Detective Berger asks, squinting his cold blue eyes, as the manager nods.

"I told you that it's parked out at the Villa Riviera."

Berger looks at the two patrolmen, but asks me, "So, you don't mind if we head over there and look for it?"

"Not at all. Here's the keys," I answer, taking the car keys from my pocket and dangling them in Williams' face. Berger returns his icy gaze to me.

"Emesis"

In a fit that shakes his flabby jowl, Williams yanks the keys from my hand and says, "It'd better not be damaged."

In fact, when we drove back from Wilmington the previous evening, 'Olevaivai'olefe'e suggested that we drop off Solstice at an alley near St. Anthony's and then drive to another alley in the back of Petal's Flower Shop, so she could retrieve a couple of buckets with water and rinse any dirt or dust that might have stuck onto the car during the Wilmington sojourn. But after dropping off Solstice, we started to make our way for Petal's, and at that moment, a brief shower passed over Long Beach, cleansing our car, and so we headed immediately for the Villa Riviera cooperative, parked the car and walked in through a back door, unseen, and took an elevator to 'Olevaivai'olefe'e's top-floor suite. Soon after entering and drying from the rain, I fell asleep on a rather comfortable leather couch, shoes off, warmed by a handmade quilt. I woke up before dawn and she bid me goodbye, kisses on either cheek, standing slippered in a bathrobe. I felt too tired and too ill to drive the car the few blocks back to the boarding house. So, truthfully, I walked home. "It's not damaged, Williams. I hardly drove it. I already told you fellas: we took the car out for a cruise down Ocean, down the beach area some miles, then headed back, parked the car, went out for a walk along the beach, and I spent the night at her place, because I didn't want to sleep in the car."

Berger starts his interrogation, again.

"Did you see Dennis Carpenter last night?"

"Who?"

"Dennis Carpenter."

"Who lives in this house?"

"Why, you know more than one?"

"No, I never saw him after he left the house for work."

"He's dead. Murdered."

I suppose Detective Berger shared that information with me in a short, shocking manner, to read my reaction, to gage whether I was surprised, indifferent or somehow guilty. I chose the middle response, even though I was upset at being involved in yet another violent, homicidal episode coming so close to me, this time in the home where I lived, and then thoughts of Carpenter's family. I breathed heavily, stifling the urge to vomit again.

"Is that why...?" I asked, looking at Williams, who shrugged his drooping shoulders.

Detective Berger looked at everybody in the room, and asked, clearing his raspy voice first, "You thought we were here about the car?"

"Well, it seems rather obvious if Williams reported it missing...no?"

Williams responds, "We'll handle the car later, Camaratta."

"Just a second, Daryl," Berger jumps in. "So, you're telling me, Camaratta, that you spent the night with someone at the Villa Riviera?"

"Yes. Her name, and pardon my pronunciation, is 'Olevaivai'olefe'e Manu. She's from an island called Samoa, located in the South Pacific, but lives and works in Long Beach. She gave me permission to tell Mr. Williams she may be called upon at Petal's Flower Shop or Vogue Salon, if you need assistance retrieving the Ford vehicle. Of course, be kind with her. Her English is not so perfect, as you might imagine."

Berger tries to hold my attention like a vicious dog holding a bone. In an accusatory tone, he points his fist at me and says more than asks, "You two are romantically involved?"

"What?" I reply, acting shocked. "Romantically... why heavens no. She is presently in a romance with a United States Navy Captain, who owns the particular residence where she lives. Perhaps, I've said too much already. But, to answer your question, no. We are just friends. She was doing me a kindness by allowing me to sleep on her leather sofa, since I was out after ten and was forbidden entry to my own bedroom." I stare at Williams, disapprovingly. He folds his arms across his chest. In fact, 'Olevaivai'olefe'e gave me permission to reveal, and insisted that I explain, to any authorities asking about my previous evening's whereabouts, that she is the paramour of United States Navy Captain Stewart McKelvy, the actual owner of the spacious apartment in the Villa Riviera cooperatives, just a couple blocks from the boarding house. Her villa, as she likes to call it, is filled with windows overlooking the ocean and beyond, from the top floor of the second tallest building in Los Angeles County—the first tallest building being Los Angeles City Hall. There is hardly much competition for skyscrapers in Los Angeles like there is in Manhattan, owing to the frequency of earthquakes in southern California, but the architect of the Villa Riviera, mindful of the ever-looming possibility of tremors and aftershocks, studied in Japan the science of building design in earthquake-prone geographies, and implemented his knowledge of such matters in the erection of Villa Riviera, 'Olevaivai'olefe'e reports. Although we were quite drunk when she said all this, I recall her seeming very proud of her lavishly-decorated, architecturally quake-proof dwelling. Before we fell asleep, she showed me her shrine to her gentleman, to whose enormous oil portrait she prays every night by reading aloud a random passage from the Bible then silently meditating, hands clasped together, for his seasonal return to her embrace, safe from his voyages around the globe. "Detective, I am simply aghast at the news. Truly, I'm thankful to be so lucky. Does the Department have any suspects, may I ask?"

The detective gives up a long sigh and relaxes his time-worn but fit body into the broken boarding house sofa. "We don't have anyone in custody, but..."

I look at the two patrolmen and Williams, giving a slightly frightened performance. "...If there's anything I can do..."

"...I was just about to say," Berger interrupts. "We might call on you again if we have some questions. Are you going to be home today?"

"Why, no I won't be," I reply. "As a matter of fact, I have to leave the house soon, regarding employment."

Berger asks, "An interview, at six in the morning?"

"No," I laugh, before excusing myself for laughing. "A job. Working up on Signal Hill or somewhere near abouts there. I don't know exactly. It's the first day."

"Quite a walk," Berger rubs his chin. He looks at the two young patrolmen, who both raise their thin eyebrows in unison, if such a thing is possible. "So, tomorrow?"

"Well, as I have to be flexible, I can't promise tomorrow. How about in a few days, say, the coming Wednesday, or maybe Thursday would be better for you?"

Berger stands and directs the patrolmen to the front door. "We'll be in touch, Camarrata. Just let Mr. Williams know if you, ah... plan to move out. Before you actually do so."

"Oh, yes, Detective Berger. Yes, of course." As the police make a slow exit and I change into more casual clothing, I ponder the fact that the boarding house manager, only a few months ago, lost a bloody fight to Dennis Carpenter, and in my pondering, my skin pimples with a paranoid realization that, rather than Daryl Williams, I am the suspect in a murder investigation. And then, I think again about Dennis Carpenter's relations, their sudden loss, their eternal powerlessness, wherever they may live in this city, this country.

I long for Abraham, hating his cowardice. Time?

* * *

Before making my way directly to Farmers and Merchants, I walk a northerly path towards Signal Hill, up Alamitos Avenue, the Villa Riviera fading in the distance. When I approach Fourth Street, I turn to the west, and check to see if there are any police observing me. Seeing none, I keep walking, and follow alleys, until I come to the intersection of Pine and Third Street, where the bank building stands. I am late, as I recall being told to appear at six o'clock, but I see from the bank clock that the time is now seven. I wait as the minutes pass. I don't know what I am waiting for, but at least I feel fortunate to see neither police vehicles nor patrolmen on feet. Then, after about fifteen or twenty minutes, a speeding motorcycle approaches from the north on Pine. It weaves through traffic, and finally stops at the corner where I stand.

"¡Oye! ¿Es usted Antonio?"

The motorcycle still runs, emitting a muffled purr. There is a seat for a second person, and the rider slaps his left hand onto the extra seat, around his back. I mount the bike, and he takes, first, my right hand and places it around his waist then repeats the same maneuvers with the opposite hand, until I am holding on, snugly.

"Prepárate..."

His feet and hands operate the vehicle, while he accelerates to a slow speed, at first, to turn a successful about-face in the light early morning traffic, then, riding in a northerly direction, we take off, occasionally passing through intersections without any reduction in speed, and after a couple turns, we travel north on Long Beach Boulevard. He wears goggles, so I can't see his eyes clearly above his large, wide nose, but sports no helmet, so I protect my eyes behind his thick black hair, clean and wet. At some point after passing Pacific Coast Highway, he frees his right hand, which appears dry, chafed, then reaches into his brown leather jacket to take out a bar wrapped in aluminum foil, which he then passes over his shoulder, I presume for me. It feels soft and warm.

He yells, "Cómelo. Es un tamal." Feeling comfortable, I take my hands away from his waist, as we pass intersections, and he continues, without slowing down. I remove a portion of the foil from one end, and, unwrapping corn husk, I inhale an aromatic steam of corn, pork, chiles, cilantro. Placing my left hand around his waist, I use the right to hold it as I begin to eat. Meanwhile, the movement of his body against my thighs begins to arouse me. Without intending it, I grow hard and push against his bottom, occasional bumps in the road stirring me further, and at one point I sense him pushing his whole body backwards towards me, against me, more than possibly, more like probably, on purpose.

By the time he reaches Willow Street, he leans his body, and the motorcycle, to the right. The sights and smells of the busy oil derricks overwhelm me, and I soon lose my appetite but finish eating anyway. When we arrive at our destination, he brakes gently to a complete stop, and then waits. I lean forward, and he follows suit, so that I can throw my leg over the side and dismount. After I stand on my two feet, I wipe my mouth on the sleeve of my shirt, then extend my hand outward, as if to shake his, but he throttles the bike and speaks from his thick lips, "Gracias, fue mi placer..." Within a second or two, he speeds away, and disappears.

In the morning haze, my eyes feast on this unfamiliar, Dantesque vista of barren, muddy roads covered with trailer trucks, filled with impossibly long timbers and hollow steel tubes, all of which extend over the ends of the vehicles. Men wearing khakis and blue jeans walk about without smiles, giving orders, slapping each other on the back. One heavy man in particular stands taller than the rest and constantly points his large hand in different directions, talking out his small, thin lips at various volumes, and making jokes, without smiling but causing laughter. Eventually, he notices me standing alone, and he demands my attention, "Hey, you! Over here." I approach, he scans my black pants and white collared shirt, and runs his fingers through his premature thinning, gray hair and laughs, "You Italians always like to dress up. What's your name? Is it 'Anthony'?"

I wait a few seconds before answering, "Yes."

"Right," he nods. Then he starts giving instructions, "I don't have time to break you in on the drilling work, which you might not even get, so I hope that just because Cornero told you that you'd be working for me, that you don't get to thinking you'll get the good work right away. You'll be paving roads, with the other Latins. You speak Mexican?"

I am not sure what I am supposed to say, as I don't know who Cornero is, or why I'm talking to this man, or why he even knows me. I assume Cornero is either the one whom I met at the club the previous evening or Cornero is somebody whom the one I met at the club knows. "English. I speak English," I answer.

"Good. You speak Italian, too?"

"Yes."

He sighs, "If it's all the same, you'll be working with the Mexicans. It's like Italian, Mexican is, right?"

"Sure."

"Name is Watkins. J.D. Watkins. It's me you'll want to see at the end of the day to collect your pay. See that truck over there?" he asks, pointing his hand towards a flatbed truck, loaded with gravel, about fifty feet away from where we stand. Around the truck pace four men, talking and laughing, holding shovels in their hands. "We got a new road starting from the main one and then winds down Signal Hill going to the derricks at the bottom. Should take a week or so with a few strong wetbacks."

"Got it," I reply. Watkins seems like an unpretentious man, giving clear work goals, but who also organizes work crews into platoons of similar folk and orders them to stay with their own kind and get along, I imagine. As he talks, I watch teams of white men, covered in grease and dirt, move skids, pipe and chains with trucks and hooks, yelling and laughing without smiling. I start walking towards the flatbed truck, and as I come close, I lift my hand up to say cheerfully, "Buon giorno," words which instantly cause confusion and a bit of laughter among a group of short, stocky Mexican men.

A chorus of "¡Hola!" One man, perhaps in his forties, approaches, extends his dirty hand, which I shake, then he asks, peering from his tight eyes beneath his heavy brow, "¿De dónde es?"

"Di dove? Where am I from?"

No answer.

"Italia..."

"¿Italia...?"

"Si... e New York..."

"¡Ay, New York!"

"New York... Brooklyn..."

"Brooklyn. Me llamo... Alejandro..."

"Anthony."

"Mira, vas a trabajar con nosotros. Toma la pala," he orders, handing me one of the two shovels held by his hand, then adds, "y síguenos," as he turns his back to me and waves in my direction, I presuming asking me to follow him.

I remember hearing, in the short time I have been living in Long Beach, someone mentioning a famous California writer, whose name escapes me, but who put pen to paper describing Pincushion Hill, about the barons exploiting the land for its oil, about the heroic work of thousands of men moving equipment measured by the tons, often failing, causing death and injury, and yet it continues. It always takes a certain perspective to see the world in a certain way, then to represent it as great, American literature. It takes a certain intimacy of things on the inside, where people move according to the risks they take with capital, in and out of jurisdictions covering whole continents and beyond, and coordinating the daily rhythms and conflicts of whole families with them. And yet, here are four men who will likely never read such literature and who perform a small, forgettable task in some untranslated, master narrative, like the janitor who cleans the courtrooms, who keeps the law seeming neat and clean, to add to its professional objectivity, its near-medical sterility. Without graveled roads, mud stymies heavy trailer trucks carrying even heavier supplies and equipment, measured in tons, and prevents them from moving easily, quickly. With delays arise losses of profits, and increases in anxieties, all of which adds to urgency and more employer risk-taking, and a heightened sense of danger among those assuming responsibility for the life-altering consequences of such risk-taking, outweighed only by the possibility of whatever meager rewards employers sanction.

My task is to copy what others are doing, driving the shovel into the pile of gravel, and adding rocks to the dirt, spreading them evenly, creating a road about twenty feet wide, and eventually descending several hundred feet, downhill southward. I keep silent, going no faster, and no slower, than anybody else, as we work foot after foot, hour after hour, while the men talk and occasionally sing in Spanish. We share a couple of large bottles of warm water, and each of us occasionally asks to be excused to use the shrubs for our private necessities. But except for those brief moments, the shovels move in regular patterns, and as the temperature rises, a couple of shovelers roll up their sleeves and unbutton their shirts, exposing their brown, hairy, sweaty chests to the soft breezes. I feel tempted to stare longer, but I take only a few glimpses of their tight muscles bulging. I open my shirt, too. If they, too, study my body working, I don't notice.

With the sun sitting tall in the sky underneath a few welcome clouds, Alejandro says to a young boy, sporting a wispy, black moustache, about maybe fifteen or sixteen years old, "Gracias a Dios que llovió anoche, Pedro."

Pedro stops shovelling and turns his large, oval eyes to Alejandro, "¿Por qué?"

"Porque nos hace fácil el trabajo," Alejandro answers, all the while working his shovel, back and forth between the truck and the road under construction.

"¿Por qué?" Pedro stands still, scratching his fat head.

With a slight whine in his voice, Alejandro replies, "¡Ay, pinche cabrón! Porque la arena gruesa pega mejor debido al lodo. Pregúnta le a Antonio qué va a hacer esta noche."

Pedro turns to me and slowly asks in English, in his heavy accent, "Antonio, what you going this night?"

I look Alejandro in his black eyes and give my answer, "Niente."

"¿Nada?" Alejandro responds, packing the gravel firmly in the ground with his shovel.

"Nada," I affirm. "Niente. Nothing."

Alejandro whistles and calls the men to attention. They stop by throwing their shovels in the back of the flatbed truck. Pedro runs to the truck door, opens it, and his well-developed arms pull out a large canvas bag, which has a dozen tamales wrapped in corn husks. After passing them around to the men, who take seats some feet away from the new road, Pedro retrieves from the same bag several bottles, one at a time. I remove the top to the one he hands me, and take a sip then pass the bottle around. It is home-brewed beer, which leaves me feeling warm, relaxed and comfortable under the hot sun. I listen to the Spanish spoken, but otherwise keep quietly to myself. Finished eating, I lay back on the ground and close my eyes, feeling exhausted, knowing the day is hardly over. Within a few minutes, Alejandro gently taps his boot against my shoe and wakes me back to work.

"¡Petróleo!"

By the end of the day, the road has been extended about one hundred feet from where it was in the morning, leaving hundreds of feet to go. I am covered from head to toe in dried mud and gravel dust. My clothes, like my whole body, smell raunchy. Alejandro gestures to follow him, after we throw our shovels on the back of the truck, which Pedro moves off to the side and then parks, ready to be started up again. Finally, our crew meets up with Watkins, who hands single dollar bills to white men and gives our crew members each two quarters. Watkins asks to talk with me, and he tells me that I should return for work on Monday, that Sunday is a day off. Alejandro asks me to follow him again, and we approach Pedro.

Pedro smiles kindly, then tells me, "Los Angeles, you went there?"

"No."

"You come this night, ok?"

I pause and realize that any chance to avoid the boarding house is welcome, and I presume that, unless I have told Williams otherwise, that I may sleep anywhere I like and expect to keep my bed for myself, as long as I have paid my rent, which I have, although I reckon that fifty cents per day building gravel roads on Signal Hill will not keep me fed and housed at the boarding house for long. "Yes, Los Angeles."

Alejandro, watching the conversation, says to my surprise, in English, "Pershing Square."

"When?" I ask Pedro.

He looks puzzled and laughs, "Now."

Chapter Eight

"Digs"

"Oh seventy. Oh, seven, zero," the caller shouts.

I continue talking, "It's all a game, gentlemen, if you're healthy enough to play. Take for instance the rent on my downtown place, just sixteen bucks a month. Now, if you think about it, that's only four dollars more a month than what I was paying at the boarding house, but I get my own tiny room, a toilet down the hall with a sink, and a working hot plate for some rice and beans, or a can of soup, if I can't order the blue plate at Pekin or wherever. But I have my own clean cot, a good lock on my door, a closet for my clothes, a cup, plate, one silver spoon and a sharp, sturdy knife. There's a window that looks out over an alley, twelve feet down, no fire escape, and I get blue sky up in late mornings after the fog burns off. I keep a small potted plant on the sill for decorations, hell, I'm even thinking of painting a picture one day, when I can afford it. When I shower, I walk to the bath house, where I also take swimming lessons. When I need my clothes cleaned, then I go to the Chinese down the street." The only thing I neglect to mention about my new dwelling is that Dr. Parks honored his promise to send me a few of my old belongings from New York, at the good doctor's expense.

"Bee eight. Bee, the number eight."

"I am hardly ever home, basically to sleep or nap there when I have to, and sure, I don't sleep hard, but I don't hear snoring. And I don't have fights breaking out in my room, and I don't have Williams barking up my ass. Yeah, I don't have a car, it's true, but so what because it wasn't like I was using his anymore after what happened to Dennis Carpenter. And I don't need a car, because I have the bread truck, which I've been driving for three months now, so I ain't a freeloader. I work six days a week, eight hours a day. It's all working out fine, really. I don't miss a thing at the old house. Now the game of it, that is to say, the moves I have to make to keep everything in motion to make this all possible, is just that, a game, and I don't want to give my hand away, but let's say it's a bit of da da da da da, and a bit of do do do do do."

"Aye twenty-nine. Aye, two, nine."

Sitting at my side, Solstice ignores what I am saying to my former housemates, Carl and James, sitting silently across from us, and she focuses her light brown eyes on her handmade deck of magic cards, which on one side, and one side only, she has rendered intricately and colorfully hand-drawn pictures. The cards, she tells us at the table, are cut from blank pieces of white paper ripped out of St. Anthony's copy of the Encyclopedia Britannica and then trimmed to a small size to complete a set to her satisfaction. Her smallish pink fingers select a first card revealing the drawing of a yellow star, and her manner of interpreting this card shows her absolute absorption in her tiny deck of homemade mystery. "Good omens," she says after a few seconds of contemplation, and she runs both her hands through her sandy-brown, bowl-cut hair.

Pulling down a lobe on one of his large ears, Carl asks her, "Do you even know what's an omen, kid?"

James laughs beneath his hand.

"Bee thirteen. Bee, one, three."

"Uh huh, yeah. It means a sign of the future," she says.

"Ooh!" Carl joins James, who now is laughing openly.

Solstice scowls her young face at both men. "Look, don't make me put a curse on you two." She sticks her tongue out.

I try to manage the conversation, "Carl, James, you obviously came here to talk with me, and not play cards, but..."

Solstice argues, "...I'm not playing cards. They're magic cards."

"Gee forty-nine. Gee, four, nine."

An older, thin lady, excited, stands slowly from the crowd of three of four dozen players seated at different tables in the basement, and her raspy voice screeches, "Bingo!"

Carl suggests, "Actually, we could just talk while playing bingo instead," which causes Solstice to show a look of dismay. "At least we might win some money," he jokes. "Should we buy some cards?"

I explain, "They call numbers really slowly here, huh. The sign says the pot is only two bucks, but if you want, it also says it's a nickle a game. But, not my game. Did you bring nickles?"

Carl looks at James, and they both rub, then shake, their shaved heads.

Solstice persists, "The star card is a good omen that means somebody is going to make money, or fall in love, or something good is going to happen." She turns over another card. It shows her own hand-drawn picture of five glasses of pinkish milk, she explains, two of which are spilled over. "See, this

"Bingo"

means there's no use crying over spilled milk, and you should focus on good things. See, I'm trying to help, fellas."

An ashy cat sneaks along the basement floor, brushes against my leg and purrs loudly while the hall of bingo players move about getting ready for the next game. As her tail sweeps my shoe, she rubs against Carl, then James, and finally, she sits next to Solstice and meows, as if asking to be picked up. Solstice ignores her, "Ok, so this next card tells me there's a period coming of very hard work." Her drawing on the card shows eight green circles, in each of which there is a five-pointed red star. "So basically, I see good things coming, and you should focus on the good things, and work very hard to get them, Anthony."

"Me?" I reply, looking at her directly.

Her pale brown eyes stare back at me, "Of course. This is for you."

"Huh," I reply, shrugging my shoulders. "There it is fellas, good rewards, hard work. Like Solstice says." The cat leaves our table, and scurries away quickly, chasing shadows some feet away.

Carl clears his throat, prepares to speak at length. "Anthony, I'm glad you have decided to keep in touch. Basically, we need to talk about Williams."

James nods in agreement as the bingo caller announces the next game.

"What about him? I haven't heard anything from anybody about him. What you got?"

"First number... En forty-four. En four, four."

Carl continues, "Well, it's good that you got Solstice helping you out, otherwise, we'd have no way to reach you."

"I figure I might still get some letters coming to the old place," I explain. "I just asked her to check in at the old house to ask about them."

James asks, "Why, you expecting letters... from who?"

"Maybe... New York. But what is it you wanted to talk about?"

Carl looks at James for a long second. "Well, the reason I asked Solstice if we could meet with you, when she came by looking for the letters, is that we got some news for you. It's about Carpenter."

"Carpenter?" I ask, shocked to hear Carl say his name. After being first questioned by Detective Berger about Dennis Carpenter, three months ago, I didn't hear much about him. The Press-Telegram which published a short, one-paragraph story a couple days after his murder, kept the story out of the papers afterwards, for whatever reasons. Although I lived in the boarding house for a few weeks after the murder, I spent most my time working in Signal Hill, surviving on tamales and beer shared with me while earning just enough money improving roads to pay my weekly rent. The weekend hitchhikes to Pershing Square, at day filled with scores of the unemployed and several loud radicals, and at night haunted by perpetual drunks and desperate perverts, meant meeting men who used the underground bathroom there for the quick illicit nighttime rendezvous, when they were too secretive or cheap to use the downtown bathhouses or speakeasies. It was there that I met Don. Don and I took our business to a nearby hotel, where he rented a room. He loved to lay on his back and mould breasts from his hairy chest, begging me to lick his large brown nipples, while I drove myself between his fatty thighs and underneath his extremely large, low-hanging sac dripping with sweat and saliva, until I caused him to spill jism over his big belly. After a couple of our hotel visits, he revealed he was the owner of a bakery factory in north Long Beach, and he helped me get a decent job making deliveries of bread, and alcohol, in one of his trucks. After getting that job, I gave notice to Williams at the boarding house, finished up working on Signal Hill, and started driving for the bakery, which earned me two dollars a day, more than enough to rent my own small place and save money, too, so I feel quite legitimate. Now that summer has arrived, I think I almost forgot all about a dreary winter and the murder of Dennis Carpenter. "What about him?"

"Oh sixty-nine. Oh, six, nine."

James takes over the conversation, "You know, Anthony, our folk, over at Christ Second remember these things. Dennis had a temper, and maybe he shouldn't have shown it when he wrestled with Daryl Williams, but he was a good man, sent money back to his family in Texas, every month, and he didn't deserve to go, and he didn't deserve to go like that." James chokes back tears.

"What James is saying," Carl explains, "is that Williams knows more than he lets on."

"And you should know that, Anthony," James adds.

"Aye, twenty-three. Aye, two, three."

"I should know what, exactly?"

"Aces!" Solstice shouts, who has pulled another card from her deck that, this time, shows a single glass of pinkish milk. "I'm feeling a lot of love at this table," she says to herself aloud.

Carl and James look at her quietly.

I repeat to James, "I should know what, exactly?"

"Anthony, Dennis was murdered," James says, emphasizing the last word. "By two people, at the same time. It was a conspiracy."

Carl reinforces James's point, "By definition a conspiracy."

"But what does it have to do with me, so unless you expect me to start speculating, tell me what you think, James... Carl?"

"It's not what we think," says James. "It's what we know."

"Bee one. Bee, the number one."

Carl, brings his hands on the top of the table, making gestures, as if drawing a map. "Look at the bigger picture, Anthony. Williams has a fight with Carpenter, Carpenter is murdered, and the police ask you questions, then they stop asking you questions, and the story disappears from the papers."

"Gentlemen," I clear my throat. "What, you think all that didn't occur to me, too? I just don't talk about it, because what's the point in talking about it."

Exasperated, finally, James says, "Anthony, Williams set you up."

"How do you know that?" I ask.

He explains, " 'Cause it was the goddamned Klan that killed Carpenter. The ones they got inside the Long Beach police department, been there a long time. He was killed by some white-hooded cops. Hell, the police chief used to run the Klan not ten years ago."

"En forty-five. En, four, five."

James continues, "And Williams gave you the car that night, to use, so that he could be free of any suspicion. Without a car he lacked opportunity, even if he had the motive. You had the opportunity, and he can always make up a motive. Now, your alibi, about spending the night at your friend's house, well the police checked that out."

In fact, I knew that to be true, since 'Olevaivai'olefe'e told me herself a few days after my interrogation that she was visited by Detective Berger and asked about my story, which she confirmed, as Berger understood it, except he also embellished it, inventing some facts, claiming he misunderstood what I had reported, and she corrected the detective, firming up the whole narrative. "I know they did. I thought it was over after that."

"Bee seven. Bee, the number seven."

Carl says, "James may not say it, but Anthony, the police think you were there, where Dennis was killed. They just can't prove it."

"I know you were there, Anthony," James adds. "And I can prove it."

Solstice blurts out, "Oh, no. I see change coming." Her finger points at a drawing of a blue tower, which appears upside-down, either because of the drawing, or the way Solstice has oriented the card on the table. "Anthony, you need to hold on. Hard."

Before James speaks, I interrupt him, "James, before you go further with that, let's say I was there. Let's say I lied to the police, that my friend lied to the police, that I happened to drive the car to a place where Dennis was murdered, let's say. That doesn't mean I saw anybody do anything. That doesn't mean I even saw Dennis' body. It means nothing."

"Gee fifty. Gee, five, zero."

James, pulls back, "Oh, you saw the body. I'm not saying you did anything. But, you were there, because I was there, too, in the confusion, when everyone was screaming to leave. I brought Dennis there with a car that a lady friend of mine lets me drive. She used to live on the second floor of the boarding house. Now, she's a proper Christian married to some shyster. But, she goes to clubs—like those—to meet girls anyway. I go just to drink. I'm a ladies' man. Sometimes, most usually, I just drop her off, but this night I stayed around until everybody panicked and left."

"But…" I start to protest.

"Enough Camarrata! You think you're special," James accuses me, agitated. "You think you're the only one who's ever fucked Williams? We all heard you two that night. We talked. Williams knew about the party in Wilmington before that night. He set you up with his car, so you could be framed."

"En thirty-eight. En, three, eight."

Carl puts his hand gently across James' chest, easing him back into the chair. "Anthony, listen, we have got to get rid of Williams. He knows people in the police department, and he plays with our lives like he's playing chess with nobodies on the Pike. All he has to do is tell one of his cop friends that somebody pushed him or slapped him, true or not, provoked or not, and the next thing you know, they end up in jail, disappearing there for good, or they end up dead or just missing, forgotten about."

"Anthony, we need you," James begs. "Christ Second needs you."

"En thirty-three. En, three, three."

Solstice turns over a card, showing a drawing of her image of the Pope. "Anthony," she says, "you're being asked to do the right thing."

In long silent seconds, I meditate on suffering, while the three of them study my face. Christians have made a profession out of suffering. They project onto the world all of their need for compassion and for justice, which however you look at it, never quite abandons the taint of vengeance, the sense that the world is in some sort of proper alignment, some sort of proper balance, which must be vigilantly preserved and maintained, by human forces if necessary, meting out some unwritten law, even if it requires enduring suffering and adding more suffering still. But I see the world exists in an equilibrium chaotic, as irrational sequences of order and stability appear out of an otherwise jumping spontaneity created from universal forces too vast and infinite to fathom. That we can breathe at all, after our tenth or twentieth year on Earth, is itself a wonder to me. That I should direct my breathing to satisfy the yearning for justice, either coming from within me

"Tarot"

or surrounding me in the presence of god-fearing folk, seems often wasted suffering, an endless repetition of rehearsed visions resurrected from the past. I begin to doubt this meeting playing church bingo.

"Oh, sixty-four. Oh, six..."

A mature man, stout and moustached, raises his right arm out and above, "Bingo!" The basement is flooded with a chorus of disappointed sighs.

"What you are asking for, gentlemen," I begin pompously, "is vengeance. And while I may have been framed, as you suggest, and as it previously occurred to me, I am not persuaded that the wisest course of action would be to eliminate Mr. Daryl Williams, as surely such an undertaking would involve a great deal of effort. Also, it occurs to me that merely leaving him incapacitated might stir further retribution, either from him or his allies, and thus perpetuate a never-ending sequence of actions which will likely lead to no good for anybody."

Carl rubs his chin in his hand, "Perhaps. Perhaps not."

"Anthony," James says, pushing his finger into the table. "The point isn't to put slugs into him, although it isn't like he doesn't have it coming, since you don't know a tenth of what I know about him. The point is to entrap him in his own vices, publicly, so that he is not only disgraced, unable to continue his role as manager of a shitty little boarding house in Long Beach, California, but he also is treated with suspicion and contempt among the Klansmen assassins in the police department. Forever."

Carl says, "Amen."

"The Queen!" Solstice says, showing yet another card, with one her drawings. "Anthony, you should focus on home, the cards say."

"Yes, indeed, gentlemen. Solstice makes a good point, that whatever fate we devise for Williams, it cannot interfere with my investments to make my California home. I have done enough cowardly running. I can't keep it up forever. No more 'hits and runs,' as they say."

Carl smiles, "We're not asking you to do it alone. We're here to help."

"You may count on my congregation to help," James smiles. "We're your home."

Just about as Solstice is to turn over another card, Carl admonishes her by swiftly moving his thick-fingered paw over her deck, and retrieving it from her grasp. "Enough with the cards, kid," he barks, which causes Solstice to protest in silence, pouting by folding her arms across her chest.

"Carl, give her back the cards," I request politely, and he complies.

"Hrmph," Solstice pouts.

I look at her and sigh, "Hrmph."

* * *

July 3, 1932

Dearest Glamour Jackson,

Deepest apologies for not writing you a reassuring letter sooner, as I intended. Keeping our heads above water here in California has proven the challenge I knew it would be, and so you might imagine that I wanted to write you at an appropriate time. It was my intention to do so before one year's time passed since our departure from the East Coast, and I'm sure you were expecting the same, but please accept this late letter without receiving any offense, which never has been nor ever will be intended. I merely wanted to share the good news that Solstice Meridian and I are safe at long last.

How we miss you, terribly! Solstice, who has taken residence at an orphanage with the assistance of St. Anthony's parish, the oldest Roman Catholic church in Long Beach, and who is too often truant, but manages to avoid trouble, sends her very warmest regards and begs me to tell you that she longs for you and cannot imagine spending one more year without you nearby. She also tells me to tell you that she senses you approaching in her dreams, that she knows you are up to something, and that your reply to this letter will bring long-awaited news. As for myself, I cannot say that I hope differently.

You promised, when we saw each other last year, that you would meet us in California. Of course, I realize you were expressing a wish more than anything else, being in no position at that time other than to hurry us on our way for safer shores. California seems so far away, indeed. And I can't imagine a place more different from New York than here. The weather is almost always cheerful and pleasant. Even the poverty seems to put on more color, a more happy face than Brooklyn. And certainly, there is a falseness to the local pretense of public beauty and private joy we see on display all around us, but it does compensate somewhat for not having a more comfortable life, inside well-furnished dwellings, shared among the company of the mischievous and mirthful well-to-do. But all is not boring sunshine all the time. You would like it here, I imagine.

Indeed, I am also motivated to write this letter to inquire about your intentions at this time. I realize that you may still be suffering from a lack of means, and so please understand that there is no pressure I seek to exert. Nonetheless, I miss you. If it is possible to hasten your decision, by securing room and board for you prior to your departure, I can share with you that it is possible to make that happen. And while there are always negotiations of favors involved in these matters, I owe you so much already, regarding your assistance with the old truck, that it goes without saying that I am at your service. Please accept the two twenty dollar bills enclosed with this letter and put them to whatever use you deem appropriate. If you manage to put necessary events in motion resulting in your relocation to southern California, I can promise you business opportunities await. In fact, there is one waiting for you presently, about which I would rather discuss in person.

I look forward to hearing from you at the soonest.

The lipstick kiss appearing below is from Solstice, who made me promise I would save enough space at the end of the letter to allow her to leave it for you. Yes, she wears lipstick now, occasionally. She likes this ruby color. She asked me to ask what you think.

All my love,

Anthony Camarrata

* * *

RECEIVED AT LONG BEACH, CALIF
OKLAHOMA CITY, OK

AUGUST 23, 1932

ANTHONY CAMARRATA

COMING TO CALIFORNIA STOP I WILL ARRIVE BY TRAIN AT UNION STATION IN LOS ANGELES A WEEK FROM TODAY IN THE AFTERNOON STOP ONLY TWO PIECES OF LUGGAGE STOP SEND SOLSTICE TO MEET ME WEARING LOVELY LIPSTICK

GLAMOUR JACKSON
1145A

Chapter Nine

"Blackmail"

The seeming weakness of the octopus.

* * *

Chasing October nocturnal moonlight snaking around curves of tiny, crisp, elevating bubbles from the province of Champagne, I heed solitary voices braided in a conversation, cut from the gentle fabric of gossip, secrets and ancient wisdoms learned from previous lives lived in the rush of migrations great and small, from Cleveland to Brooklyn, from Pago Pago to Long Beach. I hesitate to speak the word "you" to either intimate, a form of address that would cut the braid and leave one voice acknowledged, the remainder ignored, hence my attention is drawn, as if by gravity, to the riddle of recognition and inclusion and equality demanded impossibly by these two beautiful heiresses of my affections, comfortable at my side, their smooth brown legs pushed outward and split apart, beneath their low hemlines. In this moment I sense that rare feeling, aphrodisiac and erotic, more penetrating than the ether of champagne and reefer liquidating our atmosphere, about a dozen stories higher than the shore. All guilty hauntings feel banished tonight.

Giddy, Glamour laughs, "Fe'e, girl! Oh, I could go on about my Anthony stories. And then... the tales I could tell about train cars... May I please serve myself another glass... where is this from, might I inquire?" She pushes her long wig back from her brow, and finishes the last dram from the bottom of the flute, bringing her free hand, holding the reefer cigarette, to her nape revealed by her contemporary, low-cut, black evening gown, satin.

Sliding her legs together, 'Olevaivai'olefe'e smooths out the creases in her red and white puletasi, satin also, and tilts across the long glass table to reach for the champagne bottle, which she tauntingly dangles before Glamour. "Please, manamea. My honor." She drops the nozzle of the bottle up and down quickly, synchronizing this with her oscillating chin, in a gesture calling for Glamour's attention. "Northeast France. I don't know the price but to me is certainly priceless."

Smiling out of a corner of her mouth, Glamour's eyelashes peer directly in my eyes, "Priceless, Anthony." She tips her lipstick-stained flute towards 'Olevaivai'olefe'e, who obligingly fills it, causing the bubbles to excite and spill onto the table. "Oh!" she cries. Then, Glamour hands me the cigarette.

"Don't worry. Anthony, would you go to the kitchen and return with a clean towel. On the counter, to the left. Also, there's a plate in the oven. Would you bring that, too?" 'Olevaivai'olefe'e directs me, before stretching out her hand, summoning the reefer.

"Champagne"

"Of course," I answer, satisfying her desires. And as I leave, I hear a chorus of cackling laughter, feeling paranoid I am its object.

Before I walk beyond the radius of their hushed conversation, I hear 'Olevaivai'olefe'e say to Glamour, "You're smoking Mexico, sister. Tijuana."

"Fe'e, you don't say! Oh, child... Tijuana?" Glamour laughs harder.

While they become more familiar, sharing stories and jokes, raising the energy in Captain McKelvy's whole home, I enter the kitchen and place the towel over my shirt sleeve, rolled up to make my skin feel more cool. I open the oven door to retrieve a merely warm plate. Taking longer than need be, letting them grow more comfortable without me, finally, I return to their company, but at that moment the ladies turn their heads away, both scratching their necks and giggling quietly to themselves. Softly, I place the plate on the glass table near the bottle, where my flute has been already refilled. The spill disappears into the towel I push across the table surface, before 'Olevaivai'olefe'e takes it, folds it and moves it to one side.

"So, Anthony," Glamour starts, clearing her throat after exhaling, but maintaining her magnificent bright smile.

I stick to short utterances, "Yes."

"I have been waiting for two months now, since August, for some definite word from you about business, while I've been boarding with the Baptists, as you arranged."

'Olevaivai'olefe'e interrupts, describing the fare on her modern, ceramic plate, "It's called palusami, formally, lūʻau is the more common name. I purchased the green taro leaves with the help of a Japanese friend who buys our chrysanthemums for the Buddhist church."

"Delicious!" I coo, after eating one portion. "What is that inside?"

"Coconut cream, onion, and a pinch of salt," 'Olevaivai'olefe'e replies.

Glamour takes one polite bite and holds the uneaten portion in her hand, acting coy. "The time has come, darling Anthony. Let me have it," she says, furling her brow and handing me the reefer.

'Olevaivai'olefe'e, uncharacteristically, butts in. "Blackmail," she blurts out softly. Glamour looks puzzled, returning her half-finished serving to the plate. Then, she gazes coldly at 'Olevaivai'olefe'e, and in an accusatory tone, utters, "What... ?"

My hand holding the smoke brings the flute to my mouth, "Yes, it might possibly be put that unlikely way. Or, a different way." I stifle the impulse to stare reproachfully at the evening's hostess.

Glamour stands, "Anthony, I am not interested in one of your crazy schemes that always fail. I didn't come to California to be treated like a common criminal. Mafioso intrigue means nothing to me."

'Olevaivai'olefe'e, "'Auē! It's my fault, Glamour. Forgive me. I should have let Anthony take control." She turns her head down, staring into her lap.

Glamour returns to her seat, "No, not at all. Apologies if I acted selfishly, Fe'e."

I squeeze the last part of the reefer between my fingers and finish it. Placing the butt on the table, I then bring my hands together, "Ladies. My ladies, my allies. I am not here to cause trouble. As Fe'e said, Glamour, she didn't mean anything. Look, let me start with a story. When I started driving for the bakery, I didn't receive my pay right away. In fact, I waited three weeks, then finally, I asked to meet with the owner, Don, and I told him I needed to get paid and said I didn't see how we had an agreement if he didn't come through. Right there, he gave me about half what he owed me, and a couple days later made good on the rest. Hasn't been a problem since. Now, what was that? Was that blackmail?"

'Olevaivai'olefe'e nods, "Such a sad word, 'blackmail'. My mistake."

Glamour jokes, "Were you sleeping with Don, Anthony?"

'Olevaivai'olefe'e and I both laugh. "Don, sleeping with him? What?" Then, I sigh, "Oh... I sometimes miss the old days, Glamour."

"I don't know where this is going, Anthony, Fe'e, but a simple disagreement over wages is hardly blackmail," Glamour reasons underneath her scowl.

'Olevaivai'olefe'e replies, "Manamea, Glamour. Let me talk. There is a very bad man. And this man will be at a party on Election Day. We just want to show him for who he is."

Glamour, pushes her back in the seat, "Why does this involve me?"

"It doesn't," I explain. "Unless you want it to. Look, this is about more than us three in this room. If we succeed, then it will benefit many other people, but I'm not looking to profit from it, because I won't. You, on the other hand..."

"Have you heard of Commodore Records, Glamour?" 'Olevaivai'olefe'e asks.

Glamour leans forward to join the conversation. "Commodore Records? New York?"

'Olevaivai'olefe'e continues, "People know people. I can get you an airplane ride to New York to record a song. I should say 'we' can."

Glamour reaches her hands across the table, cocking her head to one side. "New York City, Fe'e? What would be worth an airplane voyage so far away?"

Taking her hands between her own, 'Olevaivai'olefe'e reassures her, "One of the owners has a nephew here in Long Beach, and if he can tell his uncle the right story, it can get you an audition recording. Anthony has real faith in your talents."

"Tony?" Glamour, still held in 'Olevaivai'olefe'e's hands, asks me.

I nod silently, before I bring my hands to theirs and lift the three of us to our feet, and promise, "It's not blackmail, Glamour."

"Opportunity," Glamour smiles, warily.

'Olevaivai'olefe'e pulls out her hands and embraces both of us, "Opportunity." Then, she kisses both our lips, "Opportunity." Glamour kisses back, and I kiss them both.

"Dreams," someone whispers.

* * *

The seeming weakness of the octopus.

It could happen now; it could wait.

The sun is shining, filling the bedroom with grey-yellow light. My mind stretches into what was immediately before, reaching past memories retained by the body, sore in some spots, radiant in others. It was about an hour before dawn, when the last one came. At midnight, we shared palusami. And now, the sun is shining.

How I see the future: languid, blurry, soft.

It could happen now; it could wait.

To rehearse the immediate past for a future already happened. The past comes again. Life is a perpetual habit, a knitting pattern. Repetitious gentle breathing of a pair. Routine morning hunger. Structured reflections grammatically lapsed. Hanging in the air, musk and flatulence and cannabis. Pigeon noises.

Unconscious morning stiffies.

It could happen now; it could wait.

Stir the peaceful deities before they become wrathful demons. Too late, a hand moves a digit across my prone figure. A flickering finger twitches the taint between my legs. The nervous system discharges pulses across a million molecules.

I imagine floating in the sea.

It could happen now; it could wait.

One finger's nail traces an imaginary tattoo across my back, starting in a grand arc and coming back, and building zigzagging angles aiming upwards, detours to circles inside circles inside circles, tinier, more like spirals. Then, dots. And straight lines. I take my trim pinky and repeat the same patterned gestures over chocolate skin, stirring the peaceful deity before becoming a wrathful demon.

I think about vaseline.

It could happen now; it could wait.

In a lucid state, I dream I am out of my body, like a camera, hovering, focused downward on its scene, a bed, California kingly, dripping in satin, atop the Persian rug underneath, its sides hidden in satin garments, and three immobile bodies, different tints and hues, one up, two down, a circle without beginning or end, disconnected but entwined, until my vision returns to my sockets, fixed upon a small undiscovered mole on soft skin, hairless, some inches from my nose.

I sniffle.

It could happen now; it could wait.

The kisses return. At first, my ankles wiggle underneath the gentle pressure of moist lips, softened by a dry tongue. Again, the flickering finger twitches the sac between my legs. My arm props me up, sending power through my muscles, stretching, and I return my head down, aiming for the teardrop leaving an erect brown size for fun, a perfect average, not at all exaggerated, bouncy and playful by itself. It meets my open lips before I move further, depositing a sticky strand that remains connected until my smile pulls my lips apart, breaking the bond.

I purse my lips into a pucker and blow a steady stream of air.

It could happen now; it could wait.

Behind me, nipples atop chubby little lumps, dip into my calves and retreat, only to return again dipping, at the same time dark, rough fruit push on the small of my back, as a wide bone glides along the curve defining my fundament. Kisses on my toes.

We three are awake.

It could happen now; it could wait.

Removing twitching fingers from my taint, they push down on the wide bone gliding along my fundament, plumbing. Another hand reaches around and returns greasefully easing inside. My breathing ceases, as I gasp for air, and at the same time I feel filled with a full force, my head wraps around this playful perfect average fun and makes soaking wet, bending slightly upward, forcing my teeth to retreat and my tongue to move in tandem with the motion of my hips. My breathing returns.

They kiss, only my double slurping disturbs quiet moaning.

It could happen now; it could wait.

Manifesting supremacy, a selfish generosity, hands not my own force my head away to assume their own position on all fours, suddenly, without speaking, bent facing me, hot mouth wide open and pouring spittle down over me, slowly at first, then swallowing, further and further until gagging, and repeatedly gagging becomes breathing becomes gagging, and one arm, free, moves behind me and gestures a request to fall in line, behind bent knees, spread apart, free fingers diving inside, glistening with remnants of vaseline. I lay back, my hands grab long hair and move the head, gently

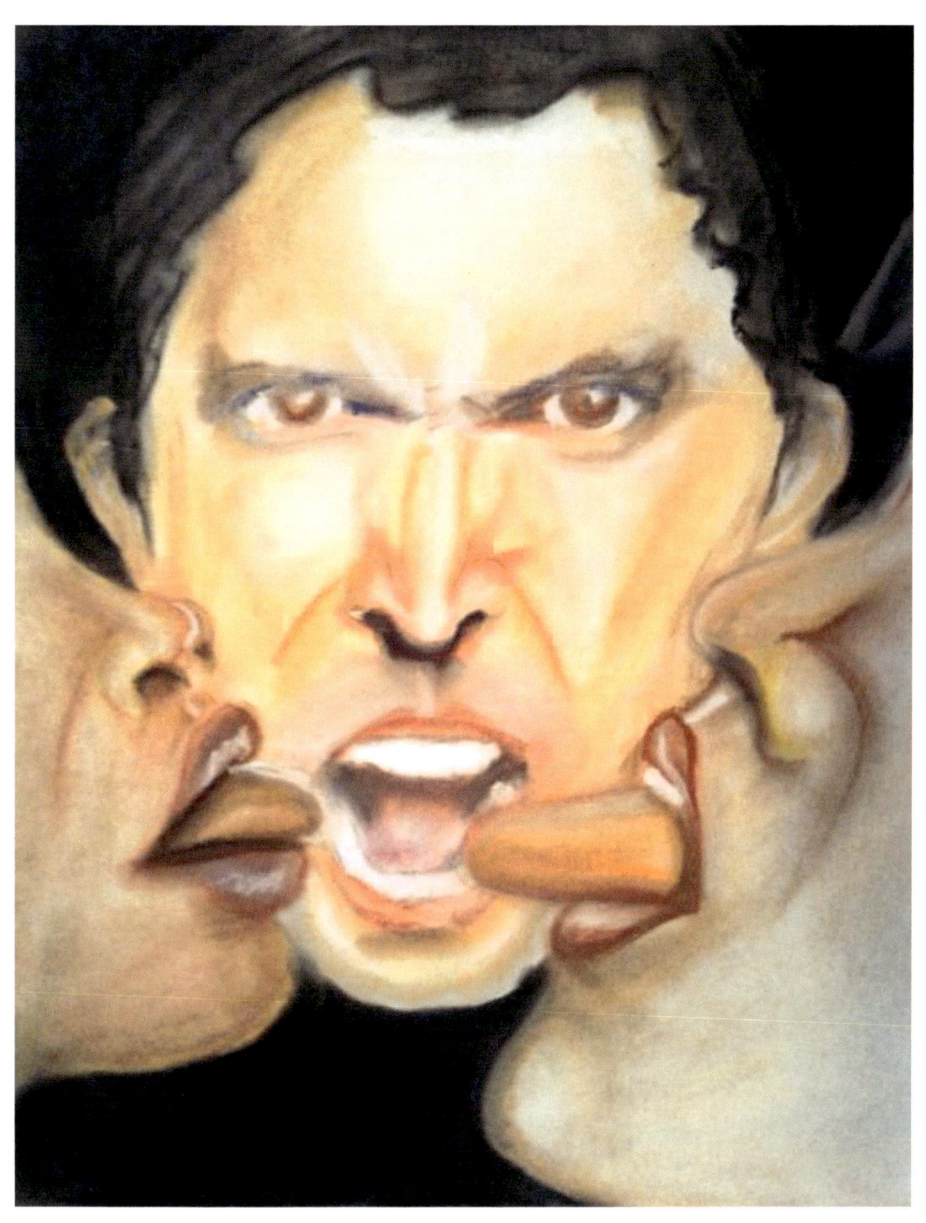

"Menage a Trois"

in sync with my needs, while the bottom dances against darker rigid flesh pointing downward.

We dance.

It could happen now; it could wait.

A cat spine in heat springing up and down, pushing the head forward and back and the back towards the head and out, inside without and within an inner tubular slide, filled with petroleum, the remnants of industry, working one hard moving hand up and down, exciting, sucking harder, faster, gagging and breathing, stealing time for an ecstatic eruption, echoes bouncing across the room and out the windows of the Villa Riviera, a dozen stories high. Orgasms join, grunting before yelling once, then shaking and grunting more. Behind and inside, pushing out and down, fighting back fast as can go, turning inside out, screeching, pulling out, and spilling over back, streaming down.

We collapse onto the bed. Glamour buries her head into my shoulder, wanting more, waiting for more. 'Olevaivai'olefe'e jumps up for the bathroom, then the kitchen, and returns, wrapped in a cloud of reefer and holding a glass of water. I feel sleep returning, in my heavy eyelids, at peace with Glamour in my arms. I think about the evening's unfulfilled needs and whether I have enough strength for Glamour.

It could happen now; it could wait.

"You asked last night. My name," 'Olevaivai'olefe'e announces without any prompt, wiping a spot of perspiration from the brow. She grins, "The seeming weakness of the octopus."

* * *

The fat, timid capon, as Hoover had been named by Franklin Roosevelt, falls to defeat on this eighth day of November in the year 1932. In California, Democrats deepen their power in the United States Senate; the state's booming population during the previous decade adds to the Party's momentum, with new Democratic House seats and less Republican; and rumors have it, only one county in California, and that would be Riverside, votes for the loser. Meanwhile, the Eighteenth Amendment is certainly doomed, the Klan which had dominated the National Democratic Convention eight years earlier seems politically marginal, and yet the confidently capable paraplegic must wait four more months before seizing power from the incapable rooster.

In Long Beach, both parties organize campaign headquarters to coordinate precinct workers, celebrate winners and console losers. The city's

Republican Party, which Reverend Dr. George Taubman has served ceaselessly by advocating on behalf of Prohibition, feels a loss of power in the unity of his flock, though it is not fatally wounded. Daryl Williams, who had served as a dutiful Republican poll-worker in each election since 1920, escapes his party's malaise over the death of America. He believes in the defense of individualism. He believes in the American Revolution. And he believes if Prohibition were to end, as Roosevelt has hinted, then it is his duty to hasten its end even faster than the President himself. Or, so I speculate that such inchoate thoughts circulate in his head after the polls closed, though it does not take speculation for me to see that he is drinking on board a gambling ship on this night.

Away from the lights and commotion, under the cover of darkness near an open window overlooking the outside deck, I stare at Daryl Williams, across the poker and craps tables inside the SS Lily, one of a dozen ships anchored some three miles off the shore of Long Beach, in so-called international waters.

I only feel pity, a condescending pity towards him, which is but a perverted form of empathy, especially if you can foresee his future. It is a matter of time, literally minutes, before his life, as he understands it, will end, and his life's next chapter, if he doesn't kill himself first, begins soon after. Of course, I suspect he believes otherwise. He seems jolly right now, secretly believing that, even if his party loses at politics, he still holds his position as boarding house manager, and can continue to hide his low social status at the gambling tables by standing near one of his black tenants, laughing in sync with Williams but otherwise stoic, serving his pseudo-superior soon-to-be-legal cocktails. This tenant, thinking about Commodore Records and New York City, reluctantly plays the role of a black houseboy and privately projects all of his revenge towards Daryl Williams, whose troubled past has been revealed for what it is. Now, there is only a pervasive sense of reckoning hanging in the air, as a radio plays the Paul Whiteman Orchestra for the passengers.

Milton Jackson, yet another time in his life, stands lacking comfortable loose clothing and colorful makeup, instead taking on the appearance of the sterner gender, utterly alien. Disguised in a plain black suit, Milton has already assumed the quasi-manly affectations necessary to survive two weeks thus far in the manager's boarding house, trading sexual favors for Williams' devotion, earning his abusive attention, and his provisional trust. Milton persuades Williams to wield a knife during intimacy because, he lies that he likes it, because he needs to submit to it, slavishly. The imminent possibility of white violence makes his black cock hard, he lies, and he calls it his black cock. That is enough, and Williams has confessed his sudden, irrepressible infatuation for his adult houseboy, who hates Williams for it, counting the hours until it ends.

In the distance, towards the nighttime shore, among the water taxis which ferry gambling boat passengers back and forth, I hear through the open window the barely audible sounds of a motorboat, and the faint, muffled sinuous whine of sirens. At that unremarkable moment, Milton's eyes meet mine, between the roll of the dice, and he tugs gently on the sleeve of Williams, who nods towards him. They take to the shadows and disappear, into the men's toilets. A minute later, the sirens grow louder, noticeable. The passengers scurry in confusion. Boat workers try to calm passengers and grasp at currency on the tables, stuffing bills and coins into large rubber purses, which when sealed, trap enough air to float over the side of the boat, under the cover of darkness, until the morning sun. The alcohol is efficiently dumped into the ocean. Gambling tables knocked over. By the time the two police boats arrive at the SS Lily, a couple of nervous gamblers head for the deck to jump overboard.

The boat is boarded and searched by a dozen uniformed and armed officers, acting on an urgent anonymous tip, with reports of orgies and violence, and not one of them is a member of the United States Coast Guard or Customs Service. When they open the door to the men's toilets, they find the only clear evidence of an unambiguous crime: two men with their drawers dropped. Intoxicated, Williams is bent over, smiling, holding the toilet seat, while Milton, eyes closed, screams loudly from behind, fucking him. The officers likely suspect the two men may not have even known what was happening on board until they were discovered, but rather than proceed by accusing Milton, as they would in most situations, the police stop themselves after seeing the large knife in Williams' hand.

Speaking so loudly he can be heard some feet away, one of the officers exclaims, "Williams? What the... hell?"

Milton breaks down, crying, insisting he has been rescued, that Williams has threatened him with his life, and Williams, in no position to defend his sobriety or his sanity, keeps silent. Rather than arrest the two men, because they lack witnesses and are otherwise unwilling to open a case against Williams for a miscegenous, homosexual sex crime, the police ignore most everybody else, too, and merely bust the boat captain for operating a gambling boat at the border of territorial waters—a dubious legal charge, given the unsettled law regarding the State of California's reach over validly-licensed ships anchored some miles from shore (which just happen to allow gambling and illegal drinking on board). As if to add insult to Milton's alleged injuries, the police officers publicly offer to ferry to shore Williams, who declines, probably paranoid with the thought that the police will report his behavior to a clandestine—according to long-standing rumors—Los Angeles County registry of uncharged, but suspected, sexual perverts. Perhaps I give him too much credit. Perhaps Williams hardly feels paranoid at all, and rather is overwhelmed with feelings resulting from his lost masculine reputation after being discovered forcing, at knife-point, Milton's fat, timid capon up his tight, white cunt.

A skiff silently approaches under the cover of midnight, pulls alongside where I stand. Milton finds his way through the useless confusion to hold my hand, shaking with emotion. He turns to my face and ominously confesses, "Right now, I've got three words for you, Comarati, and they ain't, 'I love you'." Anxiously, we wave our arms out the window and towards the skiff, on which a person holding a lantern reveals herself plainly for whom she is.

The seeming weakness of the octopus.

Chapter Ten

"María de Tijuana"

"Friendship. Where do I begin?"

"We've already started, Miss Ordaz," I tell Maria, seated across from me at a table, inside the Pekin Cafe, some time after closing, on Christmas Eve.

"I sound like a broken record, huh?" she smiles, her eyes keeping focused on my face, while her smile moves with her whole head, tilting slightly to her right, coyly, in a flirtatious manner. "Haven't I asked you, Tony?"

I push back into my seat and laugh, "I'm still waiting." I bring the coffee cup to my lips and take a long sip. "If you need to think about it," I finally sigh, "how about pouring us another before you turn off the percolator."

Maria Ordaz stands dignified, pushing the wrinkles out from her waitress apron. I stare at her hands, which have healed from the fungus that had destroyed her nails only one year ago. She proudly lifts two cups from our table, as the kitchen cook moves about some distance away, causing commotion, clinking pots and pans, trying to clean up as quickly as possible, before closing the cafe for the evening. She turns to walk to the counter, showing her beautiful shape, her long calves below her round hips and thin waist. Her black hair, kept inside a net, swings back and forth as she walks. When she gets to the counter, she bends forward, showing the top of her deep cleavage. She removes a bottle stowed below and opens it to splash some tequila in both cups, before pouring more black coffee. Again her ruby grin, which is self-confident but also somewhat self-mocking, as if she understands she is her own worst enemy, and yet she appears confident, bringing her eyes up and meeting mine, before dropping them back down on the table. When she returns to her seat, she says, "Merry Christmas," placing the two cups in the center of the table.

I nod.

"So, how come you never come in here with a girlfriend?"

I take my hand to my mouth. "Oh, you got me there with that one. Why do you want to know, do I need one?"

"Do I need a boyfriend?" she laughs, and I join her.

"I bet… " I start, thinking of flattery, "you could have anyone," I continue, before choosing to alter my slowly-spoken diplomacy, "but you choose wisely, since not anyone would do."

More laughter, "Tony, you are a sly one. But it can't be all my fault. Maybe it's me working in this place."

After taking a long sip of hot deliciousness, I swallow hard. "You can't blame this place. Besides, what else would you do?"

"María Ordaz"

"If it was you, what else would you do?" she asks, holding her cup between her two hands, keeping them as warm as possible.

"Not my choice to make, fortunately," I quip, but then wonder what choice she has. I think about her family, if she has one, and what unexpressed obligations she might owe them. "May I ask you something, Maria?"

"You just did, Tony." She stares, "Yes, what is it?"

"What's the difference between friendship and family, for you?"

In a careful gesture, she returns the cup to the table and rotates the handle in a complete circle, contemplating her next words. "Are you free next week?" she finally asks, squinting her eyes, as if anticipating my possible response, perhaps painful rejection.

"Next week is a long time away. What is it you have in mind, my lady?"

She breathes, "Tony, I have a funeral to attend. Have you ever been to a funeral?"

"Yes," I answer, thinking about my father's uncelebrated affair, and then my mother's equally simple ceremony. "Surely, everyone has by our age."

"No, I mean in a chapel."

Before I answer, I reflect on how our conversation has drifted, as if it lacks art or conscious intention, as if we are talking like school children, testing each other's feelings, uncertain of the seriousness of intentions. "Before I answer," I begin, "there's the matter of the broken record. What is it you wanted to ask me?"

"Children. Want children?"

"That's it?" I ask, pretending as if her statement is obvious, universal.

She points her finger directly in my face, "So?"

I question her question, "You know that young girl, who comes in here sometimes? Sometimes I'm with her, buying her dessert? She's about thirteen or fourteen, once in awhile sweeps up at the Cash & Carry, up on Pine?"

Maria pulls her head back and looks over her shoulder, "Let me think..." she pauses in long thought, reflecting upon the many faces of people who come into Pekin Cafe, some more often than others. Turning back in my direction, she guesses, "Sally, is it?" Wincing with the thought she might have been incorrect, she pushes skeptically, "She's your friend?"

"Solstice. Solstice Meridian."

"Solstice," she affirms. "Yes, skinny kid, brown hair, big eyes. Nice girl."

"Yes, that seems about right to me." Maria looks pleased, making me feel happy Solstice has managed to avoid trouble in the cafe. "We're not precisely friends. I'm her uncle, in a way."

"Well," Maria giggles. "Uncle? Are you, or aren't you?"

"She has no family, Maria."

"Ah, an orphan girl," she realizes, then brings her coffee up to take a quick sip.

I repeat her gesture of drinking, thinking about how much I should reveal, how much I should trust her. She probably is thinking the same about me, I calculate, though clearly there is an effort to understand one another, and the possibility of a mutual exchange of confidences seems alluring, helping me bring my guard down, in increments of revelation and deception. "Yes, I accept your invitation…"

"…to the funeral," she interrupts.

"To the funeral, on the condition that I may invite Solstice," I explain, gauging her response.

She twitches her nose, "That might be hard to explain to my family."

"Well, if it's a family funeral," I reply, indicating that perhaps regarding this matter between us, there may be no place for me to exist among the members of her family. "I completely understand."

She protests, waving her hands in the air, "No, no. It's fine. I just need an explanation. Solstice is your niece, you say, so… her mother and father?"

"Both dead. New York City. Catholic Charities relocated her to California in the late twenties," I dissemble.

"With the Long Beach Day Nurseries?"

"Too old for them. I have been working with St. Anthony's to raise her, or socialize her, as they say."

Finally, Maria seems relieved, "Yes. Good. So, yes, please bring her."

I finish my coffee, "Very good. And as for you?"

She also empties her cup. "What about me?"

"Well…" I draw out my speech. "Is ours a friendship, then?"

"A friend. For now," she sneers. "Thank you."

"And your family, what will they expect?"

Maria takes my hands in hers, "My father was a very modern man, who came here with my mother years ago, before she died, when I was a very young girl. The Ordaz brothers will not inquire publicly about you, and any gossip that circulates among the women at the funeral will be just that, gossip. But, at least they'll be hopeful for me during an otherwise sad day."

I understand now. "Your father's funeral."

"Yes," she confirms. "From Tijuana, originally." She brings herself closer to me, pulling my hands, clutched in hers, even closer to her chest, and whispers, "Juan Ordaz, member of the Communist Party."

"Tijuana?" I wonder naively.

"Tijuana, Long Beach. Once you belong, you always belong, wherever, unless you're purged. So, have you ever been to a funeral in a chapel?"

Sensing it is safe to discuss matters of religion openly with her, I answer, "Yes. Both my parents were given last rites by the same priest. However," I say, giving a long pause, as the kitchen cook has finished cleaning and now cuts the lights, turning the cafe more dark. One light remains lit in the dining area.

"I'll close up after counting the register, Chu," Maria says to the cook, who waives his hand and throws his towel on the counter, before leaving out the back door. "Yes?" she returns to our conversation.

"Let's just say, I don't care much for baseball... or Jesus."

She snickers, "What do you care for?" Then, she turns suddenly serious, "Wait! Let me guess: fast cars, loose women, and travel."

I simper, "Huh. Darling, you most definitely," I hang a long pause in the air, "are not psychic."

She jokes, "Damn Reds ruined me!" We chuckle, in unison.

"No, no," I steer back to the art of it. "In terms of friendship, can you trust me. Can you do that?"

"What?" she peers in my eyes mischievously. "Trust you? What am I, nervous?"

To release tension, I titter, "Nervous?"

She slips her hand underneath the table and places it on my knee. "Nervous?" she asks.

And she repeats this question, moving about one inch up my wool pants each time.

I mimic her, moving my hand up her exposed knee, then underneath her skirt, echoing the same word each time she utters it. Finally, both our hands reach far enough forward, then I surrender. "Maria, please. Your brothers."

She pulls her hand back abruptly, confused. "What about them?" Then she leans back in her seat and crosses her arms. "I don't care about them right now."

"Ahem," I clear my throat. "It can't happen."

"I'll get to you somehow, Tony," she warns. "Or not," she throws her hands up in the air. "What are you, one of those homos?" Upon hearing the last word, my face grows instantly hot, as I watch Maria's mouth open wide as she studies my flushed-red cheeks. She surges to her feet, sending the chair backwards a few feet. "Just my luck," she says.

"Maria, please. I'm damned if I say anything more, damned if I don't. Surely you understand."

She returns to her seat, but stays some feet away from the edge of the table. I feel studied by her penetrating gaze. "What is it you want, Tony?"

"Your friendship," I plead.

She shakes her head, "You sound like a broken record."

I bring my arm to the table, dive my chin into my palm, and rest my head like a sculpture. We wait in silence, alternatively staring at and looking past the other. I think about the meaning of truth, the possibility of words to express sensations accurately. I think about self-preservation, the freedom of anonymity, the habit of calculation. Finally, impulsively, I ask her, "Do you want to get drunk?"

"Thank you," she breathes a sigh of relief. "For sure!"

We get up, she hurries to the register, counts the money in about sixty seconds, makes some notes, and locks the register closed, before throwing her apron and hairnet on the cook's towel already on the counter. She turns the lights out and draws the shades closed. We leave, locking the door behind us. Outside we walk around the Pike and go in and out of a couple of unlicensed establishments, she tells me, she rarely visits. Inside, in the company of others avoiding the holiday, we enjoy cocktails of watered-down gin infused either with citrus or bitters or honey. By the end of the night, we concoct our own banter of private jokes, more chatter really, while I constantly tell her sternly to "be good" while she always rhymes, like a naughty school girl, "you should."

After accompanying her home, which happens to be about a three blocks from the old boarding house, I make sure her key fits into the lock on the building, and in one last embrace, her drunken lips fall towards mine, but turning my head at the last moment, I let her lick my cheek and promise myself not to remind her of any of it. Instead, after a solid squeeze, I remove her locked hands from the back of my neck, prop her shoulders, and gently shake her until her droopy eyelids pop open. "To bed," I tell her.

"Fart on friendship," she whines inside the hallway, before turning her back on me, farting, and ascending halfway up the stairs, then all the way down, before proceeding another halfway up then disappearing around the landing.

* * *

The moment behind the backseat inside Daryl Williams' black Model A Ford lasted long enough for me to learn that Glamour spent Christmas with the Baptists during daylight before catching a ride to Pershing Square that evening. Two days later, she hitchhiked back to Long Beach, in a new dress, shawl, hat and shoes acquired as gifts, before leaving Los Angeles. Fortunately, she was clever enough to make a copy of Daryl's keys to the doors of his vehicle back in late October, without my even requesting it, as if she recognized then the more she held over him, the more she was taking care of her own, best interests later. She believes, in a few days on New Year's Day, she will ascend into the skies on board a plane bound for New Jersey, eventually, weather permitting. Until that day, there is a matter of local Long Beach blackmail which needs settling. And this time, she is comfortably dressed.

Before I even have the chance to describe my dull holiday to her, the boarding house manager enters his car, parked in the early morning darkness, on a curb outside the boarding house. His resident, Carl, conniving with our intentions, previously convinced him to gather groceries in the early winter morning before the sun completely rose, in exchange for Carl's offer of spending all morning and afternoon preparing a grand, holiday dinner, since Christmas had come and gone without much fanfare, as New Year's Day would likely would pass without celebration, too. At the moment Williams tugs the ignition switch, moving the motor parts to begin their noisy routine, Glamour and I properly sit up in the backseat, startling the driver, who has not yet engaged the gears to produce motion.

"I need to borrow the car this evening, Daryl," I state, as though my words are uncontroversial. Meanwhile, Glamour, seated behind the driver, extends her left arm, dropping her hand on his shoulder and massages it. "And I need it for New Year's Day, too, while we're at it, here." At Glamour's side, I take the keys from her closed right fist and jangle them in front of his face. "These, in fact, mean I will be using the car every now and then."

Daryl Williams turns his head to the side without removing his hands from the steering wheel. He takes a deep breath, looking askance but towards my direction. "Why don't you just take the whole goddamned thing. For good."

Tempted to scrape the keys against his face, I vibrate them, closer to his ear. "Don't talk stupid, Daryl. Listen. We need to know who's got your back in the police department."

"Jeezus, Camarrata. Who the hell do I know?"

Glamour edges towards the front of the back seat, bringing her mouth to Williams' ear. "You remember that cross burning last month, Daryl, on East Third Street?"

"What about it," he says, turning forward in his seat. His head moves back and forth, trying to catch a reflection in his windshield.

"What about it? Did you read those names in the paper?" Glamour removes a small piece of the Press-Telegram from the top of her dress, and she recites the names like poetry, "Clarence H. Brooks, Samuel J. Sampson, Owen J. Stearns, Ernest A. Buttram, James Henry Russell, Dale H. Elliott,

A. P. Tyler, Audrey L. Jenks, Homer D. Turner, Charles H. Clark, Clyde D. Dunn, Walter R. Brooks, Earl Amos, John Lindberg and Waldo King."

I interrogate him, "Ever clash with any of them?"

"Clash?" he stalls.

"Yeah, got any old grudges with them?"

Williams shifts his weight, uncomfortable in his seat. "What the fuck are you talking about?"

I see Glamour's hand tightening across the front of his neck.

"We're talking about you, Daryl," I reply. "Right now, they probably don't know about your predilections. Maybe, but probably not. How about it, if they did. In the papers?"

Glamour asks, "Daryl, have you ever thought about killing yourself with carbolic acid?"

He exclaims, "Milton?" Without waiting for an answer, he says finally, "Look. If you want the car tonight or whenever, you can have it, for crissakes, Camarrata. Just leave me fucking alone, okay?"

"My, how we have lost the art of conversation, Daryl. We're not through, though. We want names... of the police... who killed Carpenter."

"Why don't you fucking ask Yancy yourself?"

Glamour and I look at each other. "The Chief," I mutter.

"Fucking figure it out, Sherlock," Daryl chortles.

"Out of the car," I command while Glamour's fingers squeeze tighter, making Williams' breathing difficult. "Out!"

Unhappy, he wriggles his neck free from Glamour's grip and turns around to find Milton wearing cosmetics and a lovely dress, blowing him a kiss. He scowls, mumbling, "Perverts."

As he exits, Glamour and I leave the back seat. Outside, I shake the keys once more, taunting Williams, "Back before midnight." I open the passenger door for Glamour who takes her seat gracefully. Then, making sure all the doors are closed tight, I take the driver's wheel and head for Pekin Cafe to meet Maria.

Upon our arrival a few minutes later, I park the car in front of the windows of the cafe and get out to help Glamour exit. Maria, already dressed in black for the funeral, sees me with the car and throws her napkin onto her breakfast plate. She waves goodbye to the cook and steps outside and wraps her arms across my neck, kissing me on both cheeks. After she satisfies herself, she lets go and pauses before introducing herself to Glamour, who immediately extends her hand courteously and says, "Jackson. Ms. Glamour Jackson, charmed."

Maria silently shakes her hand.

Glamour, focused on her imminent return to New York, forces a polite smile then waves goodbye in my direction, as my head gestures the same, repeating aloud, "Soon." Then, I wink at her, before she walks past Maria and me, towards the east, under overcast skies growing brighter.

As I drive the car through Long Beach, first to find Solstice at St. Anthony's makeshift orphanage, Maria fidgets in the passenger seat, questioning me about Glamour, whom I describe as a singing talent soon to fly in a biplane, with stops along the way, from Long Beach to New York City, to record a number of vocal tracks for a couple of original jazz compositions. This has the effect of impressing Maria. In minutes, we arrive at the residence of Solstice and park the Ford. Solstice runs outside a building door to greet us. Soon, Maria is asking Solstice about funerals and her familiarity with them, questions to which Solstice gives short answers. Quickly inured to Solstice's disinterest in the conversation, Maria distracts herself with questions for me concerning New York City, which I describe with enough detail but without showing much interest in the conversation itself. Exhausted of small talk, Maria falls still.

When we arrive at the chapel entrance, I open the doors politely for Maria first, and then Solstice. Solstice intuitively understands the formality of the somber occasion and she grabs my left hand, as if I am leading her. She is wearing clean clothes, including a neat, simple brown dress, which although a little large in some respects, does not fail to flatter her. Maria takes my right arm and walks proudly in black. I am wearing my only suit, newly cleaned, and in the moment, if someone were to take a picture, I suppose, we would appear as a family. Once inside, I watch a gathering of a dozen people moving about, variously speaking Spanish and English, emotionless and tearful. A few move their way into the pews, while Maria's brothers, close to her in age, stand quietly in the same place, greeting visitors and extending their arms in repeated embraces.

I explain to Maria that I will not be participating in any mass and would rather remain outside, while Solstice seems anxious to join her. I apologize to her: if my behavior seems rude, I beg compassion. She grins. Making good on my intentions, I escort the two ladies to a pew and return to the waiting area near the door of the chapel, passing her brothers, one of whom engages me in conversation.

"Ernesto," he says, taking my right hand. Ernesto stands about my height, broad shouldered. His face displays a gentle kindness alongside its wide curves and tight, dark eyes.

I place my left hand on top of his already holding my right, and I say, "Anthony Camarrata."

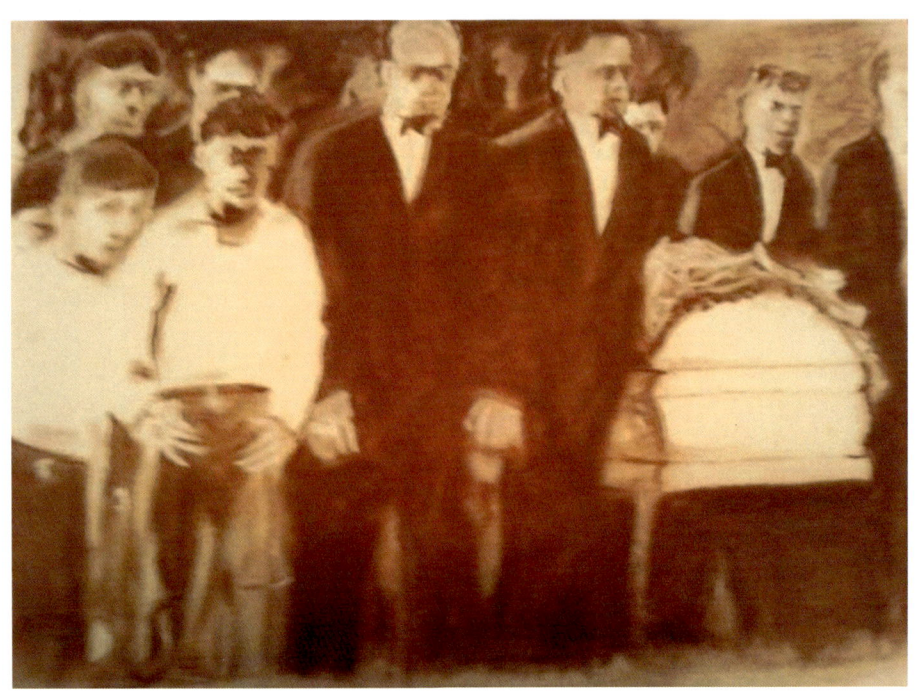

"Funeral"

"Thank you for coming. This is my brother, Rafael," he says, pointing at the gentleman standing a few feet away. If possible, Rafael is more beautiful than his brother, though he is more stocky, and about a head shorter. I gesture in Rafael's direction, as he greets a few more guests arriving late to attend the mass.

At this point, Maria has turned her attention in my direction, and seeing the conversation between us, she excuses herself in the pews to join us. I wait for her. "Anthony," she says, "I see you met my brothers, Ernesto and Rafael."

"Yes," I reply. "We've already introduced ourselves."

Maria explains to Ernesto, "Anthony's from New York, originally."

"You live in Long Beach now?" he asks.

"I do," I say, without giving further explanation. The less I speak, the more appropriate it seems to me on this occasion.

Maria, somewhat nervous, fills the silence, but keeping her composure. "He has a friend who's a jazz singer flying back to New York on the First," she says, apropos of nothing in particular.

"Oh," Ernesto says in a hushed manner, pointing his finger up. "That reminds me. I have a question for you, then. You think your friend might take a package from me on the airplane to New York?"

"Can we talk after the service?" I ask, seeing that the priest has taken a position behind the chapel altar. Ernesto agrees quietly, as Maria apologizes for starting a conversation interrupting the ceremonies. She appears strong, but somewhat distracted, and I accompany her, again, to her seat next to Solstice, before I walk past Ernesto and Rafael seated already at the back of the chapel, as the last few invitees arrive.

Listening to Latin sung and spoken from outside the closed chapel doors, I imagine what the contents of the package might be and if it presents an opportunity for an exchange of favors. I reflect on the car in my temporary possession, the consequences of gaining its use, in the manner which I did. An escalation of controversy in Long Beach feels somewhat inevitable to me, requiring thoughtful management and careful alliances. Speculating that Maria understands my overall predicament, about which I have revealed little detail, I contemplate whether her family presents a source of stability and trust.

After pacing for some time, mulling such matters, the service finally ends before the rituals of interment proceed. Somewhat leaving me shocked, Solstice exits the chapel crying, holding Maria's hand. After some commotion over dividing people into cars, the Ordaz family and their guests drive to the municipal cemetery off Willow Street. We reach a hole in the ground, and stop the vehicles, get out and stand together in a group. Ernesto and Rafael help bear the weight of the casket, as they remove it from the funeral coach, with the assistance of other sturdy men. I reflect on the funerals of my parents, who were visited only by a handful of intimates. I feel numb, estimating the measurement of any life, whether in terms of years or wealth or reputation. I dwell on memories of Abraham. The priest continues the rituals, speaking more Latin, as the casket is lowered by ropes into the ground, before the pall bearers use shovels to throw dirt, until finally the hole is firmly sealed, as Ernesto and Rafael stomp their feet across it. Solstice, fascinated by the whole scene of it, turns to me and dives her weary head into my gut, while I gently caress her soft hair, leaving me completely surprised by her reaction. I return to thoughts of Abraham and imagine if he were standing next to me, and if I could express my feelings honestly to him, I would whisper privately in his ear something mocking, something like, "All religions are death cults." And he would recoil, repulsed at my lack of manners.

When Solstice lets go, I approach Ernesto, explaining that I must return downtown, but that I have some moments to discuss the matter of the package. He assures me there is nothing intoxicating about its contents. Then, he asks me about the French Revolution, whether I know much of its history. I confess my ignorance, after which Ernesto gives me an impromptu sermon on Donatien Alphonse François de Sade, Marquis and his father's personal, pet theory that among the many causes of the Revolution, libertinism surely is misunderstood as having played an insignificant role because he believes it was far more important than not. Confused, I listen as he clarifies the point, explaining that the package contains revolutionary materials, and he inquires about my feelings about revolution, a subject about which I can only shrug my shoulders, an honest response. Ernesto then asks me if I know about the comic "Betty Boop" and, after I indicate I know about it, in a general way, since I read newspapers rarely, he tells me that his brother has designed, edited and printed two thousand copies of an illustrated comic called "Betty Poop" and he asks if my friend, the jazz singer, can deliver it to a specific address in Manhattan, without any excuses. I try not to laugh, just smile, and assure him that there will not be any difficulty with his request, before I ask him if I can make my own.

He catches me staring at his brother in the distance. "What you got?" Ernesto pointedly requests.

I move my fingers across my lips, searching for the right words. "I've the needs of Rafael's artistic talents," I begin, suddenly realizing my fortune. Ernesto stands motionless, while I continue speaking, "Yancy, the Chief of Police, Long Beach."

He shifts his weight to his other leg. "What about him?"

I confirm that we are alone, by scanning our vicinity. "For getting Rafael's work to New York, I need several thousand copies of a commissioned, but anonymous work of his revolutionary illustrated literature, in Spanish and English, calling attention to the presence and influence of the Klan in our city, by illustrating police handiwork in the murder of a Negro guarding the entrance to a speakeasy full of fairies. Burning crosses, illegal liquor, queens, all of it."

He smirks, "Mexicans too, eh?"

"All of it."

He lifts his hand towards his brother, still consoling Maria, who in turn consoles Solstice.

"You got it," he agrees, as they dutifully approach.

Chapter Eleven

"Friends of Friends"

Shrouded in rolling fog interrupting cold, clear morning skies over Hangar No. 2, Glamour Jackson's copper eyes blaze through her fresh mascara. "I won't likely see you again, soon," she warns me between the maroon borders of her mouth biting the lower lip and leaving a stain on the bottom of her front top teeth. I stare at her long perfect Cleopatra forehead, her roots pulled back, hidden beneath a modern, wide-brimmed black hat with white accents, pairing an equally modern white dress with black stripes. An ill-matched, wooly grey shawl, hand-knitted, she was gifted in Los Angeles, falls upon her shoulders under two complicated, golden earrings. Finally, after turning her head as the airplane propellers spark and smoke in their starting mode, some feet away, she resolves to say, first inhaling clean air deeply, "There is one thing, Tony, I need to share before I go." Vainly waiting for me to speak, she gently, ambiguously huffs, and then continues talking, "Remember, back on the SS Lily? I told you I had three words for you..."

I interrupt, "...and those words weren't 'I love you', you said." I stand arms crossed, nonplussed, causing her distress, forcing her to furl her brow. "Don't do that," I beg her, then joke, "You'll wrinkle too soon."

She giggles, "Tony..."

Knowing she wants to reveal, and knowing she wants me to want her to reveal, I ask, "What were they, your three words unspoken?"

She speaks with intention, "You blackmailed... me," then dips at the knees, placing the luggage already in her right hand on the ground, while the other reaches for the strings tying together the thick butcher paper insulating several reams of Betty Poop which Ernesto previously delivered to my possession, now clutched in my fingers. She takes both items and stands, studying my facial expressions, smirking, sensing I know she speaks some truth and expecting me to confess.

Rather than argue or mislead her emotions, which merely would arouse her paranoia some minutes before ascending into the heavens, I simply shake my head, shrug my shoulders and stare at the Boeing Model 80 trimotor biplane boarding a group of eight passengers. "If I did, and I mean 'if'..." I begin, turning left and right searching for truthful words, finally settling upon her skeptical countenance, "It's because I believed your talent." Before losing my composure, I direct her towards the future, "I'll send your other belongings soon," is all I say, all I can really bring myself to say, lamely, before she turns at the waist intending her departure. Instantly, I rudely grab her shoulder to forcibly pull her towards me, to her complete surprise, and eyes closed, I dive my mouth forward, greeting hers, our tongues quickly move like precious, hungry goldfish, intimately swimming inside the same small universe.

She pulls back, our eyes wide opened, turns her chin to the side but staring into my pupils, and licks her front teeth. She smirks, "Good bye, Tony."

First revolving on her heels, the jazz singer walks towards the biplane, and I yell, "Happy New Year, Glamour Jackson!"

Settled in line, among the last of the passengers, my diva still refuses to turn towards my direction. The final glimpse I catch of her is her ankle lifted from the top stair as her whole body disappears inside the shadowy entrance of the craft, shortly before the door closes. The stairs are pulled away by two husky engineers.

Three whirring engines help the biplane to taxi some feet, then it turns and picks up speed, negotiating the paved airfield, preparing to ascend. I stand motionless watching, until car headlights out of the periphery of my vision appear to be approaching quickly, through the thickening mist. It finally stops some yards away. The driver, whom I do not recognize through the glass window, wears a formal Navy uniform, which hardly seems out of place, as the Long Beach Airport is used for both commercial and military purposes. The driver exits, not acknowledging my presence, and opens the door behind him. An officer, greying, clean-shaven, stands tall and pulls straight the gold-leafed sleeves of his black, ribbon-studded jacket tightly. He leers at me, walking around the vehicle and opening the other rear door. Taking his arm, 'Olevaivai'olefe'e stands next to whom I presume is her devoted paramour. Selfishly, I consider how much she has revealed to him about me, as they approach. I peer through the mist searching for the runway to find the biplane readying for take-off, and immediately I hear a loud, commanding deeply masculine voice.

He bellows, "Hello!"

Rather than immediately respond, I extend my hand and wait for his. Finally, after we shake hands, I introduce myself softly, "Anthony Camarrata."

"Stewart McKelvy," he responds, without smiling. "This is 'Olevaivai'olefe'e," he says, looking in her direction. "I won't pretend the two of you haven't met."

'Olevaivai'olefe'e controls her emotions. "Glamour?" is all she asks me, scratching the back of her neck. And I point my finger at the biplane speeding quickly away from our direction as it disappears. "Well, at least Solstice might get some spiteful happiness that we also didn't get to say goodbye," she declares.

The Captain comments, "Damn weather made us late, I suppose. Once the Boeing reaches three or four thousand feet, according to harbor reports, flying should be clear, likely through to Arizona." It's difficult to discern from his manner whether McKelvy is sympathetic or indifferent towards me.

"If they don't fly into Charles Lindbergh inside that soup," 'Olevaivai'olefe'e whines, looking up into the moving fog bank.

I ask her, "Solstice didn't want to come along and say goodbye?"

"Too upset Glamour's leaving, she said, Anthony," 'Olevaivai'olefe'e explains, returning her eyes towards my direction.

I nod my head, as McKelvy studies our exchange of words, closely. Finally, he says, "Right, so. I have matters to attend at another hanger, so... Mr. Camarrata, it was a pleasure to meet you. Thank you for alleviating some of the loneliness of my Fe'e," he grins. The three of us stand for some time, searching for words, uncertain of how to proceed.

"Long Beach Airport"

"Off so soon, folks?" I ask.

'Olevaivai'olefe'e responds, "We're flying to San Francisco for a few weeks, while he's still on leave. We just got back from San Diego, after a month of holidays."

"I see," I affirm, understanding now why it has been so difficult to reach her since the end of November. "Well, happy New Year, of course."

"Of course," the Captain politely rejoinders then shakes my hand a final time. The driver who had been patiently standing at an open door salutes the Captain as he takes again his back seat. 'Olevaivai'olefe'e winks at me once before returning to her seat. Ensuring that his passengers are safe and comfortable, the driver gets behind the wheel, and closes his own door before steering the car through the impenetrable weather, almost impossible to see beyond.

I fear my life has settled on some sober plateau, almost mechanically sober. Abandoned by Abraham, Glamour, and now 'Olevaivai'olefe'e, I evaluate this lonely feeling, walking towards the Model A, parked at the side of the Hangar No. 2, feeling separate from everything. The fog fills the air densely now. I step inside the isolated car, and before touching the ignition, reach for the flask of tequila in my jacket, open it and sip, seal it closed and drop it. I close my eyes. My left hand instinctively digs below my belt, reaching down and fiddling my flaccid cock. My forefinger wipes a strand from the slit, and I carefully recover it to stick it successfully to my tongue tip, which I roll around inside my teeth, savoring this juicy, viscous droplet. I long for the calming influence of 'Olevaivai'olefe'e's reefer. I long for her chocolate pyramids, her palusami and champagne. My hand returns, my eyes keep closed, and I get harder and longer, while my other hand lifts my shirt and opens the buttons on my pants, releasing the full weight and girth of it. Happiness falls upon the crease of my lips. My mouth practices suckling invisible nipples while my fingers caress the tips of my own, tugging their hairs gently and harder, back and forth, as I stroke the full length of my long trunk, flickering a knuckle against my glans. Downward jerks, fist hits scrotum, precise measurements of pressure, not too soft, reaching the threshold of pain, a multiplication of velocity and pounds per square inches, a weakening grip holding loose, supple Latin skin, pulling up, spitting, and resuming, manual manipulations in sinuous motions like a piston. Eyes still closed, I imagine all eyes on me. Concentrations deep inside, movements of tendons and unknown muscles, tightened sac, elephantine, upward, downward, faster, faster yet. A building sensation, the synaesthetic tastes of cocoa and amber and tympany, bitter, addicting, veins narrowing, fundament clenching, ounces squeezing through channels burning, fire spinal bolts. Magenta, violet, titian. Aaaaaaaye!

I yank, the first release explodes a couple feet directly upward, as I open my eyes, it travels in an arc, landing on my open face, I moan, loudly into the wheel. I yank, the second gush gurgles over my grip on the trail of hair leading up and down my center meridian. I yank, a feverish burst oozes an ounce outward, pooling on top. I shake, quiver, shrinking, quaking aftershocks of involuntary spasms, each one echoing the last, echoing. Grunts, echoing, pull me back to my sober, mechanical senses. Eyelids collapse. My wet hand falls on the leather of the seat. Gasp. Breaths deepen.

The sound of someone rapping their knuckles against the glass window on my left side. "Huh?" I mutter. The knuckles come again, so I roll the window down as far as it can go, halfway.

A man's voice speaks mellifluously, "Fist full of dollars. Money comes and goes quickly. A handkerchief cleans." Then, a wrinkled hand comes into the cabin, dropping a white handkerchief which parachutes to my lap. As I clean myself and reclaim my modesty by buttoning my trousers, a head falls to the level of the window and peers inside. I do not recognize his pale face, which has been weathered unkindly by the sun, flaky and dry. The lips appear cracked. Only the man's green eyes, beneath his grey, bushy brow, retain any sparkle. "You will leave the car and come with me," he says coldly. "We shall return the vehicle to where it belongs, and I do apologize for the sudden inconvenience, but it is the simplest solution and therefore for the best." He rubs his bald head, covered in brown spots, then stands aside, waiting for me to exit.

I hesitate a moment, reflecting on a life of taking orders, adhering to another's discipline, and consider whether my recent actions, first subjecting Williams to humiliation and then making use of his car against his will, are in fact minor rebellions against ingrained habits as old as the Roman Catholic Church, which itself I have rebelled against all my adult life. I could ignore the request of this man, who so rudely observed me enjoying privacy contrived inside this vehicle. It would be a simple matter of starting the ignition and proceeding about my business, but then, I wonder, what would I be doing, except more rebellion. Discipline and the reaction to it must yield to more careful motivations. I choose to yield, in the end, so retrieve my flask and step out of the Ford. A younger, short, husky man standing behind the bald one some feet, holds his palm out, letting his fingers move up and down. I presume he wants the car keys, so I walk towards him and let them go to his possession. He promptly walks past me and takes the driver's seat, before starting the engine and driving into the fog, as I silently observe, uncertain of my own future.

The bald man, who has already started walking away after the Ford began moving, stops and turns in my direction, beckoning. Where else can I go? I follow his shadowy figure instinctively, anxious, cautious. At length, we arrive at another vehicle. The rear door appears already open, and in the fashion of a valet, he gestures for me to enter through the open door, which I duck into and make myself comfortable as much as possible, given the mysterious circumstances. Without speaking, he closes the door, and takes command of the car. We travel slowly, as the atmosphere is quite formidable, rendering reality opaque and invisible. Without incident, he takes us to a quiet place near the beach and parks in a spot where there are no other cars nearby. I can't guess where we are. I recall wearing the blindfold to last year's Valentine's Day affair, and at that moment, the bald man turns in my direction.

"Head for the shore. Wait there."

As if caught in a flow of events beyond my scrutiny and understanding, I submit to his simple directions and leave. The sky and the ocean form a solid monolith. Even the sand eventually bleeds into the miasma of a perfect monochrome nothingness, one solid hue, without much differentiating shades. If it were an oil painting, the scene before me would make for rather dull art. Only the sound of waves crashing, in the distance, beyond my vision, orient me in this non-space. A few yards away from the car, I turn back, to see it entirely disappear, slowly, into the fog. I feel utterly alone, vulnerable, with only the sound of the waves growing, as I walk in my intended direction. Finally, at the edge where sky meets land meets water, the impermanent boundary dividing all earthly realities, I stand looking out some feet onto the Pacific. There is nothing else. There is nobody else. There is me.

Minutes pass as the sun lightens the sky, and I scan thirty or forty feet of shoreline I can actually see. Finally, to my east, a lone figure appears as a silhouette growing black in the grey. I turn squarely to face him, as I see his black suit more clearly, his polished black shoes leaving footprints along the water's edge, his black tie against his bright white tab-collar shirt. His hair appears equally black, combed and greased with a substance as heavy as marfak. A clean-shaven countenance, handsome, a dark tinge to his complexion, his full lips mimic some sort of smile.

"Mr. Camarrata," he states, matter of factly, waiting for me to acknowledge, as he ceases walking at a distance of about three feet in front of me.

"Yes?"

Finally, he reaches his hand forward, "Tony Cornero."

I reach forward and he grasps my hand firmly, crushing it in his. "If I knew what to say…"

"You may start by saying, 'thank you,' and before you ask, 'for what?', I can give you an answer. The car you stole from Williams, we have returned to him. Mr. Williams is no longer a matter for your concern. Let's go for a walk," he says, extending his open hand in a westward direction. I follow, expecting him to talk and for me to remain silent. "I'm the owner of the SS Lily. Nice work you pulled off there, setting up Williams like that with the cops. Well done. But, before you say 'thank you,' I want to know what you're up to."

I match his easy pace, walking on his right side, unsure how to converse. "I'm done with Williams, if that's what you want to know."

"Sure you are. What's this I hear from some of your friends about you going after cops?" he asks, gazing into the fog ahead of us. "You got some sort of death wish?"

"I figure a couple of them have it coming to them," I state honestly. Some of my friends? Whom does he know?

"Mr. Camarrata," he begins ominously. "Don't mess with my ships, you got that?"

"Right," I state simply.

"Listen. If you decide to do what you are going I'm trying to do my part to keep 120 million people from being poisoned to death. Let me make you an offer. Whatever you got going on, we might be able to help each other out. How much you make as a truck driver? Ten or twenty a week?"

"About that," I admit.

"I'll bump to 100 what they're paying you, if you work for me, and that's just to start with." He stops walking and places his hand on my shoulder, turning my body towards his.

Without looking anywhere else, I stare into his eyes. "What you got in mind?" I ask, figuring that there is no harm in learning his intentions, though obviously I understand my choices in this matter are limited. "I mean, sure. What do you need me to do?"

He grins and nods his head. "You can't see them, but there's a dozen craps and poker boats about three miles or so offshore. Some of them are mine, some of them are not. I'm not sure what future they have in the liquor business. Some Navy people talk about making the harbor the permanent home to the Pacific Fleet, maybe turning some of the islands out there into shooting ranges, securing the Wilmington oil fields for military purposes, building up Long Beach into a jazz spot for sailors. You read the papers?"

"Occasionally," I reply.

"Look at Japan. Or, the communists. Look at Italy, for chrissakes. Sure, Hitler lost the November election, but you think that's gonna keep him down for long? Ain't happening. The Navy is going to make this harbor home. And Prohibition? Over with Roosevelt. By next year or so, I'd say. Let's keep walking."

As we move forward, a young couple walks past us through the fog, and Cornero keeps his silence.

"I need a bigger crew than the one I got now," he starts finally, "to help me diversify. It ain't gonna be liquor anymore, it's gonna be a lot bigger than that, maybe that whacky weed they got in Tijuana. And the gambling ain't gonna be kept on ships. We're trying to move it to shore. Somewhere it all can be monitored and controlled, in the City of Long Beach itself. So, the folks from Los Angeles can drive down here, spend their money easily, rather than head out to Vegas, where Luciano has rigged everything. The point is, Camarrata, I am the future."

Suddenly, my skin pimples as I relive memories of the terror I felt standing before Caligula in Brooklyn, declaring he was the future and then instantly shooting orphan Joe in front of me, as I panicked and ran away. Once again Cornero stops, but this time reaches into his suit jacket and removes a handgun which he holds at the barrel, pushing its handle into my chest.

"It's unloaded, here," he says, opening the empty cylinder, showing it, before snapping it closed in one smooth gesture. "I want you to keep it, especially if you have a vendetta against cops."

My hands don't move.

"Here!" he says, forcing it into my sternum, causing me some intended discomfort. "Smith & Wesson, .38 Super. Keep it. Just gotta find the right bullets for it. The nickel ones slice right through a car door, 'cause they got about forty percent more cartridge pressure than the brass the old guns used. Get the nickel." Finally, I lift my left hand and take the handle, as my right hand caresses its edges. "Put it away, would you? Now!" I stuff it between my belt and my stomach. "Here's the deal. You are going to keep walking to the west, eventually, you'll reach Rainbow Pier. Sometime this summer, we'll set you up as a lifeguard in Long Beach, get you out of that truck. You'll like it, perched up there. After the summer ends, we'll talk again. You may thank me, now."

"Tony Cornero"

"Got it," I state. "Thank you."

He stops our walking his last time, warns me, "Just leave Williams alone. Now head west." I turn away and starting walking into the fog in the direction given. After some yards, I turn my head, and see that his figure has completely vanished into the mist. Once again, I am alone.

In this nothingness, I imagine Solstice's deck of magic cards, predicting the future, leaving me open to fate, as if my intelligence and will are so supple that they merely bend to forces seemingly beyond my control. I merely talked a good game all my life, slipping into and sliding out of situations and emotions that are only partially of my own making, relying upon the impressions of others, always coming to some terminus, some failure or reckoning which leads to another vista, opening up and beckoning, vain promises and illusory realities lacking foundations or even the semblance of permanence. It is though I am as a boy, once again, listening to wise and clever priests, offering this and that in exchange for these and those.

I pull the gun from my pants and, as I walk, I aim it forward into the nothingness. If it were loaded, and I were to shoot it and hit something, someone I don't see who it is I hit, am I the true cause of destruction, the agent of death, lacking malevolent intention? I picture my body like an enormous weapon, discharging illness into unknown bodies shrouded in darkness. I am becoming a weapon, towards what end? Dennis Carpenter was a sort of weapon, protecting others, ready to discharge himself at a moment's notice, into the dark if necessary, until he was sliced and stabbed, left bleeding to death. If Cornero is right, all of Long Beach will soon become a weapon, discharging seamen like semen into some future sinkhole filled with communists murdering fascists murdering communists. Bump my salary, get a job as a lifeguard, dispatched to Tijuana.

Is there nowhere to hide, but behind a wife and children, like Abraham? Is there no release from a life sentence of masturbation, masked as anonymous liaisons? I see nothing around me but the shoreline. I am at the center of the universe. I am alone. I don't know what I am.

I return the gun to my waist, as soon as I hear the sounds of birds flying overhead. Where do I acquire nickel bullets?

Chapter Twelve

"Abalone Cove"

RECEIVED AT LONG BEACH, CALIF

NEW YORK CITY, NY
JANUARY 21, 1933

ANTHONY CAMARRATA

ARRIVED HOME STOP WEATHER, EQUIPMENT AND WHITE MEN FORCED DELAYS STOP DELIVERING PACKAGE NEXT WEEK STOP SEND LUGGAGE TO COMMODORE RECORDS STOP COMMUNICATING FURTHER TOO COSTLY

GLAMOUR JACKSON

0435P

* * *

 Pastoral vistas guard restful intentions some distance ascending over pools caught between high and low tide.
 The miracle of turquoise edging inward, variously foaming and flattening, receding back into glassy reflections of verdant desert cliffs, haunted by low frequencies emanating from the horns of vessels gliding in the channel between San Pedro and Catalina. Inside that flat plane extending above water and away from shore, a crumble of stone juts out, forming a lip holding it, in it, pouchlike, ponds hidden and revealed in six-hour cycles of common swells. If I were as enormous as Pantagruel, I would straddle the land, and kick my feet wet, throwing sand and seafood everywhere, opening my

codpiece and pissing into the sea, reaching for the sun and pulling its radiant salve across my skin, a feasting glutton, sinful, until over tired, so bending down lenticular clouds from blue skies and stuffing them underneath my head like pillow feathers on which to repose before sleep.

My midwinter's sobriety yields no joy, no tears, just constant ruminations on the wonders of gulls, whose calls resemble mocking. Nature cackles on the boundary of the Pacific. An entire continent mapped by Vespucci's guesswork ends here, and yet two more could fill the ocean before touching Mount Fuji. The accidents of history to which I am enslaved surround me. Repeating, if I were as enormous as Pantagruel, I would stand up and walk into the harbor to submit Catalina to my will, once and for all. Yet being small scale, I slay the monsters of epic horrors, because at this moment, all I want for myself is a century, at least a twentieth century, of peaceful indifference and common sense.

"Abalone"

Maybe I will never visit Catalina. I can accept that. The sun is constant, too. Thinking of common sense, I stare across half the spacious cove, able to accommodate dozens of skiffs perhaps, and spot my two friends, Maria and Solstice, balancing themselves on the edge of shore, occasionally squatting down into rocky tide pools below their feet. From this distance, they appear to be about the size of large ants, dancing up and down. Each carry a machete, as Maria wields it carefully, showing Solstice how to devour urchin and abalone, caught with bare hands. My belly, already full, extends outward an extra inch, pleasantly gurgling with the sounds of a contented digestion. Maria's brother, Rafael, drove the car of his brother, Ernesto, to bring us all here to Portuguese Bend. He was my machete master not an hour earlier, while the ladies were busying themselves with gathering wood for the fire pit he is now tending some yards beyond me. The method is simple. For urchins, the machete blade falls down with an appropriate force to split the inedible shell of the creature's underside but without causing injury to one's hand holding the spiny thing. All of the orange matter is instant raw food, suckable and delicious, the ocean brine seasoning the meat naturally, plus some squeezed citrus. Along with peels, too, the shells are thrown whence they came. As for the abundant abalone, each is removed from the rocks by the machete tip, carefully, and the grey-pink flesh is lifted by the weapon's edge, cleaned of underlying black matter, juiced with lemon or lime, and dropped between the lips, slipping around and sliding down. Instant ceviche.

As there are no other visitors to the cove on this day, the four of us remain, through sunset.

In my presence, Solstice fusses sulking about the shore of the cove, but generally so since Glamour returned to New York a month ago. Now that February is upon us, I had been hoping Solstice would have shown me signs of improvement in her disposition towards me, sharing her effervescent personality and cheerfulness, but these emotions she keeps private from me, and instead, she gives Maria more of what she formerly had shown towards me. Solstice's sensitivities are staggering to my mind, and I speculate she is channeling the transcontinental coldness of Glamour, whose January telegram stays folded inside the pocket of the trousers I wear, cuffs rolled up to my knees. Of course, I tell myself I am merely speculating, being offered nothing explicit in the form of conversation from her. But, every once in awhile, in an odd moment, I catch Solstice staring at me, before she averts her gaze on some unimportant detail otherwise occupying her attention. It is as if she is studying, measuring me for some inscrutable long-term purpose, to such an extent that, if Solstice had ever proven herself capable of harming other people, I would feel somewhat nervous. Allotting her the benefit of my doubt, I tolerate my unease. Maria wisely has counseled my adult patience, and I have kept my feelings distant, satisfying myself with platitudes about masculine ignorance.

For behavior that seems typical to me now, Maria improvised this cove adventure, sharing her desire that we escape the familiarity of Long Beach and to imagine ourselves living lives like Crusoe, taking from nature's bounty and starting a beach fire to keep us warm through an early winter sunset. Her brother Ernesto had been previously obliged to complete a number of errands and was unable to join us this day. Rafael, however, she explained, was eager to share some of his art with me, and although he hardly spoke on the ride from Long Beach, he has kept an eye on me, and his gaze remains fixed once it meets mine.

"Anthony!" he shouts, poking at the fire with a tree branch narrow as my thumb but as long as his arm. "Come here for something," he adds.

Rafael is dressed in rolled-up trousers and a white undershirt. His skin below his neck and across his broad, heavy shoulders is covered in deep-blue tattoo art, some of which appears abstract and geometrical to me, while its other parts represent animals, including a snake, bear and eagle, and flora, like cacti and roses. The Ordaz siblings must have been born within a few years of one another as they all seem near my age, and despite this, Rafael displays remarkably youthful, well-developed muscles pushing against his clothing at every point. His black, bushy eyebrows circle his lids in wide arcs, always making him seem aloof yet metaphysically attentive. His nose, wider than my own, is similar to mine in length, and his lips, reddish brown, burst outward and taper to points further than the ends of his flaring nostrils. A small dimple in his chin adds to his attractive qualities. Without smiling purposefully, he always manages to appear happy, calm. It takes me a few seconds to center my attention on initially standing up from my day-dreaming and then complying with his request, by walking towards his direction.

I approach, when he reaches his thick-fingered hand into a trouser pocket and retrieves a notebook, somewhat bent, so as to fit. Then, standing at his side, and gathering in his pleasant odor, mixed with sweat, ocean and now smoke, I feel my stomach brushed by his hand moving us both some feet away from the fire. He explains, "These here… are some drawings for the book. This one here," he says, pointing his finger at one page, depicting a heavily muscled man wearing a blue mask and trunks, walking into an illuminated doorway, "He is what we call a luchador… a wrestler." Rafael turns the page, showing the Luchador throwing bodies dressed in Klan hoods across a dark room. "So, here he is, destroying the bad guys. His name is Salvador." As he continues turning the pages, Rafael shows images of his nocturnal masked avenger nailing Klansmen with his exaggerated phallic weapon popping out his loins. Red stains, presumably blood, squirt out from each rape scene, and Rafael grins above each page leafing between his fingers. There are scenes of cops and Salvador wrestling them into submission in moonlight, scenes of bullets stopped with his bare hands, scenes of squads of blue-hooded Negroes following Salvador into battle. "These are just ideas," he shrugs his shoulders, dropping his notebook on the sand. "The moral of it is, Anthony... Salvador is unable to love anyone. All he can do is win fights his whole life. He doesn't have room to believe in love, because he believes so much in justice. Could say, he's a tragic hero."

The quality of Rafael's illustrations seems to me exceptional and noteworthy. It is obviously popular in style, but not rudely crafted. The depictions of perspective appear consistent, the lines drawn are clean and near perfect, the principal characters' colorful faces are distinguishable. Though the drawings lack dialogue, I expect this would be added later in his creative process. Recognizing I am standing next to a genuine, talented artist, I catch feelings of prejudice rising within me concerning what I regard to be Rafael's simple conversation. Ernesto, whose diction is precise and learned, must protect his brother's gifts by representing them with clever discourse and intellectual artifice, but certainly Ernesto realizes, as the businessman in their family partnership, that Rafael possesses powers of expression that are worth publication and praise, in the service of higher ideals concerning what I recognize, more quickly than in my past, to be cultural subversion and social revolution.

"Can you swim?" he asks me.

I suddenly perceive irony to his question, having just received an invitation to perform the duties of a lifeguard. Though I have used the Long Beach Bath house for its showers, I have not made much use of its pool, just usually wading my feet and cruising men. "I could use some lessons," I truthfully admit.

"Right on. Want some?" he laughs, pulling off his shirt and trousers and throwing them some feet away from the fire. Instantly, he takes off, running away, further from the gaze of his sister and Solstice. Without much reflection, I follow his lead, undress myself and jog in his direction. We travel like this, under the late afternoon sun, today's winter air neither too chilled nor sufficiently warm, and stop after a few hundred feet, where plenty of sand comforts our feet. Then, he leads, splashing his skin with cold water, yelling into the sky to release the shock of it, and finally dives headlong near the shore, immersing himself in one quick swim, before standing and beckoning me to follow. Not to be outdone, I run into the water, past him, causing chaos, before I flip my body and dive backside, arms thrown out either side, showing my swinging cock, before it predictably shrivels in the sea. When I surface, I scream as loud as I have ever screamed, and Rafael laughs, screaming louder.

At such shallow depths, I easily support myself standing on the sandy bottom. Rafael approaches, first walking, then falling forward and paddling his way. He gets close, his hands bump my thighs, he apologizes. "One first thing you must learn… " he begins patiently. "You must learn how to float. Do you know how to float?" I shake my head. Placing both of his arms out, he explains, "I'm going to put my arms out like this, so you come to me and put yourself in my power. Can you do that?"

"Sure," I smile. I move closer and settle between his arms. I lean backwards into his left arm, while my legs still support my weight by pushing against the sandy floor.

"Now," he continues. "Your body will float by itself. You just need me to show you how. I'm going to reach underneath the back of your legs and lift them off the sand. Okay?"

I nod, understanding he has become my master yet again.

"Your job is your breathing. Nothing can happen to you out here. You can always touch your toes on the sand if you get nervous. So, here I go." Rafael dips his right arm underneath my seat, triggering a wiggle in my sac. Then, his hands guide the backs of my long legs up, and he kindly directs my attention to my breathing. "Now, your hands, they are floating. Put one of them on your belly, feel it go up and down, in and out as you breathe." I comply, while he continues to support the weight of my body in the ocean. In the open air, I feel my skin pimple, but thankfully there is no wind, and I become quickly comfortable with my breathing. I notice the blood flowing to my cock, which lengthens, aroused by his gentle touch and earnest attention. He says nothing. Instead, he continues to hold me as I breathe. "Float," he commands, releasing his support slowly, allowing me to maintain my buoyancy under my own effort, though my feet sink slightly. Satisfied I am floating, Rafael takes a position floating backside, next to me, spitting water up into the sky. "Now, move your hands in circles, like mine, to help," he says, touching my fingers with his and extending arms outward, bodies separating. Aroused by my curiosity, I turn my head in his direction, and throw myself out of balance, causing me to stand on my two feet, staring down el general standing tall, reaching for the sun.

His erection is beautiful. The big, wide, purple head atop the shaft extending downward wider and darker, still smooth and veiny, quite firm. It bounces up and down, probably by his command. I see he is simply smiling to the sky, utterly happy to be alive, floating under his own will, able to express his desire and to know of mine, without words, without expectation really, when suddenly he sinks below the surface and pops up, amused, before moving towards me, gazing deeply into my pupils and kissing me, first nibbling, then falling inside momentarily, then pulling backwards. "I'll see you on the beach," he says taking off, swimming into the Pacific, beyond my reach, beyond my skills, heading for deeper water, but also at a near constant distance from the fire on shore. Having no choice to follow him, sensing the obstacle I face copying his skills, but also knowing I have the opportunity to learn more, I settle agreeably on feelings of uncertainty and possibility and walk to the shore. I move a couple feet, but practice floating by myself one last time. I am successful. A headstand, my eyes open underwater watching air bubbles ascend. Flipping, causing a splash, I stand a second time, and head for land, feeling pleasantly teased.

The flames have simmered to a state of low burning, and some of the wood has charred, some of it has turned ashy white. Maria stokes the coals, using the machete. She wears her hair loose and long, and the fresh air brings out her natural happiness. Without looking directly at me, she stares into the fire, engaging me in conversation, while I use my undershirt I had been wearing to remove, slowly, excess saltwater from my naked body.

"Tony, it's called Portuguese Bend. Not Portuguese Bend Over," she jokes.

I walk towards my trousers and, standing, I pull them up to my hand using my toes.

Before I am able to dress myself, she makes a "tisk" noise, reproaching me.

"How many inches is that?"

I smile upon hearing her vulgar question. "I haven't measured." Pausing, I vainly wait for her rebuttal. "About ten, when aroused," I finally admit.

"¡Ay de mí!" Pause. "Perfecto," she murmurs, ambiguously whines.

Looking up at the sky, I ask for permission to don my trousers and receiving her nod, I proceed. Meanwhile, Rafael is swimming closer to shore, in our direction.

"Solstice is still eating?" I ask.

"Yes."

I wonder if I should mention more about my uneasy feeling. "Maria, is this a time to ask about her? And before you say, 'what about her,' I'm talking about how cold she's been towards me all day."

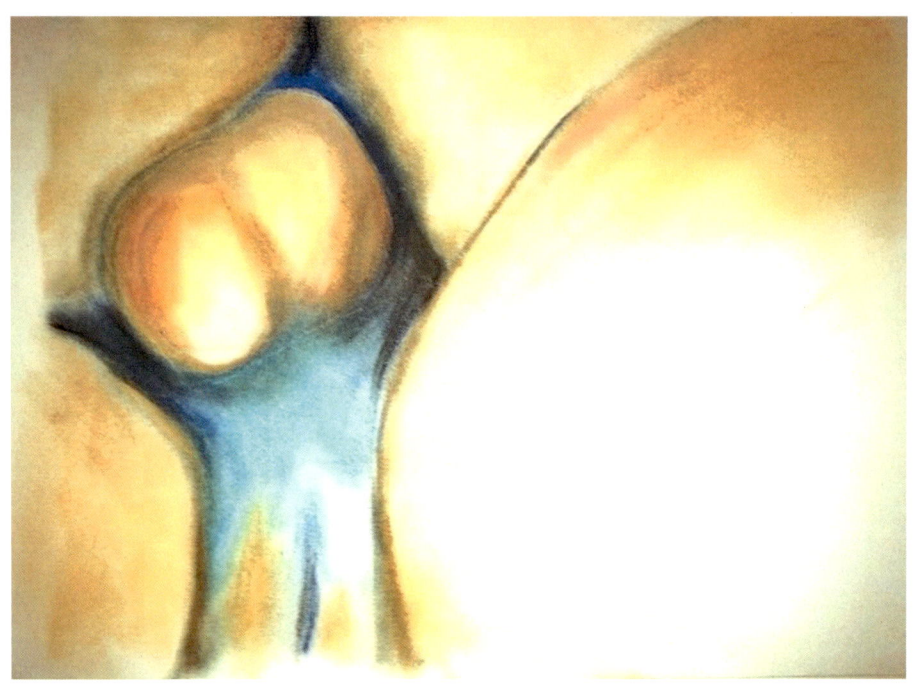

"Rafael from Behind"

For the first time, Maria looks directly at me, inhaling deeply. "She's upset. She's upset Glamour left. She's feeling homesick, I think. Or something. I'm not quite sure, to be honest. What do you think of Rafael's luchador?" she asks, in an attempt to steer the conversation away from Solstice.

"Does he have a name for his comic yet?"

Maria returns to stoking the coals. "I told him it should be 'The Stranger,' or something like that."

I stare at Rafael now walking closer to us. "Did you see the actual drawings? Too fierce."

"That's it." Maria drops the stick and claps her hand, "'Fierce Stranger'," she announces. "It should be 'Fierce Stranger', Tony. I'll share my idea with him later."

While Rafael takes his place in our tiny cypher, he hesitates before donning clothes to warm himself, positioning his hips a very short distance from my head, while Maria wilfully attends to stoking coals, signaling her unwillingness to acknowledge the obvious. Exercising the extremes of my peripheral vision, I study his curly black pubic hair, dirtied by gritty sand, draping his genitalia, still loose, relaxed, occasionally twitching. I wonder what it is about men that demands my attention, and then I consider whether it is all men, or whether it is just some men around which I shape my preferences. There are some men who seem more desirable, showing their intellect like Abraham, or their creativity like Rafael, or even people who transcend themselves, making a life by living their free-spiritedness like Glamour and 'Olevaivai'olefe'e, more than men and in some ways women, too. But beyond these qualities, there is the fact of chemistry, alarm substances catalyzing below consciousness, that draws my attention. And in that special instance where a reaction occurs, where a physical conversation transpires without words, the impulse to act evokes a feeling greater than hunger or addiction, more like the urgency felt holding one's breath under water, which can only be held for so long, until the body instinctively resists what the mind compels it to perform and acts nearly of its own accord, racing for oxygen.

Rafael longs to feel my wet skin against his warm flesh.

"Will you two stop?" Maria begs, still refusing to direct her eyes at us. Rafael proceeds by slowly walking towards his trousers and dressing himself. "Oye! ¿De qué significa esto? ¡Sin vergüenza! ¡En este momento, ya no me estoy orgullosa de ser tu hermana!" Maria scolds him.

Without speaking, I stand, stretch my arms towards the sky, yawn, and turn my back to walk away from the fire, away from the shore, towards a path that gently ascends to the cliffs some height above us. A few moments later, without checking behind me, I sense I am being followed. At a distance of some yards, covered completely by shrubs and short trees, I stop when I feel Rafael's warm hands fall upon my shoulders, massaging them. Removing one hand, he releases his pants, which fall down, as he begins to whip me from behind. Instantly, I drop my trousers and scan around me, searching for something to hold on to, finding a tree trunk, a few inches thick, sturdy enough to resist my weight. I kick off my pants and walk towards the tree, spreading my legs far apart, taking one hand to my mouth and pouring spit inside, without turning around. Rafael walks behind, repeats the same gesture of applying moisture to my furry crevice, rotating his finger around the edge of my hole, pushing spittle inward, slowly at first, his other hand pressing down on my shoulder, inviting me to slide backwards, adding another finger inside, pushing further, edging myself closer towards him. In time, we create a rhythm of intimacy, his probing feeling more comfortable, taking longer, adding a third finger and more saliva, I moan in baritone registers. Silently, he removes his fingers and inserts his head, dripping, close against my skin, gently rubbing back and forth, mildly, gently. I spread my legs further, as he dips at the knees and dropping spit on himself one last time, he prepares his way, and then dives inward, my muscles tighten, resisting at first, but then relaxing, nerves pleasing every meridian. He takes his time, moving one inch forward every few seconds, and withdrawing at an equal speed, spitting on himself every minute or so, until I command the pace of the motion, using the tree trunk to extend backwards, arching my back to pull him out and myself forward. Then, at a sudden moment, all thinking stops, and my movements synchronize with his, and in a loss of control our flesh yields to spastic, sinuous, grunting, cooing spasm. I laugh spontaneously, without intention, my cock bobbles up and down, growing harder, he leads our movements deeper, faster. Spontaneously, I release myself on the tree, the shrubs, the sand. Reaching around my waist, he pulls out one last time, my muscles clenching. I relax, but he dives and dances so quickly that his strong hands force me to arch my head backwards at the moment he climaxes deep inside tempestuous waves. We slow to a stop, remaining docked, he rubs my motionless back, enjoying his strength. Some moments afterwards, he steps backwards and I turn to face him, to approach, to embrace in forward kissing connections.

Pastoral vistas guard sexual intentions some distance ascending over pools caught between high and low tide.

Returning to our fire feels like going backwards in time. Dressed, Rafael and I arrive, seat ourselves, cross-legged, upon the sand, and wait until Solstice returns from her expedition, finally standing next to Maria, who gives her brother a disapproving look, while he merely grins, ignoring her emotions, seemingly uninterested in speaking to her at the moment.

The orgasms have released all tension from my body, filling me with youthful sensations, illusory sympathies with the living ocean. I am a tide pool encompassing conflicted emotional species, ensconced temporarily inside some stable niche, a momentary equilibrium of feelings, a welcome indifference to the unhappiness of the unhappy. My loins, beneath their garments, burn like a volcano. Simple satisfaction subsumes poetry and the encumbered grammar and vocabulary of unrequited desires. Now, here, I bid farewell to this moment, thankful for the garden of the sea, for the nourishing urchins and abalone in my creamy interior, thankful for Rafael, and Maria and Solstice, too. At peace with the Pacific intruding.

This fierce cult of California, trembling strangely underneath my skin.

Chapter Thirteen

"First and Subsequent Shocks"

The thing about earthquakes is that they never happen all at once.

* * *

5:54p Shock!

Awake. Brutally stirred from my light nap wearing my clothes, my half-empty flask in my hand, a loaded gun in my pants, thinking about the inauguration of the new President, and three-two beer, after the bed moves abruptly upward, slams down, everything, including me, slides side to side in my small bedroom. I remain calm, watching the walls teeter back and forth. The alarm clock flies halfway across the room, smashing the glass. I crawl on the mattress, as best I can, towards the door, confused, vainly trying to reach the door handle. Finally, after some effort, I succeed in grabbing it and twisting it until the door pops open. The swaying slows briefly, I quickly throw my body in the frame, the most stable part of the room. The swaying then speeds again, lasting a few seconds, sending my dresser crashing to the floor. I hear awful sounds, crashing, violent, explosive noises down the hallway, out on the street, through the open window. Women and children screaming. Men shouting.

In the first moment of calm, my first thought concerns Solstice, to my surprise. Friday is the start of the weekend, so she must be working at the Cash & Carry on Pine, I imagine, if she happens to stick to her routine this day. My room appears a complete mess: clothes strewn everywhere, broken glass from the window and plaster covering everything in a white powder, turning the air into an unbreathable fog. I turn my head into the hallway and see more chaos, people stumbling out of their rooms, trying to steady themselves against walls in the common area, as minor motions keep things liquid, unsettled. Finally, I stand and make my way to the stairs, which are intact. The first floor is no less disturbed, and when I exit the building, my mouth gapes at the sight of whole frontages collapsed into piles of brick, cars crushed beyond recognition, a couple of bodies lie motionless underneath heavy matter. Already, gawkers approach, try helping.

It is a matter of walking a few city blocks to reach Solstice, but I can hardly move down the sidewalk, which seems practically invisible. Traffic moves randomly, selfishly, hurriedly. As I walk, a whole building face collapses suddenly a few yards in front of me, forcing me to take shelter by dodging to the other side of the street and covering my face with my arm, as projectiles of small bits of stone and wood and glass fly at some velocity from where they were launched. Sudden, brief, mild tremors make the earth seem constantly viscous. Occasionally, I misstep, not even knowing what it is my feet are touching. Two cars suddenly crash behind me, so I turn. After some yelling, they ignore the accident and continue their intended routes, urgently.

Finally, upon reaching the Cash & Carry, I make out the signage to the business collapsed among the rubble of glass and brick covering the street. I call Solstice's name and hear no response. Perhaps rather than working, she was at St. Anthony's. I scour the rubble for signs of life, finding none inside, just people scurrying around the exterior, I venture in the store, climbing over bricks, calling her name, loudly, hearing no response. The sounds of gunfire suddenly echo in the distance. I leave the structure, and look up at the sky, in the direction of Signal Hill, spotting billowing clouds of black smoke against the grey, cloudy March sky. Signs of fire. I continue walking, passing people whose faces are bloodied, holding the bodies of weeping children, walking in groups.

Block after block, I travel. Ten blocks later, or so, I arrive at Olive and Sixth wondering if there is more to come, and how bad it could be. By this time, fire trucks and police cars can be heard all over the city. A few looters take advantage of the temporary loss of government, braving buildings that appear on the brink of collapse to take whatever they can carry. I look towards the ocean, and thankfully, I see that most tall buildings are still standing, including the Villa Riviera, and I think about 'Olevaivai'olefe'e. After I find Solstice, will I find her next? Or Maria?

Solstice first.

In this manner of uncertain reflection and utter amazement at the spectacle of destruction, while maintaining a thoughtful regard for my own safety by keeping my distance from the fronts of buildings, I finally reach St. Anthony's Church, the roof of which has collapsed.

* * *

6:05p Shock!

My first instinct is to hold my body as low to the ground as possible, as a major new shock sways everything on the street back and forth. Trees sway, as if the wind were exerting hurricane forces against them. St. Anthony's architecture seems frivolous, toyish, as it moves back and forth, causing the pillars of the church to crack, and now its edifice falls to pieces before my eyes, letting loose a cloud of grime, billowing out into the street, in my direction. As the swaying settles, again, I move careful towards the building, calling for Solstice.

The front of the church now lacks any recognizable structure, so I head for the side and rear of the building, still calling for Solstice. Finally, upon reaching the rear, I discover dozens of sinners huddled in an open lot, keeping safe distance from anything and everything standing.

There, among the crowd, Solstice responds to my cries, by waving her arms, at first, and running to greet me. We both embrace as long as possible, nervously anticipating future disturbances and eager to share information.

"They say there's gonna be a giant wave any time now. Some people are going up to Signal Hill, to take the high ground," she says, earnestly.

"Nonsense, Solstice," I try to reassure her. "Even if something like that happens, we are about fifty feet or so above the Pacific, so we're probably safe here." I am familiar with Long Beach to know that downtown rises above the sea to that height, maybe a little less, but enough to thwart any major onslaught of water, I estimate. I feel certain I am not lying to her.

"Where's Fe'e? Maria?" she asks, genuinely concerned.

I sigh. "I don't know to be honest. Look, I wanted to reach you first, you hear me? You, first. You understand?" waiting for her to nod. When she finally shows she understands, I place both my hands on her shoulders. I continue, "Fe'e is probably okay, as her building is designed to withstand earthquakes, and as you can see..." I point towards the Villa Riviera.

"I still want to find her, and Maria," she pleads.

"Of course. Do you want to stay here?"

She looks back at the crowd, disorganized, splitting into two groups, one of which seems to be ready to take the long walk to Signal Hill for safety. "No. I'd rather be with you."

I nod. "Fine, but if we find Fe'e, you stay with her tonight, okay?"

"Yes."

Solstice and I leave Olive and walk straight down Alamitos Avenue, surveying the destruction and suffering. It is only a fifteen minute walk, under normal conditions, from St. Anthony's to the Villa Riviera, but under these circumstances, of course, the path is no longer direct, and Solstice finds herself constantly distracted. I try to keep her eyes looking at the unbroken majesty of the second-tallest building in Los Angeles County. I wonder, privately, how far the earthquake has traveled, and where it originated.

Finally, at Ocean Boulevard, which is clogged with vehicles driven mostly by men who hardly pay attention to anything other than their own purposes, we negotiate the danger and successfully reach our intended destination. When we enter the front doors, past throngs of people inspecting the exterior of the building for superficial damages, we find the lobby slightly disturbed but structurally intact, nonetheless filled with dozens of confused and scared people. Solstice and I both shout "Fe'e!" repeatedly.

*　*　*

6:29p Shock!

Trying to steady herself against the frame of the exit from the stairwell, 'Olevaivai'olefe'e appears distraught and confused. Her makeup is running down her face, from tears she spent, walking down stairs in a panic, barefoot. Solstice grabs hold my waist, as I pull us down to the ground, yelling at the crowd to get down to the ground, cover heads, remain calm, this will pass soon. And this shock, which softly sways the walls of the building, makes safe standing nearly impossible, and yet soon passes.

"Fe'e!" I cry, after the erratic movements stall.

"Anthony?" she yells, uncertain where to look. Solstice follows me, as I stand straight up, both of us looking in the direction of the stairwell, where 'Olevaivai'olefe'e still wobbles. "Toni! 'Oi, fa'afetai lava 'i le Atua 'o lo'o soifua pea 'oe! 'Auē! Ta fia ola e! Nā 'ou popole tele 'auā le mafui'e. Sā 'ou māfaufau 'o le 'ā leai ni isi 'o a'u uō peleina! Fa'afetai, fa'afetai, fa'afetai 'i le Atua!"

'Olevaivai'olefe'e pushes through to our direction and opens her arms wide, and begins sobbing uncontrollably, happy to be able to hold us in her arms. We embrace for some moments that feel endless, thankful to have found each other. I break the spell of comfort by speaking words. "Fe'e, I'm so relieved."

"Yes!" Solstice cries. "You're safe!"

'Olevaivai'olefe'e looks down at Solstice, "We all are, thank God. Fa'afetai tele 'i le Atua!"

"Fe'e, I don't know how long this may last. We may need protection all night," I explain.

She finally composes herself, "Of course, si o'u alofa! You two are spending the night here. Where's Maria, have you seen her?"

I shake my head, and look at Solstice. "No, not yet. My first plan was to bring Solstice here. If I find Maria, I may stay at her side."

Solstice nervously complains, "There's going to be a giant wave, some people are saying."

"Will you stop saying that, Solstice," I chastise her.

'Olevaivai'olefe'e exercises her most confident, commanding voice, trying to convince herself more than anything else. "Fēfē, Solstice. We are in the Villa Riviera, we can survive earthquakes like they have in Japan. Besides, we are too high up to go under the water."

"I want to spend more time, ladies," I continue. "But I want to find Maria. Solstice stay with Fe'e, and take the stairs, if need be. Stay out of the elevators." Solstice nods.

I immediately exit the Villa Riviera.

As Maria almost always works the dinner shift at the Pekin Cafe every Friday night, I walk down Ocean Boulevard, as nighttime descends on Long Beach. The destruction is even worse than before, because the subsequent shocks have loosened whole brick walls already weakened by the first quake. Business signs litter the streets everywhere. I pass a couple of still bodies, half covered in debris or cars, or both. Fire engines now appear on scene, attending to small fires and extending ladders to the second, third and fourth floors of buildings lacking exterior walls, revealing bathrooms and kitchens and offices, some of which are populated with victims trapped inside, unable to escape, waiting for rescue.

Finally, after passing Vogue Beauty Salon, I spot Maria searching desperately through the rubble of the Pekin Cafe, calling out the name of "Chu" her chef, unable to find him. When I call her name, she comes running in my direction.

" '33 Quake"

* * *

7:07p Shock!

Maria's shoulder is hit by a falling brick. Grabbing herself in pain, crying for help, I race through the streets, unable to move without slipping to my left, then my right, tripping on debris. Trucks and cars either stop or run into each other, impatiently. Finally, I reach her, and pull her down to the ground, inspecting her wound, which is likely not severe, as there is no blood flow, and she appears to have the ability to move her arm. I examine her whole body, and she seems unharmed. We watch as more bricks crash upon the earth, throwing dust into the atmosphere.

"I can't find Chu," she tells me urgently.

"Then let's look," I say calmly, knowing that without strong sunlight, or at least a flashlight, it will be nearly impossible to search inside buildings. "Do you have any candles? Or matches?" I ask.

"No," she admits, biting her lip, aware of her own limitations.

"What about your brothers? Have you seen them?"

Maria sighs, then throws her hands up in the air. "No, I haven't. I suppose I should look for them, too."

"Maria," I say sternly, taking a deep breath. "You have to make a choice. How much time do you want to spend looking for Chu?"

"But..." she pleads, vainly. "Until it's completely dark. Completely," she asserts, knowing that inside the cafe it is nearly impossible to distinguish anything, as I guess the tables are thrown about, probably with the exterior side wall crushed to the ground, the roof collapsing to the side, glass thrown everywhere inside and out.

"How long have you been looking for Chu?" I ask, but she doesn't answer, shocked at the loss of the cafe. "How long, Maria?"

"An hour, since the first one hit," she nods, caressing her sore shoulder. "I know," she whines, looking in my eyes. "I have to keep looking, until it's completely dark," she insists. I begin to wonder whether she's in some sort of shock, so I remove my shirt, and throw it over her, to keep her warm. At first she resents my gesture, but then realizing she is feeling cold, she accepts it, and sits down on the ground. I sit next to her.

"Was he working in there with you?"

"Yes," she says. "The whole time. We weren't busy, and the couple of people we had in there, made it outside, without getting hurt. But Chu was in the kitchen, and..." suddenly she stops talking. The truth hits her. "I looked for an hour. I couldn't get into the kitchen. The kitchen just... wasn't there." I take her head and pull it to my chest as she begins sobbing uncontrollably. "I couldn't get inside the kitchen. I tried. I tried. I know he was in the kitchen. I know it." An ambulance, sirens blaring, approaches the destruction on our block, but parks near Lord & Taylor's, some distance away.

"We can't stay here in the dark," I beg her. "It's not safe. We need to find your brothers. Do you think they're home, expecting you?"

Like a child, she nods, pained by the thought of ending her search.

"Let's go. We'll look for Chu in the morning."

"Can we just look one more time?"

I agree, "Yes. Just one more time tonight." We stand and head for the rubble that was the cafe, looking about the bricks. I fear more shocks causing more destruction, possibly fatal, and unable to even see the uneven ground I walk upon, I head as far as possible into the cafe, touching the counter, but blocked by too much debris to make my way into the kitchen. I stop, listen carefully, at length, for the sounds of help, for breathing, for any life. Finally, I resolve to end my search, and I exit the cafe, pleading to Maria that it is best to return early in the morning, just before sunrise. She agrees.

It takes us just shy of an hour to arrive at the corner of Anaheim and Atlantic Avenue, about a block or so from Rafael's residence. Seeing him standing on exterior of his house, his figure lit by a fire he has started in his front yard, we wave, relieved to be greeted.

* * *

8:40p Shock!

Rafael's figure vibrates in this late quake, as I jaunt towards the trunk of a small tree, yanking Maria's hand and pulling her closer towards me, as we hold on.

Though it is nearly impossible to see anything, except the glows of private fires dotting the darkness, we hear more crashes, involving buildings and traffic, above the low tones of the earth's rumbling. When the shaking stops, everything becomes eerily quiet. I swear I can hear my own heart beat.

"Thank goodness! You're safe! We were wondering what happened," Rafael says, approaching us after everything has stopped moving.

"Ernesto?" Maria asks urgently.

Rafael laughs, "He's fine. He's fine. He's out helping neighbors, but we were about to go looking for you, if you hadn't made it in another hour. Where you've been?"

As we approach the fire, I look at Maria's worried face. She appears still in a state of shock. I explain to Rafael, "The cook at the Pekin, Chu, seems to be unaccounted for."

Maria cries, massaging herself on her injured shoulder.

Rafael takes her in his arms and consoles her. "Thank you, Anthony. For bringing her," he says to me, then coos to her, "Mija."

"How is your house?" I ask Rafael.

"Some minor damage inside, but I inspected the building, and it looks okay," he says. "I have some bad news, Anthony. A water pipe broke the second floor, and spilled water all over my desk on the first, where I keep my art. The 'Fierce Stranger' drawings are practically ruined. So, I have to start over."

I smile, "The least of our worries, eh?"

"Yeah," Rafael nods.

Finally, I demand Maria's attention, presently buried in her brother's chest. "Maria, hey, you should sleep here tonight, at Rafael's. It's best." Without speaking, she gestures her hand, acknowledging my suggestion. "Okay?"

"Yes, okay," she confirms, somewhat annoyed.

Out of the darkness, a flashlight beams towards our direction. Rafael shouts, "Ernesto?"

* * *

9:08p Shock!

Carefully placing at his feet a basket he holds, Ernesto accidentally drops his flashlight, swiveling back and forth on the ground, while it remains lit. Maria and Rafael call for him, and he answers, saying he is okay. Meanwhile, we crouch as close to the ground as possible, waiting for this more than mild tremor to pass.

Ernesto picks up the light and steadies it towards us, as we stand ourselves, keeping still until he approaches. In his other hand, he retrieves the basket, and when he greets us, he removes the cloth on top of it, to reveal a pot of hot soup, unspilled, and a loaf of bread that he was given by a neighbor motivated by kindness. He explains he has heard rumors of ocean waves inundating Long Beach, but proven false. He also has heard that the Navy is already dispatching sailors to assist with police and fire rescue operations, and to maintain general order. He warns us to expect more shocks yet and to stay outdoors for this night, keeping warm by fires. He asks about Solstice, and I tell him she's safe, but that St. Anthony's Church has been nearly destroyed. I explain that the Pekin is unrecognizable and its chef is missing.

The four of us share our meal, while an exhausted Maria keeps close to her brother Rafael, who caresses her hair and comforts her with gentle kisses to the forehead. Soon, she is sleeping. Ernesto enters Rafael's house with the flashlight, to search for blankets, pillows. When he returns, he arranges what he has found on the ground outside, and the two brothers invite Maria to stretch herself comfortably, laying her head on a pillow. I explain that I feel a strong need to visit the boarding house, to check in with my old mates, and although they protest, emphasizing the dangers of walking about in the dark, with looters and police roaming, I insist I simply must know the truth. In all likelihood, they are fine, but I need to show my concern. They make me promise to return and spend the night with them, and I agree, after deciding that 'Olevaivai'olefe'e and Solstice are likely sleeping, if at all possible, and will be safe until morning.

Ernesto hands me the flashlight, and I embrace them both strongly, promising my return. As I head east, towards Alamitos Avenue, down Anaheim, I keep my eyes on fires to guide my way, saving my flashlight for occasional use only. Few vehicles travel the streets. The night air is gentle, chilly, and quiet. In the distance, I hear occasional crashes and sirens. Most people have settled into small groups, here and there, thousands of people gather around individual fires, staying away from their homes and apartments. Finally, reaching Broadway, I turn the corner and walk towards the boarding house.

* * *

10:52p Shock!

This instant, I hear people all around me cry in panic. Though not as powerful as the first one, this largest of all the secondary shocks wrests from sleep those already suffering a state of near constant anxiety, likely exaggerating emotions universally. Again, the faint noises of crashing walls in the distance. Habitually now, I keep low to the ground shaking unpredictably back and forth for a few seconds. Soon, it recedes. I stand.

Seeing the boarding house door ajar, I enter. I recognize Carl, who seems to have made this his semi-permanent home, sitting in the dark living room, and eating food likely distributed by a neighbor. He doesn't recognize me at first. In the open door leading to the garage, Williams has arranged candles everywhere, keeping a few people huddled together, chatting.

"Pssst, Carl," I whisper.

He stands at attention. "Anthony? What are you doing here?" he asks softly.

"Just checking in. Everyone okay?"

He gestures, leading me out the front door. "You shouldn't be here, Anthony. You know better."

I nod in agreement but choose not to reply. Finally, we stand outside.

"Basically," he says, "most everybody panicked after the first one, and headed up to Signal Hill. I don't know if they're spending the night there, but probably. That last one was big, huh?"

"Yes. And how are you?"

"Me? Well, I figure if the ocean's gonna come, it's gonna come, but that we're so high up off the water, it's not probably gonna happen."

"Smart," is all I say in reply. "How's Williams been?"

"Him? He's been fine, much better now, actually. Has been for months. Didn't yell once throughout the whole day, except when most people headed up the hill. Nearly had a fit, but then stopped after he realized he lost. He's in the garage with a couple guys. They're drinking gin."

"And James?"

"He's sleeping, if you can imagine that. Both of us still live here. Besides Williams, we're the longest residents of this dump. But, James, yeah. After the first couple ones, decided to just sleep through it, later aftershocks and all."

"Give him my regards," I say, saluting him politely.

Carl smiles and approaches me for a hug, "Shucks. I will. Thanks for stopping by. Means a lot. Really. Maybe bingo sometime?"

"Sure," and I turn the flashlight on, beaming it upwards to our faces, startling Carl, who laughs. "I better get going then."

"You bet," he says. "Thanks again."

As I walk back up Alamitos and head for Rafael's house, I intend to cut a corner where Rafael's street intersects with Anaheim, near a large building, whose outer wall appears unstable, when I flash my light upon it. At that moment, two vehicles approach.

* * *

12:02a Shock!

This latest tremblor causes the building some feet in front of me to lose its wall. The bricks come crashing down into the street. The two vehicles behind me swerve to avoid impact. The first one, an old Ford, veers into the other lane, away from the building, and stops. The other one, a military Dodge cargo truck, turns abruptly in the opposite direction, heading straight for me. Without time to jump out of the way, I dive to the ground and roll, but the car veers even more sharply to its right and hops the curb, running over me accidentally at a slow speed and planting its left wheel on my chest, forcing the air from my body.

At first, I suffer a tremendous pain, then shock from feeling I have been injured. I take inventory of my body, noticing growing warm sensations. A man jumps out of the driver's seat. I feel the hinges of the door opening, and each of his steps vibrates my nerves, exquisitely sensitive. He pleads it was an accident, and in his confusion, asks me if I need help, to which I reply by squeezing words from my chest asking him to reverse the Dodge and remove it off my chest. Instantly, he complies, and every motion he makes, before even the wheels turn, I sense. I sense the arrival of strangers, I hear the commotion of chatter and concern. Finally, the car backs up, and in my relief, I check my arms, which appear to be fine. My toes wiggle. But I can't breathe. I struggle to heave my lungs, in and out, but they refuse to budge. I am overcome by warmth, relaxing, my eyes closing. My ears ring with the familiar voices of Rafael and Ernesto, echoing, mixed with orders from invisible soldiers.

Last words I remember hearing: loud declarations my heart has stopped.

* * *

The thing about earthquakes is that they never happen all at once.

"Death of Anthony Camarrata"

ACT II:
Sixth Dimension

> O, fortunate one, recognize.
> The time of death has arrived.
> Now let your compassion be limitless as space.
> Let your mind be at peace.
> Rest in this – the vast empty luminosity of mind itself.

As I move, I think I must be dead. And it is this thought, rather than my dead body, that transforms into light, a narrow, tunneling light vanishing into a bright point, towards which I move.

A cavernous expanse, literally cave-like but without any floor, opens before me, filling my eyes with new subdued hues, broken only by an expanding energy fixed in space, shapeless and intelligent, from which vomit mysteriously pours endlessly into a suspended, giant, wood and steel vat rocking back and forth underneath the entire cave. In the vat's sinuous movements, I recognize that which exists beyond the horizon of nameable phenomena. An ever-flowing distant evil, colorless, putrid-smelling like rotten eggs mixed with petroleum, emesis in epic form, an unbounded, fathomless sea perturbed by turbulent undercurrents and cresting waves. Across this far-flung sea and swinging vat, there is no path to follow.

In this state, I resolve to remain patient and ignore my aversions. I fix my imagination upon the image of a statue, rotund and happy, grinning a fat grin from ear to ear, naked and cross-legged, ancient and infinite. In a process of emergence from an empty space before me, I sense movement, then heat, light and moisture, when a statute appears exactly as I previously imagined it, in the air, hanging some moments until an omnipresent voice speaks, "I am Lord Buddha. To assist you here, in this Womb Realm, Lord Ganesh shall guide you on your path towards Emanation."

Then, "I am Lord Ganesh," a formless figure announces in a clearly articulated voice. "I am the Remover of Obstacles and Guardian of the Aspirational Prayers for the Intermediate State. Is your path to act for the good of all sentient beings?"

"Yes," is the reply my lips offer to Lord Ganesh, not involuntarily, but not cleverly either. I am calmly abiding my own patience. "Lord Ganesh, what is the sea rolling beneath us?"

"The Sea of Amnesia. Once entered, by choice or inattention, there arise all-consuming emotions: a feeling of aversion arises simply by treading the

Sea of Amnesia and a feeling of attraction manifests as the byproduct of the mind's endless devices vainly plotting escape, end, finality, permanence. Over time, lasting first hours, then days and anon, consumed by feelings based on only these two emotions, a person's memories of the past and intuitions of transcendence are lost. Eventually, all drown there. But master the greatest art of all the arts, that is the art of patience, as you have demonstrated by summoning my mere appearance, and then you may travel this Womb Realm, escaping the Sea of Amnesia."

Taking my hand with his trunk, we ascend upwards, above the suspended, giant, wood and steel vat rocking back and forth underneath the entire cave. There, where the cave is directly above the vat, a tiny hole, no larger than my eye appears in the stony ceiling. I peer inside, through shadows appearing in a moving mist of gentle, bluish light, and Lord Ganesh softly speaks, "There once was a king called Jayarahman. He was the most powerful king in all of the Khmer Empire. By the very strength of his supreme body, and the cunning of his unspoken mind, he ruled every subject in his kingdom, meting out justice swiftly and honestly, for the better of all his kind. Three different jovial, beautiful, buxom women in his court bore him three sturdy sons, who alone were his possessions, shared among the wet nurses, as the infants' mothers were banished but bestowed with lavish gifts and mighty castles each. In time, the fierce king taught his growing sons how to assert themselves like generals and conduct politics, forming temporary alliances among their respective armies, two against one, only to be broken and reformed along another axis of shifting interests. He was so successful that he grew very old, until such an old age that his sons begged him to let go. Finally, this he did. Yet the sons fought terrible wars and had their own sons, who begged them to let go, too. Finally, this they did. The myth of this dynasty was told through the centuries, until one day it was written down, by a playwright. Still, I am telling you, here and now, that none of what I just mentioned, including the playwright, ever happened. I see you seem puzzled."

I fix my puzzled gaze upon his large, happy head. "Then, if it never occurred, why are you telling me?"

His eyes grow over his tusks. "To whom does it make a difference, if the king and the jester had never existed? This ceiling above us does not exist; that hole is the only singular existence, for it points towards what is possible beyond the ceiling's absence, in the direction of the mind's luminosity itself." We rise through the ceiling and disappear into the ever deepening hues of blue.

Not sure of my own meaning, I involuntarily ask, "Is it possible to live a cloud-free life?" Ganesh responds by making a low guttural noise, a hum, vibrating in bass notes, then ascends the tones of his humming and drops it all back down again before falling silent.

Letting go my hand, the deity illuminates, "Semiquaver Gat of Contemplation."

In the radiant, deep-blue electric light emitting the faint odor of jasmine, Lord Ganesh appears before me, more magnified than before and grows until his head and shoulders reach beyond my restricted tunnel-vision, and so too his enormous trunk and belly, until all that is left before me are his legs as long as now skyscrapers, one on either side of his elephantine codpiece, stitched from entire bolts of multi-hued taffeta, pure white cotton, and black satin fashioned on the top triumphantly, fastened with two jeweled clasps in each of which was centered a great amethyst as large as an eggplant, suggesting an erective virtue and comfortative of the god's natural member. The ject appears the length of a yard, lacy and fuschia, sagging at the base, intricate needlework purl and carefully interlacing knits, trimmed with platinum, jade, precious rubies, obsidian, gallant, royal, plump, engorged, blossoming. Long and wide, embarrassingly abundant, incomparable next to any classical Greek or Roman divinity phallus hypocritically sculptured small, de-figured to the great prejudice of admiring Europeans.

In a sudden, a gigantic, gold and steel broadsword, larger than Lord Ganesh himself, pendulates in the empty vertical plane that separates the both of us some feet. All I feel is the quiet whoosh of the passing weapon, as it moves just past the surface of the god's boyish skin. Then, a resounding thud, when the blade, after only one slicing arc, succeeds in removing the contents of Ganesh's codpiece, as well as the codpiece itself, from his torso. Deafening laughter, thudding echoes, faint slurping noises.

The Uranian Diva, Great Glorious Heruka, organically emerges from the detritus of the oversized bloody phallus of Lord Ganesh, who himself vaporizes before my eyes. Reaching as high where Lord Ganesh's waist reached, Heruka, without speaking, projects a silent aura of the power to judge those who have committed crimes. His body, blazing in a mass of light, is dark brown in color, having three heads, six arms and four legs, which are apart, firmly. His right face is white, the left is red and the central face dark brown, full of lesions. His nine eyes are fixed in a fearsome wrathful gaze, his eyebrows quiver like lightening, his fangs are bared and gleaming, and he is laughing loudly, "Behold The Information, so that you may know whence you came," this says. "Ego! Is your path to act for the good of all sentient beings?" His apsara embraces his body, her right hand clasped around his neck and her left offering a skull-cup filled with blood to his mouth. I am not afraid.

"Yes."

"What is the nature of this truth?"

I yield no answer, and this Uranian Diva commences laughing, but a certain kind of laughter, a repetitive series of a "ha" noises motivated by some intention, and yet, spontaneous and infectious, waking inside me by a rising volume and piercing strength of silliness, deep feelings of jealousy, a compulsion to possess my own laughter here completely lacking. I want to be on the inside joke of this, this Laughter only growing bolder, mocking, chaotic.

Heruka's apsara, Bryanton, approaches to take my hand and guide me closer to the Diva, whose limbs open, inviting me closer, to feel the Daemon's heat and smell his stench and taste his breath upon my lips. Bryanton turns me around, gently pushing my back against Heruka's belly. My skin melts, like wax, from the heat of Heruka's body. My chest sags. I begin to grow breasts. Heruka moves two fingers, one each caressing the lengthening tips of my tits. My genitals shrink, shrivel, then invert. Another finger caressing inside me. Probing deeper, until I am overcome by his probing. I feel like a cute, little girl.

Bryanton speaks while I enjoy being probed and massaged by Heruka, "We start with a point. Like the point we know from geometry, it has no size, no dimension. It's just a projection of your mind, indicating a position in a system. A second point indicates a second position, but it, too, has no size and no dimension. A line passing through these two points is a projection of a first dimension. It has length only, and no width or depth. If your mind projects a second line perpendicular to the first, we have identified a second dimension. Your mind recognizes a shallow surface with no width or depth, like a piece of cloth or paper. Your mind now perceives an ant walking on this surface. Imagine this surface twisted into a shape, like a ring, but with another twist, so that the ant can walk on the same surface over and over never finding an end. Though the ant moves about in the second dimension, your mind perceives that it lives in the third dimension. This third dimension is the twist or fold of the lower, second dimension. You call this third dimension life or reality. And yet still, your mind may continue imagining on in this fashion, until you recognize that no matter what order of dimension you perceive, a higher order dimension represents a way to move instantaneously from one position to another. The fourth dimension is made of two opposing directions, like the second is made of the first, but your mind only perceives one of these directions of the fourth dimension in a linear fashion, which you name as Time. If you imagine your body's shape in the fourth dimension, it would…"

At this moment, my body changes shape yet again. My eyes project like tubes extending from my head, then my whole body transforms into a giant worm, tapering at one end with the soft skin of a newborn infant, trailing into a single, infinitely-thin tail unraveled at two ends, and tapering at the other end with the wrinkled, worn skin of a 78-year-old man covered in his flesh, decaying, dessicated, bones exposed, and finally dust blowing away.

"… resemble a snake," Bryanton continues. "But your mind only perceives your being in the third dimension, or life or reality." My body instantly snaps back to my previous shape, age and gender, as Heruka gently pushes me away. "Like what in your day and land you call a movie, each frame is still, while motion creates the illusion of solidity."

The Diva speaks, "Emptiness cannot be harmed by emptiness."

I speak, "Apsara Bryanton! I am not afraid, but you have not finished speaking, no?"

"The fifth dimension is known as the Land of Many Worlds, but in fact it is merely two opposing, intersecting fourth dimensions. Recognize: there are fourth dimensional beings, like yourself, which exist perpendicular to your ego-snake life. The Land of Many Worlds, which you cannot perceive, is just as real as the Earth where your mental body is formed of habitual tendencies, so much so that you can be moving upon the Earth and not even be aware that your ego is also moving in the Land of Many Worlds. Therefore, even if you are slain and cut into pieces on Earth, you will not die in the Land of Many Worlds. Thus, a multitude of paths are open to you at any given moment, influenced by mind, chaos and other beings."

I ask, "Is this, then, where I am, the Land of Many Worlds?"

"No!" Heruka screams deafening noises into my brain, sounds reaching deep inside my body, vibrating me, testing me for fear and terror, but my ego remains unperturbed, recognizing the internal noise of anger that can arise when confronted aggressively with the fact of my own ignorance.

Bryanton concludes, "The sixth dimension you can imagine, again, like a fold or twist of the Land of Many Worlds. So, if by imagining to twist the Land of Many Worlds, a sixth dimension appears: where you are now, the Womb Realm, where all possible states of this universe exist."

Heruka bellows again, "Behold The Information, so that you may know whence you came."

Ganesh's invisible voice, "This way out, Anthony…"

* * *

Are those words for me? Where? Is what? What?

"Oh, fortunate one, recognize…"

What is that voice? Is someone betting against me, like my life hardly has a story to it – though storied lives are not the only ones worth living – a coherent, compelling biography, the stuff of novels, even the cheap ones about ladies' love affairs with villains and escapades with rogues, or am I simply hearing things?

"Hey! Can you hear me? They called out 'Anthony' back there."

I try to speak. I fail to summon the necessary sounds to resonate across my palate. At least, at the very least, though, I can breathe. The sweet gift of breathing. My heart is pounding.

"If you can hear me, move your finger in my hand."

What is this envelope that surrounds me, this boundary between that which seems conscious and that which is penetrating into my ears with sounds. Is it moving? Is my finger moving? I doubt I can even tell if it is moving.

"Good. You can hear me. Move it twice."

I don't even know who it is that is moving my finger. Is it me? Am I moving my own finger? Is it moving twice? My eyelids refuse to move. They are there, I can tell, but they resist my commands, like they are pushing against weights many pounds heavy.

"Very good. Do not feel as though you have to move. You are here. Stay here. You are in good hands. My name is Gregorio. Ensign Gregorio. We are currently en route to Seaside Hospital. When we get there, we will make you feel more comfortable."

I notice that my body vibrates, as though in a constant earthquake, leaving me disoriented and lacking any coordinates. I feel lost in something, traveling forward, until at a certain point, the forces which apply during a speedy turn in a vehicle dominate my consciousness, and then at that point I hear the voice again, calling my name back to my body. The endless repetition of pain explodes in my chest. I want to ask "where am I?" but I simply feel unable to move any muscles in my face. And yet, I am still breathing, my heart still beating.

"Don't leave us. That last turn was difficult, but we're approaching our destination here on Chestnut. Anthony? Anthony! Alright let's get him up… Shit, we've lost him again."

***

I bow with respect to the spiritual teachers, and assembled meditational deities. May they effect liberation in the intermediate state!

As I move, I think I must be dead, again. And it is this thought, rather than my physical body, that transforms into light, a narrow, tunneling light vanishing into a bright point, towards which I move. In motion, my mental body grows radiant but shows scars, the first noticed being the one on my forehead that healed after I jumped the turnstyle in Manhattan. Then, childhood scars from fighting. I wander Brooklyn. I wander around Prospect Park and the Heights, and Borough Hall and the Bridge, into Manhattan, and up along the Chrysler Building, up through the clouds, into the sky, and in an arc, I fly down to the Atlantic Ocean, and the Mediterranean and... Mother! Father! I call out to them, I call out to Abraham! Glamour! Rafael! But, I feel like a fish writhing on hot sand. Days seem to pass in a fearsome, turbulent utterly unbearable hurricane spawned by the violence in my voice, my coldly calculating heartbreaks, my disloyalty to America, my drunken foolishness. Congenital anger.

Homosexual.

I hear chants, "Strike! Kill!" I imagine a pack of wild animals, a swarm of carnivorous ogres brandishing broadswords and machine guns, yelling, "Strike! Kill!" I hear the sounds of mountains crumbling, of lakes flooding, of fire spreading, and forceful winds, making me want to flee, towards nearby precipices, as if on the verge of falling.

Lord Ganesh speaks, "O, fortunate one, there are no precipices. You are variously feeling aversion, attachment and delusion." Then, a bounty of riches extends, like a golden bridge extending beyond the precipices. "Whatever objects of desire or blissful or happy states appear before you, do not be attached to these, too. Do not cling! There is no shelter."

I am dead. I meditate on my death. My lack of body. My ego floating then recognizing the projection of my mental state. "If you continue to be distracted, the lifeline of compassion, suspended to you, will be cut off and you will move on to a place where there is no liberation. Take heed," Ganesh warns.

I meditate upon innocence, and imagine I am as though an infant, wise, in an empty white room, alone in swaddling clothes. Contented, at peace. Newly born. The inner radiance of sixth-month-old skin. The emptiness of mind. The recollection of Glamour's talent. Of Abraham's separation. Solstice's fictional uncle. Dennis Carpenter's faithful witness. Raphael's patron.

Alas, with one-pointed intention I concentrate my mind, and resolutely brandish the residual potency of virtuous past deeds. Lord Ganesh again speaks, "Fortunate one. At this moment, this singularity of intention is by itself the most important factor, like a horse pulled by a bridle. Concentrate. There are four modes of Emanation in the Womb Realm: from an egg, from a womb, from warmth and moisture, and supernormal."

Appearing in front of me are a woman and a man engaged in sexual union. I hold at bay feelings of either aversion or attachment. Then, appearing below me and rising to lift me are four continents. An Eastern Continent adorned by male and female swans, happy and peaceful. The Southern Continent boasts splendiferous mansions. The Western Continent features lakes with male and female horses. The Northern Continent is filled with cattle and bulls drinking from lakes. On the horizon surrounding all the continents, vast armies of assassins and Daemons descend over the distant hills, growing ever closer.

The Diva Heruka appears at my side with thick limbs, standing upright, in a terrifying wrathful manifestation, racing to meet and pulverizing the daemonic armies as they attack, affording me time to make a choice of entering a continent. But, in between the continents, I perceive a small archipelago. I make my choice there. I stand upon an island and attempt to enter one womb, realizing the risk of error, the potency of past actions, and the uncertainty of the ones to come, yet feeling equinanimous.

Clingy.

Though pushed by the force of war and suffering, I cannot enter the bushy, pink labia, soft, wet and warm. I just do not fit. At her side, a beautiful, chiseled godman smiles in my face, moves closer to her, taking her place, taking her same position, but the slit of his urethra explodes before me, plump and cavernous. My whole being, cock and balls first, dives forward.

Lord Ganesh declares as I disappear, "Sarva Mangalam."

ACT III:

Last Incarnation

Chapter Fourteen

"Martial Law"

"Damn, I still lost the bet."

* * *

Are those words for me? Where? Is what? What?

"O, fortunate one, recognize..."

What is that voice? Is someone betting against me, like my life hardly has a story to it – though storied lives are not the only ones worth living – a coherent, compelling biography, the stuff of novels, even the cheap ones about ladies' love affairs with villains and escapades with rogues, or am I simply hearing things?

"Hey! Can you hear me? They called out 'Anthony' back there."

I try to speak. I fail to summon the necessary sounds to resonate across my palate. At least, at the very least, though, I can breathe. The sweet gift of breathing. My heart is pounding.

"If you can hear me, move your finger in my hand."

What is this envelope that surrounds me, this boundary between that which seems conscious and that which is penetrating into my ears with sounds. Is it moving? Is my finger moving? I doubt I can even tell if it is moving.

"Good. You can hear me. Move it twice."

I don't even know who it is that is moving my finger. Is it me? Am I moving my own finger? Is it moving twice? My eyelids refuse to move. They are there, I can tell, but they resist my commands, like they are pushing against weights many pounds heavy.

"Very good. Do not feel as though you have to move. You are here. Stay here. You are in good hands. My name is Gregorio. Ensign Gregorio. We are currently en route to Seaside Hospital. When we get there, we will make you feel more comfortable."

I notice that my body vibrates, as though in a constant earthquake, leaving me disoriented and lacking any coordinates. I feel lost in something, traveling forward, until at a certain point, the forces which apply during a speedy turn in a vehicle dominate my consciousness, and then at that point I hear the voice again, calling my name back to my body. The endless repetition of pain explodes in my chest. I want to ask "where am I?", but I simply feel unable to move any muscles in my face. And yet, I am still breathing, my heart still beating.

"Don't leave us. That last turn was difficult, but we're approaching our destination here on Chestnut. Anthony? Anthony! Alright let's get him up... Shit, we've lost him again."

* * *

"Anthony? Anthony!"

My name, this parental gift pulls me out of myself. Born a second time, to choose their lovemaking. I listen to my heart.

"Whew! Listen, we are trying to make you stable. You are on the lawn of Seaside Hospital, on a stretcher. You probably know there has been an another earthquake. Destroyed most of the city, including the hospital. But you're with me now. I know this is difficult for you. I expect you must feel a great deal of pain."

Although I do know I am in pain, I hardly cry or moan. My body feels liquid, diffuse.

My mind drifts easily, as my eyes dart back and forth while my lids squint into the darkness.

"I need to keep you awake. Do you understand? You possibly have a concussion, at least. You need to stay awake with me. I have your trigger finger in my hand. Can you move it two times?"

I have no idea whether I am moving my finger. I feel a burning thirst.

"Good. So, my name is Gregor Gregorio. Actually, it used to be another name. But I kept this one when I joined the Navy. Actually, I used to be Army. I was in the war, but was discharged after it was discovered I enlisted using the false name I use now. But since then, I've kept it. Even convinced a court to let me keep it. I realize these details may not interest you a great deal."

Inside my body, I feel jiggly. My heart pounds but at times jumps at incredible speeds, dominating my thoughts, and then slows almost to a stop. Cold sweating.

"I have to keep talking to you. In addition to having a possible concussion, you left us there for a moment. You may remember the last thing you were doing, when the last aftershock struck right after midnight. Do you remember? You dove into the ground, hitting your head on the sidewalk, shortly before our truck came running up the curb and landing, unfortunately on your chest. As a matter of fact, your breathing stopped and we couldn't find your pulse. Your heart actually stopped working. In terms of science, there is good reason to say you died. But obviously, you returned. You're practically a Frankenstein."

As Gregorio speaks, he lifts my droopy eyelids far apart, flashing light into my pupils, and lets my eyes close again. His act of gently moving my face presents me with the opportunity to arouse my tongue inside my mouth and throat. And in one act of great effort, I move my muscles as I naturally exhale to utter the word in a whisper, "water."

"I'm afraid that's not possible, giving you some water. Listen. When the National Guard truck landed on your chest, it caused a great deal of damage. We had to cut your chest with a knife on the side, and then insert a small tube to let out the air which was putting pressure on your heart. It's called a pneumothorax, if you want to know. That was probably one of the reasons your heart stopped working. The first time. You might remember the ride, which was bumpy. En route, we had to improvise a risky blood transfusion, my blood, right away, as you looked about to succumb to shock. We lost you then got you back a second time."

"Water," I whisper.

"Thirsty, well all I can offer you is for you to give thanks that at the least you have thirst, which we can't satisfy right now. Listen, you are a very lucky individual. In most situations, after you are hit by a car and lose your cardiac rhythms, most people would have left you for dead. In fact, there's a makeshift morgue opening up in an old train station a couple miles from here in Long Beach. They're finding injured and dead bodies everywhere in the city. But consider it your good fortune that I was on the truck. As soon as I recognized the injuries you sustained could be treated, I went to task immediately. Removing the air from your lungs was only part of it. I also had to push down on your chest several times with the hope such movements would restart your heart. It worked. But you also have some cracked ribs, so my pushing down might've aggravated some internal bleeding, causing shock, which is why we probably lost your rhythm a second time. The transfusion and my gentle compressions helped start it a second time. You have a quite a strong heart, I must say. But, I suppose if an earthquake was going to happen to you, it's fortunate it happened near the San Pedro Naval Station, where

I'm assigned. I'm drafting experimental protocols for the Navy regarding battlefield traumas, like shock or crush syndrome. Actually, I studied with Dr. Alfred Blalock, and worked closely with Vivien Thomas, both of whom are changing the entire science of wartime surgery out east. Squeeze my finger, twice, please."

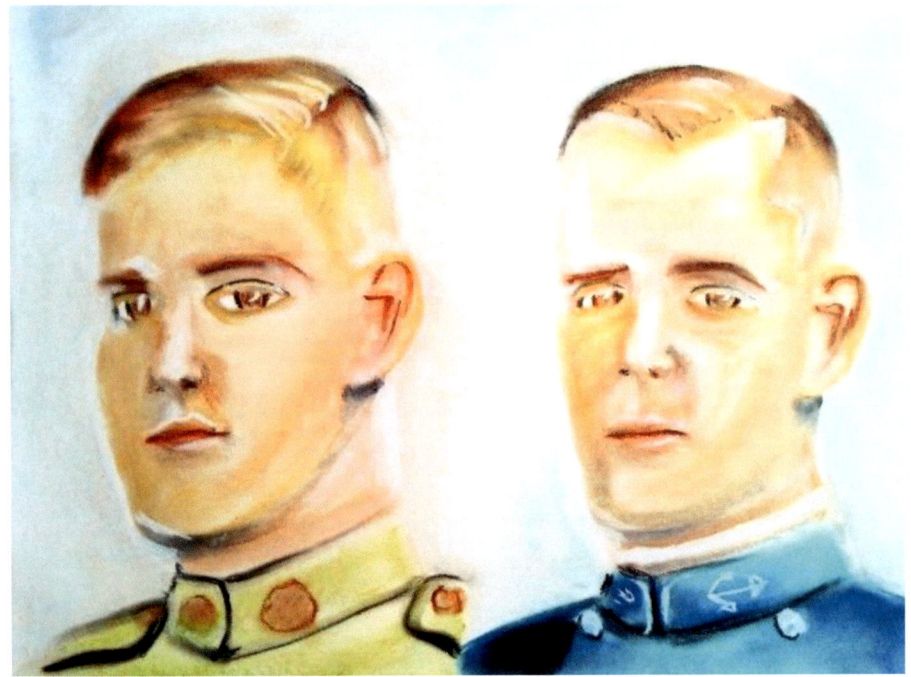

"Gregor Gregorio"

This time, I sense purpose behind my muscular contractions. "Cold," I say, spontaneously, without reflection.

"I'd share some tequila if I could. I found your flask in your jacket I had to cut off you. Tequila. Thanks for sharing, by the way. Good stuff. And I also see you keep a .38 Super. Just listen, because I'm not expecting you to say anything. I'm not only interested in medicine. I was once left for dead, too. In France during the war. I underwent an impossible recovery, thanks to a kind nurse. When the war was over, I spent a great deal of time searching for purpose, for meaning, shall we say. But I'm not a godly man, Anthony. I don't know if you are, but while I was treating you, I was also speaking to you, preparing you for the end. I don't know if you can remember what I was saying back on the sidewalk, then on the truck. 'O, fortunate one, recognize...' that sort of stuff."

Unable to recall clearly, though shards of images surface through my mind, unclear, more reflections of feelings of peace and liberation concluding in pain and suffering.

"I'll guess you can't remember. But this loaded gun I stuffed with your jacket and trousers in a pile over there, I hope it's only for protection, and even so, I'm not sure it's a good idea. If you have other intentions for using it, all I can say is that you should know I feel responsible for your use of it, now that I have saved your life. Don't misuse it. I'll return it to you at the appropriate time. Don't worry."

I lift my whole hand an inch from the ground.

"Good, movement. But, not too much. Your job is to rest and survive the night. You've just had a quick transfusion with my blood. Universal donor. I know, an implausible series of coincidences, to you. But the way I see it, I didn't come here to help you specifically, but rather you were the first casualty I came across. Actually, I was thinking about the Soviet Union right after the quake. The Russians have developed this clever scheme of encouraging its population to give their blood to the government, so that it can create a sort of storage system for individuals who may need blood for surgery or following some sort of traumatic event. The Navy has me working as an administrator conducting efficiency studies on adapting something similar for the American military. I don't think they would have ever let me enlist, if I hadn't had the good fortune of working at Vanderbilt with Blalock and Thomas. I suppose my own wartime experiences set me up on the path that I am, I guess. You could look at it that way. And yes, I'm from Tennessee originally, in case you were wondering."

"I... I..." I mutter.

"Yes? What is it? No, I can't hear you. Still can't hear you. It's fairly brave of you to try to communicate, but truly, all that matters at this moment is that you just stay awake. What do you like to talk about?"

I feel confused, not sure how to answer the question, not able to speak clearly, and not allowed to even try.

"You like baseball? I bet you do. I bet you love... Let's see, the Pacific Coast League, that would be the Angels. You an Angels fan? Squeeze twice."

I don't squeeze.

"You don't, eh? Let me see, are you interested in my reciting Bible stories? You like the parables?"

I don't squeeze.

"Hmm. I'm afraid I'm only going to bore you with more medical talk. Vivien Thomas is one of the most exceptional men I've met, for instance. Listen to this: he's a Negro who works and earns as a janitor for Blalock, but who treats him like a scientific colleague, an equal. The two of them proved that shock, the experience you just had, is not caused by toxins, but is due to loss of blood, which can be remedied by transfusions. In fact, Blalock is looking to go further and see whether the remedy for shock requires whole blood, or whether part of the blood is needed, in which case some of the logistics of inventory might get solved. You there? Don't sleep! Wait, dames? You like to hear about dames?"

I don't squeeze.

"Well, if you were a dame yourself I'd ask if you liked men." I squeeze twice. "What, you like horror stories?"

Listening to his laughter, I still don't squeeze.

"Just men?"

I squeeze twice.

"Aw shucks, Anthony. I don't know if you're foggy-headed right now, or just joshing with me. How about this, I could talk about dames, and if you get confused about certain things I'm saying, well, then you're confused."

I squeeze twice.

"Imagine this. It's France, the Great War. A young, Army nurse works inside a hospital, tending the sick. She's dressed in pretty white, and everything she touches is white, as if she has never been dirty her entire life. And the men she serves are burned, or broken or sick. Everything around her is so white almost to call attention to the slightest spot of disease. And one day, this beautiful officer comes to her, asks her if he can spend time with his men, comfort them, make sure they keep in good spirits, focus on the future. Imagine a painting. This officer stands tall, handsome, strong in the center, surrounded by beds of the fallen and weak. And this nurse is rendered in such a way, in the painting, that she notices this officer, and yet, she is not the center of the painting. She is doing something else. And yet, you know they are the story of the painting. One day, on one of his last visits, he conspires to lead her outside the tents where she works, long hours, dutifully, and it is this occasion where they take to the camouflage of the trees. He's firm with her, taking her by the shoulders and bringing her close to his face, as he stares longingly into her eyes, her chest heaving fearfully against him, as he pushes his body against hers, causing her to whimper as their lips fall forward. His hands fall down her arms as she passively yields to his driving passion..."

I cough, which instantly shoots pain throughout my whole body. It is the first time that I not merely know I am in pain, I feel pain everywhere. The shock of it is so overwhelming, air forces up through my chest into my throat, surfacing as moans, gurgled outward, creating more coughing, causing more suffering.

"Too much, hold on. Maybe you do like the men. Let me see if I can get you a wet cloth to at least suck on, so you won't choke."

Gregorio shouts at people, demanding a sterile, wet cloth. Within a few seconds, his request is answered by an anonymous silhouetted figure running through the dark. He kindly takes it, and squeezes some of the liquid on top my lips, before they crack open, my tongue parched, then relieved with each drop, offered slowly, carefully. After this attention, my coughing eases.

"We just have to make sure you don't get pneumonia, too. Let me ask you a question, Anthony. Tell me, did you manage to eat a meal last night, if you remember. Okay, so I see your finger is telling me you did. Is that right? Yes, okay. Well, I'm not sure if you realize it but you may need to relieve yourself. It probably hasn't occurred to you. So, let me tell you what I'm going to do. I'm going to be right back. Now you keep still for just a minute. I'm going to see if I can find someone to help us. Don't fall to the temptation of sleep."

If there is a feeling that keeps me company in the absence of the never-ending drone of his voice, it is helplessness, the feeling of lack any power, of being entirely passive before my fate, all my memories of who I have ever been existing as thin, flimsy details floating somewhere inside my prone, fragile body. I want sleep, the peacefulness of it, its vagueness.

When he returns, I hear very little except his descriptions, particularly his nouns naming the objects of his attention. Penis. Alcohol. Catheter. Urethra. Vaseline. Glans. Slit. Insertion. Pain. Breathing. Breathing. Breathing. Urine. Without speaking, he moves his left hand, first, tugging barely at the catheter, placing the gentle fingers on his right hand around my soft column, pulling down on it, towards my hairs. The forward insertion preoccupies my mind some minutes, competing with the painful sensations otherwise emanating from my chest. At one point, he stops tugging and actually reverses his movements, removing the catheter further some fractions of measurements, and then resumes his insertion, nudging my testicles randomly. Finally, I feel my interior emptied. But, the patterned movements of the catheter repeat, gradually growing faster, but not so fast as to arouse my discomfort.

Without sensing the presence of anyone close by, I hear him ask me, "You don't mind this?" He then reaches for my trigger finger, and once he has it firmly in his grasp, I move it twice.

"You like this, don't you?" He asks, and I respond by moving my finger, again. "Sorry about not wearing gloves, but we lack enough of them at this moment. Have to save them for surgeries."

The application of the catheter is a welcome interior distraction, and after some moments, feeling the most relaxed I have felt since the trauma began, I note the pleasantness of his contact.

"It's much easier, and less noticeable, to distract you this way, rather than use mere words to entertain your mind. Now, I am going to withdraw the catheter. For the moment."

If there is any noticeable benefit from the application of this device to my body, it is, first, that the invariable sense of empty time that burdens me, measured by recursive excruciating waves, dissipates into something else. As he slips the catheter out, I feel slightly tickled, even, wanting to laugh, but instead, falling into a series of coughing spasms, which Ensign Gregorio ameliorates with his trick of the moist towel dripping water to my lips and open mouth. Sated and calm, I return to my normal breathing, and though thankful to have even just that, I long to fall asleep, to lose consciousness and to drift somewhere else, dreaming of something else. In my breathing, I catch the scent of my own urine pooled some feet away yet in the vicinity of my body. Under the cover of darkness, surrounded by bodies moaning, occasionally wailing, soldiers and nurses and doctors scurrying, volunteers and families helping, Gregorio removes my socks. He unfurls a sheet over my naked waist, and gently spreads my legs apart. Disconnected from his touch, I hear the snapping sound of rubber.

Kneeled at the side of my body, lying prone on the stretcher, he takes my finger again, and asks me, "Yes?"

I squeeze my digit twice in his rubber-bound hand.

He then takes his hand and slips it underneath the sheet, first caressing the curve of my buttocks, then reaching the edge of my anus.

"Yes?" he asks again. Without touching my hand, he says, "I see your finger is moving. Very good."

After removing his whole arm, his fingers return with vaseline, pushing inside my rectum, carefully, repeatedly. If there is any distracting pleasure from his catheter, his finger feels tenfold so. Whole moments of him some inches inside me, still, then only slightly squirming his knuckles, vie usefully with nausea emanating from my broken ribs, discomforted with each inhalation. At length, he remains there, comfortably. Finally, after a few soft rotations, he pulls out. This time, when he returns and settles in, I sense the little prick of a thin piece of a rubber nozzle. Teasing the outside of my barely puckering hole, he pricks its tip inside some tiny distance. Then, the vaseline he previously inserted helps ease the nozzle inward some inches, hardly as satisfying as his whole, warm digit. But, his initial preparation left my rectal muscles more loose than they would have been had he inserted this new device first.

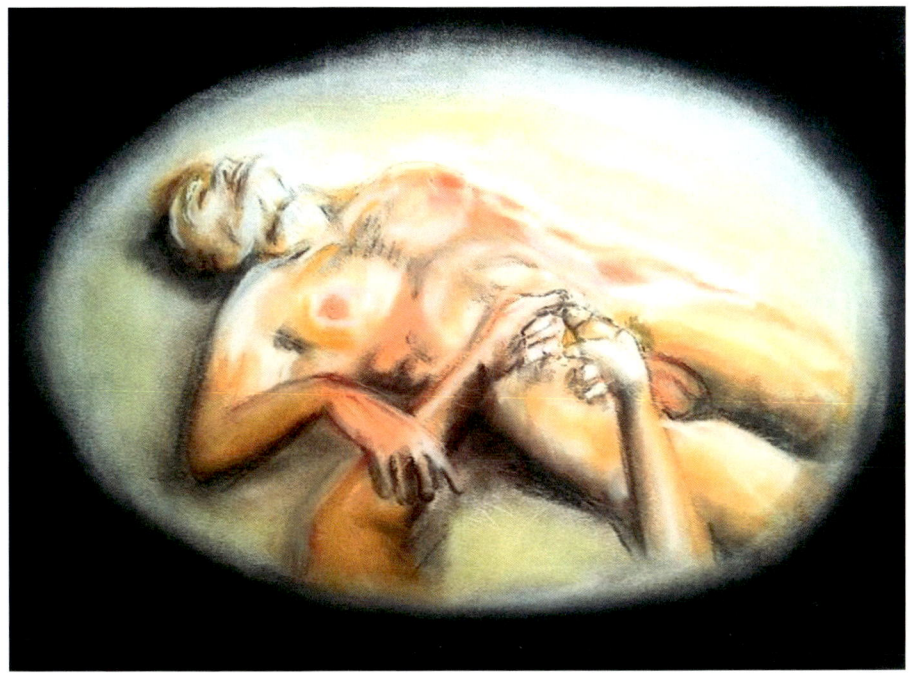

"Catheter"

"It's called an enema," he explains. "I should have turned you on your side, but in your present condition, this is probably the second best position. In any case, it's what it is."

At that moment, there is an internal sensation of something warm, not hot, filling the interior of my rectal cavity. It continues at length, completely focusing my attention off my chest. Seconds pass while I notice a continuous liquid filling feeling.

"Okay," he asks. I move my finger, which he must be observing visually, because without touching it, he is able to read my attempt at communication. "Good. Let me know if the feeling gets out of hand."

I want to know what to expect of this undiscovered pleasure. Does it increase? Does it turn to pain? What consequence will it have, until I realize that the likely intended purpose is to produce a movement of my bowels, releasing me of whatever digestion of the previous day's meals remaining in my body. And then, at the moment the pressure reaches a point of particular intensity, the muscles in my thighs twitch, and he ceases adding more liquid matter inside me. Slowly, he withdraws, and upon exiting completely, I feel an overwhelming, urgent, pleasurable need to let go of all the poop inside me.

"Yes, right here. Go ahead."

If it had been possible to mimic the reward of achieving ejaculation elsewhere in my body, then I am certain that such a discovery would have shown itself to me by this point in my life, but to my utter surprise, my nerves fire pleasantly up and down my spine, killing the evil nausea, the paralyzing agony, and leaving me eyes open, automatically smiling, releasing every possible tension inside my lower extremities, as a river of diarrhea pours onto the stretcher, causing Gregorio to laugh hysterically, and at the end of it, I find myself laughing involuntarily, shortly before I succumb to another paralyzing coughing fit requiring the ensign's caressing attention and thoughtful ministrations of oral water droplets.

Intending only quiet and calm, Gregorio takes as much time and attention as necessary to remove the traces of offal from my body, the stretcher and anything else close by. He rinses my flesh with buckets of lukewarm water, dries me as quickly and warms me with a dry, clean blanket, but not before sterilizing the stretcher with alcohol which, though slightly unpleasant to my nose, does have the effect of riding most of the offensive odors from our presence. At the very least, he has kept me awake and alert, without using words, yet also introducing me to discover something new and perhaps (no, not perhaps), it must be admitted: most certainly desirable.

"And," he says, after finding a moment to rest. "At the end of it all, you are now ready for surgery, if necessary, which may be yet avoided if you manage to avoid both sleep and shock until morning. And that shouldn't be too hard for you. I put a half cup of coffee in the enema. Should keep you alert."

* * *

Some hours later, after another pleasant application of the catheter, and dull conversation about some ancient text of oriental provenance, birds begin their morning conversations, even before sunlight appears in the sky.

Shortly thereafter, one of Gregorio's colleagues approach him, seated next to me. "Sir, you still there with this one?" he asks.

He says, valiantly, "If not me, who else? To my credit, this man has made it through the night."

Looking over my injuries, the stranger mumbles and whines, "Damn, I still lost the bet."

"That's the second time you've complained, Guardsman."

Chapter Fifteen

"Bath House Plunge"

"What was it like?" Don asks me in the antechamber to the men's shower at the Long Beach Bath House, both of us naked. Too cheap to pay for my own changing cabin, I use Don's rented space to ditch my clothes next to his. In the two months while my body recuperated from my wounds, I spent intermittent moments trying to recollect that liminal state.

I reply, somewhat deceptively, "From what I remember... So, there was simply nothing to it, but also a feeling as though I had left my body and visited some other place, except there was a blur between the accident and what came afterwards, before I woke lying on the lawn of Seaside Hospital." After some hesitation, I speculate, "Perhaps it was all just a dream." More than that, it still haunts.

Stretching his thick arms towards the sky and looking upwards, my employer, Don, pushes his large belly forward and bellows, "Perhaps everything is just a dream." As his shoulders fall down, his fingers immediately dig into the fold of skin above his waist, slide down, and grab his hefty cock and tugging at it a few times, jostling his sac up and down.

I stare at his provocations a few seconds, then turn my head downward and mumble to myself, "Perhaps."

"Aw, Anthony, is that it? Anything more stuck with ya?" he smiles.

I look into his eyes, "Just the ensign's voice, I think."

"No divinities, no demons?" he tilts his head to the side and grimaces skeptically.

"Perhaps." The subject makes for uncomfortable discourse, as I am wary of describing phenomena I never consciously, directly observe in fact. It occurred to me when I was a child that "dream" is a word for those who are awake. We can never really observe dreams directly, since observation itself presumes conscious activity. The feelings and images and sensations we recall of sleeping are themselves impositions from a non-sleeping mind which, to me, is only too favorable towards tidy storytelling, as ambiguity and uncertainty require emotional toleration to earn their recognition. Predicated upon active mental discipline, the recollection of dreams implies a verbal filter, itself a social heritage, so that the unknown and unknowable can be organized, depicted and chronicled for the benefit of the gullible. Of course I know I dream, but I just never quite know what it is I dream. Similarly, I died, but the I experiences accompanying what happened when that happened are not quite fixed in my reflective mind. Even so, I feel happy with that irresolution, its socratic wisdom: knowing that you do not know. The difficulty lies in persuading others of the same. "If it serves the purpose of putting your mind at ease, Don, I can tell you that, yes, I retain images of things and places, but they appear to lack sense to me, and whether or not you accept this, I have no interest in solving such a puzzle because there is no puzzle to solve."

"Just a soul machine." Taken aback by my stern tone, Don scratches his elbow nervously. "Listen, Camarrata. I'm just trying to do you a favor. I've given you two months now off of work, paid you anyway, until this place passed final inspection after the quake, so you could finally come here, swim and get fit, and work those muscles," he says, slapping my abdomen. "I'm just hoping you could show a little appreciation for my act of kindness. Surely, you can understand that. Hell, you volunteered at the city's makeshift, outdoor telegraph station just a few days after the quake."

"Five days after." I slap my taught gut. "Well, volunteered just a couple hours. Let me say something. Everything you've done for me, since you hired me for the trucks last year, has been very good. I appreciate having your support during these last weeks, especially. And I intend to pay you back for your temporary assistance."

"Sure. Just helping you in your situation, right now." He places one of his arms on my shoulders, "No worries, fella. You've lost weight, huh?"

"About twenty pounds," I answer, before changing the subject to what I need to discuss. "But, I'm letting you know now that I'm taking on a couple of jobs starting sometime in June."

He steps back, crossing his arms. "June? What you got going then?"

"I've got a job as a tagman this summer, then…"

"Dutch Miller?" he asks. "But, I ain't ever seen you swim even."

"Starting lessons today, with Nick Dallas, and every Saturday and Tuesday. And, then probably serving near beer behind the counter once the tourist season ends. Rumor is… liquor's legal hiatus… over by year's end. Look, I know we've worked well together. But it's time for other things, Don."

Don takes a seat on a bench, throwing his legs on either side, then invites me to sit across from him. When I finally comply, he begins to talk. "That's just the thing, Anthony. What are you doing? I mean, look at me. I could almost be your father, and you could have a son by now. It doesn't matter to me that you ain't married. Hell, I used to be married. That's not important. But, what are you doing with yourself, planning to work as a city lifeguard and privately peddle beer?"

"It is what it is, Don," I offer as a lame rejoinder. There is a long pause inside echoes of shower water splashing on the floor, mixed with muffled conversations.

"But what's that mean, Anthony?" He starts diddling himself, as men walk around, ignoring us all the same. "You just died, for chrissakes. Does that mean anything to you? You act like you're going to live forever."

"Not forever," I disagree. Then, finding my wit, I add, "Just for now."

"Childish." Don stands, causing his genitals to swing back and forth between his thighs. "Could join the Navy. Or finish college, Anthony. Or grab a job in the port."

"Or, I could move to Tijuana and pay to slice this off," I mock him, playfully assaulting him with my cock in hand.

Don chortles, "Oh, please don't go and do that. Now, THAT would be a crime! Honestly, Anthony."

"Long Beach Plunge"

"Honestly, Don?" I ask, also standing. "Where are the decent jobs you talk about? School, to study what, for how long? The Navy, for whose war? Perhaps to you it seems I am covering the craps table, hedging my bets, but I don't see a clear purpose in going after any of those, in all this poverty."

Don sighs and shrugs his shoulders, then finally, he dresses himself in his bathing suit. "The purpose would be to take care of yourself, truly, for good. This depression won't probably last forever. But, have it your way. Before I head for the showers, though... I think it's a matter of motivation and confidence." He grabs the towel from the bench, then he turns his back on me and walks into a wall of steam inside the shower room. "Drifter," he shouts loud enough for me to hear at a distance.

"I ain't a drifter!" I yell back, feeling a little hurt by his casual insult. Then, I mumble to myself, "Fatso." Still undressed, I turn to the doorless partitioned toilet stalls, before I occupy a seat, not to do anything in particular, just to spend a moment collecting my thoughts, before getting dressed, showered, ready to learn swimming. Upon reflection, I consider that I met Don at Pershing Square, and he dares share with me his thoughts about responsibility. At that moment, I hear a wet foot tapping a puddle in the adjacent stall. The staccato cycle is insistent, beginning with short, soft sounds, then a loud splash, and repeating, demanding my attention. Drifter. The word conjures images of hobos, the sick poor, Long Beach after its earthquake. It hints at freedom and solitude. Deception and impermanence. Endless transience. More tapping, after a long silence. Impatience. What is a decision, after all, but a willful movement of muscles, according to criteria established by intellect or by passion, I reason. Drifter. I'm late for my lessons. More tapping against the wet floor. The sounds of men, laughing, arguing, pacing in the distance. Tap tap. Patience. I decide to stand and don my swimsuit before heading for the showers.

My muscles move, guiding me through passages. I dress, put my towel on a hook, then enter the showers among a couple boys and several men, only some of whom will be entering the pool area, while others have already left, removing their suits to rinse themselves. In its most technical, elemental fiction, a shower should only last a few seconds, rinsing sweat and grime if entering, or pool water if leaving. But here, a shower lasts that and continues much longer, with men and boys rubbing hands across multi-hued skins, armpits, massaging chests, tugging hair ascending above waists. Fountains of water jet from more than a half dozen nozzles, under which bathers hide faces, peeking sneakily to look, to stare, but soon retreating to camouflage gazes. Everyone mirrors everybody else, keeping at bay sensations of panic, as cleansing takes longer than seconds, lasting whole minutes, enduring the pretense of thoroughness, the obliqueness of desires, the accidents of nudging each other. An erection is always a curiosity, sometimes stirring another in kind. If it could turn into an orgy, it would at any moment, because hardly any bather lingers and loiters merely, genuinely for the sole purpose of cleaning themselves.

In that instant, it occurs to me that in the Long Beach Plunge the men's showers figure as the perfect philosophical metaphor for the intermediate state between life and death.

From the other side of the chamber, Don approaches. I turn my back and stick my head under the cascading water. He spanks my bottom. "Drifter!" he cackles, then cracking up with hearty laughter.

"Basta!" I joke. "Bossy fuckhole."

Still teasing, he says, "Anthony, the soul machine, adrift." Then, he disappears through the doorway leading to the pool, towel in hand. I follow.

When I enter, I find myself engulfed by a familiar expanse of steel trusses supporting a translucent ceiling, allowing sunlight to fill the pool, itself filled with ocean water, but cleaned regularly by a vacuum pump, and slightly off-center, an invigorating, bubbling, warm salt-water fountain, on which sit or stand four, five, six or more people, of various ages, at any one time. There is a shallow end, filled with children, a jumping joyful chaos, attended by a special lifeguard, Bunny Miller. In the deeper portion of the pool, which constitutes the vast use of the entire facility, adults playfully congregate and exercise. Meanwhile, lifeguard and sometime instructor, Nick Dallas, teaches the basics of swimming on one particular day, and then adds levels of difficulty on specific days, repeating the teaching cycle every month. As I have previously learned to float, thanks to the kindness Rafael Ordaz showed me in San Pedro, I am able to tackle the next level of education, focusing on mastering strokes necessary to produce controlled motion in water. As I observe, mimic and rehearse, I am distracted by the near infinite supply of young bodies falling down a chute starting on a platform a dozen feet above the water surface. I am not alone in watching. Surrounding the pool's edge, one story higher, a platform gallery surrounds the entire pool, accompanied by seats on the inside of a protective wall. Although I have been to this bath house before, making use of the changing room to arrange liaisons later consummated in T-rooms variously dotting the Pike, this is the first time I have not merely waded my legs across the pool's edge. Instead, today, I put my entire body into the pool, and though I am not afraid of learning, I feel anxious due to the surrounding commotion, noise. Nick Dallas, however, is a hands-on instructor whose strength steadies me in the water, putting me at peace with my decision, and giving me specific tiny goals by which to measure progress self-confidently. And, of course, like others, I enjoy his personal attention.

Towards the end of my thirty-minute class, I am abruptly hit by a small body landing directly, irresponsibly on my back. I fall forward, under the water, holding my air in a moment of agony in the area where my ribs had been fractured two months earlier, and when I turn and surface, I see Solstice Meridian bouncing up and down, pleased with her wet demonstration of power to herself, and poking fun at my vulnerability. Immediately, I submerge and, holding my breath, I use my newly learned swim strokes, underwater, to chase her, as she runs away, too slowly, for me to avoid taking hold of her legs, tugging gently twice before finally, pulling her underneath the surface and immediately releasing her. When I surface, wiping water from my face, she pops up, gasps for air, and as soon as she catches her breath, she turns in my direction and laughs, splashing water at my body.

"Clingy!" she yells, diving towards me and trying to pull my legs down, too, before abandoning her attempts and rising again for air.

I laugh, too. "Oh, yeah? Who's clingy now?"

"Ha!" she yells.

"You're in a good mood," I say, pleased to see, finally, the conclusion to the period of silence between us she caused after Glamour's departure. Even after I began my recovery from my injuries in March, she remained distant from me, unsure how to show me emotion, as I remained as strong as possible in her presence, admitting to nothing and giving her no details of my traumas. Certainly she heard rumors and likely talked a great deal to Maria and 'Olevaivai'olefe'e, but we never talked directly. Suddenly, her disposition changes, and she finds the courage to ask me, "How are you?"

Feeling relieved, at length, that her old self seems to be back, I smile. "Good. Thank you for asking, milady."

"You are most welcome, kind sir," she says.

"Solstice," I begin. "I don't want to dwell on the past, but I have to ask you. Are you mad at me?"

Looking puzzled, she shakes her head. "Mad?"

"Yes," I say sternly. "After Glamour left."

"Oh, her. Well... I want to tell you, but I don't want to do it here. Can we go get something?"

I nod. "Yeah, now that my lessons are done, we most certainly may... some ice cream? Ready now?"

"Yes," the young swimmer chimes, happily.

I check, "Are you alone here, today?"

"Yes."

I think about a plan. "So, let's meet underneath the big sign out on the Pike. You know, the one that's in the shape of an arrow and reads 'Plunge', right?"

"Got it. Twenty minutes, or so?"

"Sounds right."

Solstice, who already knows how to swim slightly better than I do, heads straight for the pool ladder. I scan the room for Don, and spotting him talking to a couple of young men, I yell his name. I believe he hears me, but refuses to acknowledge. So, wading in the water, I walk up behind him and splash, but just before I douse him in the face, he surprises me with a backwards flick of his hand, drenching my eyes with water.

I state, "I'm done with Nick Dallas today…"

Interrupting me, he says with an affectation, "…Yeah, but is he done with you?" Two young men, both of whom appear in excellent shape, laugh at his banter, before briskly swimming off themselves. "Wait!" he cries, unheeded. "And they took the train, from Silver Lake…" he whimpers.

"Don!" I demand his attention. "I need to get my clothes. You getting out?"

Humbled, disappointed, he sighs, "Guess so. See you in the showers."

"Right," is all I say, before walking to the ladder, grabbing my folded towel from the floor and entering the showers.

As soon as I enter, I ditch my bathing suit and hang it on a hook, with my towel. About four men occupy the showers at the moment. Standing underneath an available nozzle, I rinse ocean water from my skin, watching them watch me. One of them ogles my cock, and feeling relaxed, I encourage it to grow longer, aided by my occasional tugs. Don enters, choosing a shower next to mine, mesmerized by my erection. Rather than censor myself, I keep stroking, moaning, while my free hand caresses my wet chest. Two light-skinned men, heads shaven, about the same height and build, approach my sides and fondle my nipples. Meanwhile, Don gets behind me, massaging my buttocks. Deprived of intimacy for some weeks, I moan, feeling the building urge to explode, and selfishly, Don races around to the other side of my body, wielding his girth in such a manner as to shove rudely the two others back, before they return tapping my tits. Boss Don kneels and opens his mouth, licking my glans, slurping my jism, his face instantly washed by the shower pouring water over our two bodies. Standing on my toes, I balance my weight until I finish, when Don stands, smiling. "Greedy queen," I mutter, as two new men enter the showers from the antechamber, and the other two fallen rinse themselves.

"As my employee, it is your duty to serve," he jokes, standing up.

"Former after June," I say, washing myself in a last few seconds. "But I guess that erases my debts."

"Whore," he cackles, leaving the showers, wrapping his towel around his waist.

"Who?" I respond, following his lead.

*　*　*

After taking some time to dress sharing the small space of his rented cabin, Don and I exit the Plunge, and once outside, shake hands and part ways. A few steps later walking in the direction of the promised meeting place beneath the sign, I find Solstice standing there looking impatient. "What's your craving?" I inquire. "Strawberry, vanilla, chocolate? Something else, like peppermint maybe?" She merely shrugs her shoulders, less a matter of her being indifferent to my offered choices, I speculate, than a matter of her anxiety concerning her need to share.

She starts with a grand, impossible question. "Anthony, do you believe in heaven and hell?"

Taken aback by her forward manner, I stop walking. "This is what you wanted to share with me? Are you getting religion, now?"

"Bath House Men's Showers"

She takes my hand in hers and gently pulls me in the direction of our intended walk, towards the ice cream vendor, some yards away. "I..." she says, not so much confessing, as expressing herself confidently, and wanting me to know. "I bet you wanna know why I'm going to you with that, huh?"

Again, I stop. "Solstice, I just don't get why we are having this discussion. Even if you have your beliefs, there's no need to share them with me. It's okay to have ideals. But just remember not everyone has the same ones you do. And that's just a fact. How you handle that fact will determine what happens to you when you get older, pretty much." Standing there, looking up at me, I catch her face turning red with embarrassment, a nervousness overcomes her demeanor.

"Glamour says..." she tries to say, but I interrupt her.

"... Listen, Solstice," I interrupt. In a paternalistic tone, I assert, "What you and Glamour talk about is not my business."

"But it is," she argues. "She's right... There's something I just got to tell you."

I sigh, "Well, if it's that important, tell me. What is it?"

Her legs shaking, she looks both ways. "She told me it will make me feel better. I don't know."

I grow impatient. "Well, now that you started, what is it, child?"

Finally, she asks if she can whisper it in my ear. I bend down towards her. She leans forward to speak, then says softly beneath her hand covering my ear, "Caligula didn't burn down the apartment building in Brooklyn." Seconds slowly pass. "I did."

Startled, I stand properly, aghast at her confession. Afraid to speak, in order to protect her secret shared in public, motivated as well to prevent myself for acting foolishly and uttering some regrettable nonsense, I arch my eyebrow to express my surprise, purse my lips to prevent them from speaking. I want to ask her "why?" Reasons she could give me would hardly be meaningful, I decide. Perhaps she is wanting my forgiveness. Perhaps she understands the chaos she has caused in our lives, overwhelming her with the sense of her own power, the responsibility that comes with it, afraid she is losing her childhood, her innocence.

"I see. Well, then. Do you feel better now?" is all I ask in reply.

Honest, fearful, she grimaces, "I don't know."

Wiping my chin with my hand, calculating my next move, carefully, I ask, "Have you told anybody else?"

"Shhhh," she scolds, bringing her forefinger to her lips, furling her brow, shaming me. I shake my head, raising my eyebrows, sticking my neck out, silently insisting she answer my question. "Just Glamour," she adds. "Have you heard from her or anyone else since the earthquake?"

I pull my body back, give my honest reply, "Just exchanges of telegrams. You?"

"The same," she reveals.

I bend closer towards her and whisper, "St. Anthony's doesn't know?"

Again, she scolds, "Shhhh."

Standing, I scratch my head. Finally, I resolve to be her strength. "Don't worry, Solstice. You got a problem, you come to me. Always." What other choice do I have at that moment except to plunge into her universe, to inhabit her world. "Do you really want ice cream?" I ask her.

She looks up and stares into my eyes a good long time, not so much like a child, but a young woman. "To hell with ice cream," she boasts.

I laugh. "To hell with ice cream," I repeat, validating her wishes. "Tequila?"

"Can I?"

"This one time you can. Let's turn around and walk down to the beach."

So, I guess she is hardly clairvoyant. I figure that somewhere along the way, thoughts of escaping Brooklyn and living in California pushed her to act, and rather than let fate guide her course, she saw an opportunity to burn down a whole building, risking the lives inside, for the purpose of protesting her circumstances, causing chaos, gambling on some sort of escape. I appreciate her good fortune that she avoided the burden of causing actual loss of life. But still, she assumed that risk, and has been only lately coming to feel guilty, perhaps due to living at St. Anthony's. That realization leads me to wonder whether the guilt I have felt since the murder of orphan Joe has been of my own manufacture, exaggerated in an attempt to construct a caricature of childhood more precious for Abraham than for me. Is guilt so easily abandoned, so easily overlooked? Maybe orphan Joe was murdered not because of anything I did, but because in spite of what I did, failing to act, failing to cause my fate to happen, separate from Joe's. Then, I consider, as Solstice and I walk quietly upon sand, how it is I am so gullible that I merely believed Caligula caused the arson, after being told so by an adolescent girl. Whence do judgments of evil and innocence arise, except in our own imaginations. Was orphan Joe himself so innocent, after all? He carried his own weapon, used it, in front of me, demonstrating his power to take life, and not be bothered by it – an effortless action of a pathetic child defending his gratuitous life.

I hand her the flask, which she takes, opens and pours into her mouth. Involuntarily, she spits it out. "Try again," I advise. "More slowly."

"It's not my first drink, you know," she brags.

"Sure," I support her. "More slowly." She complies and this time is able to handle a couple swigs, without difficulty. "What was that like?" I ask her.

"Nothing," she bravely lies. "Burns."

Staring into the Pacific Ocean, I wonder to myself what Glamour might have told her, upon learning her truth. I ask, "So, what did Glamour say?"

"When I told her?" she asks, delaying her answer.

I nod.

"Glamour closed her eyes," Solstice begins, before enjoying another swig and scowling. "Then, after a second, she opened 'em as big as I've ever seen, and she said just the one word, 'Breathe'."

"Breathe?" I repeat. "Such a stupid word."

"She told me to stop smoking cigarettes."

I grin. "What did you say to her then?"

She returns the flask. "I blew smoke in her face then told her, 'Breathe'."

Chapter Sixteen

"Guilt"

While my little arsonist tags behind me on the nighttime deck of the SS Lily, I recall the words, offered for my comfort, written in Abraham's final letter: "There is nothing natural about protecting oneself. All homicides, even later construed as not immoral, necessitate a living soul either to execute or to allow to be executed in one decisive moment some obviously concrete criminal action, which reveals the lexicon of self-defense, coercion and even incapacity serves no other purpose than judicial artifice."

I enter a private room on this gambling ship remade from an old, mediocre barge, which Anthony Cornero-Stralla has begun marketing on half-page advertisements in the Long Beach Press-Telegram and the Los Angeles Times as "All the Thrills of Riviera, Biarritz, Monte Carlo and Cannes Surpassed." Sitting at a large, round table, directly across from where I stand like a lifeguard, Cornero smiles confidently. Though he has been subverting Prohibition for years now, expanding his operations to include Santa Monica, Culver City, and Las Vegas, he conducts himself as would any sea captain. He acts vain because he has built a successful reputation offering entertainment legal as it can be and has bragged, for years now, that he is prepared to offer one-hundred-thousand dollars to anyone who can prove that any of the games played on any of his ships are rigged. The more folks play for ten and twenty dollar payouts on the up and up, he reasons, then the faster and more secure his business will grow. To keep the gossipy Long Beach public at ease, and to conduct a portion of his politics in this part of Los Angeles County, he asked a few of us to invite one friend each to observe a casual, private seven-card stud game, played with a five-hundred-dollar minimum, on board the SS Lily. A special, one-time event, invitation only, secretly repeated every now and then, also on boats out past Santa Monica, too. They are already playing cards, when Solstice and I arrive a half-hour past the time of the game's start.

"Gentlemen..." Cornero interjects, standing and pointing his open hand in my direction. "This is Anthony Camarrata, as some of you may know."

It is clear to me, from his weathered grin, Cornero appreciates the obvious risks he has taken in the past and will likely to continue taking in the future. I have heard, since first meeting him, that he was once sentenced to prison and is known to repeat his famous tale of his escape to Canada and eventually Europe, where he lived for a couple of years, before returning, to turn himself in and serve his sentence. Later, Nevada taught him both to evade the law as much as evade east coast competitors, like Charles "Lucky" Luciano, who burned Cornero's Vegas casinos during Prohibition and threatened him with worse. So, he settled, making peace with certain bosses running things along the Los Angeles coastline, from Santa Monica to Long Beach, now with an eye on Baja California, and ever always, the Las Vegas come back.

Although he never openly displays it, the gun Cornero carries often shows itself through its outline pushing against the fabric of his fashionable clothes, and then it almost looks reflected in his slick-backed hair.

Remaining on shore himself, my former employer, Don, has sponsored me for this game, covering my chips worth up to one thousand dollars, if necessary, by private agreement with Cornero. If I lose his money, Don has promised to take me out of Cornero's corner and to force me into living straight, probably by enlisting in the Navy, if I can pass examination at my age, and if not, then junior college, "whatever my age," he demands. But I am not interested in losing. And to some extent, I am only slightly more interested in winning. Rather, Cornero previously instructed me that my main purpose is merely to stay in this game and show smarts, make nice with Jim Bonner, Long Beach's City Manager, appointed only last month, and now public enemy of Jack Yancy, Chief of Police.

"Anthony, this is Jim Bonner," Cornero introduces. The politician and I shake hands. "Jim, Anthony's a city lifeguard."

Bonner is a long-time Democrat rumored to have ambitions for statewide office to be secured by turning Long Beach into southern California's premier gambling capital on-shore. Cornero believes the key to success can be found by catching some of the dirt that Bonner may be willing to uncover about Yancy – a cop for over twenty years, former president of the California Peace Officer's Association, and a long-time opponent to legal gambling and drinking. "Poker on lifeguard wages?" Bonner chides me, then turns around to introduce his southern belle, smoking tobacco cigarettes from a long ebony, ivory-tipped holder and drinking bourbon and lemonade from a wine glass. "The missus," he says. "You bring anybody, Camarrata?"

I gesture for Solstice Meridian to come out from the shadows in the room. "Just my niece," I reveal, which sparks laughter and jokes about nannies, except for Cornero, who keeps calm.

"J.D. Watkins, to the right of Bonner," Cornero butts in. I doubt Watkins recalls meeting me, but I certainly remember him working as the foreman on the Signal Hill oil fields. He brags he now runs paving operations in Wilmington, which is expanding quickly, exploiting even greater reserves and creating bigger opportunities for oil men earning wages easily spent gambling and drinking. "He brought one of his lieutenants," Cornero adds, pointing to the stocky man standing behind Watkins.

Watkins who is chewing a half-smoked cigar, mutters between his teeth, "He's Alejandro." I recognize Alejandro from working together on the roads on Signal Hill, and we nod to each other politely, quietly.

"Captain Stewart McKelvy, U.S. Navy, next to Watkins," Cornero continues. McKelvy and I pretend not to know each other, so acknowledge each other by superficial glances. McKelvy introduces 'Olevaivai'olefe'e simply as "Fe'e." In fact, 'Olevaivai'olefe'e and I agreed to find some way to get McKelvy invited to this game, after Cornero first invited me in July, in the middle of serving out Cornero's summer lifeguard patronage. I doubt Cornero knows of my liaison with 'Olevaivai'olefe'e, although I cannot be sure, as I divulged its existence to the police, and so their snitches, on the morning after Dennis Carpenter's murder. McKelvy succeeded meeting Cornero, privately on shore, by couriering word through me that the Navy tolerates gambling boats operating in international waters, beyond the impotent protests of state and local officials. Cornero, looking for more customers, sees sailors as business, and looks for the Navy's tacit support, at the least. With this poker introduction, 'Olevaivai'olefe'e smiles in my direction, and I nod.

"Finally, Anthony, I believe you know Daryl Williams."

Williams reluctantly stands at attention and approaches me, by going out of his way to walk around the table and shake my hand, which I offer after some hesitation. "And I didn't bring anybody," he admits, his eyes looking down to the floor. "Last time didn't work out so well," he mocks himself, causing everyone, including me, to laugh around the room.

Cornero finishes the introductions by saying about Williams, "He's the Republican at the table," a comment which sparks another round of chuckles.

"Anthony," Cornero interrupts, gesturing. "Take this seat here, to my left."

"Poker"

* * *

"Hitler?" McKelvy skeptically asks Watkins, who throws in the towel by taking a mighty drink from his whisky bottle and flipping down four upcards on top his short stack of chips. Then, he takes the cigar stub from a tray and tries to light it with a match.

"Fold," grumbles Watkins. "Why... you don't believe he had absolutely nothing to do with it, do you?" Watkins ribs the Navy captain, who hangs in the game with a couple hundred dollars after two hours of play. "You buy the communist angle?" the oilman doubts.

"Why not?" Williams yaps his big mouth. "They're all over Long Beach, for crissakes, excuse my French." Williams grabs my flask of tequila that I passed to McKelvy a couple hands ago.

Cornero, who deals this hand, draws attention back to the game. "Captain, it's back to you."

The Navy captain stares a long time at the two cards he holds in his hand, before returning them face down to the table. "Well," he muses. "First I was in fifty, now I'm in another fifty." If I discern any particular personality trait about McKelvy it is that he seems distracted easily, and pays as much attention to the conversation around the table as to the faces and gestures of others playing the game. He tosses in four ten dollar chips and two fives, showing a pair of sixes as among his upcards. "Call."

Williams shows a possible mixed-suit straight among his up-cards of a four and five followed by a seven and three. He studies his hand carefully, perhaps contemplating a raise, prior to calling Bonner's bet finally. "The hell do communists care about the Reichstag? They'd burn it first chance they'd get." Williams looks at me directly, and I return the gaze, blowing reefer smoke in his direction, provoking him to cough.

Holding a pair of red queens, only one of which hides with the two cards against my chest, I think about whether I can win with two pair, because my four up-cards show two black jacks, plus a nine and one of the queens. Do I risk a full house?

Then, Williams bets cocky, which is probably why his stacks have grown a bit since the game started. Remembering Cornero's warning for me to stay in the game, but seeing that my stacks have remained about as even as since I started, I make a dramatic move tossing towards the center a hundred dollars in chips, one of which is sullied by ash, then drawing extra attention to my bold gesture with a rejoinder to Williams, without looking at him directly, "It's more like the Klan would burn the communists."

'Olevaivai'olefe'e walks behind me, takes my smoke and returns it to my hand after a few enjoyable moments.

Cornero, who is about as much up in the game as Williams, quietly folds his unremarkable hand. Bonner, up on the night most of all, almost a thousand, doubles my raise, showing three hearts and one club. Immediately upon hearing the click of the chips hitting the table, McKelvy squints his eyes and studies his hand, then folds, keeping what he has and hoping for a better hand next time. Bonner and I study each other, while Williams calculates the deal, finally, without speaking, calling the raise, leaving me to put in at least another hundred. His wife places her wine glass in front of Bonner. He lifts it to sip.

Bonner says to me, before he drinks, "You resurrecting that cross burning incident last November on Third Street. Is that right, Anthony?"

"What was it?" I ask him. "Seven people, two women, beaten inside their own homes for being Jews and communists, by Klansmen?"

Bonner smiles, passing the glass of wine to his spouse. "Anthony, I bet you don't know why the Los Angeles District Attorney had to get involved in that one."

Challenged, I call his raise. "'Cause Yancy's lackeys were forbidden to do it or just wouldn't," I reply. Before Bonner bets, he studies me smoking a long while, furling his brow, likely wondering how it is I come to know what I know. I continue, "But what I can't figure out is how Anaheim and Santa Ana boys know where communists live in Long Beach." Williams fidgets in his seat.

At this point over the final call of the penultimate bet, Cornero deals the last card for the showdown, without speaking. Bonner casually picks up his last downcard, reads it without moving any muscles in his face, and returns it to the table. I take up my last card, see the black queen, and add it to the weapons resting against my heart. Full house.

Bonner, having started the last round of betting, opens wide the whole game, tossing up two hundred. My eyes ignore Williams, who grabs his mouth, thinking about what to do, then I look to Bonner, whose cold stillness reveals no useful information. Finally, Williams folds.

"To you, Anthony," Cornero says.

I pick up a stack of chips in my hand, when Bonner speaks, "You said it."

"Said what?" I ask him, keeping my fingers calm, letting the demon smoke snake about.

"The crux of it," he says.

Williams stands up, "This is crazy talk. I ain't listening to this."

Cornero calmly asks him, "You out?"

"No, but the hell does this bunch care a lick about Reds?" Williams asks. While Williams makes his show, I reach across the table and retrieve my flask, tossing back a gulp before I put it down.

Captain McKelvy orders Williams, "Sit down, Daryl, for crying out loud." Impatient, Williams complies and folds his arms.

I almost call Bonner's bet.

"You want to know how I know," he teases. "Before I take this hand."

Upon his last words, I throw in another two hundred on top of my call. "Sure," I tell him.

Bonner snortles, "Yancy used to spend time with them. It's like they're in snowy white heaven, when they all float together. He lets them off easy, move about the city and the port easy. He thinks they're just good Americans, fighting for the America they love, the same one he loves. Angels."

Looking in Bonner's eyes, I point to everyone in the room, "So, they need to know."

Bonner replies, "So, Yancy needs to go."

I puff, throwing in another two hundred. Tired of the escalation, he calls my raise and shows the nine of clubs and the seven of spades, and a flush of hearts: ace, two, eight, ten, king. Near the pile of chips in the center of the table, on top of my cards—the two black jacks, the nine and red queen—I throw down with a cocky smirk the three beauties held against my chest. Queens over jacks.

Pleasantly surprised, Cornero chortles, grabs his empty drinking glass, stands from the table and walks behind me, patting me on the back as I gather my chips. He walks towards the bar near us and fills his glass with more gin, while I talk confidently, catching Solstice smiling in my direction. "You know," I say, as though such intelligence is my own, "in the French Revolution, what helped bring down a king turned out to be a rather simple solution."

Williams butts in, "The guillotine?"

"Well, that, too," I respond, popping my cherry ember to the floor, stomping once, and pocketing the remainder. "But something more insidious, revolutionary, simple and far less bloody." At this point, I have the entire table enraptured by my speaking. Bonner, who has lost, hardly seems sore, as I simply had the better hand. He listens respectfully. "Pornography," I say.

Cornero returns to his seat, quietly, and turns to me, repeating silently the word he just heard. "Did I hear you right? Pornography..." he snickers. "What exactly do you got in mind?"

"Gentlemen," I begin, "and ladies," I add, nodding individually, acknowledging Bonner's wife, 'Olevaivai'olefe'e and Solstice. "I am in possession of five reams of what they call these days a 'comic book', except this isn't Betty Boop. The thousands of copies of this book I have are the illustrated story of a marijuana-smoking wrestler from old Mexico who dons a mysterious savage mask imbuing him with super sexual and athletic powers, of both genders, beyond anything anyone else can summon, on a mission to avenge the sufferings caused by the police department in the City of Long Beach, sufferings in the name of sobriety, in the name of sound money, in the name of America."

Bonner cackles, "A comic book?"

McKelvy, who previously conferred with me about the books which Glamour had taken with her to New York, adds, "I understand they're called 'Tijuana Bibles' out east. Very popular genre."

"What's yours called, Anthony?" Bonner asks.

"I didn't make it," I answer, arranging my newly won booty into three neat stacks. "But I know who did, and I'm happy to take the fall for making them, if they get distributed and help take down Yancy, who appears in them. By name."

Pressing for an answer, Cornero breaks his silence, "What's the comic title?"

"Fierce Stranger," I answer.

"You got an author name on them?" Cornero checks, gathering the cards on the table and shuffling them into a tidy deck.

"'Clingy'," I respond.

Williams shouts, exasperated, "No... that's it! I'm out."

Watkins scowls at him, "What?"

"Pornography? Featuring the President of the California Peace Officers Association?" Williams adds.

I remind him, "Former... president."

Cornero addresses Williams sternly, "First, Daryl, you were never 'in', so you can't be 'out'. Second, why not pornography? What's the cost, especially if it's already made? If a public official like Yancy can't take the heat, then he shouldn't have his fucking job. Third, you say anything about this to anyone, Williams, and you can forget about coming on any my boats again, at the least."

I study Bonner's reaction, which shows interest and concern. "Bonner?" I say, asking for his participation.

The Long Beach City Manager takes a deep breath, and addresses everyone seated at the table. "Well, to be honest, some of us are planning to get Yancy out by October, and if we were to get these out now, in early August, that should be enough time to hit his reputation in terms of public opinion, enough time to give us a chance to build deeper voter support to get him out of there, and discredit his politics. But, Anthony..." he looks me squarely in the eyes. "What about you? Can you take the heat if everyone knows you're the author? You could get the California AG... maybe G-men, even... involved in this matter. It could get out of your control."

I look at McKelvy, who had been paying attention to Bonner. McKelvy shows me a disappointed face and nods his head, reluctantly agreeing with the politician. 'Olevaivai'olefe'e places her hands on McKelvy's shoulders, her face showing me concern, too.

"Well, if they call this genre 'Tijuana Bibles,' then the author should live in Tijuana, BC instead of Long Beach, USA." Watkins stares deeply into my gaze.

Instantly, Cornero and Bonner exchange knowing glances. Corner hands me the deck of playing cards. "Deal," Cornero tells me, as I catch out of the corner of my eye Solstice's fist sticking her thumb into the air.

* * *

In one corner of the same private poker room, following the conclusion of the game, Bonner and Cornero conference with me, privately. Bonner grabs my attention, "Hey tagman... so, really. Who wrote this book of yours?"

"Can't say," I reply honestly, as Cornero pulls out several fifty dollar bills, having counted my chips at the table and found that I came out nearly five hundred dollars ahead of my buy-in, doubling Don's sponsorship, and allowing me to make good on some debts I owe. Impressed with this one display of my poker skills, he rounds up his count and evens his pay-out. "Let me just say that my going to Tijuana would be appropriate, if you follow?"

"Is that so..." Bonner muses, letting his words drift into quiet self-reflection. "About that," he turns to Cornero double-counting the bills before handing the whole stash to Bonner, who takes his cut before handing the rest to me. "It would probably be wisest if you left sooner rather than later. Are the actual printing presses here in Long Beach?"

"Not exactly... not too far out of town, either."

Cornero hands me the bills, smiling. "Congratulations," he offers warmly.

I accept. If the game we just finished, or at least just a few hands of it, had been rigged, I never noticed, not that I was paying close attention. So, feeling fairly confident, I take my evening's last chance. "Listen, fellas. There's another matter I have to ask you guys. About a year ago, last Valentine's Day..."

Bonner checks, "Would that be '32?"

"Yeah, that's about right. Back then, there was a murder of a man... black. His name was Dennis Carpenter. Out in Wilmington."

Cornero looks skeptically at me. "What about him?"

"I think, now that you mention it, I might have heard something. It wasn't in the papers much," Bonner recalls.

I respond, "That's right. But it was two men who killed him. Any chance that any of them also happened to join the cross burning back in November here in Long Beach?"

Bonner and Cornero back up. Cornero starts, "Now wait a minute, Anthony. What's this got to do with you?"

They wait for my answer. "I was there, at the scene. Later, Williams tried to frame me as the suspect for it." They look over at the table to see that everyone is standing up, ready to leave, although Williams appears to have left the room already, by now probably sitting inside a water taxi headed for shore. "I want to find out who did it."

Bonner explains, "You're asking quite a bit about an old murder case. How did this Carpenter fellow die?"

"Knifed and garrotted," I answer.

Cornero sees I am serious. "Let it go, Anthony."

Bonner answers, "I'll see what I can do, but no promises."

"If you ask me," I speculate. "I'd start with those names mentioned in the papers about the cross burning. Who else would have the guts to pull off a murder, and successfully disappear, the incident not really talked about in the papers, unless they also were willing, possibly, to assault people inside their own house, believing they'd get away with? And, I might add, who exactly knows who, that the occupants of a private residence in Long Beach can be identified by police officers living in Orange County?"

"Hmm. We'll see," Bonner muses, scratching his chin, while Cornero departs the conversation to give his regards to his guests, anxious to leave the boat for shore.

* * *

Seated on a water taxi leaving the SS Lily, unaccompanied by friends or acquaintances, except for a sleeping Solstice, leaning slightly against me, I reflect upon the late night lights coloring the city coastline, while contemplating my life changed by following through and committing an actual murder, wondering what sort of motivations would suffice to put into motion a relevant chain of events.

If I were intellectual, logical, something not exactly unlike Nathan Leopold and Richard Loeb, perhaps I could let my intelligence guide me through a series of actions culminating, finally, in a simple exercise of finger muscles gripping the handle of a weapon and squeezing the trigger – and equally as important, later remembering the murder only as a chain of events, mere physical movements occupying the space of the universe, the residual of a consciousness flowing like a vast river surrounding me, liberating me from all responsibility yet also clarifying my actions as uniquely my own, like childhood tales about Abraham readied, under Yahweh's command, to take his boy's life, steadied.

If presented with the opportunity, if I create the opportunity, what would I do with it? I consider acting from motives of empathy: as if caring deeply for the life of Dennis Carpenter and risking my own by emphatically drawing a punctuation mark larger than a tiny period at the end of his short sentence, or as if I figure him, in my own imagination, as some tragic representative of Africa in the Americas requiring my rebellion against centuries of colonial adventures from ancient slavery to Somaliland under Mussolini's Italy. Feeling empathetic, I am captured by a redemptive, heroic mood—a Race man—but such emotions soon evaporate as they lack a compelling,

"SS Lily"

honest justification, leaving me to realize at that specific moment I am just superficially distracting myself.

"All homicides, even later construed as not immoral, necessitate a living soul either to execute or to allow to be executed in one decisive moment some obviously concrete criminal action," Abraham wrote, I recall. At an unavoidable ignorant distance, across space and time, he communicates, I tell myself, the specific predicaments of my anarchic situation, lacking any morality of self-evident context or common sense. The significance ascribed to participating in the act of ending the life of another person, like orphan Joe, is, he seems to say, always imposed after the fact, while at the same time such action, in all cases and at all times, is inescapably criminal, as if criminality is a universal feeling with which all killers must cope while living among the dead. Meanwhile, my arsonist snores. Law, morality: edifice. Or at least, this is what I take from his words, at this precise instant.

If I could, I might deal death decisively and allow time to pass in anonymity, not merely to allow the murder to escape historical note, which it more likely could if it was believed it was impossible I had committed it, but most important to allow me to accept the consequences of my actions, to make peace with my past about which could never be spoken or remembered, and certainly not celebrated. If such were the conditions to my actions, then I might accept them, not so much as heroic but as merciful: bullets taking two lives to the same ethereal place at which I hovered, in the earthquake, but in their case, doing nothing to pull them back from the precipice - the opposite of that which Ensign Gregorio did to me, for me. I let them bleed into that abyssal vomitous cavern, showing them genuine compassion as they expire, as if their lives already no longer belonged to this world, confident that all that remains is my steadfast wit to erase my deed's public memory and a diamond core of flawless will to tolerate its private consequences as long and as frequent as strategy dictates.

Visions of the planet. Late night hunches. The universe hurtling towards some violent direction. Repetitious apparitions. A global earthquake and tsunamis. Time's trajectory.

Perpetual apprehensions. That vaguely reminiscent priestly textured place where violence is piously renounced. I accept responsibility instead. Pick the good side. Distinguish an undistinguished solipsistic existence. Thieving competing human geographies. Mystified exercises of might.

May such a deadly deed dispel submerged feelings passive, inactive.

May a path, in time, both lead to some new life opening and yet move me beyond it, towards an honorable retirement of outstanding debts in old

Brooklyn and the enjoyment of a self-congratulating pat on my own pocket, financing my advancing years passed in old Mexico.

May it be all of this, yet it may also be, despite everything, simply irreversible mortal error.

E ancora, Solstice respira involontariamente.

Chapter Seventeen

"Contrivance of Vengeance"

RECEIVED AT LONG BEACH, CALIF, USA
TIJUANA, BAJA CALIF, MEX
DECEMBER 5, 1933

SOLSTICE MERIDIAN

SENDING EARLY CHRISTMAS WISHES STOP SETTLED IN FOR WINTER STOP TRYING LONGER STOP CANNOT MAKE PROMISES ABOUT RETURN STOP APRENDIENDO ESPAÑOL Y LO DEBES APRENDER TAMBIÉN

ANTHONY CAMARRATA
1011a

* * *

The ruse of Fierce Stranger permits me to invent a new identity for myself. With the assistance of Ernesto Ordaz, and his extended family and allies in the Communist Party, I am allegedly living in Tijuana, BC, Mexico, escaping the repercussions of distributing pornography featuring the Chief of Police in the City of Long Beach, California, USA. The telegram bearing my name, sent by communists to Solstice Meridian, serves as a piece of evidence which she will believe is accurate and which she will likely share with others, including 'Olevaivai'olefe'e (and so US Navy Captain McKelvy), usefully commencing a rumor misleading public officials and city dwellers aware of my name and reputation into believing I am on the lam south of the border, when in fact I am caring for a long beard and moustache, occasionally enjoying tequila and reefer as well as Your Hit Parade on board an old bootlegger anchored several miles off the Long Beach coastline and awaiting possible conversion into a gambling boat. Cornero and the Ordaz brothers, separately, are the only ones keeping safe the truth of my present physical whereabouts. Trips to shore are deliberate and rare.

Long Beach City Manager, Jim Bonner, finished a hushed, arms-length snoop around things and passed its results to Cornero, who shared with me the names of two Santa Ana officers who in fact attended the cross-burning that occurred near Junipero and Third Street on November 17, 1932: Ruben Becker and Calvin Dickens. Bonner quietly discovered that both Becker and Dickens are currently long-term-engaged, young bachelors attending the First Baptist Church of Santa Ana and furthermore, according to his source over at the Santa Ana Police Department, happened to be off-duty on the night of St. Valentine's day of that same year, when Dennis Carpenter was murdered in Wilmington. Such circumstantial evidence convinces me to spend additional effort contemplating appropriate theatrics to solicit a confession from at least one of these men. Without such proof, I am reluctant to act upon any hunches, since Solstice's own claims to psychic powers, and Glamour's belief in the same, clearly represent the sort of magical thinking that only leads to disappointment, especially if I accept the responsibility of harboring deadly intentions, escaping legal justice and avoiding public notoriety, all the while maximizing the calmness of my mind.

Offering his version of "devil's advocacy" but also his inspired assistance, Rafael Ordaz helps me craft the imposter Jefferson Harper, an itinerant Baptist deacon hailing from Philippi, West Virginia, a fictitious, thirty-year-old graduate of Alderson-Broaddus Baptist College, which recently merged from two formerly separate schools, a fact I discovered at the public library, and therefore, offers a delaying effect thwarting any attempt to validate whom I claim to be. Long-bearded, I present myself as Jefferson Harper at the beginning of 1934, for the purpose of assisting Pastor Harry Evan Owings as his eugenics counselor working, without charge, to advise, during weekends, men and women members seeking to enter the covenant of marriage. Although skeptical, because of popular associations with abortion, Owings reluctantly allows me to circulate, among his congregation, copies of Margaret Sanger's 1932 essay, "A Plan for Peace," in which she calls attention to the need to offer sterilization and segregation for immigrants, Negroes and white Americans known to be of an inferior physical and mental stamina—another happenstantial discovery at the public library. At the very least, if church members choose not to have themselves vetted for marriage, then I argue to Pastor Owings, members will spread the cause of eugenics thereby playing their part to prepare America for its future. I persuade Owings to allow me to administer my specialized services, on a trial basis, by hand-picking one prospective couple in the midst of engagement, awaiting their summer wedding. Enjoying the reputation of being a decent peace officer, and a former Mormon anxious to prove his wholehearted conversion to the Baptist faith, Ruben Becker agrees to invite his fiancée, Miriam Jenks, to an exclusive, closed-door meeting inside the parsonage during an afternoon when Owings is absent.

The pastor typically dresses in contemporary fashion and wears no facial hair below his small, round spectacles. My clothing, however, evokes the style favored by the previous decade. To add a further element of disguise to the appearance of my beard, I have lost weight while living on board the bootlegging ship and now resemble in appearance and odor the sorry figure I assumed when I was recovering from my injuries, by now healed leaving hardly any scars, following the previous year's earthquake. Below deck, under candlelight, I spent hours reading the Bible, both Old and New Testaments, absorbing melodic passages concerning judgment, damnation, sin, apocalypse, broken only by long mental breaks of just whistling and diddling. In my present state, sitting behind Owings desk in his personal office, I stare at Ruben and Miriam, with my head tilted forward as my eyes peer beneath my brow, hands brought together, fingers locked, breathing heavily and pausing between sentences for a great and solemnizing effect, aping Abraham Lincoln by conceit of an amateur thespian habit.

Ruben is a stout man, dressed in his Sunday pinstriped suit, hat in hand, anxious to be understood and accepted and outwardly confident with the aura of authority I superficially project. Nervously, he stares at Miriam's full, pale face, when she finds the courage to express herself verbally. Usually, she sits modestly, keeping both hands gently resting on the creases of her neat and plain dress covering her soft belly and draping some feet below her knees. Their chairs are separated with some exaggeration, by about a foot, and the two betrothed do not touch each other, even once, during our entire conversation.

"Yes, well, thank you," I begin. "I say 'thank you', for agreeing to join me in a faithful and objective conversation concerning the covenant of marriage."

"Yes, sir," Ruben replies, respectfully.

I study them both a long time. "Before we begin, I should ask whether you both appreciate the need for serious honesty in your relationship before the sight of God."

"Of course, Mr. Harper." Miriam nods in agreement.

"Very good. Now, our talk is strictly confidential. I do not intend to share what is said here with anyone, including Pastor Owings. I hope that, by offering my assurance to protect the confidential nature of our conversation, you find the courage to speak candidly with me, both of you. But before I begin, let me emphasize that the covenant of marriage is sacred, and by that, we mean it is something we set apart from everything else, as I'm sure you are aware. However, Jesus tells us in Matthew that 'At the resurrection people will neither marry nor be given in marriage; they will be like the angels in heaven'."

Miriam chimes, "Chapter twenty-two, verse thirty-three."

"Yes," I affirm. "How is it that marriage will not matter upon the resurrection, but matters here on Earth? Ruben?"

"Well, ah," he dawdles, causing Miriam to shift in her chair. "I suppose it has to do with Genesis, where God tells his children to be fruitful and multiply, and ordains marriage as his covenant."

"Indeed, Ruben. God tells us in Hebrews that 'fornicators and adulterers God will judge'. He 'will judge' it says," I emphasize. "God's prohibition of fornication is a condition of his covenant with the Jews – a covenant which even precedes Mosaic law, suggesting its universality to all peoples of the Earth. The Bible consolidates this prohibition in Corinthians, when we are reminded to 'Flee fornication' because 'it is good for man not to touch a woman'. Indeed, the covenant of marriage is meant to give us a way to avoid fornication. The Bible says, 'Let every man have his own wife, and let every woman have her own husband'. I might add, it doesn't say let every man have many wives."

"Are you hinting at the Mormon church, Mr. Harper, because if you are..."

I stare a great deal of time into Miriam's eyes, which had been formerly fixed upon me, but now look past my shoulders. "Perhaps. Does the one-hundred-year-old Church of Jesus Christ of Latter Day Saints make you uncomfortable, Miriam?"

Her gaze askance, the young woman nods irregularly.

"Officer Becker, does it make you uncomfortable?" I ask him, while I study Miriam's face.

"I don't dwell on my shame," the convert says.

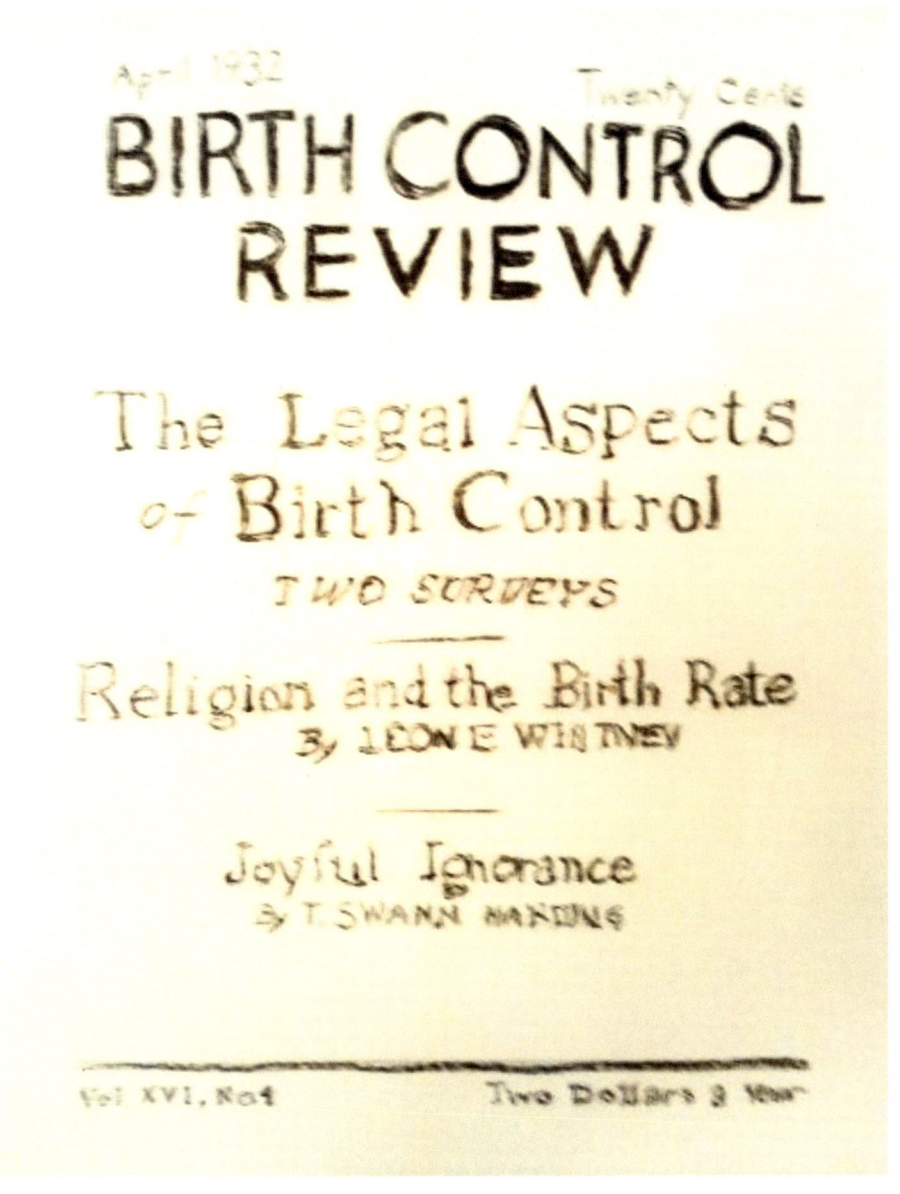

"Plan for Peace"

Still studying her face, I admonish, "Perhaps you should more, Officer Becker. Let me ask you, sir: have you touched Miriam?"

Ruben squints his eyes and leans forward. "Touched her, sir?"

"Yes, touched her."

"In what way?" he asks. Miriam folds her legs then does the same with her arms, across her waist. Turning my attention, finally, back to Ruben, I see him swallow visibly. "I mean, touched her as in just... touching her, or touched her as in..."

"...As in what?" I interrupt.

Miriam, growing impatient, mutters to her betrothed, "He's saying fornication, Ruben." She then abruptly twists and stares outside through the window, hiding her self-pity.

Ruben scratches his eye, "I mean, Mr. Harper... I mean... you're not oblivious at all."

"What's that you say?"

"I mean... crying out loud, we thought hardly anybody could see yet."

I look at Miriam who is staring up at the ceiling at this point. Finally, she stands and gently rubs her hands across her faintly protruding belly. "This, here," she says.

"You're showing me that you two have... fornicated!" I protest. Miriam collapses back into her seat, despondent and upset. "Prophylactics?" I inquire. Ruben fidgets. "Not toothbrushes. Skins, like Ramses, Sheik or Sphinx?" Ruben fidgets, wanting to reach out to her, but fighting the impulse to close the gap with a touch. "What is it you're feeling right now, Ruben? Do you want to show tenderness and touch her?"

"I want to console her, yes, but..."

"...But, the Bible." A long silence fills the room. I resume, "It is good that you are sharing this news with me. Again, I promise my discretion, of course. I suppose this is why you're getting married, is it?"

The two sinners nod at the same time.

"Are there other instances of fornication I should know about?"

Ruben wipes his lips in the palm of his hand, while Miriam shakes her head. "You're telling me, before you met Ruben, you were free of the sin of fornication, Miriam? Is that right?"

She gestures affirmatively.

"Did this fornication, giving you child, Miriam... was it painful? Did Ruben force himself into your womb, before he spilled his seed inside you?"

She shakes her head, meekly, nearly in tears.

As I interrogate her faithful soul, she forces out the word "yes" to each of my monotone questions fired in quick succession: "You succumbed to intense sensations when he first penetrated your body with his penis? Did his stimulations make you wet? Did he titillate your bosom applying his orifice? Did his erection endure hard and long enough to bring you to quivering hysteria?"

She starts to cry. "Mr. Harper, I..."

I turn mellifluously indignant, "How dare you, Miriam, to defile your body, as though it is yours. Is that it? Do you believe your body to be your body? Do you recall Corinthians, which says, 'Ye are bought with a price: therefore glorify God in your body, and in your spirit, which are...' what?"

I await an answer and receive none. "Let me give you a hint," I say. "Notice the Bible says, 'which are' after identifying both the body and spirit. Notice that the word 'are' is the plural form of the verb 'to be'. Why the plural form? Because the Bible is focusing attention on both at the same time, body and spirit. They are inseparable, and to whom do these belong? The Bible says, 'glorify God in your body, and in your spirit, which are God's'. Your body, the Bible says, is the 'Temple' of God. Let me ask both of you: did you engage in sodomy?"

"You mean..." Ruben pretends not to understand.

"You know what I mean, Mr. Becker. You answer me: was there sodomy?"

"Yes," he says simply, dropping to the floor the hat in his hand.

"Ruben!" Miriam cries, raising her hands to mouth, nearly failing to resist the impulse to strike him.

"So, was this an oral or anal crime?" I ask, letting time pass. "Or was it both?"

Finally, Ruben grows impatient with my questions and speaks assertively, "Mr. Harper, if I may speak candidly here, I was led to believe this conversation would be about whether Miriam and I are parents able to bring healthy children into this world."

"It is."

"If that's so," the officer reasons, "then why are we talking about sin? I thought we should be talking about feeble-mindedness and physical deformities and the like."

"What is sin, Mr. Becker?" I respond, smiling. "Is it nothing more, nothing less than weakness? Perhaps you suffer from a moral weakness, moral feeble-mindedness, moral deformities. Don't you believe virtue and morality are passed among the generations, too? Surely, baptism washes us clean of sin and prepares us for living in the body of the church, yet also surely, you would admit that that act alone doesn't make us all equal in all metrics, and it hardly vaccinates us morally."

"Then..." After some moments pass in silence, Ruben finishes, "I'd rather have this conversation in complete privacy, and spare my wife." He bends to the floor to retrieve his hat.

"Fiancée." I move my head up and down. "Yes, perhaps that's best. But before we do, I need to ask Miriam what she would do if you were incapacitated as a police officer?" I gaze upon this frail creature, who has removed a kerchief from her handbag and is wiping tears from her face. "Are you prepared to live your life alone, absent his consortium? Are you strong enough?" She doesn't answer. I plead, "Let me help you, Miriam. These are personal questions, to be sure, but it would be best for you to know your own answers now. Your mother and father, did they live long lives?"

She says, gathering her composure, "My father passed at the age of sixty-three. My mother is still enjoying her life, as a widow, even though she was much younger than he was when they married."

"I see, Miriam. Well, let me invite you to excuse yourself from our conversation. Please return, though in about, say, thirty minutes, after taking a stroll. It's a nice day today, wouldn't you say?"

Miriam stands, places her handbag on her arm and inhales deeply, trying to focus on happier emotions. "Yes, apologies for my breakdown, it's just that…"

"…Shhh…" I reply, bringing my finger to my lips. "Of course, of course. In a half-hour. Ruben, you don't mind sitting here so you and I may continue?"

Ruben turns and watches as Miriam leaves the room, closing the door behind her. "No, of course not, Mr. Harper. Sorry for my wife there. We're discussing difficult matters about our intimate life, things nobody even knows about. I guess this… talk… is supposed to make us feel better, right? Talking about all of this?" His questions lack a certain earnestness and suggest skepticism.

"Fiancée. All of this, of course," I reply and position my body forward continuing my stentorian manner. "I think it's rather brave of you two to consummate your liaison in the eyes of Christ and his church, rather than eloping or hiding your sins, abandoning your child to an orphanage, or even worse, to an abortionist, although…"

Ruben is stunned by this second-to-last word, "Damn it, Mr. Harper. This is such disappointing conversation."

"Well," I respond, arching an eyebrow. "Was it exciting, your indiscretion? Did it make you feel super cheerful?" I wait for his response in silence. His lips sealed tight, I speak dismissively, "Cheerfulness… such a transitory feeling, the doorway to sin and disgust. Illusory, wouldn't you say?"

He raises his brow and nods.

"Is Miriam the first one you fornicated, Officer Becker?"

"No."

"It wasn't, was it?"

"No."

"How many?"

Silence.

"One to ten?"
Silence.
"Ten to one hundred?"
Silence.
"Hundred to one thousand?"
The penitent coughs into his hand. "I'm just..."
"...No, no," I interrupt, waving my hands. "Please. Although I consider myself an educated professional, I'll spare you the humiliation of endlessly admitting evil, because this isn't a Catholic Church, and I'm not a papist hearing your confessions. But just investigating... were they all females, your dalliances?"

"Dalliances?" he asks, squinting his eyes in confusion.

I act as though his ignorance provokes my enormous frustration. "Liaisons, encounters." The lawman pauses, turns a bit red. "I see. So, you enjoy sodomy. And have you ever received sodomistic pleasure?" Silence.

At length, he says, "I have been weak in my past, it is true. I once stole a camera, when I was a boy. The camera belonged to an older man who was able to make me do things."

"Are you a homosexual, Mr. Becker?"

"A what?"

"You're saying he raped you."

"No," he says, protesting vigorously. "No, I wasn't oblivious to what he was doing. But I stole his camera because I was mad he stopped paying me each time after the things we were doing. There was another time later on, but other than that, it's strictly been normal stuff with ladies. I am not a homosexual, Mr. Harper."

"Did you penetrate... ? Show me. Your penis."

Taken aback by the question, he hesitates.

"Show me!"

"For what purpose..."

" ... so I may tell whether you are a homosexual. Now. Show me."

Ruben Becker stands, loosens his trousers and reveals his penis, pink and fat, relaxed about five inches long in its flaccid state. "Play with it." He touches and wiggles it, but it hardly grows, proving nothing of course. "I see. If you did penetrate, you should know that such action is classified as less degenerate, because you occupied the masculine position in the performance of criminally deviant genital intercourse."

"What?"

"Put your pants back on and sit down. Mr. Becker, any admission to degeneracy, of any degree, is certainly cause for the Lord's concern, and perhaps you might spend time thinking about what your proper responsibilities towards Miriam should be, aside from just going through devotion motions. But in the meantime, I need to explore with you other matters that involve aspects of your personality which possibly indicate a lack of moral and intellectual genetic stamina. Have you ever stolen anything, aside from this camera, when you were a boy, like you mentioned?"

"No," he says, shrugging his shoulders.

"Nothing else?"

"No, honestly. I am a fairly honest person."

"And seductive, I see."

He smiles, showing me contrition on top of self-love. Back-and-forth, I discourse serpentine, snaking in between flattery and shock.

"Have you ever brought physical harm to another person?"

He furls his brow, and asks, "Outside the line of duty?"

"Either way," I clarify.

"Either way? Well, I have made a few tough arrests, if that's what you're asking. And I was once caught in a fight before I became a peace officer – a knife fight. I won. There are times when I see someone get out of line, and I might... nudge them on the head... or something... to straighten them out. Nothing too severe, typically."

Curious, I delve more deeply. "You love this country?"

"Of course, Mr. Harper. It's in my blood. I would give any part or my whole life for it." I nod.

"Would you take another's life for it?"

"To defend it, I would do that in a second."

"What does that mean, defending this country?"

"What do you mean, 'what does that mean'?" he asks, defensively.

"Describe your instincts about Mexicans."

He grows agitated. "Wetbacks, what about them? I don't think they should be coming here, if that's what you're asking. And when they do, I think they should be speaking English, like Chinks, Japs, Coolies and everybody else in America. What else you got for me?"

"Well," I continue, "do you think such races inherently suffer from moral, physical and intellectual weaknesses?"

"I don't see your angle. Where you going with this? What's this got to do with my marriage?" He says, letting his voice rise in tone and volume.

"There's no need to get discombobulated, Mr. Becker. Just part of the scientific process. Let me ask you about Negroes."

"Again, what about them?"

"Let's say you saw one strike a white man."

"I'd arrest him."

"Off duty?"

"He'd remember his place when I got done."

"Would you kill him?"

He stops before giving his reply, studying my face, wondering what my motivation is. "Maybe. It depends. Would you?"

"Well," I breathe a sigh of relief, before indulging a very slight imitation of a subtle drawl, I recently heard on the radio. In a hushed voice, I speak, "I believe this is a white man's country, which boasts a heritage that should be kept pure from communists, papists, Jews, Chinamen… homosexuals. And I think an uppity coon should be reminded of his place, or lose it, and I don't give no mind nor sweet patootie to no Paul Robeson."

The peace officer hesitates before whispering, "Well, then, if I hear you right, we agree."

Resuming my normal voice, I elaborate, "The curse of Ham."

"Sounds 'bout right."

I lean back in my seat, and fold my hands behind my head. "So, again, let me ask: would you kill him?"

" 'Maybe', I said."

"Have you ever killed anyone, Officer Becker?"

He laughs, "Have I ever killed anyone? I wear a badge. What do you think? Have *you*?"

"Me?" I ask, joining his laughter, and not speaking quietly, but confidently and sympathetically. "Once." I pause a long time for full dramatic effect, as if speaking truthfully of an evil that had to be done at one time. "There was this ebony buck who raped a white woman back out in West Virginia. Well, to be honest, I didn't do the deed by myself alone. But I sure helped pull his neck up by a rope hanging from a tall tree branch." I force a slow smile out of one corner of my mouth.

"You say that with pride," he observes, more at ease with himself.

"Wouldn't you?"

"Sure. I killed one… once. And I didn't do it by myself."

"Was that back when you were a Mormon?" I joke.

"Nah," he says humbly, shifting uncomfortably. Clearing his throat, he asserts his voice, "Out in Wilmington, couple years back. With my partner."

"Your partner. And that would be…"

"Brother Dickens."

"Both of you were on duty?"

"Listen, if we're done with all of this awkward talk of murder and fornication, I'd really like to finish up, I hope you understand."

"Of course. Listen, Mr. Becker. When you act to end someone's life you have to ask yourself what the context is, wouldn't you say? I mean, if you were on duty and took someone's life to defend yourself or another person, that wouldn't be criminal homicide, now would it? And besides, there is an argument to be made that the genetic matter from creatures who are irredeemably, hopelessly morally degenerate and racially inadequate also should be sterilized, permanently, especially if their chemistry poisons the rest of us with suffering, like germs, if you get my point."

He nods. "Cleansed with super strong Ivory Flakes, yes. That's right."

Interlocking my hands together across the table, I invoke a scholarly tone, "Honestly, you might take a long, careful look at one of the copies I distributed concerning the plan promoted by Margaret Sanger. She makes a very good, solid case for a federal inquiry into this menace of racial and sexual genetic contamination."

"You mean a presidential commission, Mr. Harper?"

"Nah. Just a congressional committee." I start pointing at him. "But also, I recommend you and Miriam seek spiritual counseling from Pastor Owings. Reveal her current condition, tactfully, and in doing so demonstrate your devotion to Miriam, and brag of her devotion to you, and beg, both of you, for his spiritual protection, his pastoral wisdom and most important, his abiding forgiveness, and rededicate yourselves, truly, to the body of Christ."

"Amen, Brother Harper," he says.

"Very good, Officer Becker," I chuckle then stand. "Now, let's take a short break, brother."

* * *

...AN INCREDIBLY SHORT TIME LATER, FIERCE STRANGER RACES ACROSS THE HARBOR...

"WITH MY ARMLET OF VOODOO AMAZONA, I'LL SHOW 'EM WHAT I GOT—BETTER NOT ALL AT ONCE, AND.... SAVE... UP... YERBA MÁGICA!"

SOON AFTER...

"PATROL BOAT—BYPASS IT. WAIT... BETTER IDEA!"

ON THE RADIO...

"ROLLINS TO YANCY! MASKED MAN... OUT OF THIN AIR! ERECTION BLOCKS THE SUN! FOOTLONG... VA... VAMPIRE SPERM! EVERYTHING SMELLS... LIKE... MARI... JUAAA...!"

SUDDENLY, THE ARMLET'S VOODOO COMES ALIVE...

"CHUPA ESTA GRANDOTA PANOCHA AMAZONA, CABRÓN!"
"MAYDAY! LABIARRRRRGGH!"

"Fierce Stranger"

Chapter Eighteen

"Strike!"

Midnight.

Gentle thoughts remind me of you.

And, who are you? If I dwell on such matters, like the past and its relation to the present, I fear losing myself. But regardless whether these musings appear like narcissism, I cannot help that these caresses exchanged between us, now, provoke introspection and remembrance, as if I owned missing severed limbs which ache each time your touch falls upon a specific nerve, connected to my spine, inside an anatomy archiving a former residual consciousness.

"What are you thinking, right now?" my occasional lover but always talented illustrator asks me. His finger is drawing something. He asks me to imagine what it is, what shape it is, what form it suggests, the soft, slow movement of his finger, starting at the small of my back and riding up the ridges of my spine until turning right, or left, in repetitive cycles, tracing out something like water droplets or flames, or perhaps a large leaf, something likely natural, non-representational, non-glyphic.

"I'm thinking…" I pause to reflect upon Rafael's question, asked beneath his trim moustache. "I'm thinking… it's a flame?" I guess, deflecting my answer away from remembered feelings of past friends and lovers.

He stops moving his one finger, then applies the pressure of his whole hand, and pushes into the tissues inside my back, forcing air to rise through my diaphragm into my throat and exiting as a satisfied moan. "No," the artist says, first dropping the sound of his voice then ending the word in a rising inflection. "I mean, what are you… thinking." My body melts into his movements. His circulating massage moves in ever-widening areas, then tends to particular places, my shoulder blades, the small of my back, my ribcage.

"I'm thinking about Solstice," I admit somewhat honestly, falling vulnerable, comfortable in his grip. "I'm thinking whether she will last without me, without me being there, at any moment for her. I'm thinking it's selfish to abandon her, and at the same time, it's selfish to care too much for her."

"Right on," my lover approves. Rafael lifts the towel covering my bare thighs, and moves his hands, greased by coconut oil faintly scented with cinnamon, bottled in Mexico, imported through connections I do not understand and have made no effort to understand. His house's damp basement, lit by candles, seems to have disappeared from my mind. I imagine I am sitting on the beach at sunset, returning his affection, publicly, in some distant homosexual utopia. In a series of quick gestures, one after the other, his hands rapidly squeeze tension from my tight buttocks to my thick calves. Although it has been months since I visited the Plunge, and a couple weeks since I left the hideout of the gambling boat, I have not wasted my time in hiding by letting myself go to pot. I use a variety of calisthenics to maintain my muscles, and the food I enjoy is healthy, cooked by Rafael himself.

"I don't know if I can do it, Rafa. I mean, bring it. It's too... heavy."

He shifts his position to seat himself between my feet and applies the full force of both thumbs to relax the tendons and muscles alongside my ankle, heal, arches and toes. It seems to last for hours. I am lost to the sense of time, although if I make the effort to focus, I estimate something like thirty minutes have passed since we last kissed. "I understand," he empathizes, kneading and stroking while talking. "There is nothing special about a .38 Super. Leave it here tomorrow night. But know this, when you see Becker or Dickens, it will be a matter of having something heavy, in your hands, under conditions which will look, sound something like war, right?"

War. I contemplate the odd juxtaposition of roaring consonants separated by one measly vowel. The English word is so easily said, its consequences so easily misunderstood. I recall Abraham recalling the Great War, seated across from me at a table at the downtown Brooklyn Automat, confessing his loss of youth, haunted by his memories, imprisoned by his reluctance to share them. "Something like that," I mumble. Though it is beyond my experience, I understand the purpose behind Rafael using this word, "war," metaphorically, since in fact it is an appropriate use in these times, describing the constant, superficial demonstration of desultory violence orchestrated against human pleasures. And needs. First, the deployment some weeks ago, on the Third of May, of several city police departments, under the direction of the Orange County District Attorney's Office, off the coast of Long Beach, resulting in the arrests of dozens of casino ship operators, the closing of Cornero's competitor, the SS Monte Carlo, and the detention of water taxi captains. Then, longshoremen making just ten dollars each week walking off the job in San Pedro and every port along the west coast, an event which occurred not a week ago, raising tensions, causing employers to barrack scabs aboard docked ships, fed by men immigrated from China, and defended by barricades and local police and hired security officers, many of whom, like Becker and Dickens, are policemen hit by depressed city budgets. "Yes, that's right," I say, turning my naked body to show the front of me, all of it aroused, demanding his attentive contact. "The gun stays here."

Kissing. Calebresia and Baja California. Rafael's tongue moves to greet mine before our mouths make contact. Eskimo kisses. Tentative contact at first, then our arms force us together, as our slick lips seal. My teeth tug at his juicy lower morsel. He moans, then pulls back as I release. Taking charge, he sucks my chin, then moves inside my mouth, at the same time forcefully pushing my head in retreat. I feel his air pouring into me and release my mind to his control, letting him breathe for both of us. He relents, pulling air from deep inside, causing me to inhale through my nostrils and dominate his lungs. Assertions and surrender, one after the other. The grinding motions of writhing hips playing to win for a moment. The violent ecstasy of intercourse anticipated. Nobody gets hurt. Assertions and surrender. Cops and robbers. I give in. His gun.

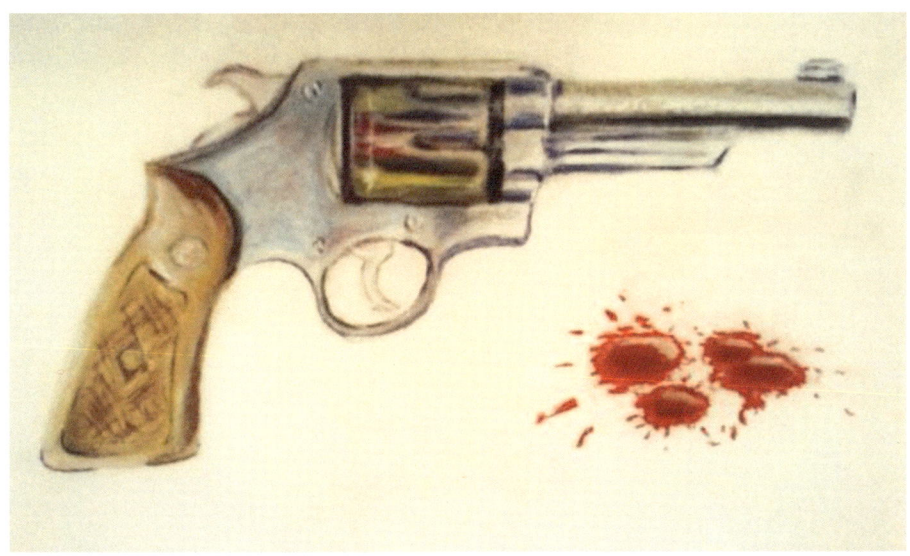

"Gun"

* * *

The next day, round about midnight.

Every major port along the west coast of the United States, from Seattle to San Pedro, sits on the brink.

Standing outside barricades surrounding the terminal office building, we – and by that I mean about one hundred brothers of the International Longshoremen's Association – have left a San Pedro pool hall, joined by a couple hundred members of Local 38-82 at White Point.

A union vote was taken, and even a new member, twenty-year-old Dickie Parker, a thick kid from Long Beach, was sworn in, last-minute, which makes my being here less suspicious to those whom Rafael Ordaz never introduced me, behind my appropriated alias, just another journeyman Jeff Harper, less the deacon's beard, keeping only a sort of baffi a manubrio. The votes led to consequences: a 300-man union raid for the scab camp at the Grace Line stockade, located at Berths 145-146 at the Wilmington Docks. We bravely chose our individual clubs, pipes, large wrenches, even torches – any sort of weapon that inflicts damage at close distances. Our lack of firearms is symbolic, though also practical, for the damage intended is meant to speak for itself but also dramatize the supposed lack of gun-toting gangsters and criminals among our ranks. In my hands, I wield a heavy-duty, jumbo combination wrench that fits two-inch bolts and weighs about twenty pounds. On the march down the Wilmington-San Pedro Road and Neptune Avenue, my arms swing my tool effortlessly, in grand arcs, in a state of heightened focus approximating meditation.

Right now, it is moments before midnight, and we spot the outline of a ship being unloaded by scabs on the nightshift. My eyes zoom to the dozen or so Los Angeles Police Department officers forming a loose confederation behind the barricades, mixed alongside private security forces and hired scabs alert for battle. We hear broken glass, shards. A bathroom window has been smashed, as one striker gains entry in the dark, unlocking the front doors to the darkened, locked terminal offices.

Instantly, hundreds of strikers storm the office building, trying to reach the docks beyond. We pass through the building, fully awake, confronting police officers and private security, launching two canisters of tear gas at our sortie, but suddenly the winds shift, causing the smoke to pour back onto the enemy. Police guns fire in the confusion, strikers engage, wielding their weapons, shouting terrible cries, cursing at the top of their lungs, demanding blood. Punctuated by sounds of explosions, screams, the unmistakable thud of a solid steel pipe crashing nearby into a skull cracking, a stomach pummeled. After holding back a few brief moments, I run into the chaos, finally spotting Becker, dressed as a private guard, taking a defensive position against the corner of a small building where Chinese immigrants cower behind kitchenware.

This is a definite moment, in this sense: everything, including the putrid smell in the air, the sight of armed men clashing, the sounds of yelling and gunfire, demands my unmitigated attention yielding no moment for reflection.

Spotting me specifically, Becker tries to shoot but misses. I rush, zigzag, and he misses again. In one perfectly athletic move, I use both hands to swing the wrench in my hands from behind my waist in an arc rising up, until it is stopped by the bony mass of his fat jaw, which cracks underneath the pressure of the blow, spraying blood into the air, causing him to throw both hands up, as he drops his weapon and falls to the earth, unconscious, if not simply dead. The firing continues all around me. The heavy, dense smoke moves back and forth in winds fostering confusion, causing my eyes to water, making it more difficult to see clearly, to breathe easily. I am stunned by my own violent power, as I scan the scene for Ruben Becker's partner, Calvin Dickens. Out of the corner of my eye, I watch brother Dickie Parker dodge bullets and wield his large club upon the gaunt bodies of a dozen Chinese cooks, overwhelmed by his fierce outburst of lethal power, between his foolish grunts, between his repeated supremacist curses. Unrelenting, he loses control of his pre-evolved animal self and surrenders entirely to his beastly passions, tempered by no human sense of proportion or justice or purpose. In the midst of chaos, strikers fall to the ground from police batons and gunfire, but Parker stands alone as a fighter with single-minded determination to destroy the entire encampment of immigrants, boasting of his intentions, and in that moment, as one Chinese cook falls bloodied and unconscious, and then another collapses paralyzed, then one after the other, the same reaction I summoned, the same vengeful anger that gave me strength to knock Becker down, tempts me, then compels me in an instant, unexpectedly, to exchange my wrench with the loaded police revolver on the ground at his side and march in a straight line towards Parker and fire three or four bullets (counting is pointless) directly into his belly, which has the consequence of ending his monstrous assault, shocking these cowering men, as they watch him fall to his knees and collapse, bleeding to his death, hopefully. Over. The location of my attacks, inside the smoke-filled chaos of the melee, prevents other strikers or scabs from particularly noticing my actions. Then and there, I stop, observing the cooking crew attend to their fallen brothers. Slowly, I trace my steps back to Becker's body, release the gun as gravity pulls it into his hand. I clench his fist around the handle. Without genuine decision, my legs bid a single-minded retreat for the terminal office and beyond, running away. Running, conjuring the face of 'Olevaivai'olefe'e.

My thoughts are racing. Long, racing, grammatically cumbersome sentences. Fast as lightening. If I could actually notice my feelings running down Neptune Avenue, if I had the luxury to express them calmly to anybody else, I would say something like I feel I have lost all allegiance to anything, anybody, anywhere. I feel as though I could vomit first, then bawl. Running. I have a headache. Ringing in my ears. There is this sense of the irreversibility to things, of permanent fate, of my inability to make any further corrections, to edit the biography, or even less to apologize. I can no longer breathe easily. I keep running. I know I do not belong here anymore. I belong to no one. I could run and run into the desert and lay down and nobody would care, and I doubt whether I would do anything than let go. No atonement, only acceptance. No compassion, only existence. No solidarity, only exile. I am more than a pawn, I am only a pawn.

"Strike!"

At the appropriate hiding place, I stop my running, waiting for Rafael to drive his car to fetch me, and take me out of San Pedro, Long Beach, and eventually out of the United States by boat. I wait, hiding in the shadows, thinking what if this were a war. What if the context were different, if I had permission to use violence, to be celebrated as a hero, to be honored and remembered and proud for being told what to do and do it because I was told to do it. But there is no context like this. There may be no one with whom I could ever share my memories of this night. This is not a war. Or, if it is a war, it is not one fought with obvious sides, I try to convince myself. But why Parker? Like Becker, he did not understand what side he was supposed to be on, and for that he died. Should I add deservedly? More than a pawn, only a pawn. Pity the pawns. Hiding, conjuring the face of Glamour Jackson.

I hate this country. I genuinely hate it, not because I adore Italy or politics or metaphysics, but in spite of these, I hate its cruel drift, its peculiar confusions, its simple-minded happiness and cheap thrills, hamburgers and motorways. Long Beach especially offers imbecilic pleasures, inviting endless war from the forces of order and morality, which in turns invites more war. Brooklyn is merely worse. I feel my gullet aching.

I feel the same fear after orphan Joe lost his head on the Brooklyn piers before I ran like a coward.

Where is Rafael, who should be here by now?

Headlights. Headaches.

I sit on the passenger seat. He takes the road and says, "We'll probably take Normandy or Western up to Manchester, then to Speedway. You leave from Santa Monica for Rosarito by boat. Tonight, now."

There is a long silence between us, as I feel unable to get comfortable. Like lying down, nearly dead, on the lawn of Seaside Hospital. The impulse to cry shakes me, keeps me from speaking, keeps me touching the tip of my nose, as if it itches, as if I am scratching an itch I cannot satisfy, and yet, I keep touching it. The streets are empty, mostly, though as we leave, we hear the sounds of patrol cars, several of them, their sirens blaring, racing towards the battle. In a matter of days, perhaps hours, reports coming out of San Pedro will likely spook the entire Los Angeles area and spread up and down the coast, and reaching out across the continent and the oceans. Something unknown, uncontrolled has begun, I perceive. I find it hard to breathe. My throat burns with thirst. "I got Becker," I dissemble by way of omissions. Breathing, conjuring the face of Abraham.

Focused on driving, Rafael talks about the ship leaving from Santa Monica, a small vessel registered to an American captain who will ask no questions, expecting me as his passenger bound for Rosarito, to arrive there after a couple days of sea travel. Then, keeping my thoughts on the future, Rafael says, "I read your poem you left me. I liked it, your talent, its simplicity." He touches softly my knee, causing my shaking nervously up and down to slow to a stop.

I start to say, "I wish I had..."

"...This?" he asks, passing me some reefer from behind his left ear. "There's a matchbox in my right front pocket."

I take a deep breath and dig my fingers into his pants, bringing a smile to his face. I light up.

"Right on," he laughs. "Just ask for some water when you get on the boat."

By the time we arrive at Santa Monica, near the right dock, I feel stoned, becoming more and more at peace with this war, with all war. Rafael parks the car, cuts the engine and headlights. We sit in the dark some yards away from the boat. He turns to my side of the front seat and scoots closer. We embrace, causing me to grow still in his firm arms. Lifting his chin, he nibbles on my cheek and slowly moves in for my lips, which are unmoved until grabbing his physical display of emotions, I take charge by, first, tonguing his face and sliding my hands to his waist, underneath his shirt and caressing his soft trail of fur which leads to his wide tits. Instinctively, he unbuttons his shirt, then mine, after which we disrobe, now tied at our tongues, eager, famished. Perhaps it was the excitement, perhaps it was the anger. Perhaps it was the violence, but, whatever it was, I force his head down to unbuckle my belt with his teeth, then I kick off my shoes and ditch my trousers in a feverish flurry. His trousers are already down. His spittle drips on my rigid cock, now surrounded by his warm throat, the sensation of cunty mansyrup, carefully, toothlessly he attends to the sensitive skin underneath my glans, dribble everywhere. His thick neck caught in my deadly hands, I yank his head up and forcefully push him against the steering wheel, audibly aching from the force exerted by my pressure. He rotates, on all fours, like a needy bitch, his pucker always clean pulsing in my hand, readying him, his spine writhing sinuously. Murderers. On my knees I dig inside him, causing him to recoil, until I jam his shoulders down, drilling him hard, raping the willing, rodgering his goddamned slippery Tijuana pussytube, massaging it long and good with my smooth Calebresian teninchfuckstick, pounding harder his shaking knees into the firm seat cushion, when I stand on my feet, bend at the knees, and dominate his tight, clean bunghole, crescendoing to a panicked detonation of bellicose murderousness, of the most dark energy, rising through cracks in the surface of space and time, bursting into the firmament light and hope and Love, inside him, and for that moment... a kind of liberation, like a fatal pneumothorax.

Shaking, gasping for air, his finger shows me he has already dropped his sticky stuff on the seat. Like aftershocks following an earthquake, my heaving panting yields to grunting shakes, I retreat, feeling the urge to whimper, like a child, then hearty, but bitter laughter. Unable to make the moment last longer than this. No longer in control of my emotions.

We dress ourselves as our breathing eases, then Rafael cuts the atmosphere with his wit, "Thanks for making life a little less lonely."

As his understatement expresses a sentiment precisely the opposite of the disconnected one I am feeling, I burst in laughter, sniffling between guffaws. "Are you kidding?" I respond, wanting to cry.

"Listen, Tony," he says softly. "I'll keep your possessions at my place until you return, but until you do, I wanted to give one parting gift." From under his driver's seat, he hands me my flask, which I open to discover it is filled with what smells like tequila, a hardly surprising discovery, except I also detect the odor of weed. "It's a special drink I make, made from messssscal, plus... you know, a little magic herbs. It takes a few weeks to make it right, so be stingy who you share it with."

Right there, I open my throat and more than a few swallows disappear quickly. "Right on," I joke.

"There you go. Right on, brother. Right on," Rafael affirms. "Oh, one other thing. I know you weren't expecting this, but Christ Second Baptist Church wanted me to pass this along to you, for everything you've done." He hands me a large brown envelope, which when I open it, shows several hundred twenty dollar bills. I feel stunned. "I just want to say... this, you deserve."

I try to speak, but catch my breath instead. "I..."

"...There's nothing to say," my artist interrupts.

"No, there is. Listen. In my possessions, among some of my papers you'll find, there's a letter from an attorney in New York. Can you get this to him, safely? Can you do this one thing for me?"

Puzzled, Rafael takes back the full envelope and places it in his lap, thinking for a moment. Finally, he nods. "Sure. You sure?"

"I'm sure," I answer. "Yes."

"It's ten thousand dollars, Tony."

"All of it to New York."

"All of it?"

"All of it."

He sniffles, "You got it."

Upon second thought, I catch myself. "Wait, let me have a couple thousand, and send the rest."

He looks at me skeptically, "With no note?"

"He'll know. If it's too much trouble to send it, just take what you need out of it, to send it safely. I trust you."

Rafael moves his head forward and kisses me lightly on the lips. "I know, I..." my lover shares. "... You better get going."

"Right on."

Rafael grimaces. "No, not quite right that time."

"A little off?"

"Crazy immigrant," he mocks, causing us both to laugh.

"Fresh off the boat," I kid. In his smile, I catch him wanting to say something but holding back. We both breathe deeply. I stuff a stack of counted bills inside one pants pocket, the flask in another, and gather the modest suitcase in the backseat. Then one last time, I kiss him goodbye. He gestures his head up and down quickly. "Nos vemos en unos pocos años," I say.

"Right on."

I leave his car, not looking back, though I hear the sound of the engine starting and the wheels turning on the ground, until those sounds fade and I all can hear is soft chatter on the boat near the docks.

Finally, a bellowing voice shouts, "You my passenger?"

Still approaching, I answer, "Yes, sir. You the captain?"

"That would be me," he grumbles.

"That's it, the one you're carrying?"

"That's it, I reckon."

Just as I approach the plank leading up to the boat, he asks me, "No firearms in that case there that you're carrying with you."

"No."

* * *

Perhaps you are a ghost
of a soul met once before
or perhaps he was a
premonition of the one
before me now
Your right ons
turn me on
flip me up
on my back
where I'm steady
where I'm stable

well-positioned
for a spirit attack
I know it is that smile
that lets me see through time
a mystical combo of
trim whiskers and squinty eyes
moving in three four time
Your right ons
turn me on
flip me up
on my back
where I'm steady
where I'm stable
well-positioned
for a spirit attack

Chapter Nineteen

"Baja"

When United Mexican States President Lázaro Cárdenas closed Agua Caliente Casino and Resort in 1935, I felt some sort of shock. To be more precise about describing those feelings, now, three years later, I must start by admitting my life has settled into dull routine, casting a shadow upon my recent past, bringing my youth into stark relief. Upon my arrival in Tijuana, I found comfort conversing in elementary Spanish, catering to the minor whims and mild debaucheries of fewer and fewer Angelenos tripping past San Diego and trickling over the border, escaping the prim certitudes of their overworked countrymen fortunate to find employment. That year-long comfort alone kept at bay memories of Long Beach. Thus, the shock resulting from the end of all this was not so much like listening to the disappearing echoes from some grand international party, which of course was true, but rather was like envisioning by way of a sudden epiphany that those bygone diversions kept me from understanding I had been struggling to commence my second life. Now, three years of obscurity have measured an era where I began to find myself making decisions differently.

I cultivate alliances reflecting calculations intended to arrive at the result of my returning north for the purpose of remaining there. My present occupation is to collect a personal fee from arranging transportation for those seeking to profit from abandoned liquor trade routes terminating in Los Angeles County, previously established by Tony Cornero's sea vessels. These days are routine—for instance, coordinating boat schedules with los agricultores de marijuana, introduced to me through vaguely extended family connections leading back to the Ordaz siblings. Like an underground railroad network ensuring that the system of payments between the two countries functions, without dishonor or indictment. It offers a sort of joy, from which at times I recognize the exhaustion weighing upon me, as I try yet again to arrange my desires into some appropriate concrete order, nagged by the intuition that all order is merely arbitrary. Predictability, in this way, becomes its own value, as the mere effort of meeting others' expectations fosters the sort of trust I need to live comfortably, commencing this second life split between one long-term residence in Tijuana's Hotel Caesar and another in a rooftop flat beachside in Rosarito.

So now, gone are Hollywood, casinos and prohibition from Baja California. Less mescal and tequila, I prefer grifa these days and, in fact, have taken daily to inhaling dope imported from India. Enjoying the black smoke helps banish nightmares of abandoning Long Beach in the violent manner I did. Yet, there is a cost: impotence visits me ceaselessly. My life is in short supply of intercourse, and worse it has necessarily become terribly predictable and increasingly barren of any fun, to say the least. I never arrived finally, fully here.

Tijuana still seems very much a lawless town, though here I have not replaced the gun given to me by Cornero and still in Rafael's possession. Perhaps the two are related. Perhaps having lost Abraham, and everyone else, it is appropriate that I choose not to defend my life with a weapon, that I choose not to subdue men with my horribly muzzled pinga, nor to allow myself to get owned exclusively as somebody else's subordinate, two-holed pooch. At times of idleness, I sit naked in my room in Rosarito, exhale smoke out the window towards the sea, and though I caress my skin, I feel no arousal, just this flaccid, limp, nearly vestigial organ, and imagine tattoos for it, as though it is a canvas for tired old dreams. I would feel sorry for myself, pretending that my life has become tragic, but as I recall from school, tragedy is a term reserved only for fallen heroes, persons of nobility, the offspring of gods, and although I can perform acts of bravery, there is nothing about my bloodline I believe to be blue, and because pitying myself only makes me laugh, I rather not laugh alone. I suppose I should take some comfort living free of venereal disease in something like the tropics. Except for cooties once in awhile, which kerosene easily rids.

At times, I imagine Solstice, whose dwindling number of telegrams have gone intentionally unanswered, particularly for the past three years, while I try to create some distance between us for the purpose that she may grow in my absence. Purposefully. To give her, at least, a chance at something else than me like this.

In the Agua Caliente's heyday, impoverished fathers hired out adolescent daughters to entertain film producers drinking poolside among bootleggers at the old casino, presently covered in desert dust, its windows broken, small animals scurrying about the premises. There is talk that, having outlawed gambling and redistributed land and finally nationalized oil production this past spring, President Cárdenas intends to bring the same governing vigor to the remains of the old Agua Caliente and build a public school, as Tijuana appears fated to settle into urban maturity. It is perhaps fitting, therefore, one of Cornero's boat operators in Rosarito informed me, a week ago, I am expected to make arrangements to transport to Santa Monica several large gambling tables, extracted from the defunct Agua Caliente, whose ballroom has already lost its gold brocade, marble decor, and grand, splendid chandeliers to thieves and swindlers. It seems my job to deliver the tables at a waiting vessel.

But, this morning, before I had time to execute my planned heist, I am warned by an errand boy on my usual Rosarito dock to meet at the old casino, without deliberation, a German perhaps tied to Hitler's government, presumably a fairly recent habitué of Baja California. "Hay un extraño alemán que quiere hablarle en el Casino Agua Caliente," the boy says. Curious and cautious, I heed the message.

Chauffeured by a handsome dockworker, a rough charro known to me simply by his nombre, I reflect privately on my shortcoming, approaching the grounds of the defunct resort, pouring dust into the air as his truck winds its way along the dirt road. At the front doors of the Salón de Oro, we park the car and I request Vicente wait until I return. From reading the occasional copy of El Universal that comes my way, I speculate that President Cárdenas is carefully accommodating the German government's interest in trade with Mexico and is unwilling to alienate them, unlike the British, who were sorely defeated this year by Mexico's move to nationalize its oil production in the southern and eastern states of the country. Cárdenas toys with Hitler to bend Roosevelt towards increasing trade between the two neighbors. It is a delicate, diplomatic dance. Since Prohibition ended, bringing a definite muteness to Baja California's economic dependency on its wealthy, protestant family to the north, a brutishness among businessmen these days renders private pleasure inherently suspect in the making of each and every efficient bargain. Impotence somehow suits me.

I exit the truck and walk through the front doors, already open, to find the grand ballroom filled with hired ranch hands causing commotion, neatly arranging several gambling tables loosened from the floor and wrapping white sheets covering the tables with rope. That these will be appreciated as antiques, one day, seems unambiguous. The German, who prefers not to speak Spanish it would seem, silently observes the work of his hired hands at a solitary distance, smoking a tobacco cigarette with a peculiar hand gesture, pinching it between his lowered thumb and overarching middle finger, pinky outward, moving it from the side of his waist to his shaved face, and back down, to and fro like a pendulum. Rather than breathing casually, he forces air in and out his lungs, as though smoking were a drill requiring not just habit, but a scientific effort of achieving pleasure efficiently.

"Who are you?" he demands in English, upon seeing me standing and waiting in the ballroom. This German is entirely unrelaxed, but not loud, standing at attention in a double-breasted suit, the color of dirt, a crisp white shirt, with no necktie. His blond hair, tapered down its sides and back, is combed and greased back on top. His eyebrows equally as blond as his hair seem to bend at a rigid, oblique angle above his squinty eyes, the color of which are impossible to discern in the low light of the room's environment.

I approach, without extending my hand. "You speak English. Camarrata is my name. Delivery, for Rosarito?"

"Coffin nail?" he offers, which I decline. "Miele. Hans," he says smirking.

"My truck is outside. I suppose this will take several trips, seeing that there are over a dozen tables."

"Hmm," he reflects, scanning the room, counting the total number under his breath, while pointing his cigarette at each individual table. "Sixteen tables. I also have a truck at my disposal, so with two trucks, one trip should suffice. Amerikanische, nicht wahr?"

I choose not to respond to his question, which causes him to fidget while waiting for my reply.

"I studied English literature at Cornell University for a time," this dapper dresser brags, breaking the silence between us.

"It might take three trips," I respond in a purposeful non-sequitur. "Our truck can only hold six of those."

"Mr. Camarrata, I think you are making an assumption. The truck will hold eight. My men will use rope to tie them down. Did you drive by yourself?"

How could he answer in the definitive tone he used, never having seen the truck? "No."

"Very good. After my workers secure the tables to your vehicle, you shall instruct the driver to follow us, travelling at an appropriate parallel speed until we reach Ensenada."

"Excuse me, but I was under the impression this delivery was bound for Rosarito." Miele throws the finished cigarette to the ground and crushes it instantly in one stomp of the heel under his hornback lizard cap toe shoe. "There has been a change in plans, il signor Camarrata. The tables will be boarded onto a vessel moored in Ensenada." He speaks this last word emphasizing the sounds "nada", while inspecting my upper body in a subtly flirtatious manner.

Keeping the interests of Tony Cornero in mind, I ask, "For... Santa Monica?"

Ominously, he grins, "As I previously stated, there has been a change in plans." Some time later, upon our slow arrival at the Ensenada docks, under dark blue sky shading into the oranges of dusk, the first of the cars, occupied by Miele and a couple of his hired henchmen, pulls up to the edge of the boards running up and over the water. He exits, and using his whole body, directs the first truck to back its way down the wooden planks as far as practical, about twenty feet. The large boat, able to accommodate many tons of cargo, and maybe a crew of two dozen, is docked some distance away, and a smaller skiff waits at the bottom of a ladder extending down the end of the pier. I advise Vicente to guard his truck at its present location, about thirty feet from Miele's parked car. After he agrees to remain patient while I survey the scene, I exit the vehicle and follow Miele, who heads in the direction for one small, nearby building sitting among others, leaving his workers to complete the task of unloading the truck and filling the skiff with as many tables it can carry in one trip.

Some short walking, then we arrive at the door of the building. He invites me to open and enter. Before I knock, I hear sounds of music through the door, spiritual sounds lifted by a familiar voice.

You hit me like

A train, a fist, a stone

The truth hit hard

And won't go...

I hear Glamour Jackson, singing, through the static but warm tones of a Victrola, amplified at considerable volume. Puzzled, I consider the coincidence, feeling slightly paranoid that I am about to participate in some staged encounter.

I turn the door handle, and in one decisive movement, I push the door open confidently, close it behind me, and cross the threshold to find one man standing dressed in a silk, grey suit, expensive, his back facing me, behind an empty oak desk, while bending his head over a polished, brown, art deco credenza, pulsing jazzy music. My hands close the door behind me and my boots scuff soft noises over dirty floorboards. The office is sparingly decorated with appropriately seafaring items, such as a stuffed marlin, a bronze sextant, and a large, nineteenth-century map of the entire Pacific Ocean. There are two chairs, one large covered leather behind the desk, the other small and splintered, in front. Suddenly, his hand lifts the arm of the machine making contact with the record. Still showing me his back, he lifts the disk nestled in between his two hands, fingers fully extended, touching its edges on either side. He turns.

"Mr. Camarrata," he says. I recognize him from my past, though there is a delay before I recall his name. "You remember hearing this? It was 1920, when she first performed this treasure on stage."

"Carlo Garcia Villa."

"You remember," he laughs. "Thank you," he generously offers, bringing the black record in front of his face, granting me credit for her art. "For this. This... this 1934 Commodore recording, truly... is beautiful. Alas, another world, most assuredly." He directs his attention to the machine, again, returning the record to where it was, and moves to withdraw the supply of electricity to the Victrola. Meanwhile, he speaks with his back towards me, "Vinyl, these new records. Quite remarkable. A little less fragile than the old fashioned ones." Finally, he claps his hands and faces my direction, before taking his seat behind the desk, and gesturing me to seat myself on the other side. "Please."

"Thank you," I smirk.

"Rumor is, Glamour polished that gem in studio, doped and gussied up like Billie Holiday, and... wearing a monocle."

I wince. "A monocle?"

He sighs, condescendingly. "Let me start with a somewhat circuitous observation, Mr. Camarrata. The flaw with Filipinos," the shipping mogul pontificates, "is not that we were colonized too much. And I say that out of love. No, that is not the flaw. Rather, it is that we fought for our race in the first place. Kataastaasan Kagalang-galang na Katipunan nang manga Anak ng Bayan! Please. Ugat daw ito ng lahat ng kasamaan. So, I congratulate you on the successful effort you have made to avoid the Order Sons of Italy, cornered up here in Tijuana," he cackles, humoring himself alone. "Tell me, as a man of some apparent thoughtfulness, do you have any notion as to the rerouted destination of Agua Caliente's antique gambling tables presently being transferred to my ship?"

I shake my head silently.

"Peking. And, before you raise an eyebrow in surprise, let me encourage you to take one moment of reflection, speculating on why that is."

I consider his manner, not quite as gruff as Miele's, but somehow less polished and gentlemanly as I recall him having shown himself in Brooklyn nearly twenty years earlier. "May I speak honestly?" I ask respectfully.

"Of course," he beams, excited that I seem to be engaging him. "By all means."

"Well, I could speculate as to your motives, or I could speculate as to general circumstances, or I could speculate as to why this involves me at all."

"Thorough. I like that," he nods, his speech betraying a slight condescension. "Why don't you cover all three. Please, go ahead. Don't be shy."

I hesitate.

" 'Over' "

"Go on!" he insists, angrily.

"As to your motive, I suspect your interests are now somehow adverse to Mr. Cornero's."

Calmly, he nods. "Indeed, and I suppose you don't know how that came to be?"

"No."

Silently, he opens a desk drawer at his side, and retrieves from it a recent newspaper. It is a copy of the Los Angeles Times, dated for August 1938, he identifies. He opens the paper to show me a stunning, Art Deco, full-page advertisement featuring the SS Rex, anchored in international waters off Santa Monica.

"I see," I say.

Returning the newspaper to his desk drawer, he comments, "Mr. Cornero seems to be doing rather well, and you might think he would return the favor of my protection of his interests, including you, here in Tijuana, by manifesting his gratitude in the form of some modest gesture. I have tried communicating this to him, but so far, the owner of the SS Rex refuses to take my calls." His eyes peer into my face, while his gaze turns sullen. I feel pleased he seems unaware of the full nature of my business associations, broader than Tony Cornero, including the Ordaz family.

"And you expect me to assist you."

"Immediately. But, I interrupted you, my apologies," he explains. "We're having a friendly conversation, Mr. Camarrata. You were saying?"

"If I am not mistaken, Peking is currently under occupation."

"For a year now. By the Japanese empire. General circumstances, as you said. The empire's interests, rather than Mr. Cornero's and those of his associates," he adds, letting his hand lazily wave at me, "are more suitable for me presently. Their representatives in Peking have offered a quite reasonable price for these gorgeous, eventually antique tables, and they also have agreed to cover the costs associated with transoceanic shipping. Of course, if Mr. Cornero chooses, he may rectify the imbalance created by his inadequate purchase offer vis-a-vis Tokyo's by recalculating his valuation of these tables and expressing his preferences more strongly. The ship disembarks in a couple of days."

"That's it. This is all about baccarat tables?"

Clearing his throat, the mogul admonishes, "Tisk, tisk. Don't be foolish. It is common knowledge that you regularly supervise the transportation of certain profitable botanicals from Baja to Los Angeles County."

Studying his poker face, I hazard a guess, "So, that's your angle. That's where I come in."

"Mr. Camarrata," he begins in a stentorian tone. "We are discussing opportunity... for you to return as you desire, and represent my interests, one way or another, so that you may secure a future for yourself. Things are in motion. Europe may fall like China any day. The Philippines may become part of Japan. Mexico might, again, join the cause of Germany. Everything is in motion. As I said, the Filipino curse is that we fought for our race in the first place. And yet, as I am demonstrating here, rewarding, golden opportunity awaits you as a single being. Let me be clear: I like you, Mr. Camarrata." He pauses to study my expressionless eyes. "By any chance, do you know the tale of the Night of the Long Knives?"

"How does this concern me?"

He smiles. "It doesn't, directly. The tale, I guess could be told many ways, but one way it might be told is through the story of one of Adolf Hitler's most trusted men, Ernst Röhm. It was an open secret, as they say, that he favored young men. It was open, because he testified publicly, in court around 1926, or 1927 maybe, against a beautiful, seventeen-year-old, blond boy who stole from him 'the morning after,' ahem. This was in the years before Röhm's party enjoyed some political success. Still, Röhm thereafter became a rather hated man, and subsequently he was framed and murdered by his adversaries during what came to be known as the 'Night of the Long Knives', a sort of purge of Hitler's party, around the time you arrived in Mexico, in the summer of 1934, isn't that the right vicinity of time? These days, of course, there are police protecting against such things in Germany, such as orgies involving Munich's boys. I suppose they might exist in Mexico, too."

Puzzled for a moment, I start to guess at his meaning, "You mean..."

"... I mean Miele escaped that purge, and is yours if you can catch him." He studies my reaction. "Don't be put off by his demeanor, too. It's all an act. He wasn't dispatched to Mexico. He asked for it. From what I'm told, he gives orders in public, but prefers to take them in private. Oh, don't be surprised I remember you from Brooklyn, Mr. Camarrata. Enjoy yourself."

"Are you threatening me, Mr. Garcia Villa?"

"That's rather bold of you to put that question to me, wouldn't you say? No, no, by all means. I think we both know you find Long Beach more comfortable, more sociable than Tijuana. Please, take a night to think about it, sleep on it."

As the businessman calmly stands up out his chair, he lifts his arm outward, letting his hand point in the direction of the door. Without exchanging words, I follow his request and depart like a gentleman while Glamour's recording starts. Before I close the door behind me, he says to me, "I'll call upon you tomorrow, Mr. Camarrata."

In the early evening air, the sky turning indigo, the moon in phase coming in view above the hills, I feel an unknown hand fall across my shoulder behind me. I turn to see Hans Miele standing. "I heard everything," he reveals. Perhaps motivated by desire, perhaps pity, but in either case I take his wrist. His free hand grabs mine holding his other. "No," he says in a chastising tone. "There will be a car to retrieve you in the morning from your home, in Rosarito, I understand?" I release all the tension in my grip, but he refuses to let go, instead he leads me to the other side of the building, away from the waterfront, away from the piers and the bustle of men transferring the last gambling tables to the skiff. There, Hans Miele brushes his palms across my shoulders, biting his lower lip, pulling me closer. "Not like this," the Nazi insists, pushing me away. He must want me to exercise power, control over his body, overcome his resistance, make me want, long for attention. Suddenly turning impatient, he insults me by saying, "Uraniaster! You think you're so special," spitting on the ground. "Go." Uncertain of what just transpired, I take several steps backwards, keeping him in my sights as he yells out of his face turning more ugly, "Macht schnell! Geradeaus!"

Finally, I turn my back and walk squarely in the direction of the empty truck, where Vicente is standing outside, patiently leaning against the driver's side door. Without speaking, I walk to the passenger door, enter and silently take my seat, waiting motionless for Vicente to decide to leave.

The drive from Ensenada to Rosarito takes less than an hour, especially now that we are able to travel at normal speeds. I imagine that, instead of Vicente, Rafael is driving. The smirk on my old lover's face tells me, without his having to even say it, that he knows he deserves me, the most precious part of his life. I imagine that his hand falls upon my knee, riding through Long Beach, returning from an outing at the movies, a premiere showing in Hollywood, the Chinese Theatre, dressed in tuxedos, both anxious to fall asleep together, perhaps, or enjoy a long, cool shower in the hot summer air, before we spend hours softly grunting gutteral noises. Banished impotence, incompetence. The end of constant surprises. Rewarding, golden opportunity. A love for all time. Love in motion. The honest, frank ocean, again and again. Gone.

When I arrive in my upstairs bedroom, alone, I walk in the direction of my opium pipe, half-full. About one foot long, it is made of bamboo with a pottery bowl and an ivory tip. I reach for a box of matches from my pocket, and start a small fire, inhaling deeply, holding it, until my body and mind turn numb, soft. Exhaling, nagging coughing, I gently place the pipe on a small bedside table, suck on a dried-out lime wedge next to a near-empty bottle of aspirin, and fall back on the mattress, thirsty for cold water, looking up at the shadows cast by moonlight wafting through smoke trails, lilting across the ceiling. What is there to think about? There is a sense of hopelessness, a sense of having been here before, the prison of imagination in repetition, impotence. The smell of fish cooking downstairs. A deficit of my attention. Old sensations of murder woven into pectorals. Longing for mercy. This prison of my imagination in stoned repetition.

Shadows in the United Mexican States.
Me pegaste como
un tren, un puño, una piedra
la verdad pegó duro
y no saldrá...

"Röhm's Men"

Chapter Twenty

"1939"

Attention, Tony Cornero.

* * *

It feels like I have been totally deprived of sex for five years, although more likely it has been two. Thank you, Vicente.

The gentle movements of the airplane, a mile-and-a-half above the California desert, and underneath the radiant azure firmament, slightly vibrate my body resting in this generous, cushioned throne, as I peer over the wings painted with the large characters, "NC13332," and stare twenty miles, in the direction of the Pacific, beyond two interior curtains slightly open. Occasional changes in altitude stir warm, nearly orgasmic internal sensations, reminiscent of feelings I used to get the couple of times I rode the Cyclone with Abraham Katza. If I could let myself go, and wet my pants, I would let it happen with a smile, but alas, I am not the only passenger on this DC-3 leased once a week from United Air Lines by a charter company, flying there and back, between Tijuana's old Agua Caliente airfield and the modern one just north of Signal Hill.

It required months of negotiations and continued patience on my part, but the timing of my return to the United States, on New Year's Day, 1939, coincided with necessary advanced preparations, if I were to avoid my previous fate of improvising an impoverishing residence at a shitty boarding house. Having maintained perfect silence with nearly everyone from my former Long Beach days, I dispatched shortly before the previous holidays a telegram to 'Olevaivai'olefe'e alerting her of my imminent return and deep desire to secure a long-term address, appropriate for my current means. Although I did not feel it was necessary to explain my situation in further detail, the truth must have hit her that I had achieved some success spending my time as I did in Baja California, because her first suggestion she offered in her lengthy reply was for me to stay at Long Beach's Breaker's Hotel, which had been recently purchased and renovated by famed hotelier Conrad Hilton. I authorized her to represent my interests and make the appropriate arrangements. Meanwhile, I settled accounts in Tijuana by orally assigning, under invisible duress, my business interests there to Carlo Garcia Villa's associate, Hans Miele, with the distant assistance of Rafael Ordaz and to the complete ignorance of Tony Cornero, whose operatives likely understood the arrangement would continue an indefinite period of time, and I felt no pressure to inform him otherwise. Even the gambling tables taken from Cornero failed to provoke his immediate reaction, and I speculated that as his profitable business of importing from Mexico was otherwise successful, perhaps he believed it would have been a bad bet for him to act hasty given the bigger picture. To satisfy Garcia Villa and thereby protect myself, I pledged to meet with Cornero personally to see if some partnership arrangement could be made between the two bosses, now that Garcia Villa was wielding a stronger hand. Relay the message, and leave the next move to Cornero in his corner.

I still believe the best way to force a meeting is to behave severely ostentatiously until unavoidably noticed with due attention.

"Clouds"

This time, my arrival in Long Beach means I possess a limited power over my fate. With Cornero's acceptance, I took as a fee a percentage of payments transacted on his ships carrying cargo from Rosarito and Ensenada to Southern California, and so effectively concealed a stash of wealth, amounting to several thousand greenbacks now piled underneath Garcia Villa's gift of Glamour Jackson's recording of "Over," inside one of my two pieces of luggage stored on board the airplane. I intend to cut the rope which heretofore tethered my fate to that of Cornero's. Beyond that goal, however, I have little vision of how I might accomplish my task. Still, I feel bold enough to imagine what success might mean, and I spend much of the flight, which lasts just over one hour, trying to perceive myself in longer, more grand phrases lasting a lifetime.

My petulant, internal tirades from bygone years waged against my old countrymen appear ended. It seems there is no point, any longer, for me to cultivate private anger neither towards them nor myself. So denying myself the energy stored in such emotions, I search other internal mental resources to fuel my forward momentum. I recognize the good fortune that comes with inhabiting a healthy, attractive body, having passed the age of forty. I fancy gliding onto some biographical trajectory flattened out like a tarmac.

Perhaps if I had the depth of experience establishing a sociable institutionality to my life, like a mason in any of the lodges of the Order Sons of Italy in America, for instance, my imagination would reveal spontaneously a course of action fitting a mature personality. But here I find myself, yet again, in pursuit of my quest for the tide of asphalt expanding like Tarzan's chest, chiseled from obsidian striations lacing the smooth, pale desert ivory hills dotted with sage. I never abandoned this quest actually, except for the fact there is now an accomplished assassin echoing distantly within me, subdued and nearly forgotten, who visits only in my dreams, among others, including my dreams of earthquakes. It is not as though I wish he would leave, like an ill-mannered dinner guest, causing shameful, embarrassing scenes. If he could only just be, remain there inside and outside of me, all of me, accommodated and received, unmasked and at peace. I would gladly forget purchasing some imaginary, superficial innocence if I could enter the coven of evil homosexuals permanently umbrellaed under veneers of common decency and middling pursuits. My life would feel more natural, more easy that way, for there would be nothing to explain, and everything would exist as if it all were implicitly meaningful and understood. Among such company, at least I would keep my laughter, authentically.

Indeed, I would insist on my need for laughter, and insist even in the most somber circumstances that all of us have the right to grieve anything in any unique way.

Inexplicably, the airplane suddenly, briefly trembles.

Drowned in the steady drone of the propellers. I laugh aloud.

Once, I loved.

This time, I will die laughing. Calm returns, as if that momentary chaos never happened.

Everything is a matter of perspective, I philosophize. What to someone of ten years appears as a lifetime also appears to someone of one hundred years as a transient phase. An airplane falls from the sky, crashes, killing everyone on board. In the long minute before the end, consciousness, I imagine, is merely terror felt by a person convinced that a painfully perfect destruction unfairly aligns with the fact that the body is very transiently belted into a cushy seat. In the newspaper the next day, consciousness, I know, is the wispy empathy generated by exercising powers of literacy upon the ink printed as symbols on purchased paper, discussing victims and accidents as factual evidence of the commonplace existence of such modern events. Chaos is, despite perceptions of order. Anxiety is, despite supplies of comfort.

A young, reassuring stewardess approaches each passenger, smiling. She asks me, "Sir, would you care for a pillow?"

"I'm fine, thank you," I chuckle.

Perhaps I am damaged, unable to accept comfort, inherently. Perhaps there is some sovereignty exercising its power over me, bringing me into a nesting circle of solitary selves unforgiven and not wanting of forgiveness, together in their apartness, separate but equal in their shared separation, coming together in fitful, grand gestures of community, like weekly soirées, or binges of orgies, occasions for accumulating remembered displays of social dependency, though in fact everyone typically lives different lives miles apart every day.

Flying causes thoughts to race?

I long for a self-made path, assuring myself that I possess the power to make self-governing choices, as if I desire to stand suddenly from my seat and dance about the cabin, dancing off the plane, out the door and parachuting down, all the way to the shore, into and under ocean waves, a disappearing dancing, remembered only as a dance. These days, there must be taverns on Ocean Avenue, bars where anyone can dance to death. I imagine taking off all my clothes, drinking, and dancing for hours at a time, making a living at dancing, and relieving the sore muscles of other dancers, by taking turns dancing on their backs. Producing pornography of men dancing with me, sharing the camera while dancing, cha cha, rumba, waltz, tango, foxtrot, two step, hula, jazz. He died dancing. From dancing to death.

I laugh aloud, briefly, then rub my beard trimmed neatly, conservatively, appropriately. I scratch an itch on my bald scalp.

A bell inside the cabin rings. The attendant advises us to remain seated and to secure ourselves using the belt attached to each seat. The descent has begun, causing a slight loss of gravity, like falling on the other side of a peak on the Cyclone, except more gradually, levelling off into a steady decline, sometimes shifting downward more severely, forcing a familiar ticklish, nervous excitement throughout my groin, bringing a smile to my face while I stifle laughter. Outside, over the wings and through the blur of the propellers, I spy beach sand, vessels some distance from land, and tiny cars traveling down roads connecting dwellings in an infinite grid of society. My ear canals fill up with popping noises.

The liberating anticipation of touching earth traces the cruelty of traveling on an airplane. Belted down, I imagine my release and fantasize I have become a skypirate, holding an entire vessel of passengers hostage, beholden to my crew of vicious and sadistic men whose goal is to dehumanize everyone's sexuality for my benefit. To that end, I conjure laws to criminalize entire sex lives, laws prohibiting physical contact except only under the most extreme conditions, the purpose of which, primarily, is to perpetuate an imaginary species already under my power and, secondarily, to satisfy my dionysian whims and exquisite perversions. Chaos is order; anxiety is comfort. United Air Lines, welcome aboard.

Yet, there is an exhaustion I feel amusing myself with ceaseless bluster and projected bravado. There is fear, a vulnerability that I am fragile and could suffer a stroke, at any moment, and rather than simply fade away, slowly lose the capacity to feel anything at all, to communicate anything at all, tossed to the side, bedridden and ignored. Perfect independence is the refuge of the deluded. The stark reality is that, despite my desires for some totalizing control, my life means more to me than it means to anyone else, and this is a glaring problem, for it should not be such. Rather, there should be some connection, some subordination, some submission, some conspiracy, somewhere. It is as if, between the two extremes of solitude and gregariousness, I have lost any knowledge, any geography of the middle ground. I am fallen off the map. I look out the window, again, the ground approaching closer, figuring cartographically in my imagination, fixing my coordinates upon a floating midpoint inside rings of concentric circles, shrinking in diameter. As it once was, and is now again: California, the good idea, so expensive.

The airfield in view, the continuing descent, the arrival of wheels upon the black road, the bounce, not once but twice, a semi-perfect landing, the reassurance of safety, the certain knowledge of arrival. Over the course of just minutes, the airplane drifts until it inches towards the hangar, where crews of men already wait to bring a short staircase to the side door and to unload the luggage safely stored away. I vaguely reek of fuel. I feel somewhat thirsty. The airplane stops. The passengers, just over a dozen in number, in a practically chiming unison, unbuckle themselves, between yawns and moans, and soft chatter, waiting for the stewardess to receive the signal to open the side door and guide everyone on their way. In my turn, I head for the door, descend the stairs, retrieve my luggage and ask for directions to hail a taxi. The late afternoon atmosphere is Long Beach in January chilly, but not cold. Inside my jacket pocket, I possess several hundred American dollars in various denominations, which constitutes a mere portion of what I have stored in my luggage. There is some formality going through Customs, but I have nothing to declare. Finally, I hire a driver, who takes me to his Yellow Cab destined for the Hilton Hotel.

Further on from the airport, I listen to Your Hit Parade playing on the taxi's expensive, fitted radio. I recognize Ella Fitzgerald's voice, from occasionally enjoying radio in my Rosarito room receiving signals broadcast in San Diego. Her song "A-Tisket A-Tasket," it's swinging introduction, her warm and inviting tones, gentle glissandos, the transition between major and minor keys, keep my toes bouncing up and down on the floor of the rear seat. Then, a change into Artie Shaw's "Begin the Beguine," its snake-charming clarinet and boisterous brass. I feel satisfied the driver makes no effort to converse, for I would hardly know what small talk to invent during the drive. I long for a thick mattress, slathered in cotton sheets, cooled by the dim light of one small lamp, windows open to Pacific breezes. But first, a long shower, steaming hot, wasteful and selfish, destroying a whole bar of Colgate's octagon soap. I shall have my clothes cleaned. I shall take a breakfast in my bed.

By the time the taxi travels south of Anaheim Street, along Atlantic Avenue, my body begins to remember walking here. And now, I notice a few more parking garages and taller buildings. Everything looks inflected in an Art Deco style. I direct the driver to spend some time cruising along Ocean Avenue, where bars dot the sidewalk. A sign for Rudy's, and another for Hollywood on the Pike, among others. Closed. It is afternoon, on a Sunday, so few people mingle about. Most of the other attractions of the Pike, the

Plunge, the Auditorium, have lost all scars of the earthquake. We arrive at the Hilton, and feeling generous, I reach into my jacket and tender the driver a five dollar bill, which causes him to smile and thank me, profusely. I carry my two pieces of luggage into the hotel and approach the counter to confirm my prior reservation register as a long-term guest, which requires a deposit of one hundred dollars for the first month's stay.

"Thank you, Mr. Camarrata," the attendant says, kindly accepting payment. "Here is your key, and welcome, again to the Hilton. Let me call you a bellboy to take your belongings to your room. If you find your room dissatisfying in any way, please do not hesitate to ring the front desk so we can immediately assist you and improve your stay to make it as comfortable as possible."

"Ocean view, correct?"

"Yes, sir." The front desk attendant gestures for a bellman, introducing me as "Mr. Camarrata."

The skinny, eager blond boy who approaches, perhaps eighteen years old, maybe less, takes both of my items, after calling himself "Jimmy." I first hand Jimmy a not-so-miniature wardrobe trunk carrying most of my clothing and an extra pair of shoes, and then, seeing he is capable, I hand him my black leather valise. I instruct him, "I need you to neatly unpack my belongings after we enter my room. Also, I have a list of errands I need you to complete, so after you finish the chore of unpacking, do not run off until I have told you to do so."

"Yes, sir," Jimmy smiles, obsequiously.

As he leads me to an elevator, I remind him, "Do not open the valise. Merely place it, locked, at the foot of the bed."

"Yes, Mr. Camarrata."

We enter the elevator, whose operator Jimmy directs to take us to the sixth floor. Upon arrival, I hand the operator a dollar bill. Jimmy allows me to exit first, and as I do so, I turn my face towards him, and say, "You need not worry. I'll be sure to take care of you, too." He grins.

We approach room number "606," and Jimmy rushes past me, gracefully settling the luggage upon the hallway floor and extending his hand forward, politely offering to open the door to the room for me. Amused, I yield to his sense of duty and return the hotel key to its employee, and in one smooth gesture Jimmy quickly unlocks and opens the door, extending his arm outward, fiddling with a lamp fixture just inside the door frame, filling my room with light and then putting his hand outward to show me the way inside. I enter first, and he retrieves the luggage, enters the room, closing the door behind.

"Jimmy"

"Inside the wardrobe, Jimmy, you will find a bag of toiletries. When you do, take them to the bathroom, where I will be showering presently." Mechanically, Jimmy places the valise, as told, upon the foot of the bed. As I disrobe in front of him, he remains focused on his tasks and settles the wardrobe near an open, empty closet. In addition to my jacket and dress shirt, I have removed my shoes, placing them by the door. "Your first task will be to get these polished and return them immediately." While he moves his hands to open the wardrobe, I interrupt him, enjoying the power he is granting me over his labors. "Oh... Jimmy, would you be so kind as to open the window a bit? Not too much, of course, as it is winter, but just enough to let a little fresh air inside." Without speaking, he abandons the wardrobe and moves to the window, following my request. Meanwhile, I continue undressing. At this point, I am standing in my pants, wearing nothing else, when Jimmy leaves the window in its properly adjusted position and passes me, without glancing, or much less staring at me, to return to the wardrobe. I see a small notepad of paper, and a pen, on the nightstand next to the bed. Before walking in that direction, I remove my pants and throw them onto the bed next to the valise, where my shirt, jacket and socks already lie. I saunter to the nightstand, retrieve the pen and paper, and start making notes, as I take casual steps closer towards Jimmy's direction.

"Before you do anything else," I tell him, standing naked over his crouched body about a foot away, "I need you to send a message." He stands from his squatted position, surprised that I am completely raw, and he moves his eyes betraying he is somewhat curious, but pretending not to be too much so, and gazes upon the length and girth of my half boner. I scribble some words meant for 'Olevaivai'olefe'e, inviting her to join me for dinner, upstairs, in the SkyRoom, at her earliest convenience and requesting her reply to my invitation. Clearing my throat, I order, "Take this at once, Jimmy. You may send it to the Villa Riviera. The addressee's name appears at the top. Finish unpacking when you return. I expect you back here in five minutes, no later." We stare at each other during a pregnant pause. "I believe you have the key. Still."

"Yes, sir," he swallows hard, nervously.

I smile, enjoying my subtle bullying, a sort of legitimate rape. "Good boy. How old are you, son?"

"Seventeen, sir."

I laugh and drop my heavy hand across his shoulder, massaging the taut muscles underneath his hotel uniform. "Hurry back," I say. He leaves as directed, instantly.

I jump for joy, the pleasure of dancing upon Jimmy's brain, and the freedom of feelings that come from the modest comforts of this room, in this hotel, in this city. I walk directly into the bathroom, turn the faucets to a precise position, raising the water to the precise temperature, engaging the shower, letting steam fill the air. Before entering, I sit on the toilet and tug at my foreskin. I recall the playful repetition of the word "turgid" on the beach, not a few hundred feet from where I am now, not quite a decade earlier, having ingested chocolate candies provided by 'Olevaivai'olefe'e. Candies infused with mushrooms producing the most pleasant mental effects. Lost in such thoughts, minutes pass, the shower steams, I stroke myself in no particular rush to release myself of the tension filling my flesh, when Jimmy returns to the room. I keep silent, still, and continue self-pleasuring. Jimmy, likely seeing the bathroom door open and hearing the shower, proceeds to retrieve my toiletries from the wardrobe, and eventually, after a minute of my listening to his rummaging around, he enters the bathroom to find me masturbating, seated on the toilet, my eyes closed, pretending I am oblivious to his presence, although I can hear his breathing. The bellboy silently places the items he carries upon a small shelf near the sink, and without saying a word, he leaves. It is too late for me to stop, and although Jimmy is only a few feet away, I vigorously massage my cock until one messy explosion douses my chest, but not before I hit my nostril, causing me to spasm and then moan, through my open, smiling mouth, the liquid of it dripping inside. I lick my lips, stand and proceed to take a long shower, forcing the young bellman to wait almost twenty more minutes before receiving his well-earned tip.

When I finish with my shower, I exit, and standing just outside the tub but inside the bathroom, I bark, "Jimmy, sorry to keep you waiting. Take ten dollars out of my jacket on the bed. Then, send a bottle of a fine wine to the same person you just telegrammed. With a small card showing my name. Keep the change. Hurry back."

"Yes, sir!" he says, taking a moment before scurrying out the door.

Alone, towel around my waist, I verify: he took exactly ten dollars from my jacket.

Chapter Twenty-One

"Return of the Octopus"

"Our menu this evening," our diminutive waiter begins pretentiously, though in no particular foreign accent, "starts with your selection of Fresh Crab Cake Cocktail or Supreme of Grape Fruit Delores, accompanied with Celery Hearts, Crissinis, and Colossal Olives, but then followed by Creme Favorite or Strained Gumbo, Royal Miramar. For the main course, we are pleased to offer you the following choices: Maryland Soft Shell Crab saute Olympic, Breast of Capon under Glass Blackstone, Sirloin or Tenderloin Steak Broiled with fresh Mushrooms, Baked Smithfield Ham Garnie Matignon, Hearts of Sweetbreads grilled Montebello. The main course you may pair with either New Succotash or Demi French Potatoes, in addition to our Salad en Saison. Our menu concludes with Creme Parfait Nesselrode as well as Sunshine Cake, and of course, Cafe Noir."

"Oh my, that's enough to make a girl light up the night sky," 'Olevaivai'olefe'e jokes, showing in her jowls, shoulders and tummy more than a few pounds since I last saw her. Nothing for me to say, of course. Clearing her throat, she sings, "I'll order a Caesar's Salad, with extra anchovies, please. Oh, and what is the restaurant wine recommendation?"

"We recommend, this evening, a 1935 Chateau Grand Puy Lacoste."

"French. Lovely. Yes, wine and just a salad, please. Maybe some Sunshine Cake, afterwards."

"Very good, madam. And you, sir?"

"Can you bring out a pizza?"

The waiter raises an eyebrow but otherwise stands motionless. "A 'pizza', sir?" I nod quietly. "Sir, may I request you choose something from our menu?"

I remove a dirty ten dollar bill from my plain brown suit jacket and place it on the table, without answering our waiter's question.

"Sir, even if I were to entreat our chef to accommodate your request, there is the added obstacle of preparation time, with regard to making the dough."

I place another ten on the table. "Your chef's got crissinis, right? So, set aside a ball of dough from the crissini dough, flatten it out to a disk, smother in olive oil, add tomatoes, some colossal olives, mushrooms, ham, and toss on some anchovies, too. Should bake thirty minutes, tops." 'Olevaivai'olefe'e and I nod at each other, while I stuff the currency in the waiter's sweaty hand.

"Very good, sir."

As he backs away from the table, I add, "Oh, and bring two bottles of the Puy Lacoste."

"Yes, sir," he acknowledges.

"What a classy hotel..." I kid, causing 'Olevaivai'olefe'e to beam with amusement then press out the wrinkles in her red evening dress.

After a long moment of silence between us, she asks me, "What's wrong, manamea?"

I laugh, "Nothing's wrong. Why do you ask?"

"Well, you seem a little blue, and I thought that, as I put our New Year's dinner off for nearly two weeks, you might be upset with me."

I shake my head, "Oh, not at all. Nothing of the sort. I've kept myself busy with this and that." In fact, I spent most of my days sleeping in mornings, wandering the Pike, and visiting Ocean Avenue's new drinking establishments, alone.

Fiddling with her small, green silk handbag, she coyly explains, "Captain McKelvy once again extended his leave, and well..."

"...Don't be silly," I interject. "It's just that..."

At that moment, Maria Ordaz unexpectedly passes near our table and releases her hand from the extended arm of a slightly pudgy, but not ugly, suited white gentleman with fiery red hair. Catching our attention, she immediately frees herself and directs her companion to the SkyRoom lounge, and she expresses her intention to join him shortly. "Fe'e? Anthony? What are you two doing here?"

We stand from our seats, and she embraces both of us and pecks cheeks. "Maria!" we both exclaim, and invite her to take a seat at our table, while I scurry to retrieve a chair resting a couple feet away to accommodate her. She accepts the invitation, but begs, "Oh, I have only a few minutes, so..."

"...Life is pieces of dreams, anyway," 'Olevaivai'olefe'e opines, causing me to reflect on the wisdom inside her trite smalltalk. "What have you been up to, Maria? It's been too long. You look delicious in that dress."

"Thanks, Fe'e." Maria looks at me, "And you! Look at you, Anthony. Last I heard you were in Tijuana."

"I was," I admit, bringing my closed fist to my mouth and coughing. "But, I've come back."

"To Long Beach?" Maria asks.

"Why not?" I realize that, although her brothers definitely know I have returned, they may not have told her, I suspect, to keep her happy.

"It's just that, anywhere you..." she pauses. "Oh, nevermind. It's good to see you. Welcome back."

"Thank you," I respond. "What are you doing these days?"

She sighs a long time, and stares at 'Olevaivai'olefe'e. "You look lovely, dear."

"Thank you," 'Olevaivai'olefe'e turns her eyes down, humbly. "I'm doing well."

Maria turns her attention back to me. "Anthony, it's been too long, truly. Well, I stopped working for the longest time. The earthquake took quite an emotional toll. But, after awhile, I decided to go to trade school, and about a year ago, I became a secretary to a bank manager... widowed... here in Long Beach. After work, every so often, we go dancing, and he takes me out dining on Friday evenings such as this. Strictly on the up and up. No shenanigans, as he likes to say. He loves the SkyRoom. Such a generous, upstanding member of the community. Oh, where are my... What a surprise to see both of you here tonight."

"Yes," I say, studying her face, slightly aged, though still her eyes radiate their old glow, and her fingernails, and general hygiene, have lost any trace of defects evident in the first grips of the Depression. "We should make an effort to spend time at the Pike."

"That reminds me," Maria says. "I have so much to tell you. It's almost too much. Solstice..." she starts to say, before I quickly interrupt her.

"...What about her? She must be such a beautiful, young woman."

"Yeah, she's about... what, nineteen years old now?" Maria takes my hand into hers. "She's... she's eloped, Anthony."

To my complete surprise, I feel my skin turn pimpled, shocked with the news. "But..."

Nodding, 'Olevaivai'olefe'e interjects, "Oh, Anthony. Like you said, a beautiful, young woman, eh?"

"With whom? Where?" I beg Maria for answers to my urgent questions.

"I don't know to where, maybe Portland or Seattle, or even Vancouver maybe? With some college senior at the Lutheran college. I think his name was Cody, or something. It happened just this past Christmas, all of a sudden, without any promise of her return. I only know because she asked me to give you something before she left, saying she couldn't wait for you forever. A deck of cards."

"SkyRoom"

Though I feel a tinge of sadness, and perhaps deeper disappointment that I failed to see Solstice Meridian before her departure, I smile, thinking about her homemade, fortune-teller cards she made earlier in the decade. Perhaps Solstice never quite let go of her younger self. Perhaps she felt Cody was in her deck of cards. In any case, her act of arson may have scarred her as a girl, but it failed to keep her from taking the chance to make herself happy as a woman. And whether that chance she took for herself will prove rewarding or not, presently it no longer involves my confidences, and that realization immediately brings feelings of happiness. "I see. Well, I wish her only the best. Hopefully, one day, then," I struggle to find the right words to say, recognizing the coldness in my awkward response. It seems normal this feeling of detachment from former intimates.

"But that's not all the news I have for you, Anthony. Oh, I'm so glad to see you. There's so much more to tell. We need to talk, soon."

Interrupting, 'Olevaivai'olefe'e asks Maria, "More? You mean, you're the one who needs tell him about Ruth?"

"You know about Ruth, Fe'e?" Maria asks.

"Of course, Maria. Don't be such a cannibal, eating up all the gossip for yourself, girl." Maria plants her two fists on either side of her waist. "Who told you?"

"Solstice, I bet," I guess. "This Ruth, she had an Easterner's accent?"

'Olevaivai'olefe'e acts shocked and questions me, "How did you know?"

"Mind reading," I reply tersely, sarcastically, eager to learn more.

Maria leans closer in to reveal, "But what you probably don't know, Anthony... or Fe'e, ahem... is that Solstice convinced this Ruth person to entrust me, specifically, to return something to you that is very, very important, Anthony, if I should ever see you again."

I look at 'Olevaivai'olefe'e and clear my throat.

'Olevaivai'olefe'e glares at Maria, "Noted."

Maria, if she wanted, could stand up from her chair and leave a number where I could reach her. Instead, she waits, silently, twiddling her thumbs, expecting me to inquire further.

"Oh, tell us already, Maria," 'Olevaivai'olefe'e chides. "You know you want to."

The business secretary leans in close to me, and I follow suit. "Fe'e, Anthony, she left..."

"...Yes?" I follow, impatient with her pausing.

"A large yellowish envelope with..."

'Olevaivai'olefe'e whines, "Oh girl, just say it!"

Maria whispers, "Several thousand dollars in it."

"Several?" I ask, startled, as I pull back.

'Olevaivai'olefe'e questions her, "Did you count it?"

"Eight thousand," Maria mouths, without aspirating her words.

I stick up eight fingers to confirm, and Maria nods.

"Precisely eight? Not seven-thousand-nine-hundred-and-ninety-five, or eight-thousand-and-five, or whatever?" 'Olevaivai'olefe'e chides aloud, crossing her arms, skeptically, but the gossip continues nodding as before. "What is this about? Who is this Ruth person, is what I want to know?"

Maria pulls back in her chair. "But that's not all, Anthony. It is what I saw, with my own two eyes, that Ruth wrote on the envelope that is also interesting."

The waiter at this point returns to our table to serve the first bottle of wine. He asks if we will be needing a third glass at our table, for Maria's enjoyment, but she declines the offer and stands up, excusing herself, saying she must join her employer patiently expecting her company in the lounge.

"Wait!" I say, begging her to remain for just a moment before leaving. "When did this happen? Where did she go? What did it say?"

The waiter serves the open wine bottle into our two glasses and then departs. 'Olevaivai'olefe'e notices the eagerness in my questions and turns to reproach me quietly, "Don't get sweaty, Anthony."

"It happened a couple months before Solstice eloped." I feel puzzled. "Ruth then just returned to New York?"

Maria stares at the ceiling, "She said she was moving to San Francisco."

"What did it say, on the envelope?" I ask again.

Maria turns the corner of her lips into a knowing smile, and while leaving the dining area, she turns her head in my direction to say, "She wrote something, my brother Rafael says, that appears to be in Hebrew."

Inappropriately, 'Olevaivai'olefe'e turns the conversation, after Maria disappears into the direction of the SkyRoom lounge. "You want to smoke later, Anthony, huh?" she whispers.

"Fe'e, please," I decline.

"Fēfē! Are you going to tell me who's this Ruth person, manamea? Manamea?"

I stare at my glass of wine, not responding. There is a temptation to become lost in thought, engrossed in my self-reflections, in the middle of a dinner that was supposed to be something else, something lighter. "Hmm." I had planned to reach Rafael soon, but now I reconsider that intention, uncertain how quite to proceed.

"Manamea, darling. What's wrong?"

"Suddenly, I don't feel...," I try to say. "...I don't feel like eating."

"Well, let's at least grab the bottle you paid for, and we'll enjoy a dinner here another day. Let's head out for the Villa Riviera and talk," she offers, kindly laying her fingers on my forearm, and gently massaging my wrist, before I stand up from my seat and walk towards the elevator, as she follows, wine bottle and green handbag in tow.

* * *

"There we were in the SkyRoom, and I was thinking, finally, to hell with Anthony's poverty and live for today, and then after the name 'Ruth' appears, you got all sad and looking for comfort like a little boy, Anthony. Now, I don't think anyone should have to keep this all inside, but Lord knows, if you came to me, Anthony Camarrata, penniless, hungry and homeless, I would have happily showed you the curb. So, how is it, you give yourself some happiness putting yourself up at the Hilton, but cannot even eat a meal upon hearing the name 'Ruth'?"

I stare a long time out the window, through the late, winter dusk settling over the Pacific, not thinking about Ruth so much, but about Abraham, and the coincidence of eight thousand dollars finding its way back to me, after leaving the same amount with Rafael shortly before leaving for Tijuana not quite five years earlier. "You set this all up tonight, Fe'e. You set this up tonight, because you knew Maria would be at the SkyRoom tonight and might tell me about Solstice." My bluff.

'Olevaivai'olefe'e admits, smiling, "Too bright, you are. Yes. But, I didn't know about the envelope with the Hebrew on it and eight-thousand dollars inside. And I still don't know who Ruth is. Nobody does, as far as I know. More wine?"

"Yes," I answer, holding my empty glass out towards her. I feel my ego collapsing, a cauldron of emotions bubbling to the surface, the impulse to speak stifled only by my need to maintain composure, a sense of decorum in her apartment. "Where's McKelvy?" I ask, breaking my brooding silence.

She walks some steps to the corner of the room, and she returns, sticking a short, automatic firearm straight up into the air but in a rather casual, comfortable pose. "The Captain has returned to duty, his extended leave was granted then cancelled after a couple of weeks. He took a plane to Pearl Harbor, Honolulu. Why?"

"Why don't you go with him, Fe'e?"

"I'm not a fan so much of flying these days, with my utter disappointment in Charles Lindbergh, that damn Nazi traitor, and the disappearance of Amelia Earhart, I don't believe in flying anymore." She returns the weapon whence it came. "I might take a boat over there this summer. We'll see. We should all use boats and trains from now on. Oh, you're bringing me down, again, Anthony. Tell me what's going on and don't make me cry."

I confess, "I'm in a mess, you might say."

"What kind of mess?" she peers, squinting her eyes.

"A messy mess."

"Auē, valea... palagi. Is this about Tijuana?"

"It... " I pause a long time, while she patiently waits for her answer. "It..."

"I don't want a lot of drama, a lot of chatter. Just say it, what it is. In a sentence," 'Olevaivai'olefe'e scolds.

"I can't... in a sentence."

"Try."

"I can't, even if I wanted."

"Want It!"

I struggle for words, simple words—a concise, economical expression of the most deep, recurring feelings. The only impulse I register is numbness. "I can't, Fe'e. Just, listen. If you're going to do this, then let me talk, please."

"Thank you for the reefer gifts, but honestly... you're so selfish, Anthony," she declares, standing up from her sofa and heading into her bedroom. "If you expect me to share your gift with you, you have a lot of nerve. But if it will open you up and calm you down, without blah blah blah forever, then, here," she directs me to enjoy one of the rolled up fatties on top her glass table, as she approaches me sitting on the sofa. I take it, sit back, as she retrieves matches from the coffee table, and lights me up. "There, valea. You would think one day that doctors will get paid for the work I'm doing for you, for free. What am I saying? They do."

"Your resentment is palpable."

"That's because you white people are such a burden. Always blah blah blah, spending money, and expecting the rest of us to take care of you, like you're babies." She seats herself in a chair next to the sofa.

I inhale deeply, my spine falling back into the cushions, my legs growing heavy, my mind at once turning calm but also registering racing thoughts, emotions arising from a deadly past I have tried everything to forget becoming a complete, perfect stranger to myself and everyone else, in a comedy, a farce, a fierce farce. I feel exhausted.

"Better?" 'Olevaivai'olefe'e asks, genuinely.

"No. Well, sort of."

"Which?"

"Then, yes."

"Superb. So, before you start, I want dinner at the SkyRoom once a week, at least until the summer season starts, when I won't be caught dead in the Hilton with all those tourists. Agreed?"

"Return of the Octopus"

I calculate in my head the expenses implied by her request, multiplying some numbers and coming to the conclusion that I will still be solvent through that time. Then I realize, that is perhaps the purpose of her request of many dinner reservations. "Good one, Fe'e. Yes, I have enough to get me through till then and beyond then, in fact. So, yes, 'agreed.' But, I suspect you were wondering whether I have a long-term plan, which I do."

"So, Tijuana wasn't all that much of a disaster," she counters.

I realize her insights are helping slightly. "True, it was only five years of my life," I retort, emphasizing the word "only," to signal my surprise at her lack of evident sympathy. "But this news about Ruth is causing unexpected concern."

"Because you weren't predicting some New York woman reappearing in your life," she asserts causing me to nod, after ingesting once more one of the last three jazz cigarettes I personally imported for her as gifts, from Baja. My fa'afāfine concludes, "That could only mean one thing."

"Her husband. The one..." I start to say.

"...who got away," she finishes. " 'Auē."

"Ruth's husband."

"So, what is your long-term plan, Anthony?"

"Insurance."

"Insurance?"

"Insurance. Like a salesman, a broker, an investigator... something like that. Licensed, bonded, legit. I figure I have enough for some tuition, start my associate's maybe at the university in Los Angeles, and a little to open a small office, here, in Long Beach. And enough to take you out to dinner through June, but April would be better."

"April?" 'Olevaivai'olefe'e studies me, passing the reefer, which I take. "Insurance. Well, then, that's it. No more Cornero's corner?"

"Out," I emphasize, gesturing with my hands dramatically.

"And Tijuana?"

"That's the thing, Fe'e. I was forced to sell all my business interests there, including my interests in Cornero's operations."

"Forced... ?"

"To some Filipino millionaire shipping mogul."

"Cornero knows him?"

I inhale a long time. "No, he doesn't. I'm supposed to facilitate an introduction." Exhaling, I pass the smoke to her, but she declines, so I keep enjoying it, growing more comfortable, and leaning now to the side, in her sofa. "It doesn't matter if Cornero doesn't know this shipping mogul at the moment, since I've been cut out from Tijuana already anyway."

" 'Cut out', you say." After reflecting on our conversation for a long minute, 'Olevaivai'olefe'e concludes, "All of this because of a five-year-old, dirty comic book?" And here in our conversation I recognize the gap between what I will allow myself to talk about, and what I know to be the deadly truth of things. She continues, " 'Oka, 'oka, 'oka. I should have invited my nephew in Honolulu to visit you, years ago. Preacher's kid. Samoan and German. He was studying to be a missionary at that time in '33 or thereabouts, but... maybe not..."

"... so then, maybe not."

"'Auē!'"

"I'm just saying, Fe'e, 'Maybe not'."

'Olevaivai'olefe'e ponders, "So, you think Ruth is a sign of things to come?"

I breathe heavily, anxiously sinking in the sofa, connecting with feelings long buried and believed forgotten. "How could I know?"

"You need to get out of Cornero's corner, whatever you are going to do, whoever comes your way. I hope you aren't so naive to believe he's going to be happy with you just giving his business to some stranger, when he was favoring you, expecting you to represent and protect him. If he's disappointed, or anyone he reports to is, or feeling double-crossed, Anthony, he won't just go after you, he'll go after anyone you associate with."

"I felt I had no choice."

"Really?"

"Water under the bridge at this point. Look, I'm trying to draw attention by living beyond my means in the Hilton, so he'll want to interview me directly," I argue, placing the last, unused portion of her reefer smoldering on the foot of the empty wine glass resting on the table in front of me.

"Well, maybe weekly dinner reservations with you aren't necessary," she advises, half-joking and yet, ominously, half-seriously.

I concur, "Maybe not."

"Hmm," she replies. "So, who is Ruth? Or better yet, who is her husband?"

"I thought I knew," I admit my ignorance, honestly.

She nods her head slowly, calculating, "Yes, I see that. But is he worth it, Anthony? I mean, would you forego any other alliance you might create just to make it with some married man, because he's that important if he did return to your life, somehow? Getting Cornero out of your way may be hard, but not impossible. Neither he nor his boss, Jack Dragna, are particularly liked by law enforcement, or by California's politicians. It might turn out, one day, that US military patience with gambling ships could be running out. Gossips claim poker makes borders insecure, that sort of thing."

Intrigued, I reflect upon her conversation, taking inventory of the possibilities, not wanting to settle into something blatantly dishonest, foolishly impractical or blindly repetitious. The only other ally available, and if I were true to myself I would have to admit that I do not even know whether my thoughts are simply fanciful, is Rafael, who shows only the slightest interest, maybe, in some alliance that could possibly endure. "Ruth's husband was once that important, but maybe, now, I would just be kidding myself."

"Maybe you are," she says, crossing her legs. "So?"

"So... what?"

She grows impatient. "Anthony, I mean, 'so nobody else'?"

I stutter, "Raf... Rafael Ordaz, but..."

Chapter Twenty-Two

"Anxieties of Influences"

"Yes?"

"Good morning, Mr. Camarrata. We apologize for disturbing you, but..."

"...my clock reads almost five in the morning!"

"Yes, we do apologize, but our front desk has received a phone call from someone claiming to be your attorney, in New York City? Mr. Camarrata, are you there?"

"Yes."

"Would you care to take the call at this time, sir? The Gentleman, Mr. Katza, has requested that we convey to you it's most urgent that he speak with you. Hello?"

"I'm here."

"Would you care to take the call at this time, Mr. Camarrata?"

"Hold on. Alright. Yes. But, wait. Wait! Operator? Hello? Yes, as you are aware Mr. Katza is my attorney, you will observe the strictest confidentiality and immediately terminate your telephone connection to ours. Do we have an understanding?"

"Of course, Mr. Camarrata. As a professional representative of Hilton Hotels, I ask that you allow me to express our recognition of your loyalty to our company. We value your patronage. You may enjoy utter confidence that we will respect your wishes and faithfully defend your privacy and security."

"Thank you. Yes, this is Anthony. Operator? Operator?"

"We are alone, Tony. Good morning."

"I don't know whether I shall call you Abe, or... your proper name, 'Abraham'."

"I should not have terminated our lease so soon. What we had was good, up to a certain point. We should have swerved in a different direction, together. To California, together."

"Right to the point, is it? I should have put a time limit in my letter begging for your return."

"This isn't starting right."

"How should it start, then?"

"Like we're on a stage. There must exist some exit lines for this sort of thing. Somebody must have written this dialogue for stage sometime, somewhere. In a modernist piece, all disjointed and chaotic, like a Cubist portrait. Or maybe something like Picasso or Brecht. Something Germans would call 'degenerate'... oder yiddishe."

"Art makes for trite talk. I think I choose to address you as 'Abraham', for now..."

"Huh. Does love always have to be a search?"

"Oh, I see, of course. I was wondering how you tracked me down, and now I realize: skip search. You did a skip search."

"You weren't that hard to find, Tony."

"I don't need your help, Abraham. Is that what you want to know? Is this phone call about your help?"

"Transcontinental"

"I could no longer help you and that is why I needed to see you help yourself. I might have been open to retaining the terms of our arrangement, but only upon another basis, as though, originally, I had failed to go far enough."

"To go far enough?"

"You're referring to the skip trace, Tony? I mean, it's hard to tell what you're talking about, since you sound confused a bit."

"I sound confused? Funny."

"A bit."

"Look. When my letter begged for your return, I didn't mean hiring a private investigator followed by your calling my telephone."

"You expected me simply to write a letter in reply."

"If you want to admit to a lack of imagination about it."

"What are you doing, staying in a hotel, anyway? The Hilton, after all, Tony? It's like you have become somebody somehow different. What's going on?"

"I've been inside this hotel a month, and I'm out next week, starting a course or two at the University of California at Los Angeles, renting a room over at Craftsman Village in Long Beach. You? You hid inside Ruth for years."

"I see."

"Abraham, you're the one who called me. And you called me, to tell me I've become somebody different? I seem confused to you, then you say you failed to go far enough? What are you talking about? You're the one not making any sense."

"I… "

"… We failed to go far enough. We did? 'We', you say? Like you and Ruth, that sort of 'We'?"

"It all seems so conflictual to you. Aren't you exhausted, Tony?"

"Now you have me laughing at five in the fucking morning, prick. Exhausted. Ha!"

"Indeed."

"Abraham, do you really want to know what is going on, or are you going to protect yourself first, always making me out as some sort of opaque mystery. Is that what you need? Mystery? Mystery to yourself? Mystery to women. Just be, just listen. Just shut up."

"I… "

"… you fucking talk too much, Abraham. Too many words."

"Me, too many? Who wrote the letter, Mr. Camarrata?"

"And?"

"And, so, Tony, which one of us uses too many words? Is that who you've been all along, a big spender of prosaic words, like they're currency, off the gold standard and just circulating like little whorish symbols of fiat nothingness? Do you even care to learn what the words in your letter did?"

"Last I recall, Abraham? Last I recall, in your reply, you wrote you were at a loss for words. So, message received. Mystery solved. My words did nothing."

"They did everything. They caused such silence. It got to the point where Ruth and I were hardly speaking. Much of the decade I spent in near silence."

"The silence of Ruth, Abraham?"

"Anthony, Ruth, and Boris and Mila, too."

"Pity the lawyer. I can only imagine. What do you want me to say? You want me to say 'sorry', to apologize? Or, do you want me to be ruthless, hang up the phone, cut off all possibility of communication?"

"Some sympathy, please, Anthony. Boris and Mila?"

"I'm no longer somebody's child, Abraham. And, I did not produce issue, I'm pretty sure. No, I'm certain. I'm neither a father nor a child, Abraham. Where does that leave me in your estimation? Am I on the inside of your world? The outside of it? Or, am I bitter as I seem barren?"

"Too conflictual, again."

"Yes, oppositional, almost obstructionist."

"Like a psychologist."

"Precisely."

"There's a melody to our conversation, as though I should be able to predict next what you are going to say."

"And what is that, Abraham?"

"You seem to circle back to your letter. It's becoming a habit of our conversation."

"What is the use of pointing that out to me? Is Abraham Katza trying to make Anthony Camarrata feel guilty for writing a love letter? Is that what you need? Some sentimental framework to interpret my words? Like some patterned grid of emotions fixing the coordinates of my utterances? My mysteriousness never ends."

"Maybe it does end. I have been offered a law teaching position, part-time, at the University of Southern California. Anthony, I don't know if you can understand, but I need to be close to my children."

"Why not all the way to San Francisco, Abraham, for yourself?"

"Too close. Ruth needs independence, from me."

"A whole state? There's Berkeley, too. And Palo Alto."

"If need be, Anthony. It's USC for now. So, therefore, I don't want to mystify anything about me. But that is why I had to find you. I need to know."

"What, Abraham?"

"About some things."

"Such as..."

"Tony, I never invited Dr. Parks. Ruth made me invite him. Psychology was a mistake."

"It was childish of me to write you an earnest love letter in the first place."

"How does that follow?"

"Psychology was a mistake, you say, Abraham? You picked psychology over me. And where did that get you? I can't... psychology... a mistake. Why didn't I think of that?"

"How could I have asked you for help then? How could I? You couldn't even help yourself, and you expect me to have asked you for help in the form of advice, judgment, or even experience?"

"Experience. Ha! A childish love letter... do you see now why I say 'childish', Abraham?"

"You're too hard on yourself, Anthony."

"Maybe I should end this call, then."

"Hear me out, please, for at least as long as your letter. This call is my reply to you. At long last. You should feel relieved. That I cared. That I remembered. Maybe it seems like a speech to you, but it's what you wanted, at one time. It's what you asked for. Your offer seemed... open for good. I took that to heart. Don't break it now. Not yet. I'm not ready."

"You're afraid, vulnerable."

"And what if I am, Anthony Camarrata? The world is too rough. I hardly survived Prohibition. God knows what's around the corner."

"That's funny, Abe."

" 'Abe', you say? Good, I like that. Yes, 'Abe'. Like when we were boys."

"Like when we were men, Abraham. Young men. Our bodies were strong. We could rrrrroger the whole night... back then. All I wanted was you. When we were men."

"Boys, Tony. Boys pretending to be men."

"Damn cocksucker. Now, you got to bring up Joe the orphan kid, don't you? Just got to bring that up. What about him?"

"Tony, let me be clear. I wasn't talking about Joe."

"Sure you weren't. And even if you really weren't... Even if I... for all I know, you're just expecting me to still need your mercy. But, I don't."

"You're holding something inside, Tony."

"I don't need your mercy, Abraham. In the end, Ruth didn't need your mercy, although I wonder, did you need hers? Is that how she took you back, as an act of her mercy?"

"Conflictual!"

"Okay, fine. I'll get off it, Abe."

"Tony, in those days, I was keeping care of you in an imperfect way, because I didn't see then we had something more deep and far beyond whatever we actually started."

"I, too, have a tendency for the dramatic, hence the letter."

"See? There."

"I do, Abe."

"I know."

"I only admit that, because you are talking about imperfection."

"Tony, if I could have, I would have done it all differently, made better decisions about Ruth and my children, decisions requiring work and commitment and time. But, I failed as a father. It is my eternal shame."

"I don't think you quite failed, Abraham. You covered your tracks pretty well. A lack of publicity about our sort of affair defers quick disaster."

"In one sense, you're quite right to imply I've enjoyed a successful private life by some measure. But in another sense, there is a relentless opportunism to my keeping such secrets, but before you ask, I'll tell you that the sort of opportunism I mean is not the financial kind... "

".... Although, surely you appreciate that was one factor affecting the decisions you made."

"Perhaps, yes, I see that more clearly now, as much as it hurts to admit it. There is my selfishness in all this. But the opportunism I mean is the emotional one. The false allure of ego, of pride, as if by honoring the duty to my family I can compensate for the dereliction of duty to myself."

"Abe, you sound utterly unhappy."

"I want to change that, Tony. Sending me the money as you did showed me I needed to change. More than your letter. I can imagine the deep effort it took to acquire that, and then for you to forego using it was equally as difficult."

"That you didn't keep the money says much, to me."

"The funny thing is that not keeping it was Ruth's idea. I needed to take my time to decide what exactly to do with it. I hid it, for years, until finally it was discovered by Ruth, accidentally. You can imagine the questions she asked. I might have showed her your letter, but when I looked for it after she found the money, I discovered it was gone from its hiding place, too. As it turns out, she discovered your letter some years before the money. The timing of these events had the effect of slowly evaporating her confidence in me, until finally hopeless…I'm placing the children on a plane for San Francisco next week, so they may join their mother, a development I regrettably failed to prevent in court."

"I listen to you, Abraham Katza, patiently. And I think, there's plenty of time for you to find happiness for yourself, wherever that is, however that is, but before you dive into California."

"You're suggesting I should not take the teaching position."

"No, not yet."

"You are my last prayer, Anthony. I am purging myself of everything, even what came before."

"Instead of responding to the letter, you should have just masturbated to it, and be done with it."

"Such vulgarity."

"I'm making a joke, counselor. Lighten up."

"Ain't so easy."

"If you find it hard to lighten up, you might start with stop praying and stop purging."

"There is wisdom in ancient things, and wisdom brings me comfort."

"I'm not interested in your traditions and clichés. You can have them, but they are not mine."

"I need you, Tony."

"What do you need from me, exactly, Abe? Parts of me? Which parts of me? Or, all of me? Do I get to know that you accept all of me? Do I even get the chance to reveal all of me?"

"I need all of you, Tony."

"You don't even know all of me, Abe. You don't."

"I believe I do."

"You don't."

"I believe you know all of me, or nearly so."

"Perhaps I do, but that doesn't mean you know all of me."

"It doesn't?"

"No. Too sentimental."

"Sentimental?"

"Sentimental."

"I care too much about you to call it 'sentimental'. It has been decided: I'm moving to Los Angeles. There's no two ways about that. Now, I would like to see you. And I will make that clear to you, until you tell me to stop."

"Stop."

"May I talk, please? Well, not hearing your answer, I give you notice that I shall assume your silence implies your consent to my talking."

"And I'm the conflictual one."

"I just want to see you. Any mention of companionship would be premature to introduce into conversation."

"Not premature. Impossible."

"Nothing is impossible, Anthony."

"Exactly. Nothing is. And what nothing is, is impossible. There's nothing to see one another about."

"You're so definitive. At the very least, are you alright? Is there something that my lawyerly advice and protection would satisfy?"

"Lawyerly protection? And what of Ruth finding my hidden letter, then, or is that to be overlooked? Should be disbarred."

"Tony, I burned the letter. It no longer exists. What Ruth knows is of little consequence."

"What she knows led her to bring me eight thousand dollars, unexpectedly."

"The events described in the letter took place in New York. Over a decade ago. But, look now. We're all talking about California right now."

"It's half-past five, Abraham."

"At times, I imagine we are speaking, on the telephone, across the country, from New York to California, and for a moment, I feel at a distance what I recall feeling in your arms on those nights I was suckling, in our apartment in Greenwich Village right before the depression took off. There was no animosity or hostility. An even cadence and volume. Soft and gentle spoken words. Acts of mutual... hypnotism."

"Do you know one of the things I admire about you most, Abraham? It is your near perfect nationalism, as though it binds everything in your world, making it whole, complete. But are you not, to any slight degree, at least ambivalent about such feelings? Do you not have any doubts about your visions and fantasies you so casually share on transcontinental telephone lines?"

"I know who I am, and where I come from."

"I see. And what if I don't, precisely? At least not in the same way as you."

"It doesn't matter."

"At all, Abe?"

"For the most part."

"Hypothetically, if a man died at my hands? Hello? You there?"

"Sometimes, it isn't easy holding on to feelings for you, Anthony. There's part of me that wants to push you away, not because I hate myself, but because I am a father. I couldn't begin to explain to my children the amoral universe you seem to inhabit."

"It's not precisely amoral… "

" … But, I would still defend you in court, at risk to my reputation, if I thought it would genuinely help. Regardless, I would still deign to talk to you, to recognize you and not abandon you. I know your heart. If you killed a man, you likely believe it happened after reflection, and even if it didn't, any impulsive action you took likely reflected what is always most enduringly good about you. That's how I think of it, as a soldier who fought in one war, shooting into the darkness, into fog, not seeing where the bullets landed, or who they hit. The war hospitals, the desire to relieve suffering to the end. I admit with near certainty to having killed, and I can quantify my doubts, mathematically. But my heart can sense the compulsion of destruction, and acceptance of that is something beyond interpretation."

"I'm not talking about sin."

"You needn't be so defensive. Nobody's talking about sin. Oooh…"

"What's that, Abe?"

"Go on… "

"I'm not satisfied by your tidy values."

"What would satisfy you? Is it possible my shelter for your feelings could satisfy you, as you take this path back to school. That's what we should have done in New York."

"Education."

"You say that with some condescension… Anthony…"

"A means to an end."

"Openness to learning is the end."

"See, Abe? Yes, you believe that. But, me? What do I believe? There was a time I believed that you and I were supposed to be the end, until the end."

"Tony, let me ask you something. Tell me, what are you going to do with the eight thousand, now that you have it back?"

"I guess I could put down on a home, or maybe hire a lawyer. Or tithe."

"Ha! Tithe to whom?"

"To the Roman pantheon."

"To what?"

"Yeah, I'm thinking 'Jupiter Insurance' as a fictitious business name. Maybe 'Venus Insurance'… Abe, are you breathing heavily into the phone?"

"Yes… Uggh!"

"Abraham Katza, you dirty, old man. How dare you rub one out while we're talking on the phone."

"It started when you said the word, 'masturbation'. I couldn't help it. Your voice, it provokes a hefty bone. I couldn't help myself. Can you?"

" 'Can I help myself', is that what you're asking, Abe?"

"Yes."

"I can be frugal, yes. I am, when it suits me."

"And right now, does it suit you, helping yourself, alone in your bed, in that hotel room?"

"You paid for a skip trace, so you could hear me moan into the phone?"

"I'm coming... to California, Tony."

"I bet you are."

"Tony, …"

" ... Abraham... "

"We never ended. We always were. We can write whatever story we want. Even whatever story about our past."

"Oh? How's this one: that letter caused your tongue to reach for me, so your ears could hear these lips renounce everything I ever felt about you."

"I don't care, Tony. I'm still coming."

"Hold on. Hold on! Whoaaa! Yeah, fuck yeah. Fuck! Ugggh. Fuck."

"Tony?"

"Thanks, Jimmy. Why don't you hit the shower, boy? Yes, Abraham, what is it?"

"What? What... was that?"

"I don't beat my meat, Abe. I pay the bellboy to vacuum it with his pretty mouth."

"I can't imagine."

"In fact, Abe, I very much believe that you can't imagine."

"I don't care. I'm still coming back."

"And I don't care you are."

"I can't believe that. I won't believe that."

"We've spoken ourselves into oblivion. You've had your say enough. I heard your reply to my letter enough. You no longer are at a loss for words, Abraham. It is clear to me now what you want. You have completely given your plans away. I can predict nearly your every move from this point going forward. Los Angeles is a big city..."

" ... Anthony... "

"... There's room enough here for both of us. You have the right to live, clearly. So do I. So, you've decided to come out to California. Welcome. Good for you. Enjoy your stay. I hope you find what you're looking for. But I don't see the point of continuing this conversation, which has lasted probably too long. I don't have much confidence in you, Abraham. Decide what you need to do, then do it. Hopefully, it will all just work out for the best. How could I take away your hope? It's all you have left, having purged yourself of nearly everything and everyone else..."

" ... Anthony... "

" ... What more is there to say? I hope all the best for you. I do. Is there anything else, counselor? No more words? Hearing none, I think we can find a polite end to this call at this point, yes?"

"But... "

"Don't blame me, Abe. Your mind is your partner. Please, I think it's time we stop."

"Hugs, Anthony."

"Good bye, Abraham. Hello? Hello... ?"

"Tony's Boner"

Chapter Twenty-Three

"Tango Showboat Texas Rex"

As I examine my feelings from the perspective of a man twice the age of his classroom peers pledging some fraternity, or sorority, I must admit my vanity somewhat blemished towards the end of my first semester at the university (which, by the way, I learned later conferred passing grades in both my classes: "Applied Mathematics" and "Law of Agency"). When I realized I would not hear from Tony Cornero in any likely version of the future, I birthed a little crush, leaving to fantasy speculations that Cornero might yank me back into the world of men my age, in their forties, a world populated with pawns exuding an appropriate gravitas. Though disappointed, I remain determined to do nearly anything except pretending to be a young lifeguard defending the city's beaches, as I had six summers ago.

The temptation to survive upon eight thousand unwanted dollars, or at least some portion of it, weighs heavily upon me. A substantial portion of my ruminations is preoccupied with my act that led to this gift returned. Perhaps I was too hasty keeping but a sliver of the larger honorarium on my way to Tijuana, but as it seemed at the time, I left with the feeling I had earned a profit, rightly or wrongly, and returned with a certain sense of having paid some sort of debts to Abraham and the cosmos, too, living and working in Baja.

When I appear to myself glib speaking like this, I consider the earlier facts of my dying and medical revival. I consider these as unpredictable, random events, and therefore, I ask myself why repayments of debt should be valued at all in a modern, relativistic view of things, and then I think about the earthquake and how much balance and equilibrium were valued during that crisis. Suddenly, I intuit that eight grand could be put to some better use than satisfying my immediate desires, a better use such as my opening my own business. That's precisely when I battle the temptation to enjoy some portion of my stash, a temptation born of the delusion that I am riding powerful surf, and its great momentum will carry me eventually out of its barrel and safely near the shore.

Fortunately, classroom routine brings with it social introductions and offers to attend beer parties held by students in private apartments. Shortly after I vacated the Hilton, I bought a Packer from a dealer specialized in selling previously used vehicles, and have met people who casually cultivate my reputation as a survivor of hard times looking to live an educated life relativistically in equipoise. I also learned, through one neighbor, where exist the best places in Craftsman Village to venture secret love. My favorite is, still, a garage known for pleasureful nighttime liaisons along a wall featuring two small but useful holes, two feet apart, carved out in the vicinity of the pelvis. Sunday is a particularly busy time. Otherwise it's hit or miss there, and that has spawned a few mad scenes, as might easily be imagined.

So, determined to do anything except pretending to be a young lifeguard defending the city's beaches, I found a job in June at the 101 Club, downtown on Pine Street, first as barback, later as weekend bartender, for the first month by just asking around one Saturday night which led to a spontaneous interview, whose highlight consisted of my agreeing to be handcuffed and then spending the next hour searching for, either one specific woman, or any of four specific men in the crowd, without at any point even giving the appearance of running afoul of our shared, decoded understanding about those folks who would enforce the city vice code deceptively. These five targets each permanently own only one copy of the appropriate key to open these cuffs, which belong to the New York City Police Department, but during Teddy Roosevelt's reign as Commissioner, and which are bona fide appraised, therefore, at well over one hundred present dollars, I'm told by Murray Caldwell, the moustached sole proprietor of both the club and the cuffs. He also warned that if I didn't find someone who had the right key before leaving, I would be charged with theft. An hour later, I discovered, or rather I should say, privately, in the loo "earned" one of the keys held by a gentleman, and upon my freedom I received a generous chorus of approbation for being a good scrum and taking a job as a barback.

Despite the desperation which hangs over my mood, my good fortune in finding work alleviates the temptation to yield to short-term pleasure over long-term interests. In fact, Club 101 seems very much like a prison. Not only is there the aspect of my physical labor organized according to the interests of the alcohol economy, yet again, but in addition to this sort of servitude, the joy that is possible in this establishment is the joy permitted under an atmosphere of an omnipresent intolerance. Not allowed in the bar are gentle caresses, much less kisses, for fear of undercover vice circulating about. Men and women mingle, but rarely in equal numbers. Friday nights are known to have slightly more women drinking. Saturday nights are known to have more men. And it all functions without explicit coercion, as if everyone knows the rules and voluntarily enforces them, struggling to hold onto what little they already possess in between infrequent raids. T-rooms, of course, are always the exception, so much so that after spending in these sorts of places a couple hundred hours one way or another, I have come to more than tolerate and affirmatively associate pleasurable orgasms with the aroma of urine and feces, and visa versa. For this mediocre piece of civilization, some will fight even the police, who can always be counted on, like a pendulum regularly but occasionally measuring superiors' calculations of supposed inebriated deviants and un-American radicals, enjoying "Over the Rainbow" and "South of the Border" while leaning on an upright piano pushing its rambunctious and semi-plastered talent closer to a red brick wall.

   I resolve to tend bar, on weekends, through the course of my part-time education. Caldwell, as grumpy as he is, does show his sense of taste in personal appearance and the overall character of his establishment, which is dimly lit, but lavished with wood and brass everywhere, gold velvet fabric on seats and chairs. Hewing to this theme, I sport a young bachelor's pose, keeping my hair short and slicked-back with a fragrant smidgen of sandalwood oil. My face stays clean shaven, above various interchangeable cotton collared shirts, and often a light tan jacket or a sweater vest, and wool trousers draped over argyle socks and saddle shoes. College-looking, perhaps professorial. Appropriate, hence inviting.

"After 21st Amendment"

* * *

A short time ago, Rafael Ordaz and I resumed communicating, indirectly. There was a long period of silence between us, and it was only the fact of my crossing paths with Rafael's sister, Maria, at the SkyRoom in the Hilton, back in January, that likely informed him I had definitely returned. If there was anyone who had stayed on my mind, it was Rafael. But I stopped myself from reaching out to him, until first I had resolved what to do about my lack of employment and so forth. Finally, after not hearing from Cornero since my return, and then eventually finding the bartending job, I contacted Maria at the bank where she worked, and she agreed she would let her brother know I wanted to meet him after dinner at the 101 Club on the first Thursday of August.

On the chosen evening, I arrive having snacked a bit before I left campus, and somewhat early, I take advantage of my luck by seating myself alone at a small table, wearing an iteration of my stock clean-cut outfit. After an hour, seats become precious, which means losing solitude, but the end of isolation helps bring me out of myself though a gradual progression of informal social exchanges. Who knows, at some point one of them might even lead to a vivid, rambling conversation, which can be its own pleasure and a welcome distraction, that is until Rafael appears and stands and waits. Or, maybe he just joins right in.

"Seat taken?" a gentleman asks, pulling one of the two chairs out from the table, holding a cocktail in his free hand. "If you don't mind," he says, resting himself, studying my appearance, as I sit stoically, legs crossed at the knees, one hand fiddling with a cocktail, not speaking a word, while he continues. "What are you, drunk or European?" In response I merely sigh. He mumbles, "Ainsi soit-il."

"Is that French?" I ask. "I used to know this lawyer who... "

" ...You say 'lawyer'? Gary's the name," he smiles politely, talks softly. "Look, page one: I'm just trying to relax by myself. That said, if you are offering your company, I wouldn't mind sharing it."

"First time here? Lotsa queers," I venture to interject.

Gary is dressed in his jacket and tie, which appear to be his work clothes. He has a tapered haircut, sandy brown in color, long bangs, and with his right hand he pushes them back, like a confident business type in his thirties. He grins, "I know, isn't it awful, all the pervs? What, are you a cop? To answer your question, it's my second time here."

"A cop?" I snicker. "Ha, no. What are you looking for? Trouble?"

At that moment, a radio on the bar counter blares a tune captivating Gary, who starts humming, then singing, "Ah, ya ya, ya yea-ooh…" At the right moment, he lifts his lips high into the air and screeches at a high pitch, for a couple seconds, "Ee…!" And for a few more seconds, Gary adds his voice when the singer leading the harmonies repeats this high note. Finally, he asks me, "Have you heard this one, yet? Solomon Linda and the Evening Birds. I can't for the life of me remember the name of that tune. On the Hit Parade, though. Alas, oh well. You asked me, 'Looking for trouble?' so, you tell me, do you think that's what I am doing, and by the way, what's your name?"

"Anthony. I bartend here."

Gary pulls back, surprised. "Is that right?" And after I start nodding, he confesses, "Had no idea. I would have guessed tutor or clerk or something like that. Bartender's interesting. So, let me ask you something, bartender Anthony. You recall the seven deadly sins?"

"I sette vizi capitali sono: superbia, avarizia, lussuria, invidia, gola, ira e accidia."

Gary sips his cocktail. "So, you aren't drunk, then."

"Italiano. E voi? Francese?"

"Sadly, no. Marin County. North of San Francisco. I've spent time in Paris, though. Île de la Cité?" Still and stiff as a statue, I yield no reply, causing Gary to stir. After an awkward silence, he studies me skeptically, then asks, "So, if you're bartending, why are you doing it sitting there, hmm?"

"I work Friday's and the next night, and sometimes on Sunday's for private parties."

Gary giggles, before clearing his throat and consciously dropping his voice an octave and an equivalent measure of decibels. "How, excuse me," he apologizes, before gesturing we both lean in together. "Private parties?" I pull back and raise my eyebrows, showing a look of slight surprise and bemusement. He adds, "I mean, if there's room for one more, I wouldn't turn down an invitation."

Gary hardly strikes me as attractive. If he were cast in a movie, he might get a background part, something like a lackey to James Cagney or Edward G. Robinson. Despite this handicap, he carries his voice with a certain subtle mellifluousness, exercising a degree of wit, cutting off my pity or suspicion. I lie, "It's a costume party, for the next Sunday party."

"You going?" he asks, sipping.

"No. I'm the fella to get you in. But in addition to it being a private costume party, there's gonna be a theme."

"I'm free." Gary tilts his head to the side, suddenly skeptical. "Wait, how do you know all this if you're not going?"

"Good question. See, I'm the neutral decider in all this, so they let me, being absent of the group, improvise its theme. Hot, huh?"

Gary leans in close, and I keep still. He asks, "What theme, Anthony? Tell me. I'm happy to bring some mood lifters."

"Some discretion, Gary." I wait, pretending to mull over a decision while Gary fidgets. "Let me just reveal this. If you decide to dress as a lackey to, say, James Cagney or Edward G. Robinson, you'd fit right in."

Bringing his finger to his lips, he squints his eyes and furls his brow. "How you mean?"

"Well, I mean, sort of like what you got on now, but something with pinstripes, right? And a fedora, you got one of those? Oh, and a smidgen of dirt, rubbed around your eyes, making you look sullen, and deadly. The party's got plenty of cops to arrest you and rough you up a bit, or you can turn the tables on them. Whatever turns you on."

Gary winces a bit. "Sounds a little dull, to be honest."

"Dull?" I ask, incredulous. "What more could any honest citizen ask for?"

"Prohibition's over, Anthony. Why on Earth would you want to choose a theme like that?"

"Who said it's over? The Constitution? What is Prohibition, at its most fundamental, Gary, my friend?"

"A bad legal experiment."

Surprised at his intelligent answer, I acknowledge, "Yes. But why? I'll tell you why, because at its core any prohibition is an incitement, not a policing subtraction."

"Incitement to what?"

"Not 'to what', but 'of what', Gary."

He huffs, impatient with the game. "Fine, I'll play. An incitement of what?"

At that moment, a short, chubby dark-haired man, sporting a goatee, interrupts our conversation to ask, "Excuse me, gentlemen, is this seat taken?" I stick my hand out in the stranger's face, to acknowledge he was heard and to impress upon him my need to have him wait.

"Of what?" I querry Gary, giving him my surveillance to see he is paying attention. He composes himself, before I begin, "Incitement of desire. It's like a kid told by his parents not to repeat some behavior, and that kid, not thinking about anything in particular during the previous moment, now goes ahead and repeats the naughty behavior, just because he was told not to do it. Prohibition—the booze, the guns, the gangsters... the panzy craze... Voila! The incitement of naughtiness, the very reverse of repression. This is why gangsters excel—selling safe liquor and safe gambling on the boats. So, the way I see it, Prohibition blossoms inside a more grand governing mindset marketing to the masses a 'normal,' statistically-centered life, but apparently beyond police power, a place where many, if not most, people dream they already live."

As I am speaking, the stranger takes the last seat, as now every table in the place has at least one drink on it, and he hardly appears in the mood to hop around for the best seat. Needless to say, his face falls frumpy when he settles in. "Hello, I'm Coach…"

I ignore Coach's introduction for a moment, so I may finish speaking to Gary. "Let's remember to talk more later about those mood lifters," I say to him. Gary nods, and then we both turn our attention to Coach. I start, "Anthony's my name, please join us." Then, I turn to Gary to make an introduction, and this continues around the table with handshakes and barroom politesse. During this commotion, to my slight surprise I notice Maria Ordaz sitting in the back of the club, talking to a gentleman. At that moment our eyes meet, I smile. She knows of my intention to come this evening, and she told her brother hopefully. She averts her gaze. Finally, Coach introduces the nameless, bearded boy standing at his side, and he insists that his boy can stand waiting and sternly forbids us to offer him any of our seats.

Coach chortles, "I was beginning to feel the whole civilized world has gone mad."

Gary tilts his head to the side and appears puzzled. "How so?"

"Oh, we could drop it," Coach pleads. "I mean, I'm glad we found a place to take a load off. But I will tell you, for example, did you hear about that battle over at Santa Monica? It's like a war out there, a drawn out standoff between a gambling boat and the authorities. Just heard on the radio, parking the car."

In fact, I had heard nothing. I remember reading in the papers, earlier in the summer, about troubles between Cornero and California's attorney general, whose tireless efforts to end southern California's ocean-going gambling empire with repeated police raids this past year have been met consistently with courtroom upsets, leaving international boundary battles unresolved and smoldering, years after the Twenty-first Amendment, but at least Cornero seems more than preoccupied. "Coach, right? When you say 'war' you mean what exactly?"

Scratching his head, he repeats widely-reported news, "They're going after his entire fleet. Their names again, boy? Which ones did they get back at the end of last month?"

"Ah, they raided the Tango...," the young man starts, then stops by drawing out the 'o' in his last spoken word.

Coach interrupts, "Tango, that's right. And the Showboat."

"Were those two here in Long Beach?" Gary asks. "I mean, they're so many, and I don't spend time out there."

Snapping his fingers upon his epiphany, the boy continues as though he hadn't stopped speaking at all, "The Tango, the Showboat and... the Texas."

"Yes, I think those were the ones off Long Beach," Coach comments. "Now, the Rex... that's a different matter, up in Santa Monica. It's the most famous of the fleet. There was a full-page ad taken out in the Times for the Rex, not two months ago. It seemed that business was going to be there forever."

I remind him, "So, war?"

"Right," Coach acknowledges. "The Rex, unlike the other ships which shut down immediately... The Rex, I say, isn't just throwing up the white flag. All the passengers on board during the raid have been released to police custody without harm, but that was days ago. They got all sorts of gawkers at the shore with binoculars and spyglasses, according to the radio reports. It's still fighting being seized with water cannons and gunfire, as of earlier today."

"Because they're putting up a fight, one guesses," Gary observes.

"No doubt," I add, winking at him. "How long it's been, again?"

Gary interjects, "Well, I remember the raid started around a week ago."

"Yes," Coach nods. "That's right, about a week. They'll end up just surrounding the boat in international waters, until they run out of food and water, then they'll surrender without a fight. Fast as lightening, or almost."

"Almost," I chuckle. "Maybe California's Attorney General might find time to surround Hitler and make him give up, too?"

Gary chimes in, "And Mussolini, Franco?"

"Come again? You mean Poland, Anthony? War there's not likely. Brits have it covered," Coach asserts. "Chamberlain has made it clear he's drawing the line at Danzig. No, I suspect the only war we're going to see is in Santa Monica."

"Probably right," I concede, out of politeness and a certain cultivated ignorance. I hardly remember reading or hearing the name "Chamberlain", which shows how much I have shun politics, since turning to my studies and part-time job.

Coach asks, "So, Anthony's a bartender, and Gary, what is it you do?"

"Photog. I just shot a few rolls on a contract for a postcard company. Pays the bills, and let's me pursue other interests."

"101 Club"

"Other interests?" I ask, finishing my gin. I see that Gary has finished his drink as well. "Erotica," the photog admits, raising eyebrows. "Acts of extraordinary coitus, my specialization."

I joke, "What are you, the Samuel Goldwyn of smut?"

"Art makes for such trite conversation," Coach complains.

"Hey, that's my line, buddy!" I protest, standing at full attention, exaggerating my indignation. Coach pulls his head back, and his boy stands behind him, massaging his shoulders twice before Coach brushes his hands away. "Joking around, fellas. Actually, the well is sort of dry," I explain, raising my empty glass. "Gary, can I help you to another? Coach?"

Coach responds first, "Oh, no. I've got it covered, if it's all the same to you, thanks."

"Yes," Gary replies. "A little tequila, lemonade, a dash of triple sec. Ice, if they still have any."

"Got it," I reply, taking his empty glass in my hand.

Photography. Erotica. I mull these over in my mind as I approach the bar, order the drinks, and wait patiently. I look again over at Maria, who now has two men, one seated, the other standing, speaking to her. I decide on an intervention. After receiving my drinks from one of the young bartenders whose acquaintance I have not yet made, I drop a couple bills on the counter and head for Maria's table, letting the drinks wait on the bar, momentarily ignoring Gary, perhaps adding to the impression I've already made. Hmm. Erotica. Photography.

"Ms. Maria, as always, encantada."

"Oh, Anthony! Here, give me a hug. How are you? Come closer, I can't reach," she begs, standing herself from her seat. "Anthony, please stay."

Looking at the two gentlemen trying to talk to her, I say, "I wasn't expecting to see you here tonight. What a charming surprise." At that point, Maria and I are gazing directly at each other, to the exclusion of her would-be suitors, and her face radiates only joy. "Rafael promised he'd be here soon, Anthony."

"Are you by chance here, at his request?" I ask, my curiosity aroused.

"Ok, I won't lie to you. He asked me to be here for a reason, in case you need someone for some support."

"Support?" I ask, pulling back with some surprise.

"Well, you know. Rafael talks to me, and I once in awhile talk to Fe'e, and..."

"... and I talk to Fe'e. But I don't understand."

At that moment she reaches down into her handbag and retrieves a full envelope with Hebrew written on the outside of it. "Here, this belongs to you, I believe. Rafael asked me to hold onto this, because he wanted you to have it tonight, and he was too preoccupied with his business to carry it around himself."

Puzzled, I accept the envelope, which from its size and shape I presume holds about eight grand, and stuff it in my front jacket pocket. I scowl before speaking, "So, you had... I mean, thank you. I'm glad it didn't cause you any trouble."

"I can handle myself, like my brothers," she says, before looking over my shoulder. "Speak of the devil."

From behind, a voice says, "Good evening, Anthony."

I turn, and to my marvelous, then stunned surprise, I see Rafael Ordaz, a little fatter than the last time we saw each other, and standing behind him, Abraham Katza, a New Deal older.

Chapter Twenty-Four

"Beer Barrel Polka"

Drunk, I believe it was Shakespeare who said, "I have no joy of this contract tonight. It is too rash, too unadvised, too sudden."

* * *

I sit on the floor in front of Abe's still clothed body. Rafael rubs his chubby gun. Abe turns to see Rafael's shirt removed. Pulling his shirt from his unbuttoned trousers, Abe rubs Rafael's bare chest and moves in closer. Rafael opens his mouth and tastes Abe's lips, reluctant to open for him. They kiss for minutes which pass more like hours. Slowly, I stand shirtless, and Rafael takes the opportunity to guide Abe to the bed.

There Rafael continues kissing Abe on his neck and rubbing his chest, and my hands open Abe's trousers and remove his flaccid, circumsized cock, gently massaging it, while he sits there, eyes closed, breathing, still. I take my seat next to him on the bed, open my legs, and Rafael helps remove my pants. A few moments more and we are all naked, as Rafael stands over me, caressing my nipples, and Abe kneels before me, bent over, intensely focused on my lap, tugging at me, eyes closed, his nose travelling up and down my thigh.

I turn my head to my left and start sucking on Rafael, who caresses my head and tugs on his own sac. With one hand on my cock, Abe pulls in closer and places his lips on my chest, until they find my erect nipple. Gentle, repetitive, wet circles on my breast. After some minutes of this, Abe pulls his head back and moves his mouth to my dick, tugging at it, coaxing it to grow longer and more firm. His technique is gentle. At times his whole mouth dives downward, taking it all in until it reaches the back, where it sits, as he breathes, his tongue pulsing in miniature waves. He pulls back and lets licks the tip of it. Spittle drops down the shaft and he pulls his hand upwards and back down, gliding. Mimicking Abe, I perform the same movements on Rafael. As if enjoying a sweet lollypop, we suck insatiably, childlike, mesmerized.

Occasionally distracted by Abe's natural obsession, I pull my head away from Rafael's body and stare at Abe, watching the back of his head oscillate slowly in its own sinuous rhythm. At peace, my instincts return my mouth to Rafael's body. As my eyes close, I sense Abe's head bobbing faster up and down, purposefully, hungrily, the twentieth-century way. His hand keeps still, while his mouth busily devours. Rafael drops his fingers to my chin, softly raising my head up as he bends over for a kiss. Abe maintains his focus while Rafael and I start kissing, at first pecking, but quickly opening our mouths, our tongues playing footsie with each other, both of our eyes closed. Breathing is effortless. Rafael has grown a small moustache, which I hardly notice, while the soft whiskers fondle my lip, my nostrils. His chin drives into mine. He pushes air through my open mouth, and I receive it, inhaling as long as he can exhale, and then, at the moment it stops, I push my diaphragm, exhaling at first slowly into Rafael, then aggressively, I put my arms around his waist, while Abe synchronizes his movements with ours. If Rafael could bite and chew my face, I sense he would.

Again, Abe continues, as Rafael guides one of my hands to Abe's chest, and we take turns diddling Abe's nipples, causing him to suck faster, then slower, alternating between speeds, adding inches to the length of it. Rafael's kissing draws my mind upwards, and we close our eyes, facing each other, moving in small, slow circles as our lips ramble across the surface of our faces. Our nostrils flair as the air passes where our lips have been, perfumed with musk. Rafael's tongue is the perfect size, not too rigid or too passive, mirroring my movements at times and taking lead at others. I can feel my own whiskers prickling his skin.

There is no talking. There is no moaning. There is only gentle breathing, and the soft sounds of wet slurping. The near silence is meditative. It is complete presence in each other's beings, whose movements feel as natural as walking or sleeping, or somewhere between.

I ravish Rafael's mouth, when of a sudden, Abe ceases sucking and slowly rises to meet us, the three of us kissing, dislocated, undefined, amorphous. Tenderly, Rafael guides my shoulders backwards as we fall together into the bed, our kissing unceasing. The stench of beer.

Comfortably reclined, I keep my eyes closed as Rafael takes his mouth and drags it down my cheek, to start, proceeding to my neck and after a moment, he lands his teeth on my areola, playfully biting without stinging, then kissing and sucking alternatively, like a child. Abe soon follows his lead and after leaving my mouth, he adjusts himself for some moments, placing his body in front of my legs, his right hand pushing my left leg up and away. Instinctively, Rafael caresses my right thigh with his right hand. My muscles relax in his directed gestures. I keep my right arm above my head and out of the way, while my left hand pulls the same leg Abe has pushed back.

In an instant, I feel the wet pressure of Abe's tongue on my sac. Tapping it in morse code. Dot dot dot dash dash dash lick lick lick. The spit falls down like a rivulet, across creases in my thighs, like mountain valleys, coalescing the viscous mess into a single stream which pools at the rim of my puckering hole. Before gravity can pull any further, Abe quickly moves to suck his own spit from the crevice of my anus. Efficiently, he sucks the excess fluids and moves his face up my taint, until the river has dried. He repeats this.

Rafael continues working the same nipple raw.

Feeling the tension in my tendons holding my left leg, Abe relocates his hand to my chest, pushing his fingers through the trail of fur leading from my groin to my navel. There is a gap between that place and my pecs, and Abe finds the hair between my breasts, occasionally touching Rafael's face obsessed on my chest.

My dick twitches, standing at attention, all of it ignored.

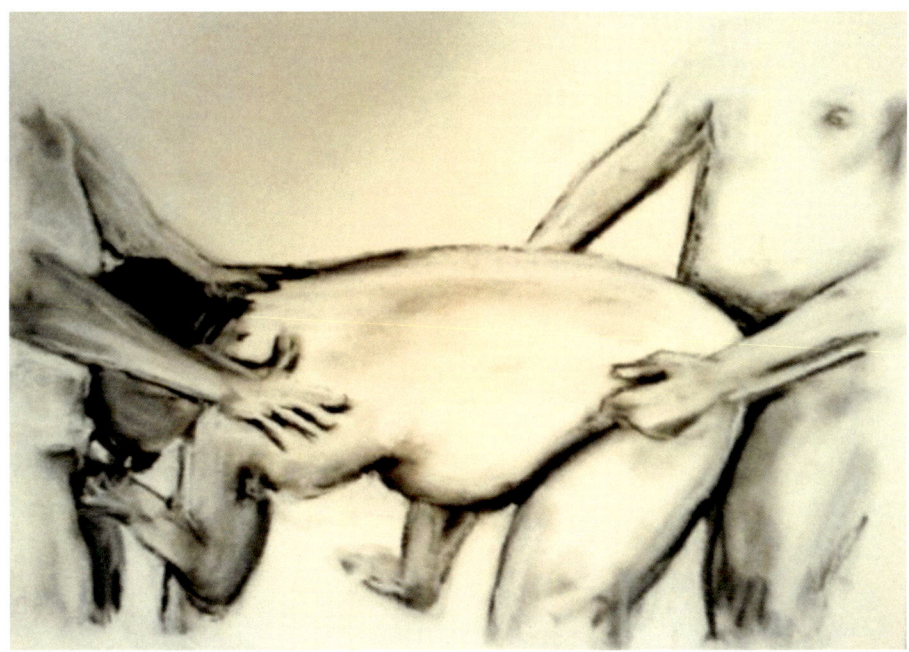

"Polka, No. 2"

I am the first to groan. It is impossible to stop. My eyelids pull tightly closed, as if I am staring at the bright sun. My lips move but cannot close. My throat feels parched but still produces a hum from inside my gut.

Rafael still attached at my breast, moves his hand along my erection. The knuckle of his thumb glides along my glans and the tip of his forefinger teases my pisshole. Abe is now hitting every nerve on my rim. As if by kissing, a rhythm emerges: he kisses, and I pucker; I pucker and he kisses. French kisses. Abe's tongue moves inside me, spreading me apart by fractions of an inch, coaxing me to relax, to accept. I have forgotten how long his tongue is, how perfectly rigid it can grow, how deep it can open me with pleasure.

I feel like a baby.

The hand over my head finds its way to Rafael's shoulder, then his back, massaging him. He moves his body in such a way that my fingers make no effort to tickle the long crescent of his crack, clean. And when I check it by smelling my digits, I inhale deeply, overtaken by the musk of his sweat. I lick my fingers over and over. Occasionally, I remove my hand and slide around the geometry of Rafael's ass. His mouth continues working my nipple and his hand stimulates my cockhead.

I am smiling.

Abe pulls his head back and puts his finger against my wet bottom. The movement of his finger copies the eagerness of his tongue, gently lapping at the surface of it, and applying gentle pressure inwardly, at first no more than the depth of a thumbnail, but carefully, almost mathematically, the millimeters increase as his drilling deepens. A second finger massages the rim of it. He pushes, as he bends over me, dropping more saliva onto his digits.

Rafael fashions a loop between his thumb and forefinger and encircles my head. He, too, pulls his head in closer and spits. Rafael's hand moves down very slowly, pulling the elastic skin back down, until at a few inches, it snaps back into place, sending electric shocks up my spine. He continues pulling downward, pushing through the pubic hairs and all the way down to the base, against the pelvis.

Abe has put two wet fingers inside me. Rafael's thumb now massages my slit. My left leg dangles without support. Abe has entered me no deeper than an inch, rotating his fingers in a slow oscillation. My eyebrows arch. Abe pulls out. Rafael inserts one, then two, then three fingers inside, while I hear Abe masturbating with one hand while the other caresses my thighs. Removing his fingers from my body, Rafael still massages my cock, but then I notice sandalwood oil drip from above onto my erection and down my taint and across my treasure.

We stop touching each other until Abe, on his knees, is able to position himself comfortably between my legs. He places one hand on either knee, my legs are now bent at the knees, pulled into my chest. At first, Abe continues making tiny pricks against the exterior of my anus. He glides upwards to get wet. Rafael takes a position behind him. At first, Rafael reaches around Abe's chest and massages his nipples. Then Rafael's hands move across his belly until they both fondle my sac. Rafael yanks on the shaft of it, forcing me to shoot, my eyes are closed and my back arches, driving my head backwards, forcing the blood to rush into my brain.

Spontaneously, I moan. Abe pushes his dickhead inside my cave, slowly, forcing me to emit a loud cry, and then, in one gesture he pushes himself inside me, one inch after the other, while I breathe purposefully. My mouth gapes, and I inhale.

The shock of his entering me causes me to wince, at first, and noticing my reactions, he stops pushing, pulls out an inch, releasing pressure and tension and filling me with the most exquisite sensations in my groin, up the small of my back. My hands instinctively caress my own nipples. After pausing for several seconds, he gently drills further inside causing my boner to stand at attention, rock-hard. Rafael reacts by rubbing very slowly, holding me loosely in his hand, tugging at my sac with a gentle pinch. Deeper, Abe dives until his hips drive into the bone of my thigh, his belly pushing against Rafael's hands massaging my balls.

Finally, Abe pulls out suddenly, and Rafael slaps my ass at the same time I hear the only words exchanged. "On all fours," Rafael barks.

I comply. Four hands caress my buttocks, various fingers probing inside me. On his knees, Rafael now positions his body between my ankles. I can hear the slippery slapping sounds of working his cock by himself. Abe, still rubbing my bottom, kneels next to my head, rubbing my back. Rafael finally approaches my rear and, unlike Abe's careful and tender movements, he thrusts his cock in one smooth, long act of deep penetration. My body spasms with agreeable feelings of being invaded. Rafael's free hands massage my skin while he fucks. Sensing that I might be uncomfortable, he pulls out and slaps my ass, again as before, but without words. I turn my head around and he rotates his forefinger, which at first I don't understand, but then I realize he is directing me to return to lying on my back. Again, I comply. Once I am comfortable and still, Rafael grabs both my ankles, pushes my legs back and my butt up. Without preparation, he confidently slides his prick into my slicked fudge hole, and without waiting, he pumps with confidence, back and forth at a moderate pace, watching me variously grin then wince. Abe's hands focus exclusively on my tits.

The electricity of it turns my mind inward, calling to mind the nerves and sinews and muscles and ligaments and bones and blood that hold me together. Abe moves his prick along my face. The odor of my bowls and his body mix, intoxicating me and without my will, my jaw opens wide, my tongue falls out and my face swallows Abe's snake. Meanwhile, Rafael is barreling inside me as fast as my beating heart. Abe moves behind my head, tilts it back with his hand, and stuffs himself deeply down my esophagus. My hands reach upwards, lightly playing with his nipples.

Still, Rafael is pushing inside me as fast as my beating heart.

I rest my feet on Rafael's chest, allowing my toes to dangle on his titties. My hands reach back to Abe's sac. At the same time I suck, my hands pull and tug at his shaft. Occasionally, I pull away to inhale deeply, but I otherwise feel myself losing air, causing me to suffocate slightly.

Rafael stops his movements. Abe this time makes the same gestures that Rafael previously made, rotating his finger in the air, signaling for me to turn, once again on all fours. Once comfortably positioned, Abe and Rafael switch positions. Abe now kneels between my legs and hammers himself through my crevice. My head rears backwards, my wide open mouth gasps for air, when Rafael stuffs his cock inside, down my tongue, forcing me to gag on it.

"Polka, No. 1"

Abe, now, is the one pushing inside me as fast as my beating heart.

Rafael pushes down on my shoulders and massages my spine. Abe is finding his tempo until his rhythm settles on some signature, a constant drumming, as if each push is a word and each pull is a breath. The walls of my rectum experience a high-pitched nervous pulse, emitting an invisible field of magnetism, radiating in circles up through my torso. Rafael now turns himself and sits lightly on my chest, rubbing his ass cheeks on my nipples and jerking himself off as fast as Abe pounds. The two find a sympathetic pattern, and match tempos, as I stare at Rafael moving his hand rapidly up and down his long, wide obelisk, and then the tear drop at its tip bounces off and lands on my lip. My tongue tastes it. Before I can even swallow, he arches his back and lifts his head toward the sky, while a long strand of his white ejaculation shoots up, in a parabolic arch and then lands between my eyes, on the bridge of my nose, just below my brow. Another shot falls on my chin, dripping down my neck.

Abe pushes inside me as fast as my beating heart.

Rafael yanks a few more times until satisfied. He cries a forceful grunt. Without pausing, he lifts his bottom up and tilts his head down, to my face, licking the jism caught in the wells of the corners of my eyes, the ducts. Licking, the sucking it up, he thoroughly cleans my face with his mouth. I open my eyes fully to see him smiling, sitting himself upright. He leaves the mess on my chin alone, while I gently take his dick in my hand and push along the urethra to force out any more fluids caught inside. I rub what emerges along my face and suck his glans.

Abe is now pushing inside twice the speed of my beating heart, when he begins to tremble and quake. Rafael distances his body from my chest, and I watch Abe squinting his eyes tightly. He moans and withdraws from my body and immediately grabs himself, jerking himself as fast as he had been pounding. Then, the first shot also hits my chin, causing me to laugh, and he spills himself over my belly, filling my navel until it overflows across the top and drips down the sides. Near the end of his explosion, his hand releases his rod and he, once again, pushes my legs apart and dives inside my derriere, violently pushing as far inside as he can, yelling grunting noises. Breathing hard, he stops fucking and collapses upon my body, rolling to the side, where Rafael is already positioned horizontally, facing me.

Rafael and Abe rest a few seconds while I sit up on the edge of the bed legs wide apart. Rafael moves himself under my ass, hovering some inches off the edges of the bed, and Abe remains and begins sucking on my nipple, massaging my cock as stiff as a steel bar. Rafael kisses, at first, then rims my butt. With one hand, I caress Abe's scapula, and with the other hand,

I pet his hair. Then, Abe moves his head downward and takes my cock in his mouth as Rafael tries to push his tongue as deep as it can go inside. Substituting his hand for his mouth, Rafael pushes his longest finger inside until he finds the prostate, which he stimulates as Abe push the back of his tongue along my glans, kissing intermittently.

At first my body feels warm inside and out. There is a warmth that resembles the feeling of wetting my bed, like a child. It overcomes my hips and my stomach and throat. My legs straighten out, causing Rafael to resist my involuntary orgasms by penetrating with more determination. Abe steadily increases his sucking velocity, and the warmth turns into a mini-seizure, like the sensation which builds before a long sneeze that never happens. Muscular contractions that overwhelm for several seconds, and then in my controlled breathing, I sense it. At first the feeling generates inside my sac, tightening, causing the skin to become rough. Rafael pokes the prostate tip at the moment the contractions start, and my growl starts to menace. Abe pulls his head away and wraps his lips around my testicles, pulling them into his mouth, causing something just below the threshold of pain, intensifying the sensation into a defined direction, an exploding feeling pointing outward. My stomach muscles spasm, contract, and then I explode across Rafael, some four or five feet across the room, as my back arches just as violently, causing me to scream, not yell, but scream. Abe lets go of my balls, causing them to snap back into place, and forcing the second shot to detonate. Second scream. He races to drink it up. My hands reach across his head and I force my cock down his throat and spill the second half of the second load deep inside his throat, causing him to gag, to cough, to struggle to breathe, nearly to choke. Unfinished, the urge to cry, as in a tantrum, takes me and then my head rocks back and forth as the third squirt trickles like a fountain down Rafael's eager face. I can hear him slurp and swallow.

There is a recursive series of tremors, as I continue to pour myself on Rafael. If there is anything inside me left, I cannot tell, as I lose myself to the sensations of this aftershock, its massive release of emotions and tensions, an exhaustion that could welcome death in its completeness. I wish I could die, here and now. I wish my heart would stop. I wish my breathing would cease. I feel paralyzed withholding my breathing. It is no effort. Finally, I fall backwards onto the mattress. My mind emptied. My heart slowing to one beat every hour. Brain starved of oxygen.

In a massive contraction, I inhale, once. Holding it there forever, and then releasing.

Everything returns to normal. An absolute stillness.

I cannot think. I cannot speak. I cannot move. Nobody is moving. Nobody is speaking.

Nobody is thinking.

Nobody. Nothing.

Death.

Paralysis.

Emptiness.

Foreverness.

Somnambulance.

Some minutes later, I break the silence to say, "I believe it was Shakespeare who said, 'I have no joy of this contract tonight. It is too rash, too unadvised, too sudden.' Fuck Shakespeare."

Laughter.

Rafael reveals, "Hey, Anthony. The night of the earthquake, when you weren't looking, I slipped some magic mushrooms in the soup you ate. Ha... just fucking with you."

Chapter Twenty-Five

"One for Her, One for Me"

There are times which demand guessing.

Reading the front page of any edition of the Press-Telegram, for instance, it becomes difficult to predict subsequent events, and yet oftentimes, they do not feel entirely surprising, even when they are detailed in black and white after the fact. Journalistic accounts suggest probabilistic outcomes of imagined futures, as if some invisible hand passively nudges a path of life still possessed of random elements. Were there a single word to describe this feeling I notice when enjoying the newspaper, I would use it universally to describe other matters, because the temptation to perceive extra meaning in facts presents itself to nearly everyone, and I do not except myself. However, it is my private suspicion that the mind tragically opposes the act of interpretation to chaos, when actually this artificial mental construction can be targeted as the cause of a great deal of popular confusion and unhappiness.

An example: for generations there has existed a thing people used to describe simply as Polish. But as of this month of September, this same thing is becoming German and Soviet and Slovakian. And so, I imagine Poland, its land, its people, its language, its god, all of it to be something like a cube of ice. For a time, it takes on the appearance of a solid state, with distinct boundaries separating what is inside from what is outside. Then by altering its ambient conditions, without crushing intervention, it ceases to be like the end of the Abraham Lincoln Brigade after last April Fool's Day; all of it melts away and the liquid joins its environs, whether atmosphere, cocktail spirits, or sewage seeping towards the sea.

Another example: for days Southern California, all of it, bakes in temperatures of such high degree that dozens of its people perish. But, in a dramatic shift (coinciding with the second week after the Soviet invasion of eastern Poland), the same geographic region is subjected to torrents of rain culminating, without much forewarning, in an exceptionally rare tropical storm whose winds and waters threaten to alter, very slightly, a segment of the contoured coastline of the eastern Pacific and take yet more lives.

I make a series of disconnected intuitions. A kind of peace can be achieved by recognizing that individual consciousness, no matter how complex or sublime, is basically arbitrary. Exhaustion and struggle arise when asserting interpretation over chaos. Neither peace nor struggle should be distinguished absolutely.

* * *

In a cotton, plum-colored Japanese kimono covering my dress shirt and trousers, I tell Solstice in a grandiose voice, "Tony Cornero explained he needed a haircut."

She looks at me, puzzled, and fiddles with the collar on her own gold silk kimono. Underneath, she sports a dark, wool pair of pants and a plaid shirt. "Is that what you yourself heard him say?" she asks, while the windows shake from the force of the insistent tempest.

"Nah, I read it in the papers. When he was arrested back in August, he said that haircut business on shore, supposedly. If it's true, you gotta give him respect for his sense of style though."

"Is that so?" she asks more as a statement, than a question. "Love these stylish robes we got on, huh?"

We spend this night at the home of Ernesto Ordaz, while the tropical storm gives Long Beach a deadly lashing. Rafael, mysteriously, happens to be far out of town. And then, I learned that Maria told Ernesto she planned to find shelter with her employer's family.

I reach nearby for my only piece of overnight luggage I have brought with me. My Craftsman Village dwelling, which has more than just a leaky roof, would have made for poor accommodations for both Solstice and I. So, I decided she stay with me at some place else, after I received a message from Maria forewarning me of Solstice Meridian's unexpected return to Long Beach, only a couple days ago. Ernesto begged me to have us share the comfort of his sturdy old house during the sudden climatic tantrum. He has spared no detail making us feel at home, while he busily tends to small tasks to secure further his property.

The rain outside turns heavier. I sit upright, from my reclined position resting on my elbow. My sudden movements startle her, and she scoots back a couple of inches from where she is sitting on the floor, sort of on top of part of me. Clapping my hands, and making a gesture calling for the flask of tequila stuck in her hand, I say, "So, enough about the battle of Santa Monica.

Besides, Cornero, a.k.a. 'The Admiral', is caught up in so much legal trouble with Attorney General Warren these days, he'll end up having to take his case all the way to the California Supreme Court, I'm sure. After that... doubt he'll be quite welcome anywhere in this state." I drink a long swig, hoping my prediction is accurate. I harbor deeper doubts, about whether my fortune is something like a woman's, whether the gossip of an octopus eventually persuaded Captain Stewart McKelvy's superiors earlier this summer to call the California Attorney General for the purpose of expressing the military's interest in disposing of the distraction Anthony Cornero presents to the security and sovereignty of the United States of America and has so presented since the twenties. After all, everybody knows Roosevelt has warned the country must now prepare for war, if there is to remain any chance for peace. These days hover in an in-between epoch, a kind of metaphysical limbo.

"Just like that? Cornero's gone for good?" she asks spookily, like she is listening to a ghost story.

"More like, gone for now. So, what about you, sister? I mean, I've said enough about Tijuana and everything else I've been doing since we last saw each other. You've gotten to be quite a young lady of the world. Eloping. Solstice?" I turn my head to the side and give her a scowling, skeptical glance. "What would mommy and daddy say?" I return the flask to her, which she greedily enjoys.

"Kimonos"

"Aren't you a card... Mommy and daddy? Ha!"

I smile, "Not that I'm letting you off the hook..."

"... for?" she expresses concern.

"For... telling me more yet about Corny, or..."

Her lips pouting, she reproaches me by interrupting, "... it's 'Cody'..." A violent gust must have picked up some debris, because at that moment we hear a noticeable but ignorable 'thud' outside.

"Yes... yes, of course. But speaking about 'cards', I have something to return to you." Rummaging around my case, I recover an envelope containing Solstice's handmade deck of tarot cards. Her face beams with excitement, and she instantly passes the flask to me, so she may open the envelope now in her hands. "Not this minute, though, please," I admonish her, and she stuffs the sealed envelope under her crossed-legged bottom.

"Promise, later?"

"Later."

"So, Cody... Where do I begin?" she begins.

I empty the flask. "You might begin by telling me where you eloped to?"

"That's just it. We couldn't settle on a place," she admits coyly. "Such a boy that Cody. First it was San Francisco, then it was Portland, then it was Seattle, before Portland, again."

I involuntarily cough into my hand, begging her to wait. "All of those?"

"We never even made it to Vancouver."

"So, how did..."

"... Let me guess: why did I come back to Long Beach?"

"I guess you read my mind," I joke. She arches one of her eyebrows. "I'm joking about the fortune-telling part. You know that. Right, Solstice?"

"Right. Well, why did you come back here... Clingy?"

I scowl with some exaggeration, before letting out a giggle. "You mean, to Long Beach from Tijuana?" Slightly impatient, I remind her, "I asked you first."

"I know you did. So, what? That's not an answer to my question."

Solstice needs to trust me. Or maybe she needs some sense of approval for making the choices she has made. Finally choosing to face my feelings, I admit with some vulnerability, "I'm not entirely sure. I think it might be because this place sort of feels like the closest thing to a home. Other than Brooklyn."

"Well, then you understand," she answers, nodding. "The wind outside is a shriek."

"Like a ghost, actually. Solstice, I do understand. I do. But, so now what? It's over with you two?"

She smirks. "Oh, you're one to talk. I wish I had a cigarette."

"They're bad for you."

"So is tequila," she comments.

"Not true. Not true." I shake my head, then point my finger at her, "Too much tequila, maybe. What did you mean, when you say I was one to talk?"

Her fingernails reach between her lipsticked lips to remove an unwanted something or other. "What's the deal with you and Rafael? Really."

I don't have an answer for her. Silently, I presume he's safe and suspect he takes comfort knowing I am here, with his brother. So, I pause without responding, waiting to see how urgent she feels her question is.

"Are you expecting me to change the subject without an answer, Tony?"

"Wouldn't you?" I ask her, resting the weight of my shoulders upon my arms pushed backed, supporting my head stuck up, eyes closed, breathing softly.

Out of seemingly nowhere, she points between her thighs and says, "There's no room for carelessness in this bush." My laugh starts as a giggle, then it moves into my belly, causing my diaphragm to spasm, emitting guffaws, embarrassingly, at some length of time. Meanwhile, Solstice repeats, "What?" trying to gain my attention, despite my evident pleasurable fit. "It ain't that funny," she tries to sternly interject, before giggling a couple of times, herself. Finally, we settle down, though the muscles in my face force me to maintain a sort of insipid grin.

"Was to me. Funny, that is. It was funny to me, to hear you talking like that."

I now look at her, and stare for a long time into her large, warm, brown eyes. She is expecting me to follow her mood somewhere. I sit correctly, and close my eyes, focusing my attention on the outdoor sounds of stormy weather. I reach my hand out, palm down, and say, "You remember, Solstice. The first time we met. At the automat, you held my hand, and told me I was guilty?" My eyes keep closed, and now feeling her warm hand inside mine, I ask, "Tell me, now. Do I still feel guilty?"

"I'll answer you first, but you must promise. Promise to say if I feel guilty, too, after you say if you are." I grip her hand, which she must have interpreted correctly as my consent, because she reveals, "Well, then. My answer is 'yes'. I believe you feel guilty. Even still, Clingy. Although it might have changed, whatever it is that is causing all this. Now, mine?"

I reflect a long time on how warm her hand feels and how easy it would be to attribute that feeling to the effects of my tequila or her youth. My hand, though, feels cold, now apparent to me in our intimate clutch. "You feel warm." Has she succeeded, somehow, in forgiving herself about her arson?

"Ha! Thank God!" A period of silence passes, although every three or four breaths of air is followed by a short burst of happiness, for each of us. "Tony, what the hell are we talking about? Huh?"

"Us," I answer, annoyed slightly by her tone.

She huffs, "No, I mean, what are we not talking about, you know? I mean, can I talk to you about Cody? Or do I have to keep that inside until I can forgive him later? It all seems so shallow."

"But what's the point, Solstice? If he's out of the picture, what purpose does it serve talking on and on about him?"

"It just does," she complains. "I mean, like, Fe'e living in Honolulu now... or, don't you... I mean, when you sort of died... but you didn't, so... But, did you ever talk to anyone about why?"

I let her question linger some time. I suppose she is looking for some affirmation, or maybe some obstacle to test herself. Or maybe, in this instance her innocence is trusting. "Are you asking me if I believe there is some purpose I am supposed to fulfill because I had a chance to live twice, one might say?"

"Chance," she mumbles, her head turned down. Her hand fiddles with the edge of the envelope still stuffed under her seat. "I don't believe that. I don't know what I believe. Who would care what I believe..."

Wincing, I butt in, "... Well... "

"... But, I know I don't believe in chance."

"I see." I can tell, without asking, Solstice Meridian wants me to want to get to know her more deeply than a good-time friend or vague guardian. Affording her the intimacy of my raw emotions, however, poses a minor challenge. I accept it nonetheless. "Alright, Solstice. Tell me what happened with Cody. I'll just listen."

"Only if..."

"... Another bargain?" I interrupt to ask.

Indifferent, she repeats herself, "Only if you tell me what's going on, the real deal, with Rafael."

I put her off-guard, "Right on. I go first?"

She looks skeptical responding to my apparent generosity. "Nah, you going second's alright. So, I guess I gotta go first. Cody. Let me put it to you this way. Being sincere, now. When I left with Cody, I left a virgin. I came back the same, okay? What? Why are you looking at me like that? Stop flaring your nostrils like that. Oh, say something like a man already. What?"

At this point, she repeatedly pushes my shoulder back, trying vainly to knock me down, causing me to smile. "Enough." I grab one of her wrists with my firm grip, forcing her to stop her wrestling and give me her attention.

"Who is Cody? I want to know." I release my hand, gently, and she takes her place on the floor, pretending to pay attention to the tempest around us, while gathering her thoughts.

"I met Cody Bixby at the university in Los Angeles."

"A Bixby of the Long Beach Bixby's?"

"He says, 'no'. Anyway, while you were gone, I was living with this nice, older couple. They fostered me, and a couple of other girls, while I went to high school in the day and worked at night. I barely did average, but enough to get into State on probation, I guess, with the aid of charitable services, and a couple of passes, I guess, on some tests. That's where I met Cody. He was a math tutor... well, then my math tutor, and others', too. He talked about quitting college and going into some Lutheran seminary. He said all sorts of things. He said I made him change his mind. About everything. So, we changed our minds, together. We talked about Vancouver. Sounds pretty dumb, like kids or something."

"Stop that!" forbidding her to throw a pity party in my company. "You still haven't explained what happened."

"Oh..." she shrugs. "He was impotent the whole time, from the day we got the wedding license in San Francisco to the day we hitchhiked from Portland to Reno to get a divorce, as a detour on the reverse back to Long Beach."

I pause to study her face, her eyes a tinge red from exhaustion, her heart perhaps a bit heavier. She has most certainly aged, grown in height, in the chest filled-out, since we last saw each other over six years ago. Still, her skin appears innocent and radiant, while each chestnut iris simmers, her long blond hair well-kept. Tiniest amounts of makeup purposefully applied with great intention. And yet dressed like a woodsman in plaid underneath her golden kimono. "Impotent."

She grumbles, "Like an earthworm."

"Not even almost at least close to once?" I inquire for innocent clarification purposes. She drops her head down and stares incredulously into my sockets.

"Not even," she smiles, finally, after a long stare. "Such a little boy sometimes."

Her story strikes me as requiring further elaboration if it is to offer me some pleasurable satisfaction upon learning the mysterious force depriving a young cock of its vigorous command. Of course, the delicacy of my interlocutor's gender and age, together, cause me to reflect upon the wisdom of presently ceasing all further inquiry for the sake of maintaining a mutual confidence.

Then, "Herpes, I thought at first," she blurts. "I found out pretty sure in San Francisco, when I had a doctor's visit before getting the license. They couldn't tell for sure but advised it was highly likely. Cursed rash, just on the one side near my bush. And I know exactly how it started. Back in high school, letting this boy experiment, you know what I mean? Stupid kid stuff. Usually the rash isn't there, but appears about once a year, when I feel like I was feeling in San Francisco. Cody panicked at first sight. That, and I was born with a big one... talking about the bald man in the bush down there."

Bald man in the... ? Her clitoris. I dwell in her present moment, as conscious as possible, projecting sympathy and attention, while at the same time, the back of my mind races with reckless self-diagnosis, visiting every bump, rash and sore on my body, mentally, since abandoning Abraham's consortium years ago. I continue in this near meditative state at length, until Solstice brings me back to her concerns.

"You there? Where did you go, there, jeez..."

I blink my eyes on purpose and summon all of my energy to take a huge breath, holding it, listening to a distant tree crack in the mess outside, and exhaling in one natural release until my muscles rest, before I push out even further, deeper, turning me red, and inhaling once more, normally, resuming breathing calmly, in unconscious, mild oscillations. I talk openly, "It wasn't as hard as I thought as it was going to be."

Solstice, slightly startled, confused, asks rapidly, "Hard as what? What are you talking about?"

I ignore her and sort of ramble. "I didn't know what to do, at first, when I saw Abe standing behind Rafael at the 101 Club. I mean, it was obvious Rafael had led him there, but how puzzled me. Once again, I found myself unsettled in my feelings, and drifting, and, maybe you said it, Solstice. Maybe all that's left is what's shallow. Rafael took charge, first, guiding us to chairs, serving us drinks, getting the conversation going. Maria, helped, too. With the talking. It was so civil, and then a marvelous party, sort of, happened. Double-entendres and hidden meanings. An old game. Easy to play. We were got drunk, of course. I offered Abe my old cock—excuse me, Solstice—if he'd give it up at the same time for Rafael. Abe didn't agree at first, then he sounded variously ashamed or reluctant for a long while, like an hour or more, before he turned to just drunk, then finally eager, an easy, horny eager. Rafael immediately fell painfully offended upon hearing the insanity of my proposal, and he was about to say something in protest, when I beat him to the punch. Right then and there, I pulled out eight-thousand dollars from my pocket, while Abe moped still reluctant about it all, and I stuffed the whole wad in Rafael's hand, and ordered him to 'shut up', which he did deliciously spitefully. So, moving on to the next morning, Rafael drove Abe to the train for Los Angeles, but not before Abe bid me 'good-bye' in this certain kind of way that I always want to see as ambiguous, when in fact I can never tell whether it is ambiguous or not."

"Hurricane"

The tempest and the downpour.

She smirks, "Ambiguous." Solstice seems capable of absorbing my revelations without expressing internal perturbations. She demands, "Eight Thousand dollars? Where did you get the eight-thousand?" I stare at her a long minute. Fixed on the audaciousness of her question, I cannot find her an answer. "I see," she mutters, breaking the silence. "You can't tell me about the money. How about Rafael, then? Did he keep it?"

I smile, "Yep. I mean, as far as I know."

"See, Clingy... You definitely got what it takes, and it don't take all you got. Without a doubt, you're going to hell."

Still smiling, "Probably... not. I mean, I don't want to get too serious about any of it. And you, still trying to get into heaven?"

Solstice giggles, lightly. And trying to catch her breath, she jokes, "Don't you think it's worth at least trying to get a reservation?"

"For what? Fish and bread? And bottomless wine? No, thanks."

"I know it's more than this," she asserts.

"What's next, Solstice?" I turn the conversation in another direction. There is a point reached when listening to words that, rather than earnestly declared from the limits of self-knowledge, instead subtly steer the non-believer into tireless debates which resolve nothing because they can never resolve anything when belief is not a matter of debate—the proposition most believers end up defending anyway. "And don't accuse me of being afraid of god, when all I really want to do is laugh just like him."

"Well, if..."

Calmly, I drone, "... Enough, Solstice. There's a storm outside. Let's show our gratitude to the host whose abode secures a peace shared at this moment for our common benefit."

She stretches her arms and also breathes in dramatic fashion. "So, let me ask you this. What becomes of it all now?"

I look at her a long time, before speaking my first word offered in reply. "It wasn't a waste of those eight thousand, I can tell you that. I don't know. I'm not going to be a card about it. Decisions take time. And education takes time, even if I try and rush it, or turn it into something else. I expect to finish my associate's degree, however, before I see or hear from Abe, again, at my request. Solstice, let me ask you. Who budged for your divorce, first?" My young lady refuses to answer, and rests stoically. "Of course. Fair enough," I concede.

She jumps up. "Clingy, among friends, playing a little game can help. Wanna play a little game with me called 'Secret Sin'? It's simple: I write my worst sin on one side of piece of paper, and you write down the worst sin on one side of another piece of paper. We count to three, then at the same time reveal our secret sin to the other person. The loser with the worse sin has to beg the winner with the lesser sin to suggest an act of penance. For fun!"

"We don't need paper, Solstice. I can just give up mine... "

"... Wait! On three. 'One, two... three!'"

"Maurrsdoenr," we blend from two different words spoken simultaneously.

"I'm guessing you said, 'Arson'?"

"You just said, 'Murder'. Are you one-hundred percent sure, Tony?"

"No."

"Tony, when was this?"

"Does it matter?"

"Oh, my. That's where... that's how the... eight? Only it used to be more, wasn't it, I bet... ha!" Solstice Meridian flaps her lashes at me, giggling in perfect disregard for the hurricane hitting southern California, the first time in nearly a century.

The thought recurs: the mind tragically opposes the act of interpretation to chaos, when actually this artificial mental construction can be targeted as the cause of a great deal of popular confusion and unhappiness.

Chapter Twenty-Six

"Dec. 8, 1941 A.D.: Rev. 13:1"

Holding the truth is the hardest thing.

To his question, I reply with a non-sequitur, "Living in Mexico required copious amounts of opiates, Mr. Katza, something external to me, something greater than my will, which I managed fortunately not to surrender entirely, despite lonely years subduing and tempting myself."

"I see. Sounds as if you found your god, in Mexico, then."

"There is no god," I insist.

He shakes his head, "There is."

"Yeah, your beloved America," I kid.

Our conversation appears outwardly fragmentary, picking up bits and pieces of awkward emotions underneath. Hardly a breeze this afternoon. A slight chill, but not cold. Under the sun, in Abraham's 1940 dark green Packard, parked near Rainbow Pier's Spit and Argue Club, we sit a few inches apart with the windows down. Abraham, at the wheel, rummages through a valise pulled from the back seat and settled atop his lap, chatting anxiously about Roosevelt who, just today, raised the work week to 48 hours. I patiently wait, clear my throat, and resume waiting, looking out the window towards the sandy shore curving eastward and southward, towards Orange County, while I slip out a fat jazz blunt from inside my jacket and hand it to Abraham.

Puzzled, he accepts it with a sort of intrigued, scientific objectivity, "Cigar?" Smells it, scowls and drops it inside his valise. He draws my attention to a stack of documents and says, "Fier, c'est ranger." The lawyer in him slowly reveals each one. "French... it means 'proud is putting things in proper arrangement'."

"Abraham, have you ever had an enema?" I ask, while at the same time, I read at my leisure, silently.

In an exaggerated Yiddish accent, he complains, "For what? In my decent state of health?"

Letter to Captain Burton W. Chippendale, Reserve Midshipmen School, Columbia University

Limited Power of Attorney

Application for California Insurance Licensing Examination

Jupiter Insurance, Articles of Incorporation

Jupiter Insurance, By-Laws

Jupiter Insurance, Minutes for December 8, 1941 Board Meeting.

I ask him, "Do you care much about survival of the fittest?"

"Such a misunderstood idea, Tony. Really. We'll probably find out, one day, that the human species evolved because of an overall sexual appeal of the demonstrably reproductive and not because it was propelled by individual stamina arranged on some imaginary ladder of Aryan mishegas."

"Though something was true in the past, its future is not guaranteed, Abe. But I suppose you and I know that already."

"Each in our own way, Mr. Camarrata." He removes from his jacket a paper-wrapped packet of Ramses skins, and tosses them into my lap.

American ships have been reported torpedoed on the high seas between San Francisco and Honolulu.

Yesterday the Japanese Government also launched an attack against Malaya.

Last night Japanese forces attacked Hong Kong.

Last night Japanese forces attacked Guam.

Last night Japanese forces attacked the Philippine Islands.

Last night the Japanese attacked Wake Island.

And this morning the Japanese attacked Midway Island.

Handing me the birthday gift I purchased in 1930 for him, a Diamond Point jade green oversized fountain pen with a gold nib, he explains, "The insurance exam application, and the various legal incorporation documents for Jupiter Insurance, I admit, except for the dates, had been prepared and sitting on my desk since I was notified I passed the California Bar Exam earlier this year, waiting for me to reveal them to you at a time and place of my choosing. So, they were, you might say, anxiously premeditated some months ago. Just sign your name by the penciled 'X' letters on those, next to the paper clips. The other two documents I composed myself very early this morning, soon after I reached you on the telephone. I hardly slept at all last night, you see. When I finished typing, I stacked everything into my case, locked the apartment and rushed to the car. There remains one incomplete matter, for which I earlier made initial arrangements, concerning the coming letter of introduction from Dean Watkins to Columbia."

Abraham appears to me, for an instant, like an Automat.

* * *

December 8, 1941

Captain Burton W. Chippendale
United States Naval Reserve
Midshipmen School
Columbia University
New York, New York

Captain Chippendale, sir:

On the occasion of Congress's declaration of an existing state of war between the United States and Imperial Japan, I write to announce enthusiastically my candidacy for Fall '42 matriculation in the Midshipmen School at Columbia University. My formal, complete application I shall submit before the date it is due, next semester.

Owing to my patriotism as an American citizen, I feel compelled to help defend the peoples of our democracy which the armed forces of the United States valiantly protect. A native New Yorker, without surviving family, I moved to California a decade ago, one American in a larger, desperate struggle for survival. Since my arrival, I established myself, served as a city lifeguard, and shepherded local businesses adapting themselves to the lawful opportunities afforded by the end of Prohibition. By the end of December 1942, I expect to complete my baccalaureate program at the University of California at Los Angeles with high course grades in my areas of academic concentration: Mathematics and Business Administration. It is my deepest desire to return to my home city and give my maximum contribution to the defense of our nation.

Attached herein, you will find letters of introduction corroborating my qualifications, credentials and fitness. The letters are from Gordon S. Watkins, Dean of the College of Letters and Science at the University of California at Los Angeles and from my attorney, Abraham Katza, Esq., Second Lieutenant, United States Army (1918-1919).

Cordially,

Anthony Camarrata
Long Beach, California
encl

* * *

Five minutes of contemplative silence.

* * *

"I lied when I said opium helped hold me together. It did, but it cannot overcome holding the truth."

"I lied when I assented, two years ago, to sleeping with you... and Rafael. That occasion was hardly sentimental, and it was ultimately not in my best interest to pursue you in that manner. The reason I did that was because... "

"... Abe, you know what the really funny thing is? Lying, it doesn't matter in the end. So then, I guess I should just sign this ass-kissing letter you wrote on behalf of my future."

Summarily, he returns to business. "Yes, of course." I sign my name to the letter. "And the Power of Attorney, please... " he adds. But I hesitate, while he continues speaking, "We would sign one for me, but perhaps later after your deployment ends."

All these quiet pieces of paper, and all these silent words written with ink, could be wrapped into a thin cylinder, tighter and tighter, then encircled several times around my left hand's fourth finger, and maybe if they were soaked in booze and tonic and left to dry, they would retain their shape, and I would be owned by something like a wedding ring.

Prior to signing the Power of Attorney, I pull out a piece of paper on which I wrote a short poem this morning at a café on the Pike, trying to enjoy my wake-up coffee, after Abraham's telephone call. To serve as a counterpoint to law, I gift him the poem. It's the same poem I memorized for 'Olevaivai'olefe'e before I saw her sail for Honolulu to join Captain McKelvy two years ago. He reads it aloud, softly, "In times like these we hear small words from hands too far to touch us now. Long sounds stretch out and push and pull and tear the ties that bind us frail. So, hold my loves to these small words and drop the ones too large to bear."

Just as he finishes reciting, I nonchalantly sign the Power of Attorney, granting Abraham authority to make business decisions on my behalf for Jupiter Insurance, Inc., until such later time that I can direct the business' affairs, as its independent Chief Executive Officer (in possession of an honorable military discharge). Additional clauses also grant him the authority to conduct any legal matters regarding the disposition of the interests of my estate, in the event of my death or incapacitation. He admits he is uncertain his plan would work, if he had to visit me in a military or civilian hospital, but he expects it to be better than nothing. The Power of Attorney expires by its own force in 1946, which I point out to him is a rather excessively long period of time, five years that is, to expect this war to last. Pointing to the decimation of the American Pacific Fleet, he convinces me of the merits of this date, and he explains, if an earlier date is appropriate, we can void the arrangement at that point. "Efficient," he stresses, then smirks, "Pro bono, of course."

I look to the surface of the ocean, some yards down and out. There could lurk, soon if not now, Japanese submarines anywhere between here and Catalina, up and down the coast. There could be, any day now, a German, then Italian, declaration of war upon the United States, or vice versa. I recall my old delusional feelings induced by pneumonia. I cough and spit out the window towards the lagoon. Hold on, I tell myself. Then, I ask Abraham suddenly, "Wait. How did you find out I used to be, briefly, a Long Beach lifeguard, as you mention in the letter I signed."

"Some investigating on my part. Been asking around about you for the past couple years. I was wondering if you were going to ask about the lifeguard reference, which is one reason I put that in the letter, so you would ask. Are you surprised I know these things, Clingy?"

"Signed"

" 'Clingy', Abe?"

"I have a question for you, Tony."

Though puzzled and irritated at his persistence, I relent, "Ask me. Go ahead."

"What I can't figure out is whether you were defending Dickie Parker, or..." I feel startled by a cold bolt of nervous energy cascading down my torso. He starts, "Los Angeles police couldn't explain satisfactorily, from eyewitness testimony, how the assault on Becker happened after the officer shot Dickie Parker at close range. Even now, Becker admits he can't remember anything clearly about that night, but he feels certain he did not shoot Parker. Perhaps some other assailant did, maybe after assaulting Becker and picking up his weapon, which was found somehow still held in his grip, despite the blow he received before he fell. Becker is still living, in Santa Ana. He's got a shattered jaw, often eats through a straw. Even simple talking is usually painful for him. Communicates with his wife, child and pastor using pen and paper majority of the time."

"Abe, if I may ask..." I start, then surrender to his interruption.

"... Tony, the smutty funnies from '34 were a hoot. I came across a copy of Fierce Stranger. By the way, was that your idea, the title?"

"Friend's idea."

"Down here in Long Beach, there's this lawyer with whom I have started some business, keeps an old Fierce Stranger stashed away in his locked office desk. Its author, Clingy. He told me rumor has it was distributed from here in Long Beach, by some local gambling syndicate. And that information led to me asking around, and now I understand you used to be known for a while by the Clingy name."

"It was just for fun, Abe."

"Ha! And for publication and distribution with the intent of ruining the reputation of the Long Beach police chief at the time, Yancy, is it? 'Armlet of Voodoo Amazona'? Where did you come up with that one? Anyway, in my digging around, I found you supposedly checked out for Tijuana. That's what a couple people told me—in Mexico, as you admitted a moment ago, but on the lam for escaping charges like pornography, defamation, possibly seditious radicalism or incitement. What I figured out was you sent me the eight grand months after the date people were telling me Fierce Stranger was first sold. Eight grand from one comic book sale? At ten cents a copy with ten-thousand printed, that's just a thousand bucks. To make your share totalling eight, after production costs, artist costs... I mean, call me naive but who ever heard of kids pooling their coins to buy some dirty comic for a buck or more? I haven't. Maybe you have. One Superman's what? A dime?

Anyway, around last winter on a whim, I went through the Press-Telegram archives from around the date I received the money, looking through stories about robberies and the like. Know what I learned? I received your envelope of cash the same month as the '34 ILWU strike started in San Pedro. An envelope from Long Beach with eight thousand dollars at the time of one of the biggest strikes in America and an unexplained murder. All that might have connected together in my head in the first place, but it didn't. Ruth and I were already falling to shambles, again, back then. But now, I meditate and wonder: coincidence?"

"Hmm."

"Now, if I were to hazard an educated hunch, I'd guess you intended to hit Becker. I've come across rumors about him being in the Invisible Empire. But, tell me, did you shoot Dickie Parker? With Ruben Becker's gun? In any case, why?"

"You're just speculating, counselor, but let's say with a nod to our privilege of attorney-client confidentiality I was there, yes, confidentially. And let's say a longshoremen's wrench shattered what I thought was the bottom of Becker's skull. Let's say Parker was some ways away, bloodying Chinese cooks until they were unconscious, at the very least: one, two, three, then four falling down. Let's say that, in the tear gas and the sound of gunfire and screaming, I found Becker's gun and stopped Parker's mindless rampage." I quietly focus on calmly breathing.

"Sounds like you know a little of war," he says, with a slight tone of condescension. He clears his throat and continues, "I also found out that earlier, during an earthquake, you actually, medically died for a brief period of time, until resuscitated by military personnel. Obviously made a full recovery. What... I... that time you spent... in between... what was it like?"

"It was like... a dream. A very real dream, but... and this makes little sense... a dream occurring throughout my whole body." Absolution before penance amidst ever-lasting guilt: nonsense, too.

Abraham takes all the documents I finished signing and arranges them neatly into a stack, which he stuffs into his open briefcase. He asks me, "Have you told anyone what this... body dream was like?"

My truthful answer, "Never. I don't lack the capacity for receiving compassion, Abe, if that's what you're hinting. But, to be perfectly honest, many of my deepest feelings, including ones about this dream, are better described as nausea than guilt."

Abraham studies my face a long time before speaking. "Nausea is something your body can learn to control and eventually avoid for the most part..."

"... my opium days."

"Yes, most likely, unfortunately. I mean, if you're anything like I was in France back in '18, you recognize that war is not fighting for your ideals much or even for your comrades. It's fighting for yourself, despite the long lulls in violence, despite nausea. You surrendered, in the moment, to what you felt was right to you. You did what you had to do, even if some hypothetical jury, in the end, might, sorry to say it, might disagree with me. Did unexpected things happen? Did something happen to you, which you couldn't expect? If those questions were put to me, I'd answer that I am not entirely the same person I was, when I was a boy."

"I killed because I could... "

"... You... can fight. For both of us. Now."

Our cards all laid out on the table. Abraham Katza, Esq. offers to take my secret to his cemetery. In exchange, he will assist me in legitimately establishing myself in southern California so that we can share, eventually, something post-war domestic, a proposition which leaves me squirming.

He explains that the decision to sign papers is a different sort of decision than to hold oneself later to what was signed earlier. In these times, there can be, however, no alternate plan of action, he insists. He asks me, at my age, to rise up to my destiny, beyond merely accepting it. He offers an end to irony between us, then points out, grimly lowering his voice, that even Canada has been at war for two years. Private thought: Would it be ironic for him to call me his "husband", when I was the one who wanted to stay the last time?

O, Canada.

Abraham says, breaking a long moment of silence, "The existence of camps, in Europe most certainly, and maybe occupied China, why not, has been known by most governments long before the beginning of America's newest war. It has been long known that the inmates in camps have been beaten, tortured and shot. Hundreds of political refugees have tried to warn governments about these camps and to ask them to do something. Nothing."

Going for a matchbook from my pants pocket, I ask Abraham, "Would you retrieve the joint I handed you earlier, tossed in your case there?"

Some yards behind the car, standing on the pier, a young man plays guitar and serenades a charming girl:

"...I don't want to set the world on fire

I just want to start a flame in your heart

In my heart I have but one desire

And that one is you

No other will do

I've lost all ambition for worldly acclaim

I just want to be the one you love..."

Abraham finishes the lyric, singing softly, just for my ears, "And with your admission that you feel the same, I'll have reached the goal I'm dreaming of... Be... "

I sing loudly, "... Boogie Woogie Bugle Boy of Company B." I share these lyrics with little irony. Abraham and I first kissed each other when we were both eighteen. Who is this middle-aged stranger encouraging me to risk my middle-aged life? After an end to the long moment of patient, quiet sitting between us, the late winter sun perhaps now rising in Tokyo comes to hover over the western horizon, above San Pedro, above the Pacific Ocean. "Are we done with this?" I wonder aloud, lighting the joint with the help of an old, lucky SS Rex matchbook. I inhale, pass to Abraham, who copies my smoking gestures.

He squints through his spectacles, then involuntarily coughs. I retrieve the joint. Smoothly, I say "Excuse me." I pause. "I meant to ask, 'So, what now?' "

"A thousand words is the worth of one picture. Paint one," he requests. "For Hanukkah."

Upon his request, I inhale once more, clear my head and search for the right mood lacking irony. I pass the joint back to Abraham, who shakes his head, but I insist and he relents. An authentic smile appears on my face, delighting Abraham, and I exhale before painting, "A stolen kiss silhouetted under a setting sun rising for an empire Japanese yet shining upon the tiny Venusian goddess more than her loyal Lune waning. He beseeches me to speak of us, again, betraying beautiful wounds and eternal years, and the wounds eternal of years beautiful. Home is here, parked at this pier, inside his valise, on paper smudged with the lexicon of law binding cosmic days into optimistic artifice, like this poem, which he asked me to improvise to one thousand words, or the price of a picture. Dickens was paid by the word, they told me in school. Dickens. Becker. Dickie Parker. Packard. If I were as enormous as Pantagruel, I would straddle the land, and kick my feet wet, throwing sand and seafood everywhere, opening my codpiece and pissing into the sea, reaching for the sun and pulling its radiant bolts across my skin like salve, feasting like a glutton, sinful, until over tired, so bending down lenticular clouds from blue skies and stuffing them underneath my head like pillow feathers on which to repose before sleep. But, I've summoned those words before, on an ancient occasion, secretly, in my mind, thus I feel compelled to reveal now, Abraham Katza, an ultra-secret, my deepest secret, of how my curious afterlife dream appeared at its start. Close your eyes. Imagine. A cavernous expanse, literally cave-like but without any floor, opens before me, filling my eyes with new subdued hues, broken only by an expanding demonic energy fixed in space, shapeless and intelligent, from which vomit mysteriously pours endlessly into a suspended, giant, wood and steel vat rocking back and forth underneath the entire cave. In the vats' sinuous movements, I recognize that which exists beyond the horizon of phenomena on which I can hang names. An unnameable ever-flowing distant evil, colorless, putrid-smelling like rotten eggs mixed with petroleum and, emesis in epic form, an unbounded, fathomless sea perturbed by turbulent undercurrents and rogue waves. Across this far-flung sea and swinging vat, there is no path to follow. This... appeared to me, only, as death's start. But even so, here in this car I now reveal to you that all your quiet pieces of paper, and all your silent words written with ink, could be wrapped into a thin cylinder, tighter and tighter, then encircled several times around my left hand's fourth finger, and maybe if they were soaked in booze and tonic and left to dry, they would retain their shape, and I would let myself be owned by something like a wedding ring."

Not far from the Packard, an anonymous agitatrix commanding the center of audience attention at Rainbow Pier's famous Spit and Argue Club is screaming shouts above the common chatter, under the fall of Pacific dusk, "... Beasts ferocious with hunger will swim across the rivers, greater part of the army will be against Hister. The great one will cause him to be dragged in a cage of iron, when the German infant observes no law... "

Retreating to our intimacy, I whisper to him, "You realize the United States has declared an existing state of war against an alliance of atheists, Buddhists and Shintoists on the occasion of the Roman Catholic Feast of the Immaculate Conception."

Abraham murmurs, "Blasphemy, like an Illuminati conspiracy theory mystery."

"Beast of the Apocalypse"

Addendum

Acknowledgements

Holding the truth is the hardest thing, indeed.

This novel would not have been put into print without the use of several companies, including: Google especially, but also certainly Microsoft, Wikipedia, Xtube, Asus, and Charter Communications. Although the images published herein are original photographs of my drawings made with pastels, charcoal, ink and pencil on paper, any visual references to other art in my drawings are believed to be consistent with "Fair Use" copyright law, as set forth in 17 USC §107.

I acknowledge and thank Sal Flores, founder and editor of GetOutLB.com, which published this novel, chapter by chapter, biweekly, from July 2012 through July 2013, without fail.

I acknowledge the kind and loving support of Rafael Lainez, without whom this novel would not have taken the direction it did.

I acknowledge and support Claudine Burnette whose willingness to meet me and talk with me and keep in touch with me helped make this novel better than it would have been otherwise. Late drafts that she provided me of her book, Prohibition Madness (2013), helped provide useful historical context about Long Beach for my storytelling.

I acknowledge and thank the staff working at the Los Angeles Maritime Museum for their assistance. Similarly, I want to thank the staff at the Historical Archives Building of the Port of Los Angeles, for letting me ask some brief questions about the 1934 West Coast Waterfront Strike. The staff at the Long Beach Public Library and the Historical Society of Long Beach also freely extended their time and attention. Last but not least, the staff of the Centro Cultural Tijuana (CECUT) spent time answering questions I had about Tijuana and the Agua Caliente Resort and Casino in the 1920s and 1930s.

Specific published work should also be mentioned. The content of "Act II: Sixth Dimension" was conjured by reading the Tibetan Book of the Dead and "Imagining Ten Dimensions," a movie narrated by Rob Bryanton and published on Youtube (2012). Chapter Twenty-Two is structured around Harold Bloom's psycho-poetic archetypes set forth in his famous book of literary criticism, Anxiety of Influence (1973). A noteworthy local history of LGBT Los Angeles and Long Beach can be found in Bohemian Los Angeles.

None of the words you are reading would have existed the way they did without the love and support of my husband, Jeremiah Taimi McMoore Malumaleumu, who not only gave me his oral history about "Abalone Cove," as well as his assistance with writing the languages of both Samoan and Spanish, but he also figured as the conscious and subconscious foil for my imagination, as all good lovers should do, to my mind. Jerry is braided to my Id and Superego.